THE REPUBLIC

THE REPUBLIC

Traitor

Remo Quaggiato

Contents

Chapter 1

THE GAME OF LIES

The sweat rolled off the pilot's face as he watched Washington DC burn. The place was a free-fire zone—a bright flash of light flared far to his left. As another car's fuel tank brought light to the night. *Damn, the place was a Goddamned war zone.*

The last two districts he had overflown in the military helicopter were a collection of random buildings burning brightly into the night, bracketed by lines of blazing cars and wild street anarchy.

Major Allan Brown glanced over to his co-pilot, who looked equally unsettled. Although it was not the bright bonfires of anarchy that made them sweat but the safety of their passenger.

He spoke softly into his helmet mike. "Agent Stevenson, I want to take her higher; we're too low." *Maybe we should have taken Marine One,* he thought but then dismissed the idea; that particular helicopter was far too easily recognized—and even that bird could be brought down with a lucky shot when they were flying this low. And there were enough gun crazies around.

This'll teach you not to be so goddamned smart. The Secret Service and he had agreed to use the military bird in the hope that the Man would have given up on the idea of flying over the capital if he knew he'd be flying in a standard military helicopter.

Damned stupid, we're going overboard to compensate. Well, what could you expect after Congress?

"I have already requested that we go higher. But the president wants to see for himself." Agent Stevenson glanced towards the silent passenger as he stared through the side window.

Hunched over, the Man stared at the ruin below with a look of ashen disbelief stamped onto his face. His expensive suit seemed too big for him. *The man's left the building and only the husk is left,* Agent Stevenson thought; *God save America.*

"Mister President, the pilot is worried about the helo being this low."

"Just a few more moments, Joe, I need a few more moments." President Clayton Prescott III continued to stare out the side window. "How could we have let this happen?"

They passed over a few more streets.

"Mister President, sir, this is not safe. I must insist that we climb." "Very well, take us back."

The pilot turned the helicopter away from the fires and began circling towards the White House, climbing to once more see the lights of Washington below. The flight passed in silence, broken only by the noise of the machine and the rasping of breath.

The helicopter landed with a dozen agents watching, so desperate to get the president inside that some were practically balancing on their toes to get moving. Even in such a safe environment, they still felt unease.

Waiting at the door was Abb Cole, the chief of staff for the previous president. "How bad was it?"

"The worst I've seen… The TV just doesn't do it justice. What's the latest from Congress?" Clayton asked him.

"Another three are confirmed. That takes us up to one hundred and ninety nine confirmed cases of the virus."

"President… Uh… Andrew?"

"He's 'stable,' whatever the hell that means when he has a spiking fever, swelling of the brain, bleeding into the brain, and muscle spasms."

"Are they any closer to finding something that'll help?" Clayton saw the look, just a passing flicker of emotion on Cole's pallid face. "I see." *Damn, damn it to hell.*

"It's the brain that's the real worry. His brain activity is going." Cole looked down into his hands. "I've talked to the doctors. Of the hand-full that are fighting it off, 90 per-cent of them will be vegetables. They'll need constant care. Help to just change their nappies. God damn it, we— They let me see him, for a second… All of them in those plastic suits and helmets. They all looked away… They know. They know they can't do a damned thing to save him." Abb Cole had been friends with former president Andrew Caine for more years than either would care to admit. They had started off on their long journey through politics together. Now, one served a brand-new, unelected president that he hardly knew, while the other man lay in an intensive care/ isolation ward.

"He's dead and we can't even bury him with any dignity. He could spend the next twenty years as a vegetable or stuck on life-support. And Helen… what do I tell the children?"

President Clayton Prescott the third looked at the man, the man he needed to run his house. What do you do when something like this happens? What do you say that could possibly help? He knew both men had been as close as brothers. They had gone through the fires of politics together, guarding each other's back for so many years in the dark corners of Washington.

"Do you want some time to yourself to sort things out? I can—"

"*No*, no, Mister President. Please, I need to work. I'd just sit at home doing nothing."

"Right, so are we getting a handle on the rioting?"

"Los Angeles, Dallas, and Washington are the main sites at the moment. Couple of other cities are warming up for a hot night. Parts of New York look ready to go up in flames. The police are overwhelmed, sir. We need to crack down on those damned anarchists before they can carry out any more sabotage."

"Sabotage, Abb? The violence is unacceptable, but protesting at being unemployed hardly equates to undermining America's industrial or social equilibrium."

"The majority may have some legitimate concerns, but the anarchists are committed to bringing this country down. You mark my words, Mr. President. They want the end of America as it stands."

"There will always be the few," Clayton acknowledged to his chief of staff. "The key is ensuring they don't grow in number. Still, we need to re-establish order. Why hasn't the National Guard made any real progress? President Caine had them deployed more than four days ago."

"Government cutbacks, I'm told, have cost them dearly, sir." No surprise really. He sighed. For years Congress had steadily reduced the funding for equipment and manpower needed to make the Guard and Army reserves even halfway creditable. Lately it was either feast or famine. He fumed in frustration. They either drowned in money or got nothing, depending on who was in charge.

"And there are some reports of Guardsmen actually joined the protesters," Cole admitted with an air of disbelief.

"Even with the cutbacks, they should have had some success by now. The situation as it stands is inexcusable," the president responded.

"There are a lot of unhappy people." Abb offered in defeated simplicity. "I know. I take it everyone is waiting for me?"

"What's left of the Cabinet or their stand-ins are here," Cole answered. "Are you sure you want all the extra functionaries? It'll be crowded."

"The more, the merrier, Abb. I need options, ideas. We need to get things moving." They walked through the doors into the White House, down corridors with portraits of men whom Clayton considered great and many he considered morally questionable.

Then again, they had lived in different times, with different values. *How many of them would look at us with scorn, even contempt, at what we have become? Would they damn or praise us for what we have made of our nation and their legacy?* The thought haunted him as he entered the meeting room.

Clayton shrugged the thought away as he went through the motions of greeting people he had rarely, if ever, met before taking his seat. He looked around the table.

At least I still have the Secretary of the Interior and the Secretary of Defence. That's something of a start. Both men were holdovers from the previous administration. They had been out of town and missed the presidential address to Congress on the day of the attack.

Clustered around the table were the acting department heads, either unsure or less than enthusiastic to be present. That was clear from the timid glances he saw from the men and women. Most were from the previous administration, with needed experience in Washington's questionable ways.

Scattered around the room were those on the opposite end of that spectrum, the ones who saw this as a golden opportunity, the young overachievers ready to show what they had.

To take the proverbial bull by the horns and with the herculean strength of youth bring it to its knees. Clayton sighed at the thought, since most were from his personal staff; unfortunately, that meant people with a paucity of experience serving within the White House.

When he had entered the room, it felt overcrowded, but suddenly it seemed to be lacking a great deal. He wanted to shake his head. Right now he desperately needed wise counsel, not wild adventurism.

Clayton cleared his throat. "My apologies for the late hour. I know most of you would rather be home with your families, but needs do indeed demand. So let's get started, shall we?" He wore a broad, confident smile that he did not feel. "I need options to get the country moving. So what have you got for me?"

The acting Commerce Secretary began. "Quantitative easing, sir. We have done this before. We just need to increase government spending…" Donald Beck had been number two at Commerce and was Clayton's temporary replacement for yet another they had lost, eager and overly direct. He would be quite capable of presenting the president's case to the public but was not necessarily a deep thinker. "We need a stimulus package… Infrastructure projects, sir… we still have too many bridges collapsing, roads crumbling from neglect… just need to pump more money—"

The acting Treasury Secretary cut him off. "With what money, Donald? We are up to our necks in debt." Gene Austin was old school, stubbornly knocking his head against the wall of political ignorance for years but had never given up in defeat. He probably never would. The fact that America was still on its legs was in part due to that very stubbornness and his skills behind backroom doors. Now he nearly snorted in exasperation. "We have been running on debt for decades; we have nothing left."

"We just need to spend enough to get the economy up and running again. Then we can talk about debt reduction."

Austin shook his head at Beck. "We do not have any money to spend." Beck raised a hand. "We could print—"

"We can't keep printing money." Austin was all but shouting at Beck. "The dollar is nearly worthless now. We print more, and it will be totally worthless."

"Then we need to borrow."

"Haven't you been *listening*? We're in debt up to our eyeballs. Half the world wants its money back, and they want it back now."

"And haven't you seen the rioting in the streets?" Beck waved his arm, in a grandiose gesture worthy of the theatre. "We need to stabilize the economy to reduce the unrest. Once we have the economy running again, money will flow."

"You bloody don't get it, do you? Instead of extending us loans, China is liquidating American assets, and once our bonds are due, they will want their money. We're the last people anyone is going to lend to. We've made ourselves a laughing stock, damn it. Tens of millions are out of work. We have an entire generation unable to find work."

"Come on, it's not that bad." Beck straightened in his chair. "Just compare us to Europe. Yes, in some parts their lowest is 23 per cent unemployment, but other states are as high as 28 per cent. That's ignoring youth unemployment, which has gone through the roof. All that with an ever-growing debt burden.

On the other hand, we have only 19 per cent unemployment. Besides, America has endured economic downturns in the past."

"We may have 'only' 19 per cent unemployed, Donald. But we have another 22 per cent working at or below the poverty line. Do you understand? That's 41 per cent who can't feed themselves or are basically living hand to mouth. What is wrong with you? Another misstep and we're looking straight at the greatest depression in US history." Austin shook his head in bewilderment.

"Let's not be overly dramatic, shall we?" Beck stated as if he were the only one with a calm head.

"You think having tens of millions of Americans barely able to feed themselves… living in cars, living off food stamps, on handouts… is a minor detail?"

"We have always had people unwilling—"

"Don't give me that." Austin was fuming in indignation. "You know worker productivity has been going up for decades. For thirty years it's been at an all-time high. We're not talking about lazy no-hopers; we're talking about people with jobs who are barely able to pay their rent."

"Once the economy picks up, wage growth will follow," Beck persisted. "Jesus, how many times have we heard that bullshit?" Brandon Keel could endure no more. One of Clayton's inner circle, he was a hothead, a firebrand, but a highly regarded thinker.

"Excuse me?" Beck retorted.

"Why? You know full well that real wages have been shrinking since the seventies. Apart from that little hiccup a few years back, name the last time we had real wage growth to GDP that was worth a damn." Keel's voice kept rising. "Well, when?"

"There were technical issues that needed adjusting, but our fundamental base is still sound."

"Have we had real, sustained wage growth for lower-income workers since the seventies?" Keel demanded even more forcefully.

"Well…" Beck sighed. "We need to understand the dynamics—" Ann Hornwood broke in. "Sorry, if I may interject? The economy isn't the major problem at the moment."

"What?" The entire room turned to look at her in disbelief.

"The main problem is the media, Mr. President. You have to get a handle on the media before it crucifies you."

"I don't think it's all that important at the moment." Donald Beck looked at her as if she were ready to be committed. What the hell did the president's mouthpiece know about the economy?

"Wrong, it's vital. To a large extent, Mr. President, it's not the public but the media that creates public opinion... so you have to take charge."

Gene Austin leaned forward. "Let's get real, the public isn't stupid." "Just easy to manipulate, by presenting the story in a positive or negative light," Ann responded.

"You're overdramatizing this, young lady." The Interior Secretary felt as if she were stepping on his toes. "I am sure the public will calm down in due course."

"I can only take that as an admission that you haven't been listening to the radio shock jocks." She turned to the president. "Sir, even the mainstream media is clamouring for the president to do something. They have been going on and on about how 'he needs to save the economy, he needs to save America, he has to save the world.'

"Mister Secretary, as you well know, the media may not be able to remove a person's bigotries, but it can reinforce them. And that's the problem, sir. The media is screaming for the president to act." She turned to him once more. "And unless you get out there, on the airwaves, the media will turn on you. Sir, as bad as the economy is, a loss of confidence in you—in the government— will bring this country to its knees."

Beck tried again. "Miss Hornwood, once the economy picks up—" "And just when will this miracle take place?" Ann felt like throwing up her hands in defeat.

"We just need to get things started." Donald was convinced he had the answer to their dilemma.

Gene Austin snapped, "With what? Where are you going to get the funds?"

"Additional revenue, by increasing taxes on those with high incomes." Brandon Keel spoke up from the ring of people in the room.

A few groaned softly. None could really argue against his abilities but most considered Keel hot-headed and volatile to the point where he was a liability. Though not to Clayton Prescott;

Brandon had always been the most willing to hold up a mirror to his imperfections. That was worth far more than all his hot-headed liabilities. Only a fool thinks he's smart enough not to take a dose of criticism.

"That will kill any chance of restarting the economy. We need tax cuts," Beck fired back.

"My God, man. We have been cutting taxes since Reagan to the point where we can't even fund government." Austin stared at the man. "You know full well we are one of the less taxing nations in the developed world. Especially when it comes to our CEOs." He shook his head. "And we certainly have some of the best tax avoidance laws in the world."

"Gene, only the private sector can create jobs," Beck replied.

"How do you know?" Keel asked. "The public sector has never been allowed to competently engage in business."

"Are you talking nationalization?" Beck grabbed for the worst possible option, certain that no one would agree to such a measure.

"Well, now that you mention it…," Keel offered, being only slightly sarcastic.

"Are you insane?" Beck took a breath to calm himself. "Government has always been wasteful. It can barely run its departments with any efficiency. How can it handle business in the real world?"

"Your staff will be delighted to know how highly you regard their abilities," Ann Hornwood put in, smiling in victory.

"Government wouldn't have to run them, sir," Keel jumped in. "We could make a mountain of money by nationalizing companies and then reselling them on the open market or selling them to the employees.

"And that'll work quite well, sir. I personally know of several companies that are owned by the employees, and they're going great—better than many owned by shareholders."

He turned to Beck, keeping his tone moderate. "Economically it makes sense: employee- owned companies tend to actually concentrate on long term stability. As oppose to maximizing short-term profits for shareholders.

"Even better, they actually serve America's interest by keeping jobs here in the country. You won't get that from your gold card–carrying CEOs." Keel saw Beck's jaw drop. *Well, that shut the asshole up for a minute.* He leaned forward, elbows on the table. "Sir, we need a radical change to the economy."

"And nationalizing industry is the answer?" Beck scoffed. "Mr. President, we can't guarantee that a nationalized business would be taken on by its workers or purchased by other companies. What do we do if we can't get buyers? We know government can't run business; it—"

"Who said it can't?" Keel gleefully cut in. "Provided we remove politics from the equation." He was still addressing the president. "What if government-owned business were run by independent boards, engaging in sound, principled economic decisions, instead of a couple hundred congressional reps and senators playing politics?" He turned to face Beck. "Better still, the companies won't be corrupt to the bone. They won't destroy the economy as your bank CEOs and captains of industry have done in the name of greed."

"How dare you? They built this country—"

"And made money all the while, just as they are now making money by plundering it, and they'll make money when they're selling its carcass," Keel retorted, to Clayton's amusement. *Brandon is the last person you want to build up a head of steam.* And, in truth, Donald Beck needed to be shaken out of his complacency.

"That is just more scandalous liberal propaganda," was Beck's response. "Yeah, such damned unjustified accusations," Keel rolled on. "Like when Enron was falsely accused of overcharging the state of California for its electricity—wait, sorry, they were found guilty of that, weren't they?" It was common knowledge that the collapsed energy giant had not merely engaged in years of illicit business dealings and accounting tricks but had also deliberately shut down power plants at critical periods so they could artificially raise the price that California would pay for its electricity. "Well, at least we know corporate America is eager to pay its taxes, right?" Brandon continued in an innocent tone. "Just look at how much most of the big IT companies paid last year. Was it 5 per cent, or was it point-5 per cent? Do tell, is our revered Apple still paying only point-zero-zero -5 per cent tax to the Irish revenuers?" This by way of reminding the room that in 2016 the EU demanded that Apple pay Ireland some 14 billion in penalties for tax evasion.

"Don't be childish," Beck warned, "and certainly do not engage in such libel; you know they paid and are paying all taxes required by law."

"And spend millions more finding ways to legally avoid paying taxes. Tell you what. Let's tell corporate America they don't have to pay taxes; instead we just double the penalties for corporate malpractice. We do that, and the country will be in the black in no time. What do you reckon?"

Beck gripped the arms of his chair as if to keep from springing to his feet. "You have no grounds to accuse the corporate sector of any inappropriate undertakings."

"You're right, it's not as if thousands of our companies haven't been fined by the government for corporate violations over the decades. —Oh, sorry. Maybe I shouldn't have brought that up." Keel hammered away, not about to let the man off the hook. "Tell me, sir, has even one cigarette company told the truth about their cancer sticks? No? How about naming a pharmaceutical company that hasn't manipulated its test data? No idea?

"Well, how many car companies are there that haven't gone to every effort to defeat clear air regulations or safety regulations or hidden defects that have led to deaths? How many conspiracy merchants and Internet trolls are quietly funded by corporations to smear their opposition? Are any major banks left that haven't been fined for some kind of criminal activity—all the way from insider trading and ignoring economic sanctions to money laundering for drug cartels?"

"This nonsense has gone far enough." Beck's voice was strained. He wanted merely to end the debate. People should be grateful to the big corporations, instead of hounding them for such minor irregularities. It wasn't as if the banks were bringing in the drugs themselves.

"Okay, how about this?" Keel kept a straight face. "We stage a nationwide corporate audit on improper conduct. The fines alone should pay off the national debt and get us to Mars."

Ann covered her mouth to hide the grin spreading across her face. "You're being flippant, while we need to be serious," Beck said, squirming in his chair." We need to make a more business-friendly environment, one with less red tape and with tax cuts."

"How do we give a tax cut to the multi-nationals when they don't pay real taxes in the first place?" Keel's words dripped with contempt.

"If corporate malfeasance is such a blight on this country, why hasn't the public complained about it?"

"They're complaining right now. Didn't you see the fires on your way here?"

"Only because they lost their lollipops," Beck snapped.

"Your sympathy is touching. You do know that *officially* you're being paid by the government and not by corporate lobbyists—at least for now." Brandon managed a half smile at his little joke.

"We are getting off track here, people." Abb Coal addressed them with a slightly annoyed look. Surprised that Clayton had not put a stop to their childish bickering.

"Agreed, I think we can all do with a recess." The president stretched out in his chair. "But I want you all to consider the real options we have, any viable ideas, by tomorrow morning." Hopefully this little drama would push people to come up with options, some alternative that he could use. "I believe I have another appointment, Abb?"

"Yes sir. You have the Joint Chiefs and then FBI Assistant Director Drywood." Abb tried to keep his voice neutral, but he was a little uncomfortable. Clayton could have waited until tomorrow. The president had to be able to think clearly, so lack of sleep was never a good idea.

"Right, thank you all," Clayton said and turned to a folder by his side. After everyone else had left, Abb turned to the president. "Well, that was lively."

"And then some."

"Covered a few interesting points, wouldn't you say?" Abb tried to bait his hook of inquiry.

"Which were mostly negative, even when they were right, damn it." Clayton then sighed in capitulation. "Okay, have Ann set up the interviews with the media as soon as possible. I'll make all the right noises and offer the correct platitudes." *As if I could wave a wand and the flowers of prosperity would bloom.* He studied the folder on the gleaming tabletop. "Well, let's get to work."

Abb Cole nodded and pressed down on the intercom.

Within minutes the grey-haired men in their pressed uniforms entered and were quickly seated.

"Gentlemen, I asked you all here so we are all on the same page. The police, the National Guard, none of the local authorities are up to the task. I may have no choice but to order the armed forces of the United States into the streets to establish law and good order. I need you to have your deployment plans ready in case I need you to act.

"Now, does anyone have any concerns with implementing martial law if ordered to do so?" He wanted to give all four men the chance to clearly state their views.

"No sir." General MacAdams, the head of the Joint Chiefs, spoke up. The others all nodded their agreement. "Although, sir, there is the legal issue of deploying the military on home soil."

"That will be addressed on my authority," Clayton responded. "Now are there any questions or concerns that you feel we need to address at this time?"

General MacAdams spoke for all four men. "Sir, we understand the need to move quickly, if necessary. But any operation of this magnitude will require time."

"I do not expect the impossible, General, just the best you can do." "Sir, will you be declaring a state of emergency? We will need a framework."

"I… Yes, General. If necessary I will enact a temporary state of emergency in parts of the country that— No, that won't work, will it, General?"

"Why not?" Admiral Kellogg looked from one to the other and then quickly nodded. "Ah, yes."

"I'm afraid it will not, sir," the general declared. "The curfew would need to be universal. As un-popular as that would be, having only parts of the country under martial law would simply see the troublemakers migrate to those areas not under the emergency protocol."

"Agreed. I will declare a nationwide state of emergency. You will have full authority to arrest and detain rioters and any other troublemakers anywhere. But General, your troops will use only necessary force. I do not want any unnecessary violence, understood?"

"Yes sir. And the… real troublemakers?" MacAdams wanted to call them terrorists but felt he should not push too far.

"We leave the anarchists to the police and FBI to track down. I want the military to have clean hands at all times, General." That should ease any concerns over improper use of the military.

"Yes, Mr. President. We will get on it immediately. But there is the question of how long you will keep the state of emergency in place, sir."

None were happy with the idea of having American soldiers on the streets. They all knew how paranoid some Americans were in regard to their own military. Clayton felt his anger rise. The public expected these men and women to fight and die for their country, yet the same spineless weasels had the gall to consider them untrustworthy.

"I can't give you an answer to that. Hopefully we can restore order within a few weeks and get things moving in the right direction by the end of the first month."

"That's understood, sir. Indeed, the Joint Chiefs and I appreciate the situation the country is in. But the phrase *unintended consequence* comes to mind if this crisis continues to drag on."

"General, I can only assure you that the moment we have re-established order, your troops will be returned to their barracks."

"We will begin developing contingency plans immediately, Mr. President."

"Thank you, gentlemen." He watched them leave. They were still unsure, hesitant. That was understandable, even expected. But he needed them to be ready if he had to send them out onto the streets—and he feared he would have no choice in the matter.

"Okay, next." Clayton addressed Abb.

A few seconds later a tall, straight-backed man with white hair at his temples walked into the room. With clear eyes he studied the room with a clinical precision.

"FBI Assistant Director Andrew Drywood, Mr. President." Abb nodded to the man, a little pleased by the man's steady gaze.

"Welcome to the White House, Andrew." "It is my honour, sir."

"Take a seat, please."

"Thank you, sir." Andrew sat with his back straight as if waiting for the order to instantly stand to attention.

"I've asked for the FBI to provide me with a personal briefing for a reason, Andrew. I've kept up with the atrocity committed in Congress. But to be frank, I want to understand. As the man in charge of the actual investigation, give me your findings in your own words." He looked directly into Drywood's eyes. "How was . . . a biological weapon used… in the halls of Congress? With all the safeguards, how could it have happened?"

"The preliminary investigation has concluded…" Drywood stopped there, seeing the look on the president's face. *He doesn't want another goddamned official version; okay then* . "Sir, it was a perfect storm, if you will. That's the best way to explain it. Dr. Arthur Quaice was in charge of—" He glanced at the file in his hands but then thought better of it, and anyway the lab's name had been on television for days now. "—in charge of the government's advanced bioresearch facility in Baltimore. In short, he was one of a very small number of people who had the expertise and the clearance. This gave him access to a variety of the most lethal viruses on the planet, which he was able to bioengineer to his satisfaction."

"Hold it right there." Abb Cole was stone-faced. "This is what I don't understand. Just where did he get government clearance? When was the facility staff cleared to make bioweapons?"

"The FBI has interviewed his staff in detail. Dr. Quaice told them that the lab had been given the go-ahead from upstairs for additional and 'specialized' bioresearch; he never spoke of creating a bioweapon. But going down the route he had outlined, well, within a matter of months they had created a monster virus. It was airborne and just needed a touch from the host to effect transfer.

"And before his staff could get truly suspicious, he had the virus and used it.

"As for infecting Congress, that was even easier. He had high-level clearance, enough to walk into the Capitol without being flagged. Once inside, he used the pretext that he had some time-sensitive information that was vital to the nation, and he needed the representatives to confirm, there and then, that straight after the joint session they would get back to him.

"And that was it; he just stood there in the hallway shaking hands with every member he met as they were strolling into the chamber."

"And his staff happily made this 'monster' virus in total ignorance?" Abb leaned forward in his chair. "I find that absurd."

"He had the correct paperwork, or so it seemed at the time, sir. We are still looking into the matter, but we are confident enough to state that the documents were forgeries, good ones. He had access to all the paperwork and just needed to forge the needed signatures. And a lot of it he could undertake on his own authority.

"Equally, he was able to justify the 'research' quite easily. Researchers do need to know just how lethal a particular virus can become. They need to know to better deal with any possible future mutation."

"Wonderful, just wonderful, they're all patriots," Abb growled. "They know how dangerous these viruses are, and yet they didn't seem to care about providing Congress with suitable defences."

"Sir, with all due respect, it would not have mattered what kind of biofilters or sensors we deployed. We just don't have a defence against this type of attack.

"In a way, the attack had already passed through our defences when the doctor infected himself. No one had considered the possibility of a person deliberately infecting himself with a lethal pathogen to attack the joint session of Congress during the president's address.

"The response teams getting there so quickly was the most we could have expected, in that kind of situation."

Abb raised a bony hand. "About that, how was it that the emergence response teams got there so quickly... and in such numbers? It's almost as if the rumours were true." Conspiracy junkies had posted wild stories that the response teams had actually been forewarned before the event. "According to one account the response teams arrived just before the alarm had been raised in the Capitol," Abb continued. Thus raising the question, how could they have known unless they were involved in a conspiracy to wipe out the people's elected government?

"The teams did arrive before the Capitol alarm was tripped."

Abb's mouth fell open. "You're saying the whistle-blower was right?" "Dr. Quaice notified the relevant response centres, sir. Just as he was shaking hands with members of Congress, his home computer was telling us what he had done online. That is to say, telling all the relevant authorities.

"Again, he had the knowledge needed to give us an effective warning by providing the information to make the threat authentic to the relevant authorities. Thus they arrived in suitable numbers.

"More, he knew how long it would take for us to seal off Congress and the surrounding area to prevent the virus spreading and timed his attack accordingly. If he hadn't provided us with the warning, then tens-of-thousands—possibly millions of Americans would have been infected if the members of Congress had gone back to their home States."

"So he's a hero now?" Abb Cole snarled.

"Of course not. All I'm saying is that it could have been millions instead of hundreds." *Shit, what's gotten up his ass?*

"Why did he do it?" President Prescott's voice was softened by a note of defeat. "Was he telling the truth?"

"We believe so, sir. As you know, his entire family, his wife, children and father were all killed in a drive-by shooting. His colleagues all testified that he had been shattered by their deaths and blamed Congress, arguing that their refusal to act on gun control was responsible."

"No chance that this was a terrorist attack?" Abb asked. "And they were using his… dispute with Congress as a cover?"

"No sir. This was no international plot or insider conspiracy. Just one man with the skills and resources needed for the job. In a way, sir, that was the only way it could have worked. The larger the group involved, the greater the chance of leaks and infiltration." *What is it with this guy?*

"Not to change the subject completely," Abb pressed on, "but how much longer before the FBI gives the all-clear for the gun factories to reopen?"

"Unknown, sir. We have come up with a rather unusual situation. We know how to detect explosives, but bioweapons—that is totally different. We do not even know which chemical or biological agent or agents he may have planted in any of the factories. We could clear a plant and still miss a bioweapon. It's going to take time, a lot of time."

"You can't be serious. It was a hoax. How could he have planted these 'biobombs' of his inside any gun manufacturing plant? They have first-class security. It's ridiculous, as ridiculous as these bombs being rigged to go off three months or six months from now."

Third-class security, more like, Drywood thought. "Sir, he had detailed schematics of most gun factories on his computer. And again, he had access to a wide range of biological agents."

"He was only one man, you said so yourself. So how could he get into all these manufacturing sites?"

"A lone wolf in his attack against Congress, sir, that is true. And his threat is probably a hoax, but he may have made contact with any one of several groups with an antigun agenda. Equally, he could have communicated with someone online. There are a lot of people that have had their loved ones shot dead in this country and could have been planting these 'bio-bombs.' A hoax it may be, sir, but we simply can't ignore the threat."

"And so thousands are out of work, the gun industry grinds to a stop, and the price of guns is going through the roof."

"Sir, we can't take the risk with their lives."

"I've already had two video conferences with their industry delegations—"

"Abb." Prescott's soft voice interjected. "They are doing the best they can."

"Yes sir." Drywood nodded in agreement. "Do you have any other questions, Mr. President?"

"I have one," Abb Cole said. "What is the FBI doing about the anarchists? When are you going to throw those terrorists into jail?"

"Sir, it's not that simple. They are well organized and hardwired into the system." *Man, this guy needs to get a life.* "As we found out in the Middle East and other trouble spots throughout the world. The kids of today are so wired into social media that they can circumvent most efforts by the authorities. Our problem is to distinguish the real anarchists from ordinary protesters and the usual troublemakers. Until we can do that, we can't really get a grip on the problem. But we are making arrests."

Abb scoffed. "A few low-level foot soldiers arrested for vandalism, trespass, and assault, while we have entire districts turned into war zones." "There has been orchestrated violence, sir, but we need proof of guilt, and someone posting a time and place on the Web doesn't constitute a crime. This is still the United States. People can't be arrested for just communicating on the Internet; it isn't a crime."

"Apparently organizing an act of violence isn't one either."

"As I explained, sir, there has to be proof of criminal intent. That's why we have only been able to take the rioters to court after the event; they don't actually put their intentions up on the Web." Drywood looked Clayton squarely in the eye. "Mister President, we need to consider a totally new approach, a new legal and social approach to the technology that is only now beginning to reach its maturity. The law is always following, never leading, and it's costing us dearly. If we had a constantly evolving framework, some legal body to deal with any future technology, then perhaps we could limit the worse of it."

Abb's view was clear and simple. "We have the House and Senate for that."

And they have done such a great job so far, thought Clayton.

Drywood responded, "But if we had a government body to constantly update Congress, keep up with new developments... if the Internet had started off with good security safeguards built into it against viruses and hacking—"

"How would that have worked?" Clayton enquired.

"I'm no expert, sir..."

"Obviously." Abb was smirking.

"I have to admit I get frustrated with computers, the damned things. I kind of wish they came with a total delete button. One press and everything goes; you're left with only the basic operating system they 'hardwire' into each computer at the factory. I always thought, that way, you'd be guaranteed to have only the basic system and any files you have personally inserted into a protected hard drive . . . At least it would have saved me the trouble of having it scrubbed." Drywood was far less ignorant about computers than he made himself out to be, but he knew it was rarely a good idea to lecture anyone. Better a more subtle approach, and clearly the chief of staff was not in his camp.

He went on, "All I know for sure is that the FBI is playing catch-up all the time, sir. We have massive hacker attacks across America. Cyberfraud... in fact, all online crime is increasing. And yet none of the Internet companies give a damn about cybersecurity or helping law enforcement." It was like terrorism: just because it was off the front page for a few days, that didn't mean it wouldn't come back to bite you twice as hard later.

"This isn't about the FBI's frustration with the IT industry—with Apple specifically?" Abb inquired. A number of recent events had strained relationships.

"Sir?" Drywood blinked.

"This seeming ongoing feud between the FBI and the IT companies after Apple refused to help with the investigation of the San Bernardino massacre in California in 2015," he reminded the FBI assistant director. The FBI had found an encrypted smartphone and tried to get the IT company Apple to break the encryption. Instead of helping, Apple had refused the FBI's request.

"Let me be clear, sir. The FBI is interested in results, not in someone's private activities. The IT companies are interested in profits, not in protecting people's privacy, no matter what they say. That incident was a storm in a teacup created by Apple."

Drywood saw the doubt on Abb's face. "If the telecom company was so worried about their decoding software escaping into the 'wild,' they could've built a bunker right under their main office. Then installed a single computer with the decoding software… having it all totally isolated, with no outside connections, no phone lines. Then they could've

Then they could've installed a single computer in their bunker, again with no external connections—no USB ports, nothing you could plug any device into, just a one way plug for the iPhone. Then create and insert the software. They could have a dozen guards monitoring the elevator door. Have five activation codes held by senior management just to use the elevator to get down to the bunker.

"More: they could put in as many regulations as they want—no other electronic devices to be taken down into the bunker. They could say, 'You need to strip and put on pocketless overalls as a security precaution.' Further, any attempt to physically remove the computer would set off a self-destruct. Hell, they could physically remove the keypad, once the code was installed. Once they had decoded the phone's data, they could send it straight to a paper printer in the same room, giving us a paper copy. When finished they could put the iPhone into a crusher in the same room, if that makes their day.

"Their excuses were all Internet self-promotion. Just like the argument that dozens of prosecutors would put their hand up to get all the mobiles in their custody decoded. They could have gone to Congress and demanded that the government pass laws limiting decoding to organized crime and terrorism. They could have asked for all the legal protection for individual privacy they wanted. Sir, the FBI doesn't need to take possession of any decoding software."

"Congress asleep at the wheel yet again?" Clayton gave Drywood a sad smile. "Yet the telecom companies do seem to have legitimate concerns." Drywood paused as he considered his words. "Sir, how many viruses in research centres all across America have escaped into the general community? Now, ask yourself why haven't they escaped? The answer is obvious: because we haven't had employees taking lethal virus out through the front door. That's what scares them… a lack of loyalty. They can add safeguard after safeguard against outside penetration, if that is their real concern. So the real question is, Can the telecom companies be trusted? And their behaviour suggests to me that the companies or their employees can't be." There, he'd said it.

"That sounds like a vote for not developing encryption-defeating software," Clayton said.

"Sir, at the end of the day, the simple truth is we are not working together. That's the real problem." Drywood took a deep breath. "These tech companies scream about government invasion of privacy, but I don't hear much about them putting in *serious* safeguards to prevent hacking, cybercrime—they're always a dozen steps behind the hackers because they're worried about profits, not security."

"Unfortunately, there are many who would disagree with you . . . and point to the NSA as proof."

"I know, sir. But if I may say: if the NSA is so all-powerful, why can't it shut down the 'dark web'? Hell, why aren't I getting a daily read-out of every crime committed on the Internet from the NSA? And who's guiltier of collecting data, the NSA or Google?" *And I haven't heard much of anyone complaining about Google.* "At least the NSA hasn't been accused of tax avoidance." To Drywood, they were happy to prevent the FBI from accessing a criminal's data, but protecting people from criminals… well, that wasn't really at the top of their list.

Drywood gave them a small smile and tried a little levity. "Sometimes, I almost wish we could start all over again from scratch."

"And do what exactly?" Abb retorted. "No one is allowed onto the net without first providing retinal scan, voiceprint, and thumbprint?" *Otherwise the bloody computer will have a meltdown?*

"Followed by blood test and urine sample?" Clayton smiled at Abb. "You must forgive Abb's levity; it was not directed at you." Clayton sighed softly, as was his wont. "Perhaps the new Congress could be encouraged to have some key members engage with a liaison team from the FBI on a regular basis. Perhaps that would start things going in the right direction." In truth he doubted it. Both Abb and he knew there would simply be too much opposition from the industry for Congress to act. As long as they were making money, why should they concern themselves with America's security?

"No need, sir. I agree with the chief of staff, especially for employees of banks and vital sectors of industry and defence. Sir, if we had a law, an enforceable requirement that people in high-security areas had to leave a digital fingerprint on all the data they accessed, downloaded, or viewed, it would be a godsend to investigators. Employees in the back rooms would be less inclined to steal money—or data—if they knew every transaction and download had their digital fingerprint on it."

"And keep the CIA and NSA contractors honest?" Abb grinned slightly. Having no more leaks from the intelligence community wouldn't be such a bad thing. *No more cocksucking traitors selling us out to the Russians.*

"An interesting thought; perhaps we should have you on the FBI liaison team." Clayton smiled a surprisingly gentle smile. "Thank you for your frankness." *And having the guts to put your neck on the line if the president was not open to new views,* Clayton thought.

He ended the meeting with his characteristic note of sadness. "Please keep us up to date with any new developments; the White House will always be open."

Chapter 2

THE DOCTOR WILL
SEE YOU NOW

Clayton Prescott III switched on the TV to watch the news channel and grew more despondent with each minute.

"…there is no other way. We need to default on our loans and begin again," the grey man in the grey suit told the camera with a straight face and absolute conviction.

"That's insane, just think about the damage that would do to the world economic system, the collapse in confidence!" his opponent for the day cried with equal fervour.

"It's not insane. It's the only way out of this mess. The government must accept that it has failed to safeguard our economic system. It has no other option but to accept its failure to act."

He sees this as an opportunity to change the entire system, wipe the slate clean, and begin again. Clayton could see it in the man's arrogant mannerisms. *Damned fool, as if that was actually possible without bring us all down with the system. We've become too interdependent.*

"And who's going to lend us anything after we've defaulted on our loans?"

Clayton sighed and pressed down on the controls to change channels.

"…what else is there to say?" The new voice shouted.

"Yes, well, Collin. What would you say to those that may argue that your group's position is extreme?" The anchorwoman was clearly not one of them.

"There is nothing extreme about my party's position," the spokesman for one of several new political parties declared." The Chinese are out to destroy America. They are responsible for this mess. They offered us all those low cost loans that we can't pay back. They wanted us to buy and buy Chinese, and now they want all the money back. No extensions on our loans, no renegotiations on the bonds we owe." The upheaval striking America was seeing a surge of new political groupings with wild agendas and even wilder views.

"They are also in an economic downturn themselves, you can't deny that," the anchorwoman responded.

"That'll only get worse if they undermine our recovery. They are placing conditions on us that we cannot hope to manage."

"Well, that may be open for debate. But as a viewer pointed out a moment ago, if they were to destroy America's economy, how could they expect to get back the billions that they've lent us?"

"By acquiring whatever land and assets we own. Along with any remaining IT properties we still own. The president must stop this aggression immediately or accept the public's anger."

Clayton pinched the bridge of his nose in frustration.

"Let us argue you are right, Collin; then what exactly should the president do?"

"The president needs to take charge and not simply go on TV to call for the rioting to stop and say that once the new Congress is established, he will work with it to get this country back on its feet. He needs to get the economy running now and tell the Chinese what's what."

The blond anchor smiled at her other guest. "And you, Clara?"

"He needs to concentrate on the political aspects of this crisis. This is going to be with us for a long time. There are simply too many problems to fix."

"But Clara, as you pointed out, the midterm elections are due, and the date to nominate any new candidates has passed. You said it could take several months, at best, before we have a new Congress. Until that time the president is limited in his options. As you pointed out before, the president can't pass any new laws, can't raise any new taxes without Congress."

"Exactly, we have a very long process ahead of us." "Surely we can make an exception?" the anchor asked. "Constitutional law must be upheld. We don't want any new legislation being held up in the courts simply due to the lack of numbers for a legitimate vote in Congress. We've never had a situation like this."

Collin jumped in, not wanting to be left out of the debate. "Let's not make roadblocks from speed humps, Clara. Fixing the economy first may help speed up the political process."

"And how long will fixing the economy take?" Clara snapped back. "Before or after the riots have ended? It could take years before the economy is up and running. Do you want to have riots going on until then? We need a political solution right now."

"And the political process will not be impeded by these very same riots?" The anchor tried to keep the two apart.

"Of course the political process will be hugely hamstrung by the public unrest," Clara declared with conviction. "It will make electing a new Congress that much more difficult. So he has to concentrate on that first." "He needs to move on the economy. That will bring law and order."

Collin countered.

"And how does he do it with no Congress or Senate—or even Supreme Court. Who knows how long it will be before we even have a new Supreme Court? Three are dead, and another four have been confirmed to have the virus."

The blond interviewer spoke up brightly. "The president can nominate new justices—"

"But the Senate needs to approve the nominations. How do we confirm new members with no Congress?"

As Clara continued speaking on the TV, Abb Cole entered the room.

He then silently turned to watch the screen.

The anchor addressed Clara once more. "But we will have a new Senate. That's only a matter of each governor selecting replacements."

"If, if the governors don't engage in politics. Republicans won't want the new Senate to be made up of all Democrats, and the Democrats won't want an all Republican Senate. And that will go for a new Supreme Court. A new Senate won't be the answer to even a few of our problems." Clayton turned down the volume.

"So how are the talking heads doing?" Abb asked the president as he sat down.

"Contradicting each other with the obvious," Clayton observed. "Splendid, they are doing their job. Confusing the dull-witted." "Abb." Clayton coughed a grunt of amusement.

"Oh, come on. We both know the facts of life." Abb gave Prescott a faint smile and then went silent for a moment. "You know, even after all this time I still remember that one classic moment that nailed it for me." He leaned back on the couch. "There was this interviewer who had these two talking heads on her program. It was over Obama's health care reforms. During the interview one said that some aspect of it will cost a hundred million. The other guy said it wouldn't cost a cent. Then they traded words on this and that. A few minutes later the same guy repeated himself about how this bit of Obamacare would cost a hundred million. The other guy, sitting next to him, said it wouldn't cost a cent. And then they argued over another part of the health reform.

"The thing was, this airhead of an interviewer never opened her mouth and said, 'Hang on, one of you is saying it'll cost a hundred million, and the other is saying it won't cost a cent. Someone is either lying or too incompetent to be here. So which one of you has his head up his ass?' But nothin', not a word; she was utterly useless."

Clayton shrugged. "I guess she was more interested in finishing the interview on time."

"And that tells you everything. How can you make up your mind when you have two 'experts' telling you straight out two different stories? We should just take the media out and shot the lot."

Clayton slowly smiled. "I can see how that would go down well with the boys and girls in the media room." Abb had a reputation for being a blunt head-kicker in Washington. Some thought of him as a dumb brute, but they soon learned differently. For all his bluntness, he had a brain and could see more clearly than most. "And I'll try very hard not to alienate the public with my overbearing attention to detail." He knew he had a nasty habit of going into too much detail at times.

"Yeah, well. At least they kept it civil, not like Fox Telly on the radio this morning." Abb smiled.

"God, you don't actually listen to that loudmouth redneck do you?" Clayton Prescott voiced his contempt for the man.

"The wife, I swear she does it to annoy me."

"So did he have a rational thought?" Clayton stated dubiously.

"Well, it was interesting."

"Okay, what nonsense was it this morning?" Clayton shivered a little. "That the recession is a Liberal, slash, Government conspiracy against the hard working middle class and the rich to force them to make concessions to the poor."

"The man's a genuine." Clayton tried to keep a straight face over the light hearted the banter.

Yet that did nothing to alter the simple truth. *Abb's right about the media, damn it. And so was Ann, for that matter. So how do you get them to put the country first? Especially when they think they are saving the country from a bunch of pompous windbags in government. Not that they're far wrong. Do you make a plea for understanding? Or appeal to their patriotism?* He looked down at his desk. As a former history professor he knew all too well that the military history of his nation held the answer to that question.

I suppose an alternative approach would be more practical. The threat of a bullet to the back of the head would get a better result than an appeal to their better nature, especially with the media desperate for ratings at any cost. Clayton shook his head in exasperation. As he wistfully pictured ninja assassins wiping out the media, the intercom buzzed.

"Yes, Kath."

"Jonathan is here to see you, sir."

"Thank you, Kath."

The young man entered in a slight rush. "Sir, Senator Walker is about to begin his interview."

"Thank you, Jonathan." Clayton nodded to the eager young man. He had wanted to hear what the most senior surviving member of the Senate had to say, potentially the Republican leader in the. The man was potentially the leader of Clayton's opposition if the Republicans wanted to play politics.

"Ah, the loyal opposition." Abb chuckled with little mirth in his voice. "Are you suggesting there is a disloyal opposition? Are we not all committed to the best interest of our nation?" Clayton asked with a straight face. That had Abb wondering if he was actually serious.

Clayton changed channels and raised the volume.

Abb snorted in reply as he once more turned to face the TV.

"We must not go overboard in our demands on the president," Senator Walker was saying. "There is so much that needs to be done, and it will take time. And remember that we have only a few members of Congress and even fewer Senators to offer assistance.

"And yes, there has been some talk about his willingness to serve, as he was considering retirement due to the terrible tragedy that he suffered, which is only natural given those sad circumstances. We can only pray for the best and give the president the time he needs."

Abb clenched his jaw, deliberately not looking at the president. *Bastard, the bastard, kicking a man when he's down. The man goes through hell, and all this bastard can do is kick Prescott in the guts.*

"But do we have the time?" one of the reporters called out.

"I am sure that he will prove himself." Although Walker sounded far from confident.

"That was generous of him," Clayton commented without real rancour.

It was politics. *If you can't attack the policies, you attack the man.*

"Yeah, real generous of the guy, ya think?" Abb mocked.

"We still need to work together." Clayton turned to face Abb without any true sense of hope.

"We'll see," Abb conceded cautiously.

"Thank you, Jonathan." Clayton dismissed the young aide, asking for a ham and cheese sandwich as he turned to another folder on his desk. He was halfway through the sandwich and still considering his options when the intercom buzzed.

"Sir, your next appointment, Dr. Peterson has just arrived at the main gate." Kath informed Clayton in advance of the doctor entering the White House as per his instructions.

"Thank you, Kath. I will see him in the Rose Garden." Clayton leaned back in his seat. *God, I need to walk, get out of here.* He dragged himself out of his chair and slowly exited the patio door towards the Rose Garden. It would be good to see someone from before politics. He smiled at the pleasant memories of his time with his old colleague, friend, and sparring partner from so many years ago. It felt like another age, another world.

He smiled as he thought of all their old arguments as he passed the bushes. *The older you get, the more you look to the past. Why? Paths not taken? Opportunities ignored? Regrets? Fear of your own mortality? Or are you just getting old?*

Clayton walked up to a white-haired man with a slouched back and a hooked nose. *Such a small man for such a great intellect.*

"Brian, it's good to see you. How are the girls? And Mariana, is she well?"

"Fine, fine . . . Mr. President. At least under the circumstances. It's all so terrible what's happened—it's almost unbelievable."

"But so terribly real. —So you finally accepted my invitation to come to Washington. I'm glad to see you, you old fraud." He did not want to talk about the horror that had taken place in Congress and now continued in isolation wards in so many hospitals.

"I know you haven't much time, so I will get to the point of my visit." "Nonsense, if I can't take a few minutes to chat over old times." "I'm sorry, but I haven't come to reminisce, Mr. President." "All right, Brian, so what can I do for you?"

"It's what you can do for the country. You have a golden opportunity to enact many of our ideas, yet you go on TV and talk of how we must remain calm and restore stability, establish a new Congress, and then begin a dialogue with the people."

"What else is there? We need a functioning Congress to get back to the business of running the country. Once the elections are carried out, perhaps I can gain sufficient support for some—"

"Elections? Clayton… Mr. President, look around you. With the mess we're in, it could easily take six months for a new government, but the country may not have six weeks. We have to act now."

"Brian, I know the violence is getting out of hand."

"Who cares about the violence? It is what's behind the violence that matters. It's the ever-growing wealth gap creating open warfare between the rich and poor that matters. The total failure of government to deal with even its most fundamental responsibilities. We—*we* are tearing this country apart, Clayton. The public may not fully understand, but you do. You know how close to the edge we are."

"Brian, what are you proposing? You know I don't have a mandate. I wasn't elected to this post. I was so far down the list that they weren't sure I was even on the list to replace the president." He was taking a little latitude with the truth but not by much. He had indeed been far down the list.

Brian shook his head. "Well, you are here, and you have a responsibility. You have an obligation to act in this nation's best interest. Remember how we talked—"

"And talked and talked about how to fix this country, but that was theoretical, debates in university. Radical thoughts on campus are one thing, but implementing them is another. Brian, you may want me to be some modern-day saviour, but I can't. It just doesn't work like that."

"If you can't, then who else is there? I know this is hard. It's unfair to put this all on you, but right now, you are all we have. Remember how we debated and postulated on how only radical change could enable America to overcome its persistent political/social stagnation?"

"That was years ago, concerning totally different parameters. Back then everyone was sick of the political squabbling, the inertia in politics. We needed leadership, not endless politicking."

"And what has changed since then? We had the answer, you saw all this years ago. It was like you could see the future."

"Brian, we were talking radical theory back then, not the real-life situation we are in now. Besides, there is the slight problem of the

Constitution to overcome, a binding contract between the people and their government, which I swore to protect when I took office."

"Please, that's absolute rubbish." Brian took off his glasses to put them away and give himself a moment to collect his thoughts. "We both know the Constitution is half the problem, if not an actual threat to this nation. You said it yourself, all those years ago. We have been twisting, mangling, pissing on the Constitution for decades to achieve our own interests." *Hell, the Founders would be disgusted by how we've reinterpreted the word and spirit of that poor piece of paper,* Brian thought with disgust.

"I am conscious of the travesties perpetrated against the Constitution to further the interests of some, Brian. And it does grieve me, but equally, people do have the rights the Constitution affords them."

"Oh yes, the people's inalienable right to be stupid . . . to be ignorant… to be led like cattle. To believe any nonsense they want."

"Brain, really."

Brain turned to his left and glanced at the Secret Service agents lingering just out of earshot on the patio. "I'm being unfair, Clayton? A bit too much snobbery from a member of the intelligentsia?" He coughed and coughed again. "Just another smart-ass intellectual who thinks he's above the common herd?"

"I never said that."

"Well, I did, and I'm right. I am smarter that the inbred yokels. And so are you. You know we need to take action. You know the fix this country is in, and you know only radical action will save our country. You can't run away from this, Clayton. You will never forgive yourself if you let this one chance to save our country pass us by. Tell me honestly that you don't believe this country needs saving? The threat to this nation is real."

"For all your 'misgivings,' the Constitution is still in force, Brain. And you know the Constitution limits my ability to act without Congress."

"Why do you keep pretending that it still has any value? You know full well that the Constitution is a contract between the people and the government—"

"And when one party no longer fulfils its obligations under the contract… blah, blah, blah." Clayton shook his head. "I know the standard line."

"Then why do you continue this façade?"

"Brian, you are asking me to violate my office. I can't do that." Clayton looked at his old friend in despair. "And can you imagine the upheaval? We'd have a revolution on our hands."

"We are already in the middle of one, damn it. Man, if you haven't got what it takes to save the country, then get out of the way."

"Brian, that is more than enough."

"Uh . . . I'm sorry, Clayton." Brian sighed, realizing his transgression. "I understand, sir, the limitations of your office. I'm sure you'll do what you think is best. And that's all I can ask. Thank you for your time, Mr. President." He turned to leave.

"Brian, don't go like this. I share your shock and outrage—the sense of impotence. The attack on Congress has affected us all. You should have seen my people last night; they were at each other's throats. This is a very trying time for all of us."

"I… apologize. You are right. It has been hard on all of us. And I think it will be hardest on you, I see that now. So, I'll wish you the very best, and I want you to know I will always treasure our friendship." They shook hands, and with sadness in his eyes Brian walked away, leaving Clayton Prescott to walk around the garden. He finally sat down on a bench with his head down as if in pray.

Sometime later Agent Wilson appeared, to begin his shift, and approached one of his fellow agents who watched over the president. "What's going on?"

"Nothing, he's been like that for fifteen minutes."

"What do you reckon he's thinking?" Wilson looked to the other agent.

"Your guess is good as mine."

That was when they saw him rise—slowly, stiffly, yet with his shoulders set, his back straight like some old Titan of legend rising from the deeps. He walked towards both men.

"Gentlemen, kindly have Abb call the Cabinet together. We have business to conduct." He paused. "But before then I will need to speak to Miss Hornwood. After her I will want to speak to the following…"

By late afternoon Clayton was making terrible progress on his next fireside chat with the public. He felt that the staff had made a credible effort, but now he was turning into a disaster. He needed to present a more caring and understanding figure. *Offer more compassion*, he thought, *present a fatherly figure to offer calm and wise counsel.* After all, if needed, he would only make it more difficult for the military to quell the rioting if he came across as a cold, unsympathetic bastard. And right now the speech could well freeze the balls of a brass monkey.

God, I'm really showing my age. Well, I feel like I was born in the age of canvas sails and brass monkeys. For a moment he pictured those strange contraptions that kept cannonballs from rolling all over a gun deck. Then he came back to reality.

The truth was, he felt miserable, he felt old. Mostly from the endless frustration. From the moment he had entered the White House, he had been pushing and prodding the National Guard, the FBI, and state and local police, all with limited success at containing the unrest.

God, what if the unrest had gotten deep into the bones of the nation? Clayton rested his head against the headrest of his chair. Agent Drywood was right, he concluded, this New Age technology could be a bloody pain in the ass.

It had given both protestors and anarchists too many options.

Originally they had preferred to stage mass rallies in several cities. That had worked until the police had learned how to handle that situation, by having a large number of police and guard in reserve to deploy swiftly and overwhelm any growing rally before it became too big to handle.

Unfortunately, the anarchists had learned as well; oh, how they had learned. Now the protest rallies began in several locations in each of several cities, stretching the local authority's ability to handle all the outbreaks. The outbreaks with the smallest government presence would then grow and combine into mega protests—which always seemed to escalate into violence. With enough experience, they had begun employing an endless combination of rioting and social unrest.

Yet all their provocation didn't stop them for blaming the "pigs" for starting the violent outbursts that led to overturned cars and property damage and often to midnight attacks on public and private infrastructure.

Clayton closed his eyes and sighed in exasperation. *If only they had kept to peaceful protests, we could have lived with that.*

Yes, if only, he told himself. But the anarchists knew peaceful protests would not get them the attention they wanted. No, they needed to continually escalate the situation.

Both sides knew it, which explained some of the approval the anarchists had amongst the average protesters and general public, even when they started their fires.

Clayton stopped to glance at the latest figures. *God damn it*—Boston with two major fires and Chicago with over a dozen houses aflame in two districts, and it wasn't even dark yet. Then there was the attack on the power grid in Detroit; so much for power and water being protected from hackers.

Clayton turned around in his chair and looked out the window. On top of all the bad news, what really worried him was that the more the anarchists scaled up their attacks, the more approval they were receiving. They were the heroes of the unemployed, the homeless, and the rejects of society. All in all, it was a top-notch "class warfare" scenario.

The anarchists are tearing America apart piece by piece. What if we can't put it back together?

Leave it, forget it for now. Concentrate on what you can achieve. He turned to look down at the document. *It's not such a bad speech. It just needs a bit more of a shine.* He was beginning to feel a little more confident when the phone rang. His presence was required at an emergency national security briefing. "Now?"

"It is important, sir."

"Be there in a minute." He hauled himself out of his chair and doggedly headed for the door. He walked down the corridor with a sense of unease. Since nothing had been slated in, it had to be an emergency. And what else would an unplanned national security meeting be? He scolded himself as he entered the secured room.

"Please, be seated, gentlemen." He sat down and nodded for the briefing to begin.

"Mr. President. A situation has arisen that needs your attention." Ethan Campbell was as grim and serious as his dark suit. Clayton's national security adviser looked to him like a vision of a Grim reaper, hunched over with shrunken eyes. But the man was competent, and he was steady.

"That, as they say, sounds ominous." Clayton's note of levity fell flat; the faces confronting him looked to have been cut from marble. "Go on." "Sir, we have been informed by our ambassador to Mexico that Texas and New Mexico, possibly Arizona and California, are planning to secede from the Union."

"Right, well—yes, of course." Clayton tried not to laugh, but his grin spread anyway. "Gentlemen, I thank you for your efforts to relieve my stress levels, but I think we shouldn't go quite so far."

"This is not an attempt at humour, Mr. President. We are serious." "Ethan, please. You can't seriously expect me to believe that Texas and New Mexico plan any such thing?" Merely speaking the names aloud made Clayton want to laugh at the absurdity of the idea. "They can't. They wouldn't?" He asked in disbelief.

"Sir, the governors of these States know they have a very large Latino population, some of it sympathetic to an alliance with Mexico."

"I am aware of the ludicrous demands of a few disgruntled troublemakers, Ethan. But they do not make up the bulk of the population."

"Sir, those States have had a massive Latino increase in the last five years. And some locals have been less than welcoming and sometimes downright hostile, causing friction between the communities."

"I do take account of the population mix and the friction it has caused." Clayton pulled his shoulders back and sat straighter in his chair.

"As do, Mr. President, the governors and the president of Mexico." "Are you telling me the president of Mexico is planning to take over two of our States and possibly more?"

"No sir. The president of Mexico was the one who informed our ambassador of their overtures towards Mexico."

"I can't believe this, what could they hope to achieve?"

"Mexico is doing rather better than we are, sir. The States feel the financial and political constraints we are under. And Mexico, of course, has a very large Latino population. The governors and their colleagues may hope to stay in power employing such a strategy."

"I cannot… I cannot accept this. It's a mistake." "No mistake, sir."

"This is preposterous; governors can't just take their States out of the Union."

"This has all been confirmed, sir. There is no mistake," Ethan Campbell declared firmly, with almost too much conviction. "Sir, as you know, in some States, but especially in Texas, there are a number of very powerful interests who do not like the current system—too much 'federal interference' for their taste. Now, a more understanding Mexican government could remedy this if it were to incorporate the States.

"And the governors and their friends could benefit greatly from such an arrangement."

Clayton understood all too clearly: *The Mexican government gets the State as long as the governor and the "special interests" get what they want.*

"And since the oil and fracking sector is suffering a massive downturn, Texas is feeling the pain. Unfortunately, this leaves the independently minded Texans wanting to blame someone for their economic failures." *And with the governor's prompting, who better to blame than the Fed?* Ethan told himself in annoyance.

"As for New Mexico, well, the governor and some… most of his closest associates are facing scrutiny from the Justice Department over certain improprieties, along, with a number of other institutions closely associated with the State. This could end up being an ugly mess involving a lot of high flyers."

Clayton looked around the table. "Still, to even consider leaving the Union… consider the risks. Consider the support from the public they would need." They were talking treason, no matter what rights of secession they thought they had.

"If I may be so bold, sir," Brian Peterson said, "America has been progressing down the road of… disunity for some decades now. We simply have to look at the escalating criminal behaviour of militia groups in Oregon and other backward States. They've been pushing against the federal government for years."

"America at its finest." *Clayton nodded in sad understanding. How many years has it been since we have come together as a nation? How right you are, Brian. If only people could see what they are doing to their country.*

Twenty years ago… even ten years ago… the thought of secession would have been unimaginable. Today, a Republican would rather see the country burned to the ground than support a Democrat, even if he agreed with that Democrat's proposals.

"And we need to consider that secession may not be their true aim," Ethan resumed. "For all we know, the governors and friends may think they can play us. They could threaten to secede but then offer to rethink it if they were to gain concessions from Washington.

"Alternatively, they may even be stupid enough to think they could join Mexico and then rejoin the Union at a later time, undoubtedly on their terms. Or so they may imagine, Mr. President." Campbell had no doubt that if they did join up with Mexico, the Mexicans would not be so forgiving if the breakaway States changed their minds.

"We have the brief from the ambassador. The president of Mexico sent one of his personal bodyguards to secretly contact the ambassador. This is the report, word for word." Ethan handed the president a thin folder.

Clayton opened the folder and read. The words took his breath away. He felt trapped as never before. And yet there was this little voice in the back of his head laughing at him. Laughing at him for thinking he could somehow escape the inevitable.

A moment turned into a minute, until finally he began to think. Then he saw a ray of hope.

"There is nothing about the governors talking to the Mexican government, just go-betweens."

"High-level individuals close to the governors," Ethan acknowledged. "But we are certain of the accuracy of this intelligence, sir."

Clayton locked eyes with Ethan and suddenly knew why the man was so strident. This was less a political issue than an intelligence matter that needed to be taken seriously by the politicians. There were to be no more intelligence failures, not on his watch; There had simply been too many in the past—especially during the Trump years.

So, Clayton thought, *Ethan is tired of failure being the default option for America.*

"I need to speak to the president of Mexico, on a secure line." "The line is ready, Mr. President."

He nodded at the words. Of course they would have set it up. They knew he would want to hear it directly from the man.

"Sir, the president of Mexico."

Clayton took the handset. "Mr. President."

"Mr. President, I was expecting your call. And yes, individuals within a number of your States have asked if we would be willing to join in a coalition with those States."

"I… don't. I don't know what to say." Clayton's elbows rested on the table with his fingers interwoven, his thumbs pressing the corners of his eye sockets. "We have people, their fellow Americans, suffering a horrible, painful death and these *individuals* would just turn their backs on them. Some of those in Congress would have been their friends. I don't understand how they can do this."

There was silence for a moment.

"I understand, sir. It has been a terrible time. I—we all share your pain. Many of us have seen those that we love suffer. I am sorry; it is difficult from me to truly express our sorrow adequately. As you know, I lost my wife to cancer. I saw her fight and struggle to last a few more days just to see her lovely children grow that little bit more. She felt such guilt knowing that she would not be here to raise them, to love them as they deserve.

"She burned in agony from the cancer, but her heart ached from knowing she would never see her children grow. When you witness such courage, such passion burn so brightly while knowing you can do nothing but hold her hand

and pray to God for another week, another day—you go to bed in tears. And the tears do not stop when they are gone.

"We suffer your pain, sir. We too have fought and struggled to overcome those that wished our country, our loved ones, harm."

"Thank you, Carlo. Sometimes it's hard to remove the politician from the man. I know that our countries haven't always seen eye to eye on some matters. But I want you to know that your honest and open hand of friendship won't be forgotten, sir.

"This is something special for me. There haven't been many moments lately when I could see the better side of our nature. I often wish this were more often the norm than our wilfulness and self-interest seem to tolerate. Your honesty is truly appreciated, sir."

There was a longer moment of silence. As if the man at the other end of the line was debating with himself. "Mr. President, I wish I could say that I have given you this information out of simple altruism. But the truth is I simply do not want the headache. Whatever we might gain by have these States join Mexico, it simply would not be worth it."

Now there was a moment of silence from Clayton. Then he said, "Again, I'm grateful for your honesty, sir. That in itself is a rare gift. Therefore, I wish to assure you that the government of the United States will be equally honest with you."

"That would be appreciated, even if it has not always been practiced." "Then the US will be honest with the government of Mexico for as long as I remain in the White House. Thank you again, Mr. President."

"I look forward to a better understanding between our nations, sir." Clayton cradled the phone and closed his eyes to think. Sometimes he could see more clearly when he could not see.

Ethan broke the silence. "We will need to act immediately, sir." "No. If we move to arrest the governors and their co-conspirators, we may have an open revolt on our hands. We have to do this right by controlling any possible backlash."

"The National Guard and Army reserves should be enough to handle any protestors, sir," Ethan offered.

"And if they were to support their fellow Texans?" Clayton had his doubts. The men of Texas did not inspire great confidence in Clayton at that moment.

"They wouldn't oppose our actions." Yet Ethan was less than certain as he spoke the words.

"Unless they believe we are attempting to stage a federal takeover of the States," Clayton countered.

"But we won't be…" Ethan stammered in disbelief.

"Won't we?" Clayton smiled that little smile he held for just such rewarding moments as this.

"Sir, we cannot bury our heads in the sand. The public will support you."

"The public is paranoid, Ethan. All they can see is federal interference.

Honestly, Ethan, how many will somehow see this as nothing but the federal government meddling in state affairs?"

"I think they'll see the difference."

"Tell that to all the Americans who still believe the world is flat. What is it nowadays? Still around 25 per cent?" Clayton sniggered in protest.

Ethan sighed. "Even so, I don't see the National Guard once federated would stand in our way."

"Unless they were dragged into this mess . . ." "Sir?" Ethan blinked in confusion.

"How many militia groups are there in Texas, New Mexico, and the rest? All ready to defend America from America—from the federal government, their government." *Ethan just doesn't see it*, Clayton realized. Unfortunately Clayton could all too easily see the senseless violence, if enough militia groups were to "defend" Texas, New Mexico, California, and Arizona from the Feds. *So how do I stop the insanity from occurring?*

"And they aren't even the elephant in the room." Patrick Oaks, the head of the CIA, spoke for the first time. "Would the state Guard back up the governors?"

"Sorry?" Ethan was caught for a moment.

"When President Obama was in office, a number of States set up their own private Guard units to defend their State. These units answer only to the governor." Patrick explained.

"Yeah, they were worried about having a nigger in the White House," Clayton declared.

There was a moment of shocked silence. Ethan's black face shone with embarrassed. "I—"

"No need to feel embarrassed, Ethan. It's the rednecks of upstanding Texas and all the other 'nigger'-fearing redneck States that should feel ashamed." Clayton shook his head, his disgust apparent. "President or no president, a nigger stays a nigger in the eyes of a redneck. More shame on them.

"But enough of that, back to the business at hand. We need to get the FBI on this immediately, to find out how serious this is. I'll ask Carlo to hold off giving that traitorous filth a reply. We will let them think everything is going their way. Get me a mountain of evidence that will prove their treachery."

"Sir, what if the conspirators decide to act before we make our move?" Oaks asked the question they all knew came next.

"I am aware of the risk, Patrick, but we need to take precautions." The president of the United States sighed in resignation, if not defeat. "Okay, I need to talk to Director Shaw and the Joint Chiefs in my office, as soon as possible." *I never wanted this. I wanted to avoid using them. It's like saying we have lost ourselves, as if I have failed—and haven't I? If we had ended the rioting on the first day, would those assholes be trying to desert the ship? I suppose it's a matter of whether you're a rat or not.*

The men in uniform appeared in the Oval Office with such speed that Clayton thought they must have been waiting for him just outside. The director of the FBI appeared a few moments later.

"Thank you all for getting here so quickly. I will be brief and to the point. It has become obvious that I have no choice but to declare a state of emergency. The military and other law enforcement bodies are to establish a nationwide dusk-to-dawn curfew on groups larger than five people.

"Daytime protest marches will need state or federal approval and supervision, along with assurances that they will be peaceful. Further, we will need restrictions on travel, especially for known instigators of violence. We will need to look into imposing communication blackouts; hopefully that will disrupt the anarchists' activities."

Clayton studied the faces in front of him, seeing the approval of some and the hesitation of others. They merely reinforced his view that it was better to tread slowly with soft steps than to impose an all-out curfew.

Director Shaw was first to respond. "Mr. President, we can't. The Constitution gives the people the right of assembly, of speech, of association, freedom of movement. Also, Congress has long since forbidden the use of the military in civilian law enforcement within our nation."

"I am aware of the law, Director. Let us say that the army is simply assisting the police and other authorities to ensure public safety."

"That will not stand any kind of scrutiny, sir."

"We will let the lawyers debate it in front of the Supreme Court. But for now we need to act.

"Gentlemen, I want as many soldiers, marines, airmen, and sailors as possible deployed on the streets, as soon as possible, along with the entire force of the FBI."

"Mr. President, we can't… you can't— The Constitution has to be protected. And as you know full well we have no Supreme Court to consider the case. We can't just ignore the Constitution. It is the very essence of the United States."

"It is a contract between the government and the people, a contract that the people have broken. Look out the window; the country is on the verge of being burned to the ground. Director, we have a crisis. Shall we do nothing or act to save this country?

"If anyone here feels uncomfortable with this, then feel free to hand in your resignation. I will give you my personal assurance that there will be no repercussions, other than your own guilt at failing your country in its darkest hour.

"I feel your concerns, Director. I know it's difficult to accept the idea of even temporarily circumventing the Constitution. It is not something I'm taking lightly. But let me be clear, the Constitution is not the country, and the country is not the Constitution—especially when the contract has been broken."

"Sir," Director Shaw persisted, "a nationwide curfew is unheard of. It is unacceptable."

"Then bring the rioting under control, Director," Clayton all but snapped at the man.

"In time I'm sure the situation will calm down on its own."

Clayton glared at him in disbelief. "How long can we afford to wait? And why should it calm down? Can you provide tens of millions of jobs by the end of the week?"

Shaw tried another approach in desperation. "The public will never stand for the curfew, sir."

"I think the people many actually welcome it," General MacAdams offered. "Many will be grateful for the end of the violence, provided the president makes it clear that this is a national emergency, and once the situation is back under control, the president will deal with their grievances." He glanced across to the other members of the Joint Chiefs, who all gave him a tiny nod.

"You support this?" Shaw retorted. "You swore an oath to protect the Constitution as well. And the military cannot be deployed against the citizens."

"Director Shaw, I have been informed that the military can, in certain circumstances, be used within the United States… even to quell rioting," General MacAdams said.

"The president is not merely talking about a few riots; he is talking about denying the right of free assembly, the right of movement."

"And if the courts declare it to be unlawful, then the troops will go back to their bases." The general leaned towards the director. "I see no problem, unless you're suggesting that the president will make these restrictions permanent. And if so, are you suggesting that I would obey illegal orders?" The general's jaw tightened as he glared that the director.

Suddenly, Shaw knew what it felt like to have a laser sight trained onto a spot between his eyes. It was discomfiting, to say the least.

Clayton felt he had to jump in, before the old general tore the director of the FBI to shreds. "General, I appreciate your loyalty to this country. Director?"

Shaw believed he had no other option. "Sir, I swore to uphold the Law." "So the temporary suspension of the Constitution is more important than saving the country?" Clayton almost sighed in exasperation. "This is the Constitution we're talking about."

"Good God, man." This time Clayton did snap at the director. "Are you truly so blind? What good is the Constitution when the very ones who should be defending it are the ones… figuratively… burning it? I should not have to send one soldier onto the streets. It should be the people condemning and opposing the violence, not sitting back and letting it happen, even condoning it. Let's get real. You have a choice: stand up, and be counted or piss in your pants. You choose.

"Anyway, we have a lot to do." Clayton breathed in before slowly breathing out. "General, you will immediately begin deploying your troops. I also want your people to present a full briefing to my senior staff as soon as possible. It's important that we communicate." *So much for my warm, fatherly speech, Clayton told himself.*

"Yes sir." General MacAdams spoke his agreement. "We will get onto it immediately." The chiefs of staff stood to leave.

"Thank you, General. —Uh, would you be so good as to ask the Secret Service chief to step in?"

"Yes sir." Everyone turned to leave, Director Shaw bringing up the rear. A few minutes later the director of the president's Secret Service detail entered.

"Mr. President, you wanted to see me?"

"Yes. Peter, I need you to get every available agent out onto the streets to help the military."

"Mr. President, with things as they are, I must strongly object. The role of the Secret Service is clearly circumscribed. There are other authorities—" "Who will all be out there doing their jobs. But one of the strongest messages I can send is to commit my very own bodyguard to help re-establish order. Look, I'll happily park my backside in the command bunker and won't move if that'll make you happy." "Well. We don't have to go that far."

"Okay, I won't leave the White House unless you're satisfied with my security, scout's honour."

"I really don't like this, sir."

"Yes, I can see that. And we will need to talk about that later on. For now, you and yours need to be seen out on the streets. Be visible; I need all the help I can get."

The two men climbed off the bus they had taken from Texas, mingling innocuously with the other passengers. In time they walked away, down the poorly lit street. Then, when satisfied that they were not being followed, they swiftly crossed over a few blocks until they had reached the location where their contact had promised to be waiting.

"This is crazy," one spat in angry frustration.

"We're here so we can wait the half hour," answered the other.

A police car came into view and stopped five houses down from where they stood. As the two officers exited the car, a tall figure emerged from behind the two men from Texas. "Wait one minute; then follow me." The man moved away without waiting for a response.

One of the officers saw him approach but thought little of it. The area was a quiet, peaceful neighbourhood. They were responding to a family dispute, just a little too much noise from one of the neighbours.

The two officers headed towards the front door of the house.

With calm precision the tall man raised his right arm and fired the silenced pistol, two shots per officer. Even as he finished firing, he broke into a run and reached the downed officers to fire one more into each head.

The two men from Texas followed as instructed.

"Check them," the tall man with the gun ordered the less plump of the two.

"But—"

"Check them," the tall man repeated.

No real need, the bullet holes had entered the skulls. "Yeah, they're dead."

The man nodded. "You have one hour before the next bus back to Texas. Again you will pay in cash. I will be in touch." The tall man turned and calmly walked away.

First blood; the conspiracy had been set in motion. The two men looked at each other and began their rushed walk back to the bus station.

Chapter 3

OPEN MEDIA

"Ladies and gentlemen, the president of the United States." The White House press secretary turned to welcome Clayton Prescott to the lectern.

The media watched as Clayton entered the room and took the podium, many taken by surprise at the sudden change in the menu that was on offer today.

"Thank you all for coming. And Ann will be with you shortly to make her scheduled presentation, but the nation's affairs call for immediate action. Thus I will be brief and to the point.

"The situation is grave. As you know, we have rioting and social unrest in many places in the United States. We have fires burning across our nation to the point where our firefighters, police, and National Guard are stretched to the limit; at times they are even overwhelmed. We cannot continue like this. That is why I have come before you today to ask that we put a stop to this violence, which helps no one.

"I know, as a compassionate people, many Americans do not want to see homes burned down and harm done to their fellow citizens. I also know that many are angry—furious at how another financial collapse has cost so many their jobs and others their future hopes. But destroying our economy will only destroy a liveable future for us all. Hoping to punish the financial system at the nation's expense is not the answer.

"Therefore I have given the police and the FBI, in concert with the military, the power to establish a nationwide curfew. From dusk to dawn any group larger than five people will be asked to disband or face arrest.

"Daytime protest marches are to be peaceful and need government approval over the route taken and other issues concerning the marches. This will require assurances from organizers that the marches will be peaceful, or else they will be barred from any further protest activities.

"Further, there will be restrictions on travel for known instigators of violence.

"My fellow Americans, we need to put a stop to the violence. Let me be clear. I support your right to peaceful protest. Indeed, I encourage you all to continue placing the spotlight on the social and economic inequality in our society. For we do need to continue the struggle for equality." Clayton saw the look of surprise on many of the media's faces.

"But it must be peaceful, nonviolent. If violence does occur, I ask you to refrain from your legitimate right to protest until the violent elements that are subverting your peaceful protests can be brought under control. Once more, I call upon you to help re-establish some level of stability, along with giving your government the time to find some solutions to our troubles.

"This nationwide state of emergency will only be in place until such time as law and order are restored. Thank you all, and may God bless America in its time of need." Clayton turned and began walking towards the door, even as a dozen voices cried out in protest at his abrupt dismissal.

"Wait," declared Brenda Carr of the *New Age* newspaper with indignant rage. "This has got to be unconstitutional. You're virtually staging a coup." That stopped Clayton, who turned to face the woman. "Coup?" he asked, matching her tone.

She was caught by the outrage in that single word. Her words had slipped out, more out of frustration than anything else. But as she thought about it, wasn't that what he was doing? "Aren't you trampling on the people's rights? I mean, what about the people's right of movement. The public's right to voice their concerns without gaining government approval beforehand? That's something straight out of Russia or China."

Watching from the doorway, Abb Cole groaned in exasperation. *Where the hell did they find this liberal idiot?* But his exasperation was more out of concern at what might happen if Clayton said the wrong thing. If he even seemed to hint at some military coup, it could all go badly. *Why did he take the bait? What the hell is he thinking?*

"Have I abolished the courts? Ordered the imprisonment of the remaining Senators and House representatives? Closed down and silenced the media? Ordered the imprisonment of any political… ideological opponents? Removed due process?"

"But to deploy the military on American streets—isn't that unconstitutional?" Carr spoke up in her own defence.

"I am using my executive authority to employ the military to assist the police in bringing the unrest to an end. I hardly think that constitutes a coup."

"But you will deny some people their right of movement," another voice announced; "that is unconstitutional."

"I am sure the public will understand." Clayton stood erect with conviction.

Another joined the baying of the pack, eager for fresh blood. "Even when the public has every right to be sceptical? How many will take this as an affront to their liberties?"

"Ladies and gentlemen, in the few days that I have been in office, you have done nothing but whine and complain about the government's 'refusal' to act and denounce its inability to provide security and safety to its citizens.

"Now, no sooner do I act that you are happy to make any wild accusations, regardless of whether there is any evidence—and refusing to consider the consequences of your words, the potential damage done by your endorsement, even your legitimization of the rioters' behaviour." "That's totally inaccurate," Brenda Carr answered; "we have just been reporting the news." Clearly she felt the fire of righteousness, surrounded by her supportive colleagues.

"There is reporting the news and there is presenting your opinions as the news. If you are unhappy with my actions, fine. All you need to do is just stop the rioting and social unrest, and I will happily order the army back to barracks and start work on congressional elections." Clayton's steady glare scanned the room, seeing the unwillingness of the reporters to even consider his words. With an even colder stare he turned to leave the room. Only too be confronted by a shocked Ann Hornwood, her face pale, her eyes wide with disbelief. Although Clayton had sufficient time to warn Abb prior to the media briefing, he had not been able to inform Ann of his decision. In truth, he had simply been in too much of a rush to consider her.

"He can't palm this off onto us…," another reporter stage-whispered to the crowd.

"Mr. President, the people have a right to know how long you intend to enforce your curfew," Carr called out to the president.

"Sir, you can't just make such a declaration without addressing the constitutional issues," barked another reporter.

The howls of the pack grew in strength as their outrage spawned new accusations.

Clayton angrily strode back to the lectern. "To the people of this nation, America faces the greatest political and economic crisis in its history. Therefore we can no longer afford the squabbling and sanctimony that allow us to act as if an individual's beliefs override all other considerations. Put simply, we can no longer waste time and money on petty indulgences. I have, therefore, three announcements to make.

"The first is that America can no longer afford its drug habit. The billions that we waste on illegal drugs can be better employed in rebuilding the economy. Accordingly, I have decided that, with the public's approval by referendum, the penalty for selling illegal drugs will be a mandatory death sentence, to be carried out within six months of being convicted of the crime."

Two reporters actually opened their mouths in bewilderment: had he actually said what they thought they heard?

"Equally, we can no longer afford the ridiculous cost and poor health outcomes of American health insurance. Therefore I will immediately create a working group that will be tasked with cutting a person's health insurance cost by half within a year. If that means nationalizing the insurance companies or setting up a Federal Health Insurance Scheme, then that is what we will do."

Brenda glanced at her colleagues to gauge the level of incredulity amongst the others.

"Finally, the massive expenditure on firearms within our nation, mostly due to their loss or theft, which often result in these weapons falling into the hands of criminals, must stop. To that end I will present a two-step solution to the new Congress or employ a public referendum." He paused for a moment.

"The first step will be to enact a new law enforcing stricter gun security. In short; if it's not in your hand, then it must be locked away in a federally approved gun safe, gun locker, or cabinet.

"The second step will be to set up a federal gun licence for all gun owners." He could almost laugh at the ridiculous looks on their faces.

"The licence will allow all the details—the owner, the type of weapon, its serial number—to be held in a national data base." Clayton's hands gripped the lectern.

"This licence will discourage the theft of these firearms, thus easing the economic burden on our police over gun theft and the associated violence." Clayton's steady gaze swept the room.

"Now, as the situation stabilizes, I hope to present further issues we need to engage with in public debate to get America back on its feet. Working together—united— I believe we will weather this terrible storm we now face, and as a nation and as a people we will come out of this stronger. I ask you all to stand firm against the storm. Thank you." With that he turned and walked towards the door.

This time there was a babble of confused, uncertain voices. For a moment all were too stunned to frame a question. It all seemed too much to take in. Yet slowly the stunned looks on their faces began to fade.

"Did he just call for the death penalty for drug dealers?" one whispered in disbelief.

"He just—the gun lobby will have a fit," Brenda Carr stammered to herself.

"Just think how the health industry will react," the man next to her mumbled.

"Shit."

"That too…"

"He can't be serious?"

"What if he is?" The baying hounds were quieted by confusion and disbelief.

A senior member of the press spoke up. "This is crazy. He can't make statements like that without explaining himself." *He can't talk to them like that; who the hell does he think he is? They're the media. They hold the government to account. They represent the voice of the people.*

While the reporters' eyes burned holes in the door Prescott had just exited, Ann Hornwood meekly stared at the lectern, bewildered, disbelieving.

What the hell has he done? Prescott's cut his own throat… Madness, this is madness. I can't… What… what can I say to save this mess? As she wondered, she heard a voice calling to her, a faint and rather unsteady voice. "Ann. Damn it, get out there and do the briefing."

"What?" She looked around to see Abb Cole glaring at her.

"The briefing." He repeated with more force.

Anger flared from her gut. She sucked in a breath through her nose and then took a small step before taking another. *Okay, girl, just do the briefing, just get though the briefing.*

"Ladies and gentlemen, I have a few announcements to make." She called the room to order. "After considerable consideration the United States will begin to cut back on some of its foreign aid. This will be a temporary measure until such time as America can afford to meet its overseas obligations. As I said, this will be temporary and depend on the situation as it develops." *God, am I rambling?* "A list of countries and their cuts will be provided, along with the cuts in dollar terms. I will go through the list with—"

"Damn it, Ann. The president can't just declare martial law; the public won't allow it."

"The president is employing his executive authority to use the military to assist the police in re -establishing law and order, as stated. Nothing was said about martial law." Her usual calm and control seemed to have left her.

"You don't need to call a spade a spade as long as it is used as one, Ann. What guarantees are there that this is not some violation of the president's authority?"

"This is not some kind of military coup, Ronald," she replied, almost stammering.

"Yet he will have the military impose a dusk-to-dawn curfew across the whole country," another reporter snapped.

"Honestly, Bob, haven't you been watching TV lately? Seen how many cars and buildings have been torched? Seen the night-time rioting? No? God, what rock have you been living under?" Ann deflected their anger with the consummate ease of a practicing politician.

Damn Prescott, he should've given me a warning. To dump this on her was totally inexcusable. *Doesn't he see he's left me as unprepared as the media?*

"For how long will you impose the curfew?" Brenda spoke up. "Given the nature of the situation, we will have to wait and see. But

I feel confident that it won't be long, provided we can re-establish order." "Will the president impose any more restrictions? Is he really talking about the death penalty for drug dealing?"

"Yeah," another reporter chimed in. "And gun control? What about that?"

"The president will further outline his proposals to the public in due course," Ann responded, then tried to change the subject, "along with answering any questions you may have on the topics you have brought up. But we will leave those topics for another day. Now—"

Brenda jumped back in. "Ann, isn't cutting foreign aid just penny-pinching? Compared to current expenditures, it's just a drop in an ocean of debt."

"Every drop helps," Ann replied. *Shit, if you're going to be hanged, you may as well get your two bits in first. Besides, she's been an asshole for years.* Then she drew a deep breath. *Calm down; this won't help. Just play along and get out of here as soon as you can.*

"Now I have a few more statements to make before we end the briefing." She smiled and calmly, slowly worked her way down the list of items before giving her usual platitudes prior to leaving the room. Behind the door she breathed out. Then, calm and composed, she threaded her way through the corridors until she reached her private office. Seated in her chair, she reluctantly turned on the TV.

And instantly regretted her decision as the news channels spent the following half hour asking philosophers, media potentates, and political psychics for their pearls of infinite wisdom in unfurling the mystery of the president's "outburst," as the media were already referring to the media briefing.

Eventually she began to write the letter she had always feared to write.

Halfway through she received a call.

"Ann, the president wants to see you."

"I'll be there in five." She was almost glad to stop writing. She stood and walked out of her office. She walked into the president's office with a tight face, hating what was to come.

"Ann, I feel that I need to apologize for not giving you a heads-up on the briefing."

"No need for that, Mr. President. Only this is very hard for me, sir. But I must sadly tender my resignation. I can't continue in my current post."

"At ease, Ann. I understand I threw you into the deep end." He sighed. "I was rushing to get this done. But that is no excuse. All I can do is assure you that you will be kept in the loop from now on. In fact, I need you to set up a series of interviews—fireside chats with one or two suitable media representatives."

"Sir, do you know what you have done? You may well have ended your career."

"Do you think I'm worried about re-election? I assure you I will listen to your opinions, as I have done in the past, but right now we have to move fast. Now, what do you think of the media's response?"

"Well, a lot of shock with a bit of uncertainty mixed in. For all their talk and bluster, I think they're treading carefully, trying to blame you without blaming you. I'd say they're waiting for someone to take the lead or for the polls to show what the public's response will be; then they'll tailor their response. This is very new for them, to say the least."

"Being publicly attacked by the president?"

"And the rest. One or two are being generous, hinting that you're under a lot of pressure. And in all honesty, a lot of people are sick of the media. Especially when they know how much certain media personalities draw in a year compared to the average worker. But the rest of it—what were you thinking?"

As she finished speaking Abb Cole entered the room. "Sir, I need a moment in private."

Ann gave him a lopsided grin and left. She could imagine what was bothering Abb.

"Sir, I know you have the right to say what you want. And you're under pressure with this Texas nonsense. But what were you thinking?" Abb almost choked on the words. He had been pacing up and down in his office, trying to work out why Clayton had gone off the handle with what he himself considered to be wild declarations. He had known about the military curfew but not the rest. He was still thinking about the fallout to the shitstorm when the sudden flood of calls began—calls he had no desire to answer. He had been close to a blind rage by the time he had hung up on the last caller.

"You need… I can't do my job if you just come up with this sort of stuff. Death penalty for drug dealers, locking up guns, nationalizing health—" Where had he got these crazy ideas? "I have no idea how to fix this."

"Abb, I understand, but there is nothing to fix. When the media kept asking the same bloody questions, there and then, I realized they were never going to truly listen to me with an open mind. No matter what I said, they wouldn't believe me."

"Where is the surprise in that? Just typical media suspicion." *He knows that, so why did he blow up?*

"I mean they truly won't listen. They were not going to meet me halfway, even in the middle of a national crisis that could possibly cripple this country for years. They were already convincing themselves of my duplicity." His eyes clouded over for a second. "You know, I spent hours going over Ann's speech, getting it just right for tomorrow—to heal the wounds and try to bring the people together. What a fool I was. Kind, sympathetic words of encouragement are not going to work. I need to take direct action."

By creating fear of insanity in the White House? Abb wondered. "So you're going to give it to them by cutting your own throat?" The thunderous look on Abb's face almost made Clayton laugh. "This isn't funny. You have infuriated just about everyone. The head of the gun lobby has already gone barking mad. I just got off the phone with the guy, who was blasting my ear off. Spent ten minutes going on about how he'll organize a million-man march against 'gun confiscation.'

"Liberal governors pissing themselves that they won't get their regular income from selling dope… Damn it, everyone will be out for blood. What were you thinking?" Abb ended up repeating himself.

"The government has to be seen doing something," Clayton offered with a calm voice. "Much more, we need to be doing something constructive."

"And your answer is guns, health, and drugs?"

"If it can keep their minds off military coups and presidents taking power 'illegally,' you have a better answer? Kill two birds with one stone. I needed to take the imitative, take the damned fight to them. Abb, I… we don't have the time to play around. Good or bad, we have to move."

"But 'shock and awe'?"

"It got their attention, Abb. And honestly, I will be damned no matter what. This way we may actually achieve something worth the effort."

Abb gave him a strange look. "So just where did you come up with all that stuff?"

"My bad old days in university."

"Your university… was it burned down for heresy, by any chance?"

While Clayton was still addressing the briefing, deep within the Pentagon, General MacAdams was already issuing the orders to his staff that would arouse the behemoth from its hibernation. A task far easier said than done; for all the talk of military precision and speed, the Army and Marine Corps were large and cumbersome at the best of times. Worse still, the military had no experience and little planning for deploying combat units within American cities to assist the police. Their experience came from the bad taste of occupied cities.

Being mindful of bad press, the general had decided to start off slowly and carefully. Small reconnaissance/liaison units had already been dispatched. These were being swiftly followed up by deploying forward headquarters. These command centres would be set up in the cities or districts where the troops were to operate well in advance of the main body's arrival.

While these timid steps were being undertaken, the Army began the inevitable briefings, along with developing their rules of engagement. Once orders were issued and operational plans were completed, the individual headquarters would hand out the riot equipment according to the soldiers' tasking. Only when the old general was satisfied that all logistics and planning were attended to could the military units begin their actual deployment.

Even with such delays, within a day convoys of hummers and trucks rolled out from Camp Pendleton, California, as the 1st Marine division began its long march to its assigned areas of operation.

Matching them step for step were the 2nd Marines from Camp Lejeune, North Carolina.

The 3rd Armoured division from Fort Hood found they needed more time, as they were not taking their heavy armour with them into the cities.

This mildly amused the 1st Infantry division, from Fort Lewis, Washington, whose officers had made more than one pointed remark about how the armour was always late for the party.

While the 1st infantry were still chuckling, one battalion of the 5th Infantry division from Fort Polk, Louisiana, had already turned on their vehicle engines for their short drive to their assigned areas.

A half hour later lead elements of the 7th Infantry division out of Fort Ord, California, rolled onto the highway.

In Colorado, the first two battalions of the 8th Infantry division from Fort Carson rolled through its gates, with the lead unit almost making a wrong turn.

On the other side of the country lead elements of the 10th Infantry Division emerged from Fort Drum, New York.

From Fort Bragg, North Carolina, the 82nd Airborne Division, minus its parachutes, took to the road.

The 101st Air Assault division, Fort Campbell, Kentucky, employed some of their helicopters to allow better movement for their ground forces at potential choke points on their route of march.

Other Army divisions and smaller independent units also rushed to turn on their engines and roll out for their bases all across the United States.

Although nowhere near the numbers of soldiers or marines, airmen and sailors from dozens of small and large bases were loaded unceremoniously into the backs of trucks and sent into the waiting jaws of the rioting taking place across the country.

Overseeing the military deployment from within the Pentagon, General MacAdams could only wait and see how the situation would develop. He did not expect to see any tangible results for some time. That did not stop him from looking up from his desktop at regular interval to glance at the clock. *Some good indicators wouldn't hurt*, he silently told his office.

He continued to nurse his hopes until a staffer entered to shatter that view with his first updates. He studied the reports with growing unease. The local authorities were not overly confident of their success.

When told of how many additional bodies they would receive, the locals and Feds expressed genuine concern. They had hoped for far more personnel.

What the hell did they expect, given the size of the Army these days? They should be grateful the military had managed to stabilize two hot spots as they rolled out across the country. *Even if it was more good luck than anything else,* he admitted to himself.

One entire infantry battalion had been driving through Charleston at the very moment when a riot had flared up.

The other incident had been just as fortunate: on its way to the designated dispersal point, a full Marine Corps company had stopped to eat and refuel on the side of the road when the local sheriff had called for their assistance.

That was the good news. The bad was the bad mood held by a growing number of the public. According to one report the Army's presence seemed to only agitate the protestors when they heard the news. *It's still too early; give it time,* he cautioned himself.

A knock on the door ended his thoughts for a moment. "Come in." Colonel Susho, one of his senior staff, entered.

"Sir, the liaison team with the NSA has reported chatter on the iNet." The general nodded. The intelligence agency was watching all forms of social media more closely than ever now—enough to see a few tentative signs and possible patterns emerge that hinted at a possible course of action. The colonel handed over a folder. "There is enough to suggest the anarchists are organizing for a major operation—two or possibly three of the largest protest marches we have seen so far, on Friday."

The general took the folder and began scanning the report, becoming ever more dejected. A real fear grew in his stomach. "The NSA obtained this much detail from some Internet chatter?"

"Actually, I talked to our team. They think some of the intel came from an informer."

The general gave a belly laugh. "Wonderful. We spend billions on electronic intercepts, and we get better intel from an informer. That just makes my day." *If only we had the communications blackout,* thought MacAdams. That was the one thing that could change the equation, but there were risks of a major public backlash, just for one.

And then there's the question of obtaining the legal authority to actually cut our own communication and Internet links. Well, early days, very early days. Still, if those potential protests erupt into violence or worse... If the marches continued into the night, ignoring the curfew, God help us then.

Just as he began to read another report, a young lieutenant raced into his office. "Sir, we have a report of a violent confrontation with some Marines."

Outside Kabul, Afghanistan

The three men sat on pillows, silently sipping on their black coffee. The young Egyptian addressed the grey-haired Turk on his right. "Our friends in Pakistan are very angry with the Americans, my friend." "Indeed? For calling them liars and the filthy mongrel dogs that they are?" The man smiled through his long beard. "How truly unforgivable of them, as if the Pakistani's word of honour could ever be questioned… the filthy, lying mongrel dogs." He turned to the young man and scoffed with contempt. "Let the dogs bark for all the good it will do them; no one listens."

"Be as it may, they are our brothers."

"They are not our brothers," Greybeard snapped back. "I spent too many years in their prisons for that." His words dripped with scorn. "They are flea-infested dogs, who swear eternal friendship and brotherhood for as long as you are useful to them, then throw you to the American dogs when they are finished with you."

"For all that, they can give us the Devices we have always wanted." "They will give us one of their Devices?" Greybeard whispered in disbelief.

"No, but they have told us how to acquire some from the Russians." "Why the Russians? Why not some of their own if they are so willing?"

Greybeard glared at the young Egyptian.

"They call it 'plausible deniability,' after the Americans. They have provided us with the location and all the details, the codes we need. We need only go in and obtain the Devices."

"Do not be so easily fooled. If it were that easy, we would have acquired one years ago. There are those who think of the Russians as dull-witted, inbred fools, but I do not. I do not take Russian security for granted."

"Nor have you reason to do so. But remember, the West is on its knees, their economy in tatters. Thus they cannot pay the Russians what they want for their oil and gas. Last year they cut over 13 per cent of their demand for Russian gas. This year it may be as high as 15 per cent. As a result the Russians are suffering greatly."

Greybeard waved the argument away. "They need only raise their price."

And the Europeans wouldn't buy oil from someone else? The young Egyptian wanted to call the man a fool. "The more the Russians raise the price, the more the economy of the West will shrink to pay for the increase; the more it shrinks, the lower the demand for gas and oil… They are like two lovers, entwined. One suffers, both suffer." He had no desire to spend fruitless hours talking about the mechanics of international oil pricing, so he gave what he thought was a plausible explanation to the older man. Ignorance can indeed be… useful.

"Many Russians are suffering, now that they cannot get their toys from the West. And so they are more than happy to sell their mothers"— the Egyptian sneered with contempt—"and happily throw in their grandmothers to sweeten the deal. Given that, is it any surprise that some would sell any information they have to their Pakistani friends?"

"Their Pakistani handlers, you mean. Whatever the truth, the Device will be heavily guarded."

"True, normally. But as they say, these are desperate times. If you agree to help, all will be explained." The Egyptian grinned with a hint of secrets yet to be told.

"Do you believe it is possible?" The grey-bearded Turk turned and asked the old man with the white bread who had not spoken a word so far.

"I have been assured that it can be done." The old imam held considerable authority and was close to men of great power. It had been his voice that had brought the Turk and, before him, the Chechen leader into this old house. The Turkish leader had been drawn from his bolthole, the Chechen leader from fighting alongside yet another Islamist group. "But only with your help. We will need a strong force to take these Devices from the Russians, I am told."

"I need to know more." Greybeard hungered for them to convince him. "Three years ago the Russians built a military training facility for their special forces about two hundred and fifty miles from their coastal city of Mezen. And it is indeed a training facility for their elite troops in all manner of warfare, which includes employing small tactical nuclear weapons. That explains the stockpile of nuclear weapons they have there."

"Special forces?" Greybeard did not like that idea.

"Less than three hundred, we are told," the young Egyptian explained. "With all the troubles in Europe the Russians have moved their more 'flexible'—or rather covert—forces closer to their borders. There is more, much more, but you must decide now."

"The rest you will know once your decision is made," the old imam pressed. "Again, will you help?"

"Have I not done as you have asked? Over thirty of my men travel from one end of Russia to the other, living as if they were Russians and never knowing why. But now I begin to understand. So yes, my men and I will help." The forward planning that must have gone into this, he marvelled.

But why should he be so surprised? He was part of it. After all, he had selected dozens of the brightest recruits to be secretly sent away in ones and twos. Not to some large training camp, but to a quiet farm where three of his best fighters had made the recruits into killers. Once the brutal training was complete, each man had quietly returned to his old life before slowly filtering into the soulless cow that was Russia.

No, it wasn't the forward planning; rather, it was the audacity of the thing. He had thought the infiltration of these men into Russia was simply a long-term martyrdom operation. A pointless effort, he had thought when the old imam had first asked for his help. *What can they hope to achieve?* he had thought at the time.

But now, now, we may actually have a chance to achieve something. His old, tired eyes lit up at the thought.

"Then my house is yours. We will need your men to act, within five days."

Greybeard hesitated for a moment. They had just given him a rough location of the target, but it was enough to worry him. "Some, a few, may not arrive in time, if they are to avoid attention." Just delivering their instructions would take days.

"We understand. It was always accepted that some would not arrive. Indeed, it may help cause confusion if the Russians are monitoring some of your men." If a few fighters were still days away from the target, it might hold back any Russian response. Even a single day could be vital.

They talked and shared food. Sometime later Greybeard left the room, as did the young Egyptian.

The old imam was left in his empty room to his silent thoughts until the man hiding behind a second door entered.

"You heard everything, Salem?" The old man took in the sight of the young face with strong features, clear, dark eyes, and full beard, a true warrior of Islam.

"Yes, it goes well." The young man replied.

"Perhaps. Tell me again why we need these men." His old eyes had seen the doubts in the Turk's own eyes.

"My imam, in many ways the Turk is correct. It is well known where such weapons are kept. Most large American or Russian naval bases would have a number, thus the unusually strong security the Turk spoke of." Salem thought it best to humour the old man. The old imam was their spiritual leader, yet of late he had become easily confused, often finding doubts in every shadow, as if there could ever be a perfect plan.

"It has always been about acquiring and using them; that has always been the difficulty. Like the 'detonation codes' for American bombs, each nation- state has safeguards. And unlike the British spy films, you cannot simply drive onto a military base and flash your false ID, order a half dozen dull-witted guards to throw a nuclear device into the boot of your car, and drive off with a merry Christmas to one and all." The young man sneered at the stupidity of Western movies.

"The Pakistanis have given us the codes, the second key if you will." He hesitated for a moment, as if embarrassed. "The Turk and the Chechen's men can be relied upon to provide us with the third key…"

"And yet they are here instead of leading their men into battle?" The accusation was clear. The old imam was becoming far less trusting, even towards men he knew had proved their loyalty to jihad many times over. This saddened young Salem. Years ago the imam's sermons had fired the blood for holy jihad. Now he had difficulty holding a thought.

"They must be here for the sake of security. We cannot risk their capture and interrogation now that they know of our plans. The couriers and I can deliver the instructions to their warriors."

The old imam shook his head. "But you know much more than they do. Yet, you are going into the jackal's den."

"They are known leaders of men who will attract attention. Indeed, their coming here could make the Russians feel safer. Put them at ease. I am unknown and will not draw attention. Even if I am arrested, I will be seen, at worst, as a courier and little else. And Ahmed wants me there." He said the name with reverence. That such a man would consider him capable made his heart beat with pride.

Salem finally took his leave of the old imam to go to his small room. Once inside, he shaved off his beard and began to dye his hair. The contact lenses could wait until his departure.

Chapter 4

Freedom of speech is not the freedom to lie.

—Arnold Whitehall

Senator Chuck Walker faced the cameras. His bearded face, red and raw, stared at the cameras with furious outrage as if daring any to challenge him. It was an excellent performance, he had long ago learned just how much outrage was needed to promote empathy with the viewers.

"I can't believe that the acting president would declare martial law, tearing up the Constitution. He is ignoring the compact made between the people and its government. The acting president must immediately lift all restrictions and curfew."

A voice rose from the crowd of reporters. "Senator, what do you say to all those who are calling for law and order to be properly enforced? Even if that means we use the Army to crack down on the protestors?"

"Not if it violates of the Constitution."

"'Acting president,' Senator? He was duly sworn in according to the laws of the land." Old Andy Moore hated the senator's guts. Anything he could do to upset the self-righteous bastard was worth it to him.

"I would remind you that he was not elected to the office. Therefore, until we have a new Senate and Congress, I call on the acting president to submit to a 'Senatorial committee' who can advise and counsel the acting president until full elections can be carried out."

"With no Congress or Senate to speak of, just how would you work that, Senator?" Andy was enjoying himself.

"We still have a few members of the Senate who can take up the role."

"Yourself, included, Senator?" Andy Moore, nearing retirement, felt safe enough to engage in extra boldness.

"I am certain that the acting president knows that we need to have a united stance at this critical juncture, so I call upon him to—"

Clayton turned off the television with an angry flick. He rose from the plush leather chair and walked towards the door, glancing at a furious Abb Cole.

"And there we have it," Abb said. "Our much-loved champion of the people wanting to work with us for the betterment of the nation. Where the hell did he get the nerve to think the president should submit to some senatorial committee?"

"We still need to work together. So let's hear him out, Abb. Give him a call and arrange a time to meet." Clayton walked through the door to find Jonathan waiting.

"Okay, Jonathan, who's on the agenda?" With so many meetings and interviews planned, he was now having trouble keeping track.

"Sir, you have the interview with Miss Brooke in five minutes. Then you have a meeting with the Secretary of Defence and the head of the Joint Chiefs, followed by a private meeting with the Treasury Secretary and the head of the Reserve Bank."

"Both? What do they want?" Something wasn't right when both of them asked for a joint meeting, given the fragile condition of the economy. He had already heard of a few rumours that were worrying. Bad news wasn't something the country needed, and he most certainty didn't need it.

"Unknown."

"I so love being kept well informed." Clayton walked into the room set aside for the interview to see a young woman earnestly watching her camera crew set up.

Sandra Brooke watched the crew with a mild sense of unease. *Come on, get over it.* She was experienced and had gone toe to toe with a lot of ugly politicians who thought they could charm the "sweet little thing" with her pretty blond hair. They often assumed she was too stupid to engage in a real no-holds-barred interview, to their regret. She hid her smile. *This one will make my career.* She took her seat and waited.

She glanced towards where Clayton stood, trying not to fidget as the woman who normally attending to the president's media appearances checked him over before giving her nod of approval. *Check his make -up all you want; it still won't save him. Lights, camera, action,* she thought as the president walked over and lowered himself into the seat. They wired him up with swift efficiency.

"Thank you for your time, Mr. President."

"My pleasure, Sandra. You have done such good work in the past, I am sure we can enlighten the public greatly with this interview."

The cameraman nodded once, and she grinned. *Here we go.*

"Mr. President, if I may get to the matter at hand, there has been a lot of talk about the media outburst—"

Clayton jumped in with enthusiasm. "Good, excellent. That's what we need, a good debate about accuracy in the media. It's well past time, I think. The media's job is to report the news, the facts, not allow invention or reinterpretation based upon a point of view.

"Sandra, one of the greatest challenges this nation faces is the total failure of the media to keep the public accurately informed while remaining divorced from prejudice.

"We already have way too much social and media misinformation that's confusing the public… and often doing far worse."

"I'm sorry, sir, but that is far from fair. We do present the news impartially and as accurately as we can. As for social media… well, they have dealt with 'fake news.' Fake news is being taken down."

"We have had questionable news coverage for many decades, Sandra, long before 'fake news' became an issue. One only needs to go back to the Spanish-American war to prove that the print media has a questionable history." Some historians had long argued that the war rhetoric in parts of the American press had been a major factor in bringing about the conflict.

"You and your colleagues have failed to realize that president Trump could slander the media as 'fake news' because the media had dragged their own reputation through the mud—every time the conservative media attacked the liberal media or the liberal questioned the conservative media.

"Facts are not opinions that can be re-interpreted by a person's ideological bigotry.

"So let us not indulge in red herrings, for therein lies our problem, Sandra, our refusal to confront misinformation, lies, and even subterfuge." Clayton smiled pleasantly at the young woman. "The news is not conservative, the news is not liberal. Opinions are conservative or liberal, *but* they are not the *facts*. How can the people have faith in the media's impartiality when our traditional media are locked in mutual opposition?

"Indeed, the mere fact that we have a conservative and a liberal media simply contradicts the argument for a free, independent, and impartial media, which we desperately need to fight the extremist rubbish that is out there."

"With respect, Mr. President, that sounds like a rather blatant attempt to blame the media for—well, the failures of others… the government included."

"Thank you for demonstrating my point, Sandra." Clayton smiled sweetly. He then raised his right hand to signal a stop. "But, this is not about laying blame. I am aware that there are some who blame the media for all the ills in the world, the violence, the promiscuous indulgences of teenagers and adults, and other antisocial behaviour.

"While others argue that the media are simply one factor in a much larger equation, there is also the family and other social, economic, and environmental factors that need to be considered."

Damn it. "One factor"? Even when he's defending you, he's still sticking a knife into you. He's turning this from an interview into a lecture. Okay, focus, girlfriend. Calm down and get back into the game. "With respect—"

"It's time, Sandra, well past time for a major change," Clayton cut in with ease. "We need to create a truly impartial media to face this new age we live in, not simply settle for a collection of social-media outlets hawking their own political views, some so farfetched—well, that you wonder what they are on." Clayton hammered away without pause. "All forms of media need to be held to account. We must remember that at this moment they are free from any form of effective scrutiny."

"Are you arguing for government censorship?"

"That is out of the question, Sandra. There must not be any government control over the media. But there must be some acceptable oversight when it comes to accuracy. Some action needs to be taken."

"But we have taken action. Social media now have restrictions on fake news…"

"It is not enough, nowhere near enough."

"Then what do you propose, sir?" *Answer that one in a hurry.* She congratulated herself. Politicians never really had answers to real questions.

"I have given that some thought, and one possible answer is some kind of independent body made up of, perhaps, retired journalists and judges—a kind of fact-checking team that exposes rather than obscures the truth."

"We already have a lot of fact checkers, sir."

"That are often ignored or contradicted, as they have neither credibility nor authority." Clayton shook his head. "We need a way to get the message across. Thus this organisation will need to have the power to hold these institutions to account."

"How would this independent body work?" She wanted to buy some time to think. She was finding it harder to get into the interview. His ruthless attack was not what she had expected. Back at the studio they had all agreed that he would try to backpedal, mend fences… be apologetic, not this raving attack dog.

"It would need to have the power to force an individual or organization to justify their claims, provide facts, or make a public retraction in all the media."

"Sir, I believe many would say the established media are accurate and impartial. And with so many media outlets, the facts will come out.

"Indeed this idea of scrutinizing the media could infringe on our fundamental right of freedom of speech." *He's talking about undermining the media's credibility;* she shivered in fright.

"And many would agree with me that parts of the media are far from impartial or accurate, and thus the *entirety* of the media is failing to uphold what you hold so dear. That is why a few have argued, privately to me, that we should not simply stop at an independent body enforcing accuracy but go to something much more proactive." Clayton deliberately avoided mentioning who suggested the idea.

"'Proactive'? That's—"

He cut her off. "Absolutely essential, Sandra, according to some senior experts I have talked with. Who've argued that it's high time the public was properly informed with a detailed analysis of all the facts without prejudice.

"They recommended the establishment of truly independently run, self-criticism programs on all prime time TV channels, correcting any misinformation… put an end to any misconceptions that may arise."

"And if there is nothing to report?"

"If there is only ten minutes of corrections then the rest of the times could be taken up by going into the background of the day's headlines… the story in detail, the politics, the actors—the entire history behind the story, not merely snippets here and there." Clayton stretched out in his chair as he considered his words.

"The internet would have a similar set up… each site would be required to have a link that can independently correct any misconceptions.

"Equally, the print media could have a pull-out section dealing with any misinformation it comes across. Indeed, this scrutiny may help save the print media."

"I'm not sure I understand, sir." He was going too fast.

"As you know, the print media are suffering a slow decline, losing far too many readers. So presenting in-depth investigative journalism could save them."

"But we have done in-depth pieces on many subjects, going into great detail—"

"Then explain the public's confusion over former President Obama's health care reforms. Let's be honest, the media totally failed to enlighten the public with the facts. There was so much misinformation and myth, lies and rumours—and very little challenging and correcting the campaign of naked deception.

"Once you have finished there, you can explain the misdirection, the multiple view points from the media outlets during the Trump years. If that doesn't prove my point, nothing will."

Sandra opened her mouth to begin her defence of the media, but her moment vanished.

"Indeed, Sandra, I would say that the media have not only failed in their duty to the public, but they have failed this nation in an even more fundamental way," Clayton went on, leaning back in his chair as if he were back in his old university giving an interesting lecture to an eager young class. "This nation has so many issues it needs to face up to. Yet so many national debates on both domestic and international matters are simply avoided by the media. America can benefit greatly by having a forum for national debates."

"With respect, that is hardly the media's role, sir." Sandra stood her ground. "And there are some media debates on television. And we do have other forums and town hall meetings."

"Nationwide debates, Sandra? A national conversation on where America should stand on the Israeli–Palestinian conflict? Our Republican leadership's refusal to deal with climate change along with inequality, social injustice, and gun violence? And what should be of great importance to us all: the people's vision of our country's future.

"We have massive issues to face, yet as a nation, have we even begun such debates to forge a consensus, a unified view, that a… future Congress and Senate would obey—instead of having policies based on polls and interest groups?"

"That all sounds very interesting, but it is questionable whether that is the media's role. Sir, many would argue that freedom of speech is more than stating facts. The right to express one's opinion, to debate one's views, is vital. We need a degree of flexibility, of freedom. Some would go so far as to say we need a ferocious free media able to take risks, even if there is a lack of credibility at the time of printing."

"True, but the media has to be more than news snippets and talking heads—"

"Opinion pieces are a perfectly acceptable form of debate."

"And would be completely acceptable if they were based on solid facts and not on an individual's opinions, Sandra. The media have to confront this deluge of misinformation, outright lies—"

"Sir, the established media are not responsible for the failure of social media providers. And I would remind you that they have owned up to their failure. They now post warnings of fake reports, in one example—" "This stubborn attempt to blame 'post-truth,' 'fake news,' and Facebook for all the media's failures is not the answer, Sandra. Allowing people to ignore the truth simply because they want to is not good enough." He paused. "The established media… all forms of the media, have to accept responsibility for their own failures."

"Would you care to be more precise as to where they have failed?" "Well, it's not for me to impose my criteria." He deflected her response. "But surely you can offer the public some clarity." *Now I've got you, you bastard.*

"I'm not sure it would be proper—"

"At least a starting point to explain your grievances, Mr. President." "Perhaps, I suppose. To avoid the objection of bias, I will pick non-

political issues as examples." He smiled at her. "How many Americans believed that the first African American president was a Muslim? How many Americans still believe that the Holocaust, where six million Jews and other minorities were murdered, never happened—despite the eyewitness testimony of our own brave American soldiers? How many Americans even now believe that the book *Protocols of the Elders of Zion* is factual and not a work of propaganda?

"How many Americans do not believe the moon landings were real? How many Americans still believe that 9/11 was the work of the CIA or Israel? How many rednecks still believe that no one of Jewish extraction died in the Twin Towers? How many believe the world is flat?

"How many still believe John F Kennedy was killed in a conspiracy perpetrated by some US military/CIA/Mafia/Russian/Cuban conspiracy? In fact he was assassinated by just about everybody except the Secret Service… Oh, sorry." He comically put a hand over his mouth. "I do believe one theory has it that a member of the Secret Service did accidentally shoot President

Kennedy. About the only ones not accused have been the little green men from Mars; I suppose they'll be blamed next year."

He chuckled. "How many believed the Ebola virus was made in a secret American laboratory? Then we have AIDS. Some Americans argue that due to the rapid spread of the disease, the virus must have been made in one of our labs. This totally ignores the case of patient zero, an airline attendant who travelled from coast to coast. This gay man is believed to have given AIDS to over two hundred gays from New York to Los Angeles."

Clayton gave Sandra another pleasant smile. "Should another virus, sadly, emerge from Africa, will the conspiracy rags and Internet Trolls once more declare that it was 'secretly made in America'? Why is it always an American lab and never a Russian, German, or Chinese lab? Why do so many Americans believe that every horror in existence was made in the good old USA?" Clayton looked straight at Sandra, leaving unasked the question of whether or not it was the media's fault.

"Indeed, I recall a toilet rag of a conspiracy magazine—some pathetic Leftist leftover of the Cold War—declaring that the al-Qaeda leader, Bin Laden, was a trained and paid CIA agent. And yes, after Russia invaded Afghanistan, many thousands of Muslims from all over the world went to wage jihad against the Russians, and one was Bin Laden. And yes, America provided weapons to the Pakistani military to funnel to the Afghan fighters.

"Now, with this 'evidence,' many concluded that Bin Laden, a multimillionaire, a member of one of the richest Saudi families, was taking pocket change to be a CIA stooge. If he was anyone's lackey, he belonged to the Pakistanis, or have we all forgot where our special forces found him?

"And it doesn't stop there. You yourself have already complained about social media. But what have the mainstream media done to confront their lies? What did they do when the Internet trolls declared that the Sandy Hook school massacre never took place?" Clayton glared at Sandra, daring her to challenge him. "Twenty children, most between the ages of five and six, and seven teachers were gunned down by one man with his so-called 'hunting rifle'? And we have the Gun loving Internet filth pissing on their graves. How low can you go?

"These are the sorts of outright lies and half-truths that often lead to paranoia in the community." Clayton drew a deep breath. "And it can be so offensive. I still remember how former First Lady Michelle Obama, in one for those toilet rag conspiracy magazines, was accused of being transgender, formerly a man—obviously in a laughable attempt to accuse Obama of being gay. Now where was the outrage by the supposedly 'responsible' media?"

"In all honesty, sir, conspiracy theories are not really our area of responsibility. And you will find that the media have indeed challenged some crazy theories in the past. We have made documentaries on the assassination of President Kennedy, to name one, arguing against some questionable theories.

"More to the point, sir, we are media outlets, not some debating platform." *He's going too fast; I need to get a hold of this.*

"Then who is responsible? The government can't get involved without being accused of censorship, Sandra."

"Aren't you simply arguing for self-censorship?" Sandra persisted.

"I am asking for accountability, accuracy. When Trump declared that President Obama was a 'founder of ISIS,' did the media demand even a shred of evidence, a public apology or he would face a total media ban?

"In some countries, making such an accusation against a serving president would get you thrown in jail; here it's the first step to the White House. Why? Is it due to the media's failure to stand up for the truth?"

"The media simply report—"

"Lies? Misinformation? Half-truths?" Clayton once more cut her off. "You want another example? What about my dear Republican friends with their constant baying over voter fraud… When will the media or my colleagues provide real proof or shut up?" Clayton tried to remain civil, but his temper was rising. *God, it's like talking to a brick wall.*

"Mr. President, I think you do not give the public enough credit. The vast majority of the public aren't easily fooled and are well informed." She tried to appear composed but was instead grasping for anything that sounded sensible. "You can't fool all the people all the time," she quoted with a smile.

"Ah yes, as long as we have that wonderful little cliché to fall back on." He smiled gently. "But is that enough? After all, 'you can fool some of the people *all* the time,' correct?" He shook his head. "We need to remember that tens of thousands believed Islamic State propaganda and went to fight in Syria; we have all seen and continue to see the bloody results.

"Of equal note, Russia and China have state -controlled media. Why? Is it for the same reason that they have purchased media outlets in the West and donated to Western think tanks and universities? Isn't it to convince enough people in the West to support their agenda? And why shouldn't they, Sandra? What have the media done to uphold their 'sacred trust' of keeping the public accurately informed?"

Sandra clenched her jaw, trying to find another avenue for the interview to take. Even she had read the recent articles bringing to light how Chinese companies aligned to their government had become part owners of an ever growing number of Western newspapers that had unashamedly promoted their interests to the world. Not that the major media outlets seemed overly concerned.

And why should they? Influence peddling was an everyday event. Big business was a whore when it came to peddling its own interests; what was the difference with Russia or China? "I think you are overstating the problem. People can get the facts if they want them."

"So I can spout anything I want, and it's up to the public to find out if I am telling the truth or not?" Clayton scoffed as his eyebrows took flight.

"Of course not; one should always be held accountable." "Just not the media?"

"No, I never said that. I simply mean the mainstream media does check its facts." *Shit, be careful.*

"I do not disagree. Some sections of the media are accurate and impartial, and that is my point. Why can't the rest follow their example? And since the less reputable can't or won't, shouldn't they be placed under scrutiny and when necessary taken to task?"

"But the diversity of options… doesn't that in a way deal with your concern over accuracy? I mean, when we have so many voices, the facts will come out."

"And think of the numerous times when the truth has been drowned out by a horde of banshees." *My God, what is wrong with this woman? She really won't listen or even try. Can't she see the problem with the media in her own stubbornness? How many more times do I have to state the obvious before she gets the message? Okay, once more, different approach.* "Indeed, those instances have not only been ignored but have caused harm."

"Sir… I think that is a totally unacceptable statement."

"So the media has never been taken to court for defamation?" he replied, an edge on his voice. "Never got it wrong?"

"The good we do will always outweigh any minor flaws." Sandra hoped she came across with conviction.

"So any damage is minor?"

"It is normally corrected by a retraction, and it ends there." She declared with conviction.

"You truly believe that?"

"Yes, absolutely."

"Good, so if someone was to turn to the audience and say"—Clayton smiled widely as he turned to the camera—"Doesn't she look like a child molester? Just look at her clothes—don't they scream slimy and suspicious?" Clayton nodded to Sandra. "I heard the whispers about you."

Sandra's jaw dropped.

"The coifed hair, the long manicured fingernails that just shout 'catty claws.' Just look at her an' tell me she don't look unhealthy, sickly in a dirty way." He inched forward, leaning into her face. "Somethin' just doesn't feel right with her. I know she molests children. I know she molests little girls. Come on, I know you molest little girls. I heard all the stories... 'never leave her alone with any little girl in her dressing room.'

"Admit it, you molest little girls. Come on, it's obvious you're one of that kind." All the time he was getting closer and closer. "Come on, admit it, it's obvious you're one of 'em." He was now so close to her face that she was beginning to pull away.

"Admit it, just admit it!" he all but cried out.

Just as Sandra was beginning to feel an edge of fear, he suddenly sat back in his chair. "Now, be honest, Sandra. If some mad shock-jock was to make such ludicrous accusations wouldn't there be some stigma attached to your credibility? Even after you had taken him to court for defamation?" His voice suddenly calm and controlled, even jovial.

"But, say you went to an independent body that had the power to force your detractor to publicly apologise on his own radio station morning and night for an entire month. By doing so wouldn't he remove any stain on your credibility and seriously challenge his own?"

He then smiled sweetly at her. "This is my hope." Clayton continued. "By having the mainstream media under such scrutiny, it with achieve the credibility needed to debunk fraudulent stories.

"We need something, Sandra, that we can *truly* trust to provide accuracy and factual details... Just look at the harm done to the nation from the 'talking heads' with their bigoted and bias opinions that have created so many doubts ... and suspicions that have festered in people's minds." Clayton shook his head as if in disgust at the idea. "We have reached the point, Sandra, where the media can no longer be allowed to ignore the needs of the nation."

"I... I... You can't attack—" Her voice was timid, deflated. She had been shocked into disbelief.

"Now don't get me wrong. If some misconduct has occurred, if a politician has lied, then expose it, but with real facts." Clayton smiled happily as if he had said nothing out of the ordinary.

"If you find little green men from Mars in Area 51," he went on, in seemingly good humour, "then take a few photos and put them on the Net. I personally would love to know that we are not alone in the universe—but I want proof.

"It is often stated that politicians must be held to a high standard. Well, what about the media? Shouldn't they be held to the highest standard possible?

"We have the tabloids, the Internet trolls, the shock-jocks all arguing that they are shining the spotlight upon the truth. Yet there is no spotlight shining upon their 'evidence,' their proof of conspiracies and evil doings. They can 'examine' the evidence of 9/11, but who examines their evidence? Why hasn't the 'credible' media done a proper forensic investigation of their 'evidence' on a systematic basis?

"And doing so may actually be good for your industry, Sandra. Remember, there are those that do not believe anything the media report, who believe the media are controlled by the rich and powerful—that they're mere 'tools of the oppressors.'" He scoffed. "Now if there were a truly independent authority, the media might actually gain some credibility amongst the doubters.

"We all know freedom and liberty comes at a cost. Well, so does freedom of speech. The price for freedom in often paid in blood. The price for freedom of speech is the factual truth. And if we do not have the truth, then we may as well forget about the 'legitimacy' of the media."

He turned to Sandra. "For too long you have taken the money and the glory but not the responsibility. Well, that ends today; American can no longer afford dead weight. The days of wine and roses are gone. From today you will hold yourselves accountable. If not, I will hold you to account by questioning your credibility. Each day of my presidency I will ask what the media have done today to adhere to the standards they expect of others— while calling for independent oversight of your industry."

"That would be a totally unjustified attack against the very bedrock of our society." Still stunned by his attack, Sandra could not think straight. She had nearly begun to shake uncontrollably from his vicious accusation.

"The rioting is a perfect example," Clayton pressed on. "On the surface you have done an excellent job. You have presented endless coverage of all the events, even given the rioters endless opportunities to give their opinions and views to the public. So much so that certain individuals have accused you in the media of legitimizing the violence. I refer to that recent article by Don Adams in the *World Post*, where he all but castigated the liberal and social media for endorsing the protestors' battle cry, 'This is the only way we can get their attention.' Later in the article he even accused some in the media of heaping praise and laurels on the rioters"—Clayton paused to smile gently at Sandra—"while other sections of the media were actively vilifying the protestors, with endless condemnations and demonization, especially some shock-jocks with their 'Lock up the lazy bums.'

"We have one side condemning, the other side justifying, and neither side seeing them as our fellow Americans in hard times."

Shit, is he actually defending the rioters? Sandra thought with glee. *He'll be crucified.*

"But hard times do not justify violence. The simple facts are these: the people have every right to peacefully protest, but that does not give them the right to break the law. And if you don't like the law, then you legally change it for a better one. Yet, I have not heard one serious voice of moderation, of finding a solution other than 'Lock 'em up' or 'Let 'em burn the country down.' Not one call for unity, for compassion or understanding from either side."

He looked straight into the camera as he continued. "Indeed, I hear no encouragement to set higher standards for ourselves instead of allowing the worst elements of society to dominate the debate and bring us down to their level.

"It is not the role of government to dictate, but we all need examples. We should all be encouraged to be the very best we can be. And we can't do that if the media are small, petty and unwilling to stand as a titan in defence of our better nature.

"I truly believe that we need to be compassionate and set higher standards in helping others to create a better future." He glanced at his watch. "Well, that will have to do for today."

"But all the other topics we wanted to discuss—the death penalty for drug dealing…" Her voice sounded small and weak even to her.

"Another time. Unfortunately time is a rather valuable commodity for me of late. I will have my people arrange another time." He stood and thanked her before turning to go, leaving her with a sinking feeling. *I wonder if this is how they felt as the* Titanic *was going down.*

"Gentlemen, my apologies for not arriving earlier, but the media can be dogged." Clayton walked into the Cabinet office in a near rush, taking in the stern look on each man's face. But what slowed him a little was the unexpected presence of the director of the FBI.

"Gentlemen." He gave them the nod to begin as he sat down.

"Mr. President," William Anderson, the Secretary of Defence, began, "we felt that the director should be involved in this briefing, as he has something that may affect the overall plan." In truth the FBI director had been a little too insistent for Anderson's liking, but he had eventually agreed.

"Go ahead." *This is going to be wonderful, even more glorious news, I just know it. Maybe if I declared war on Canada, the news won't seem so bad. And I could air-drop Sandra and the media behind the Canadian lines. Only can I really be that mean to Canada?*

"Mr. President? Sir?" Director Shaw hesitated, puzzled by the distant look on Clayton's face.

"Yes. Yes, go on." Clayton nodded once.

"We are concerned that there have been some major escalations. There have been two targeted killings, two murders that we have reason to suspect were the work of the anarchists."

Shaw brought out two folders from his case. "The first was a former bank CEO, the other a multimillionaire who ran a hedge fund that collapsed and cost its investors millions." He placed the opened folders in front of Clayton.

"Both were wealth, both on the anarchist's website, both found 'guilty' of crimes against the people. Both killed in much the same manner. I was hesitant at first, but if this is an escalation, we may have to take further steps." He had the good grace to actually look a little embarrassed.

"Go on." Clayton read the names of the two men. Yes, that asshole would be a tempting target, Clayton thought. A lot of people had lost their pensions because of his hedge fund fraud, while he had walked away with nearly a billion dollars. Clayton considered it fraud even though it had all been technically legal.

The banker was little better. He had cashed in his shares and resigned several months before the bank had to explain how it had come to carry several billion dollars' worth of questionable debts that should never have been allowed.

"There have also been attacks on bank branches during the last three nights. Thirteen fire bombs and a small truck filled with petrol that was rammed into the front doors of Bank of A, after which the fuel was ignited to engulf the first floor of the bank."

"Yes, I think I saw something about that on the TV." Clayton confirmed his interest in the case.

"We must not overlook this, sir. This is a serious escalation. The deaths of these two men and deliberate attacks on our banking structure can have serious ramifications."

"Agree, so we have two instances?" Clayton nodded slightly.

"There has also been the murder of two police officers, a cold-blooded assassination. We need to take this escalation seriously, sir."

Clayton looked at Shaw. *Two questionable millionaires, both with more enemies than you could count, are murdered. Banks are fire-bombed after ripping off the public for years, and it's the end of existence as we know it.*

Meanwhile, two police officers are murdered while doing their duty to the people of this country, and it's an afterthought. As are, undoubtedly, the numerous cars and homes that have been destroyed. Was I wrong to keep him?

Clayton tore his eyes away from the director. Am I being an ass? After all, what's the big deal if two more officers were murdered? At times it seems as if it's open season on the police.

"Have the anarchists' websites begun to target the police?" Clayton asked in a soft voice.

"No sir."

"Have they called upon the public to mount attacks on the police?" "Not at the moment, sir." Shaw sounded apologetic.

"Director, you will treat these murders as the crimes they are." Clayton saw the glances and strained looks. "I am not putting my head in the sand, gentlemen. Nor am I usurping the acting Attorney General's authority over the FBI. But equally, we can't allow the anarchists' to provoke us into taking steps we will later regret. The last thing we want is to be seen cracking down on the public. That it is exactly what they want us to do." Clayton noticed that General MacAdams actually seemed a little relieved at his stance. *Good, he's not stupid.*

"Now, gentlemen, how is the deployment going?" Clayton asked MacAdams.

"Deployment is going as per schedule, sir. We expect to be fully deployed by Saturday."

"I believe we had an incident with some Marines?" Clayton asked. "It was just a few protestors trying to create an incident, sir. They were trying to present the deployment in a bad light—make it look as if the marines were beating up helpless civilians, that sort of thing.

"The CO pulled his men back, let the police take the lead, and had his marines back up the police when they needed the manpower. We were lucky the man used his head. So far there is very little backlash from the public. But frankly, the country is huge and the Army and Marine Corps may not be up to the task." General MacAdams was his usual blunt self.

"With all the billions we have spent on the military?" Secretary of Defence William Anderson barked.

"On weapons systems, not manpower, I would remind the secretary," the general shot back. "After 'Nam, the US Army had 1,123,000 men in uniform; now we have a standing army of just over 460,000."

"Combined with the Marines, you should have more than enough men to stabilize the situation," Anderson insisted.

"That is open to debate, Mr. Secretary. We'll find out how effective our deployment will be shortly. I have been informed that we have intel on activists planning two and possibly more protest marches that could turn into a tsunami."

William Anderson huffed and puffed. "Well, that is totally unacceptable."

"Would you like to reinstate the draft? Because that is the only way I can guarantee we will get enough men on the streets to have the effect we want." *To intimidate the public*, the general thought bitterly.

"General, I don't like your tone," Anderson stated stiffly. "Or the fact that you sound like a defeatist."

"Mr. Secretary, America has a population of over 350 million. Do you have any idea how large an army we would need to quell even a fraction of such numbers? Just because the military can flatten a city with bombs doesn't mean we can occupy and control it without the manpower." *Not that the loony toons would believe that. The bloody morons*, General MacAdams thought in sour frustration.

"Gentlemen, please." Clayton addressed both men. 'Now, it sounds to me as though we need to get more military personnel out onto the streets and as quickly as possible. Agreed?"

"Sir, we have no more troops," MacAdams answered. "We can possibly get another twenty thousand if we empty every base we have, but that leaves our logistics and our command and control stretched."

"We have none, anywhere?" Clayton was slightly disturbed.

"I… I think we can get a few thousand from overseas." *When we've got the transport organized*, General MacAdams added silently.

"Yes…" Clayton went quiet for a moment. "I believe we have a few army units stationed in Europe?"

"That is correct, sir. We have restructured our forces in Europe, and then we have—"

"General, I want you to start bringing home as many soldiers as you can from our forces stationed overseas. You are to hold back only as many as you feel necessary for maintenance and security."

"What if the Russians decide to do something? They have mobilized their armed forces, Mr. President." William Anderson, a thin man with a hooded nose that made him look permanently worried, now sounded worried.

"I doubt they would think it's a good idea to invade Europe. And even if they did, it's time the Europeans did some of their own fighting." Not that it would come to that; they'd just spread their legs wide and invite Russia in like the good whore Europe had become. Clayton Prescott III had a very low opinion of Europe.

"What exactly do we owe them? We covered their backsides for over eighty years, and what did we get out of it? Just what have they done for us?" Clayton addressed them with cold contempt.

Worthless whores, the lot of them. God, what could we have achieved if NATO had been a real alliance—700 million people with the most advanced weapons in the world? How many problems and conflicts could we have solved by the mere threat of intervention on a massive scale? How many countries could ignore the threat of the combined armies of America and Europe if we were serious in our desire for peace? It was an old question he had often asked himself.

"Where were their infantry divisions when we needed them in Afghanistan?" His eyes narrowed into slits with the wonder of his idea.

"They did send some forces—" Secretary of Defence Anderson responded more out of long tradition that in gratitude for their commitment in Afghanistan.

"A handful… they may as well have stayed home for all the good they did," Clayton snapped mildly at the man, before becoming silent as he sat deep in thought.

"Yes." He whispered to himself as his smile grew. "General, you are to contact our senior commander in NATO. He is to begin sending the bulk of our men home immediately," Clayton declared with almost a gleam of pleasure in his eye. "And they are not to stop till they have a skeleton crew left… for now."

Anderson was shocked. "Sir, our alliances." *God, he's not planning to back out of NATO… using the rioting as an excuse?*

"Be damned, William, they can be damned. When we have the country back on its feet, we can re-evaluate our overseas commitments. For now I want every last soldier, marine, sailor, and airman out on our streets."

"And if the Russians do move?" *Does he mean what I think he means?* "As you are aware"—or possibly not—"under President Caine we were redeploying some of our troops and positioning our war stocks in case Russia made another aggressive move or threatened a NATO member. We can't let our equipment fall into enemy hands. A handful of security guards won't achieve anything." Not that leaving the troops in place really mattered that much. MacAdams knew America's military in Europe was a shadow of its past glory days.

We had fully equipped and manned armoured divisions during the Cold War, MacAdams silently reminisced. What they had now was mostly due to President Caine's recent army re-organization.

The corner of his lip twitched into a tiny smile. He had half joked to his fellow colleagues that the recent increase was more to placate the European shopkeepers, who were upset over the last round of US base closures across Europe than any desire to defend NATO.

His heart dropped. *Are we becoming another old empire reaching the end of its glory days?* He hoped not, but the signs were there. The wallowing in past glories, as if that would compensate for the refusal to act.

"Then you have my authority, General, to begin moving whatever equipment we have from mainland Europe to England, you can call it a training exercise if you wish. I am certain the brave French and stout Germans can check any Russian advance until… reinforcements arrive." *Or not,* MacAdams added silently. "Sir, our commitment to Korea?" "Will be fulfilled. Keep our current forces in Korea, along with any front-line counterterrorist operations in Asia and the Middle East. But the bulk of our ground forces stationed overseas will come home. General, if you feel we need to make any exceptions, I will consider each case individually.

"Tell Admiral Kellogg he can leave a carrier group on the West Coast and another on the East Coast. He is to have no more than three carrier groups at sea at any one time. The rest you can put in dry dock for repairs and maintenance. The crews are to be issued side-arms and deployed to assist our law enforcement agencies in whatever manner they deem appropriate.

"Gentlemen, let me be clear. The country comes first; there is no point defending Europe if America sinks. Once we are stable, we can consider our options. But for now, no delays, we do not have any time to waste."

"Yes sir." The men stood and were halfway to the door when Clayton spoke again.

"Gentlemen, it's not enough."

They looked at each other, now what?

"We need to do more. We need to do something to offer some kind of hope. The military and the government must show allegiance to the people." Clayton drummed his fingers on the desktop.

"What do you suggest, sir?" General MacAdams asked. "It's not what I want; it's a question of what we can do."

"The charities are providing as many meals as they can, sir," Anderson answered.

"Then we need to support them." Clayton counselled.

"Sir?" General MacAdams asked with concern.

"We support the charities. Let's see…" Clayton paused for a moment. "Suppose the army sets up twenty-four-hour soup kitchens and feeding centres. And more… we find places for the homeless to sleep, to have showers. Do their washing and other domestic necessities… all in some kind of relative safety."

"Well, we can use school gyms and even stadiums," General MacAdams offered, thinking quickly. "We have enough tents to offer some basic shelter until better accommodations can be arranged. As for security, Mr. President, I suppose we can have a squad of soldiers or National Guardsmen posted as guards." *Damn it, why didn't I think of it earlier? That's the answer.* How many of those protestors would jump at a hot meal and a decent shower? *If we can get ten or fifteen per cent to peel off from the marches. If I can get it arranged in time… Just need to spread the word. Who said only the protestors and anarchists can use Twitter?* He grinned in a moment of delight. He knew of a few young officers who were good with their thumbs.

He looked at the president in a new light. *Maybe he is the right man for the job. He's got the right instincts. That's more than half the battle.*

"Excellent, General, I'll leave it to you?"

"Yes sir," MacAdams stated with enthusiasm this time. "We also have a lot of abandoned houses and buildings lying idle. If we can get clearance from the banks, we could provide temporarily housing for some until they find permanent accommodations."

"Good, have your people look into that. They'll have White House approval. Now if you'll excuse me, I have a meeting with Treasury." *And his shadow*, thought a grim Clayton.

He watched them go. *It's not enough. Nowhere near enough, but it's a start. So where do you find accommodations for hundreds of thousands of people?* The banks weren't going to just hand over every empty house they owned for nothing.

He wanted time to think but knew full well he had a massive schedule to keep up with. The buzzer was already reminding him of that fact.

"Sir, the Treasury Secretary and the head of the Reserve Bank are here."

"Send them in." Clayton studied both men as they enter and sat in their leather seats. Both were grim and could hardly look him in the eye.

More good news, yet again, Clayton silently moaned.

"Sir, a situation has arisen that, depending on how the current situation unfolds could engender an environment whereupon necessary financial and economic steps must be enacted to ameliorate perceived concerns within the banking sector." The chair of the Federal Reserve, Tren Pat-Greyhouse, stumbled over his words.

"Just say it, Gene," Clayton told his Treasury Secretary.

"Sir, the banks may need a bailout." The two men sat waiting for the expected outburst; at first they received only silence.

"How many billions has the government given the banks so far this time around?" Clayton asked the two men.

"Well, all up, counting the—" Tren Pat-Greyhouse began.

"That was rhetorical, damn it." Clayton snapped at the man. "After all that talk about fireproofing the banking system after the GFC, here we are. Not even five months after a multibillion-dollar handout, and we have the banks asking for even more money."

Gene Austin ventured a response. "Not quite, Mr. President. It's early days yet. And may I add, it's not that simple. You need to factor in the massive economic downturn we have experienced. Even the best banks can't be expected to ride out this economic crash without some losses."

"An economic collapse brought about, in no small part, by the banking system, gentlemen. Just tell me how much of the three and a half quadrillion in global debt are our U.S. banks comfortable with?" Clayton was not offering sympathy.

Both men turned a little pale at the mention of the questionable assets and debts the banks of the world had acquired since the 2008 global financial crisis, when the world's banks had promised to be responsible citizens.

"With respect, sir, I would remind you of the massive debt the Bush and Trump era left this country with. The republican love for creating unjustified debt should be acknowledged," replied Chairman Pat-Greyhouse, a little annoyed that banks were blamed for everything that went wrong, no matter who was really responsible. "And technically many of the currently unproductive assets are sound and will in time…"

Clayton silenced the Fed chairman with a thunderous look. "A pity then that so many uneducated people didn't agree with you," he snapped. "If they had, we might not be where we are today, don't you think? European banks wouldn't be threatening to close their doors—trying to steal their depositors' money yet again." *How, how could they do it to us again?* It didn't matter how much debt they were talking about… it was the public's perception that mattered.

Still, he could not really be that angry with them. If only Obama or Trump had acted. If only Obama had prosecuted a few bank CEOs. If one or the other had broken up the "too large to fail" banks… even brought back the old Glass-Steagall Act that so many had wanted.

He had personally called for the separation of banks. Separate the old brick-and-mortar savings institutions from the high-risk investment banks. The way he saw it, if bankers wanted to gamble, then they could use their own money.

"This is only a heads-up, sir," the Fed chair said, with a rictus of a smile. "They may not need any further assistance. And only till the economy picks up, should they require any assistance."

"Thank you both for the warning." Clayton dismissed their attempts to tamp down his concerns with a tone even colder than his words. Both nodded their heads, eager to please after presenting him with the bad news.

"Now, to the issue closer to my heart, how are we going with our Chinese friends?" Clayton did not feel overly pleased but knew it was pointless to complain.

Austin's manner seemed almost apologetic. "They are unmoved at the moment, sir. We suspect they may give us a bit more time in exchange for better rates. But I don't hold out much hope."

"Gene." Clayton glared at the man.

"Yes, Mr. President."

"I need you to give me six months. Promise our creditors anything you can, within reason, but give me time."

"But—sir, six months won't save us. We need much more time." "Just give me six months. If we survive six months, then we have a chance."

"If not?"

Clayton did not need to give an answer.

The silence grew for a few moments longer. Finally the two men took the hint.

"We'll get onto it, sir." Austin stood and turned to leave the room. As he opened the door, he found Abb saying his goodbyes to Ann. He nodded to her and walked past Abb.

"Gene." Abb nodded to the man as he walked into the president's office.

"Abb." Gene barely nodded to the man. He did not have an overly cordial relationship with the chief of staff.

"That was an interesting interview," Abb began as he closed the door. "I never saw a reporter so flustered or confused."

Just then Ethan Campbell entered the room through the other door holding several folders in his arms. "Sorry sir, but you did say you wanted to go over these latest reports the moment they arrived."

"That's fine. Bring them over for my grandiose inspection. You were saying, Abb?"

Abb almost gave Ethan a dirty look. They had experts to provide detailed briefings. It certainly wasn't the president's job to go into such thickets of research.

At first he had feared Clayton would overburden himself with work, until two days ago when he had watched Clayton spend the hour and a half he had set aside for the task. To his surprise the work seemed to relax him, as though he were going over the assignments he had given to a class of less than gifted students. He actually seemed to enjoy going into the intricacy of the reports.

"Abb?" Clayton glanced at Abb Cole.

"Uh, yes; sorry, sir. As I said, an interesting interview, but do you want to continue down that path? If they turn on you, they could be a problem."

"They aren't one already?"

"Okay… So how about asking someone more impartial? What did you think of the president's debate today, Ethan?" Both knew Abb was concerned about Clayton's political future and thus needed to keep the media on his good side.

"I am the last—"

"Go ahead." Clayton told Ethan. "He's not going to stop until he's had his say."

"Well, some may think it was a little harsh, sir. The public knows the media aren't perfect, just like they know editors are as politically blind as the rest of us. And the Internet is the land of crackpots." Ethan felt the need to give Clayton some clarity. "And if I may be so bold, most don't have a problem with the media as things stand. Many feel the media perform to their expectations."

"Of course they do; that's the problem." Clayton hissed with real anger. "You think I'm annoyed just because the media won't do a better job? This is about the damned media's willingness to pander to their audience's ignorance and bigotry… to pick and choose… to self-censor… what they want to see and believe in. From abortion to climate change, oil and gas 'fracking,' drugs, guns, racism, inequality, politics… the government planning to stage a coup against itself… The media let these pathetic losers off the hook when it comes time to accept the truth. That not only legitimizes their bigotry but exonerates their guilt at not accepting their responsibilities."

He gave a short sigh of defeat. "It so perfectly suits everyone's self-interest… so what if it does divide our country just that little bit more?"

"I see where you're going with this hammering of the media to get off its ass," Abb replied. "But sir, this may not be the way to get what you want. You need to consider your position in the future. A more accommodating approach could get better results."

Ethan looked a little embarrassed by Abb's call for the president to moderate his position.

"You think I should worry about my future… such as it is?" Clayton smiled. "I'll be lucky if I do a full term. No, this is bigger than me. I don't care if they call me a murderer or a rapist; I don't care if they want to impeach me for fraud. I don't care how many Watergates they expose as long as they get it right. To quote Arnold Whitehall, 'Freedom of speech is not the freedom to lie'—even in service to our political views." Clayton swivelled in his chair to gaze out the window. "The truth cannot be allowed to become a fiction."

Abb spoke up in surprise. "I didn't realize this was so important to you."

"Abb, let's be clear. America's greatest enemies are not Russia or China but the enemies within. They will always be America's greatest threat." The words sounded extreme even to Clayton. But for all the military threat that Russia or China may or may not offer, they at least could be confronted. It was America's ingrained weakness that Clayton had long seen as the nation's greatest threat.

Even, if ironically, many saw it as the country's greatest strength. Ethan said, "The truth isn't always black and white, sir. Freedom of speech needs a degree of flexibility, expressing one's views is vital."

"And thus we justify our hypocrisy when we deliberately deny the truth."

"A thousand voices do not produce the truth.

They drown it out."

Arnold Whitehall

"On a Public Broadcast station a columnist decried the state of polarization in American society.

While ignoring the conservative and liberal media's own guilt in creating the polarization, and worse, sustaining it, encouraging it, feeding it.

(For their own agenda?)

What hypocrisy."

Arnold Whitehall

Chapter 5

GUNS AND ROSES FOR THE FUNERAL

Abb Cole came out of his office still studying the last page in the report. Once finished he placed it back in the folder and looked up just in time to see Jonathan walking down the corridor, a little faster than his normal pace.

"So what did you think of the president's media interviews?" Abb asked as he began walking alongside the young presidential aid.

"An excellent effort, sir."

"Really?"

"Yes sir?"

"How so?" *I never took him for a yes-man*, thought Abb, faintly disappointed.

"The media suddenly has a lot to focus on so they're not making such a big issue over the military deployment. And from what I saw before coming to work, they're walking on eggshells around the president to avoid looking like they're out to get back at him . . . after yesterday's interview with Miss Brooke." Jonathan then grinned. "All that could give the president some time... some room to manurer."

Abb had to grin back. *The kid is bright; no surprise why Clayton keeps him on.* Abb had spent the night going over the interview Clayton had given and slowly realized that it could be a clever move on Clayton's part, to keep the media on the defensive.

But it would have been better if he had told a few of us, Abb concluded. *He obviously keeps way too much to himself.* That worried Abb. It was not a good idea to keep everything bottled up. The man needed an outlet; else the pressure would get to him.

And equally troubling, by keeping things to himself, Clayton Prescott III was denying himself the option of good counsel—something he needed for his future dealings with the media. So far the media were on the defensive but for how long?

"We have a problem? You're walking fast." Abb stated the obvious. "Yes sir. The FBI director has asked for another meeting with the president and the National Security team. The director should be here in forty."

"I see. Well, the president's doing another interview right now, so it may have to wait." They reached the door to the room in which the president was holding yet another interview.

"Yes sir, I know." Nevertheless they quietly slipped into the room to stand there and hope the president would get the message.

"Brian, you need to understand, this is about gun safety." Clayton went over the subject with Brian Gates once more. "This is not gun confiscation. All I am proposing is that every gun will be properly registered, from the moment it is built to the moment it is destroyed.

"In the simplest terms, once the gun is built it will be registered to the factory; when sold to the gun dealer, it is registered to the dealer; when the dealer sells, it will be registered to the new owner, and so on and so on. This will put an end to corrupt gun dealers selling guns to criminals.

"The public needs to understand that we have people, with no criminal records, buying guns just so they can sell these weapons to criminals. We have to stop that, just as we have to stop criminals from stealing guns from people's homes. That is why a citizen's guns must be locked away in a federally approved gun safe. No gun will be taken away from anyone. As long as it is registered and properly secured, you will keep your guns."

"Mr. President, on the surface this sounds very simple. But the gun lobby has long argued that universal background checks will not stop illegal gun sales. What has changed?"

"We are not talking about background checks. We will be registering every gun into a federal gun registry database, along with its owner."

"But to get or keep a gun, you are saying that gun owners must have a gun licence."

"And how is that a problem for a law-abiding citizen?"

"Yet the gun lobby—the NRA has argued this proposal will do nothing to stop illegal sales."

"Brian, I have long heard all the arguments from the gun lobby when it comes to universal background checks. I still remember the one about a farmer wanting to sell his shotgun to his neighbour. Their argument was; how can you do a background check on them? Well, you won't need to. Because the gun will be registered, the farmer will already have a gun licence, and his neighbour will have a gun licence. All they will need to do is go to the local police station, hand over their federal gun licences, and present the weapon. The officer takes the licences and gun, checks the photos and thumbprints, and then puts them into the database, along with the gun's serial number. Once the details are placed in the database, he hands back the licences and the weapon. All done and all legal."

"But won't it be incredibly expensive?"

"Brain, the actual cost would be no different from a driver's licence. Once you have the licence, you just go to the local police station to register every purchase.

"And the cost of securing it—well, how much will it cost to replace a dozen stolen rifles when you've gone out for a few beers?"

"So you're saying that every citizen will have to get a license and then report every gun or purchase to the police. That's placing all the responsibility on the buyer."

And we wouldn't want all those "responsible gun owners" to be actually *responsible for their guns, now would we?* Clayton smiled at the man. "What is wrong with that? The more responsible you are for your weapon, the better you'll take care of it. You'll report that the gun has gone missing immediately, instead of reporting the loss a few months later, if at all.

"In fact, I would argue that every responsible gun owner should welcome this, to demonstrate that weapons can be kept in a safe manner. The NRA keep going on about how they are responsible gun owners. It's about time they proved it by supporting gun safety.

"And if they think my policy won't work, then let them come before the people and offer their own strategies. Give us some ideas that won't include giving even more guns to criminals, children, and people with mental health issues."

"But with all the guns that are already out on the street wouldn't it be a pointless exercise? The criminals are hardly going to go and register?" Brian offered his wisdom, with a sidelong glance at the camera.

"And why are there so many guns out on the streets in the first place? Because people like you don't believe we can fix the problem . . . so you just let it drag on forever.

"Yes, the problem won't get fixed overnight, that's true. It'll take years to register every weapon, perhaps decades, because this wasn't done at the beginning.

"But doing this can begin to fix the gun problem. If nothing else, it will hopefully prevent those with recognized mental health issues from acquiring guns." Clayton paused and seemed to stretch a little.

"Every time there is another mass killing—one that's too big to ignore— my Republican colleagues always point to mental health as the major issue, and yet they have done nothing… absolutely nothing to fix the problem. Well, it's well past time for our new Republican friends to act by stopping those with mental health issues from acquiring firearms." Clayton gave a soft sigh of regret, as if saddened that the previous Congress had refused to act. "Or else spend the billions needed to be spent on mental health."

It had always annoyed Clayton that the Republicans always focused on mental health as if guns were irrelevant—as if only American citizens were afflicted with mental health problems. *There are no psychos in Europe, Australia, or Canada… only in America. Yes sir, only in America do we have "sickos,"* Clayton recited to himself with considerable disgust.

"And if, unfortunately, some criminal gun dealer doesn't make a profit, well, that's just too bad, especially if we end up stopping a school massacre." That should shut up some of the gun shop owners.

Amanda Seals, seated beside Brian, the other half of the team, spoke up. "I have to say, Mr. President, I have my doubts. It can't be that easy to stop illegal sales. It seems such a simple solution to such a complicated problem."

Clayton smiled ever so slightly. They were doubling up on him. Now they had two interviewers doing each interview. "It'll work because it is simple. Imagine a dealer selling a gun to a criminal and the criminal uses the weapon in a crime. Now, say the police find the gun, and they track the serial number back to the dealer. They can go to the dealer and ask for the gun. Naturally, he won't have it, yet it is still registered to him. And since he has not reported it stolen in the last twenty-four hours, he gets a half-million-dollar fine and can be charged as an accessory to the crime."

"But what if the dealer simply reports it stolen?" Brian asked.

"So… every few months he's going to report a few guns being stolen? Really, Brian, think." Clayton scoffed as if insulted by the man's lack of foresight. "And even if he does, he will need to explain why the weapons were not properly secured. This is the whole point: one element reinforces the other element of the plan. Guns are registered and secured, so buying and selling can only be carried out between those who have gun licenses. This will reduce gun theft and the illegal selling to criminals and the mental impaired."

"Mr. President, many people listening would argue that criminals will always find ways of getting around the law. For example; why can't the gun dealers simply file off the serial number?"

"It's not that easy… if not next to impossible. But let us say it can be done; it won't matter if each new weapon has its serial number engraved in several different places, each one harder than the next to file off." He shrugged as if to suggest the concern was trivial. "Even guns already in the community can be 'upgraded' in this manner when they are registered into the federal data base."

"But there are so many illegal guns already on the streets." Amanda sounded defeated by the idea.

"And because they are illegal, the police will gradually confiscate these weapons. And because criminals are un able to get replacements, the number of illegal guns on the streets will slowly dry up.

"That is the essence of the plan: by cutting the pipeline, we deny the criminal elements access to more guns."

"But criminals are getting hold of guns in many ways, breaking into homes—"

"What have I been saying?" Clayton shot back. "'If it is not in your hand, then it must be locked away in a federally approved gun safe or locker.' This is the absurdity we now face with individual Americans having numerous guns just lying around the house.

"Picture it, eventually they will go shopping, go to work, or get their hair done, and what do they do with all those guns? Throw them all in the car and hope the car isn't stolen?

"Do they take one gun with them and leave the other guns just lying around? If so, just what do you think is going to happen?

"I'll tell you, one day they'll come home and—'Oh, my God, someone has burgled the house and stolen all the guns that were lying around'—if they're lucky. If not, they open the door, and they are staring down the barrel of one of their own guns. Indeed, I would argue you are inviting criminals to break in to steal your guns by not securing them. And for that matter, if those stolen guns are used in a crime, their owner is liable as an accessory because they were not secured properly.

"Even more important—much more important—locking away our guns will make it that much harder for our children to obtain guns and take them to school… or worse still, shoot their brother or sister. I remind every American that on average, eight to nine hundred of our children are butchered in so-called 'gun accidents' each year in this country. In some years nearly a thousand children die—because 'responsible' gun owners leave loaded guns in open drawers."

The president turned to the camera. "Yes, this will not work instantly; it'll take years, years to hunt down all the illegal weapons. But with each year we will make it that much harder for criminals and our children to get hold of our guns.

"Equally, we will reduce a financial burden that we do not need to endure. As I pointed out, we need the billions wasted on gun violence, all the medical costs, all the law enforcement costs, to help jump-start our tattered economy.

"And again, I can assure the public that no law-abiding citizen will lose his or her firearm."

"Mr. President, Senators Walker and Holt and especially the gun lobby have declared that a national database could be used against gun owners in a forced gun buy-back scheme. What do you have to say to that?"

"That is hard to believe, Brain."

"Sir?"

"That two of our most senior Senators can't read." "Sir?" Brain looked at Amanda in bewilderment.

Clayton's faint smile grew a touch wider. "I can only assume that the Senators can't read, or else they would have read the Second Amendment. You know; that little piece in the Constitution… 'The right of the people to keep and bear arms shall not be infringed.' As for the gun lobby—well, what can you expect from them except the usual fear-mongering lies and misinformation?

"That the media are so eager to pander to their scare tactics is yet another stain on the media's reputation." Clayton looked from one to the other. "Yet another example of why we need to re-examine the media and their multiple failures. That has so shamed and belittled—"

"Mr. President, sir—" Brian could see that Prescott was going to engage in another tirade against the media if he did not stop the man. "What do you say to those that feel they need to have their guns by their side to defend themselves in the home? Now, you have said 'if it is not in your hand,' but it is hard to cook with a gun in your hand."

"They can strap it to their hip if it makes them happy." *Is this guy stupid or deaf?*

"This is serious, sir," Amanda put in. "Many women fear an intruder breaking into their homes in the middle of the night. The last thing they want is some silly regulation denying them access to firearms."

What did I just say? Clayton wanted to scream at them both. "Is that one of your fantasies, Amanda? Dreaming of a midnight prowler?" Clayton felt as if he was repeating himself to a pair of infantile clowns.

Her mouth literally fell open at the accusation. How could he trivialize such a serious matter for women?

"Not the reply you expected? Surprised? Feel insulted even? Good, you deserve to be after spouting such nonsense. Do you have any idea how truly rare that is in comparison to how women are actually assaulted or raped?

"When I was at my old university, I saw the results of this blatant misinformation. A truly lovely young woman was assaulted, not by some phantom ninja who walked through walls but by someone she knew and trusted. She too believed in the night-clad villain jumping through the window or out from behind a bush, never suspecting that her 'friend,' after a few drinks, would commit such a violation.

"After that tragedy, and against the dean's objections, many professors advocated for all the female students to employ a buddy system. Always go out in a group, always have one or two staying sober and assigned to getting you all home safely. Never accept any drink that wasn't sealed or that you haven't seen being poured… so no one could spike it. Never go to a person's home that you have just met; exchange numbers for a meeting, if you wish.

"But the most important rule: always stay in control. You get drunk, you take drugs… you lose control, and then you become a victim.

"You lose control, you become a victim." Clayton paused for a moment as if to collect himself.

"The reality, Amanda, during my time, was that nearly 90 per cent of the young women who were attacked on campus knew their attacker. They had met him at a party, had drinks with him. Some, even, had their drinks spiked so the animal could rape her without fear of prosecution." Clayton's lip gave a tiny sneer of contempt. "Just how would a gun help if you were drunk or drugged?

"Now, the phantom ninja may be the mainstay in the movies. And if one does jump out from behind a bush, feel free to shoot him-- And hope to God it's not a friend having a joke.

"As for your midnight home invader, Amanda, a good set of locks and solid doors provide excellent protection, especially if you add a personal alarm system. May I point out, it's very hard to rape someone when you have an ear splitting screech in your ears.

"What amazes me is the number of people who will go to the trouble of buying a gun to defend themselves and their property, yet they neglect their home's security when they are not at home. People . . ." He sighed, glancing at the camera. "A good alarm system with a panic button will defend both your home and your person—and, as a bonus, will not get you or a loved one-shot by accident.

Clayton looked from Brian to Amanda. "Imagine your teenage daughter sneaks into the house late one night without you knowing. Do you really want to shoot her, thinking she is an intruder?

"I still remember the story of a middle-aged couple retuning home after a night out, and the husband saw movement inside through a window. He knew his daughter was over at a friend's house, so the house should be empty. Thus he took his gun from the glove compartment and opened the front door.

"His daughter jumped out of a closet to cry out happy birthday, and he shot her dead.

"Instead of calling the police he shot his own daughter." Clayton softly rubbed his forehead as he told the story.

"And for the record, Amanda, I do support the use of firearms, but only as a means of last resort. Just as I support reporting the facts. A pity I can't say the same about the media." Clayton unloaded himself with full force at the young woman.

"Now let's take a moment to look at why people feel they need guns." He looked into the camera lens once more. "There are two reasons why people want guns. First, to defend themselves and their property, mostly from criminals with legally and illegally acquired guns—guns that we can deny to criminals if we so wish. Or give guns to criminals as the 'gun merchants' want us to do.

"The second reason is to defend themselves against a 'dictatorial government,' the reason why we need the Second Amendment." He smiled with good humour. "Well, I'm the first to say that politicians have failed America many times in the past . . . even if they were obeying the will of the voters.

"And who knows, perhaps one day the nut-jobs will get their mythical UN conspiracy." He sneered at the camera. "And the ninja 'black helicopters' flying in the midnight sky may manage to somehow place a 'space alien' in the office of the president. Well, big deal. We have the Constitution, the Supreme Court, and the Congress and Senate to prevent abuse of power.

"But let us put all that aside and ask just how do they expect this corrupt government to take power, Amanda? How will they take control?"

"I… suppose… they would argue, by force." Amanda seemed unwilling to take the bait.

"Exactly, they will take it by force." Clayton's voice hardened, and he sneered with contempt. "Do you understand what you just said? Do you?" He bit off each word. "You are talking about a military coup, the US military taking power by force." The level of his voice rose in anger as he glared at the pair.

"I am willing to have my loyalty questioned, Amanda. But for some so-called 'patriot' to accuse the men and women of our armed forces… men and women who have fought, bled, and died for this country… to accuse them of treason, of engaging in the betrayal of this country—" Clayton stopped as if the fury of his words were burning his throat.

"It is the most loathsome form of backstabbing and deceit imaginable, and I will not put up with it." He slammed his palm down on the armrest in fury.

There was silence in the room that dragged on for some seconds.

"Well, damn it," Clayton snapped at them both.

"Ah, well, we didn't think—"

"Exactly, you didn't. Have the media or the public ever questioned the absurdity of this putrid filth—who in all probability never served a day in defence of this country or else were dishonourably discharged—accusing our soldiers, your brothers, sisters, mothers, and fathers of wilfully obeying illegal orders?" Clayton's eyebrows seemed to rise along with his anger. "How dare they have the gall to suggest that our armed forces and federal law enforcement would turn their guns upon their fellow citizens? It is an insult not worth dignifying with anything but utter contempt dumped upon this vermin." The venom dripped off each word.

"Yet where is the outrage from the media or the public when such redneck filth spouts such trash? Where is the outrage when the NRA calls our marines, soldiers, sailors, and airmen, and your local police officers traitors? I'd love to see one of those redneck scum call a Navy SEAL or a marine gunnery sergeant a traitor to his face. Just so I can buy the soldier a drink for giving the slanderous filth a broken nose."

The room went silent once more. Both interviewers were totally stunned and a little worried by the naked aggression in his voice.

"To every father, mother, brother, sister, and child: know that the gun lobby calls your soldier son, bother, sister or father a traitor to this country— just to justify the selling of guns to criminals. So they can explain away… excuse the deaths of some thirty thousand Americans each year." His eyes glared at the reporters daring them to challenge his words.

"Now let's go back to the first reason, to protect life and property. Well, have guns made the American people safe? Thousands killed each year, and are we safer than the Europeans? Look at Europe, with a population greater than the US, yet with nowhere near the gun deaths we have. Ask yourselves why aren't tens of thousands of Europeans dying from guns each year? It couldn't possibly be because they take gun safety seriously, could it?" *And most aren't a bunch of goddamned impotent dicks who feel they need guns to be real men*, Clayton wanted to add. But he considered the extreme gun owners too immature to accept such talk.

"Many in the conservative camp would argue that Americans feel safer… more comfortable with guns than with the legal system. Putting simply, the police can't get to them in time."

"Is that any wonder, given the absurdity of the Republican position?" Clayton shrugged as if he had answered the question.

Brian glanced at his partner, who looked back in equal confusion when Clayton did not elaborate.

"Sir, if you could expand on your statement," Brian asked, faintly concerned that he would regret asking. Brian felt he was beginning to lose control of the interview. Prescott wasn't as easy as they thought.

"It's true that the Republicans have often argued that the police are not there when needed. But why is that? Is it because there are not enough police? If so, the answer is obviously to hire more police officers."

Both interviewers looked at the president, visibly worried at where this would lead.

"Yet, where do we get the money for additional police? From taxation, of course, and we all know where my Republican colleagues stand when it comes to taxes.

"Take a good hard look; as they cut taxes we have reduced the number of police officers even while our population has been growing. New York City is a classic example. How many police did the city have in 1900, and now many do they have today?"

Both gave him a blank look. *This is not my day*, Amanda mentally conceded.

"Since the nineteen hundreds the city has more than doubled in population and yet has cut its police force by half. They've used excuses like we have radios, cars, technology. Well, if this technology is so wonderful, so effective in crime fighting, just why do so many people feel they need guns?"

"That may well be a legitimate point, Mr. President," Brian responded. "But what do you say to all the shooters who simply want to have the right to go out and hunt, yet feel they are constantly under attack from an administration that simply doesn't understand them?"

"And that is the issue in a nutshell, isn't it?" *The poor bastard is really clutching at straws.* Clayton smiled to himself. "What's more important to the American people, Brain, the right to go out and shoot Bambi or the life of a six-year-old child?

"Everywhere else in the developed world the life of a child is of paramount importance. Only in this country is a TV or a day out shooting more important than the lives of the eight to nine hundred children we slaughter each year. How can you justify that position? Well, go on, justify the slaughter of our children, go on." He looked at both interviewers. "I'm waiting."

Shit, Brian silently cursed. *The bastard, he keeps putting us on the spot.* "When will we put an end to this madness?" Clayton pleaded. "All I

am calling for is gun safety, and the only reply I receive is fearmongering." He slowly breathed out, calming a little in his seat.

"Now, I am in a little bit of a rush. But before I go, I need to take you to task. Amanda. Yesterday I castigated the media for its lack of accuracy. And here you are, dealing more in fantasy than reality and thus creating fear when you should be educating the public with the facts.

"Still, you have the right of reply. So Amanda, how many women were raped in their beds in the middle of the night by a stranger... as opposed to women being assaulted or raped by someone they knew and believed they could trust? Give me the facts, the statistics."

She looked at him in near terror.

"And how were they resolved, how many guns were involved, and if so, with what success?" Clayton hammered away.

She looked at him as if he was insane. *How could I possibly know all that?* "Well, I don't have the figures on hand."

"Amanda, I am truly disappointed but hardly surprised." Clayton smiled sadly, as if to say how sad it was that the media had once more failed the community. "Yes, one could say the media positively delights in ignoring the facts." He said with half-closed eyes as if reminiscing over past events.

"Sir, that is totally uncalled for. We provide the public with the very latest—"

"Stories, yes, but what about the facts? I didn't mean to offend, but I just don't recall seeing the latest statistics on shootings on any of your media channels. Indeed, I don't recall seeing any reports on the four hundred and thirty-two children killed in 'gun accidents' this year. Or the nine thousand, eight hundred and forty-six adults killed by guns so far this year. The more than five thousand accidental gun discharges reported this year. The two hundred and twenty-three 'responsible' gun owners accidently shot or killed by their own guns, so far.

"If you're not careful you'll have the public believing you're conspiring with the gun lobby to deny the public the facts." Clayton smiled to suggest he was just having a bit of a laugh. But behind the smile lay a level of genuine contempt.

"Indeed, why are you not reporting the crime rate figures . . . instead of letting the public guess?

"I could go further and ask, have you reported on what is being done to combat such violence? Do we have enough crime prevention programs, training programs, and education programs in place to prevent future crimes, and are they having an effect? Or are we simply asking too much of the media?" *To be kept accurately informed*, Clayton wanted to add.

"Well, time unfortunately waits for no man or woman." Clayton began to stand.

"Mr. President, now that you have brought it up"—Brian jumped in before Clayton could extricate himself—"do you really believe that the media can truly change the public's view? Yesterday you talked about media shortcomings and said that by dealing with them, we could enlighten the public. Do you actually believe it could work?"

Clayton was struck in place for a moment, before he relaxed back into his seat.

"I was not talking about some universal epiphany for the American people as much as fighting the lies and half-truths. The ignorance and..." He nodded, as if he finally saw something that had been kept hidden. "Yes, the bigotry.

"Again, I go to the Nazi holocaust of World War Two. How is it that after all these years we still have people who actively deny the Holocaust?" "With respect, the media have done their part and more than their part." Amanda was almost offended.

"Have they, Amanda?" Clayton let out a small sigh. "Have you brought the deniers face to face with Holocaust survivors and the once -young soldiers who saw with their own eyes the truth and challenged the deniers to prove their Nazi-propaganda?

"Put simply, Amanda, has it been enough? And the answer is that it is never enough.

"Consider this: if we can open the eyes of even one person to the bitter diatribe of a bigot or an intolerant group, then isn't that an accomplishment?

"From there, who knows? Perhaps that person may begin to challenge the prejudice of his friends." Clayton's body seemed less tense. In this area, he felt, they were more or less on common ground.

"I am not calling for government-promoted propaganda. I am calling for an end to propaganda. I am calling for accuracy and facts. Brian, is fighting for the truth really that hard?"

Clayton shrugged, and then glanced at his watch. "Ah, time waits for no man, unfortunately . . ."

"One final question, sir." Brian saw the easing of Claytons shoulders and decided to take advantage. Better still, if the President was in a hurry to deal with other matters, he could be more open... and more likely to fall flat on his face. *If I'm lucky.*

"The economy... many pundits are arguing that you will be forced to raise taxes and cut spending. Do you agree?"

"Once we have a new Congress, we will need to raise taxes, but we can cut back on some spending now."

"In what areas, sir?" He almost choked in surprise at Prescott's frank admission.

"We will not be hiring any new government employees. Equally, some congressional and senatorial staff will be let go. Once we have new congressional members, the staff can apply for their old positions."

Amanda took an interest. "You're firing the congressional staff?"

"I find it hard to justify paying thousands of people to just sit around until new elections are held."

"Will military spending be cut?" Brian asked. "During your political career, many critics have attacked you over your opposition to high-tech weaponry. Has your view changed?"

"My personal position still stands. And I am not against high-tech weaponry. I have long supported the US Navy's electromagnetic rail gun to replace conventional naval cannons. I am told the rail-guns are superior to conventional guns… and they are actually cheaper, since the rail-gun projectiles are cheaper to manufacture than conventional Navy shells… at least I was, until we discovered that the actual cost of each shell was triple what had been promised.

"If only our weaponry were as in-expensive as first advertised, then I would be overjoyed. But EVEN then, we still need to make changes to our expenditure before we make it impossible to defend this country"

"Mr. President," Amanda asked, resisting the urge to scoff, "don't you think you're exaggerating somewhat?"

"Am I? I remember a delightful little story. During the NATO bombing of Libya to remove Colonel Gaddafi, our NATO allies had to ask us for some of our guided missiles. They had run out of smart bombs."

He chuckled. "Now, as amusing as the story may be, how long before that becomes a reality for us?

"Consider this, a cruise missile costs nearly a million dollars. Nearly a million dollars spent just to deliver a few hundred kilos of high-grade explosives. That's insane. We need to give the military a wide range of options, from cruise missiles to delivery systems that cost… from a thousand to ten thousand dollars a warhead.

"Just look at our air campaign against the Islamic State in Syria as an example. Should something similar take place, do we really want to be in a position where the only option is to use a seven-hundred-thousand-dollar missile to blow up a Toyota hatchback?

"With the retirement of the A-10 Thunderbolts and their nose-mounted guns, what low-cost options will we have? We have to do better, or we'll bankrupt ourselves in the next war.

"Right now our main emphasis must be on research and development of future weapon systems at an acceptable cost. Not on building everything and anything, no matter the cost."

"But many politicians have stated that we need this high-end technological advantage."

"Oh yes, and they are probably the same ones who called for America to end the Afghanistan war because the cost in 'blood and treasury' was too high, 'treasury' meaning money.

"That is the problem we face. How soon will it be before we are making weapon systems that are so expensive we may not be able to deploy them? And it's already started. The Air Force wanted to build 750 of the F-22 stealth fighters, but after endless cutbacks, they ended up with only 183.

"Then we have the F-35 debacle. It was to be the wonder plane of the twenty-first century. What did we get? Endless delays and cost overruns. And even more to the point, we've had to make compromises just to get them to fly.

"Worse, how many problems have we had keeping them flying? Maintaining the delicate darlings…" Their complex systems did require considerable attention.

"Is that really the way we should be running military procurement?" Clayton asked, not expecting an intelligent answer.

"We need a totally new approach to acquiring military hardware, and it can be done. Military spending can be cut simply by saying that military contracts will be honoured. If the system is overdue, fine; it goes over cost, fine; it does not perform as advertised, another fine. The company is fined, fined, fined, until corporate America gets the message that it must deliver on time, on cost, and as advertised."

"But sir, critics have complained about government inappropriate—er, indeed… mismanagement for decades. How it often changes the agreement on the number of battle tanks or planes it will buy… thus increasing the cost per unit. As you know, the more you buy, the cheaper they are per unit. Then there is the government's habit of changing the design or the capabilities that were originally called for." *What have you got to say about that?* Brian tried to keep a straight face.

"I just gave you the answer, Brian. I just proposed that binding contracts be honoured by both parties. That way neither government nor manufacturer can change numbers, costs, delivery dates, or capabilities. The only way to change the contract would be if a new piece of technology came online that could be easily inserted into the fighter jet or weapon system that was being developed. And even this new technology should pass some kind of independent evaluation.

"Equally, as you pointed out, it may actually make sense to buy more than we need. Originally the Air Force wanted 750 of the F-22, but if we had purchased a thousand, resulting in a lower unit cost, and put two hundred or so into deep storage, how many more years could we have gotten out of the F-22 fleet? And if we did go to war, we would have extra planes to replace our losses, instead of waiting for new planes to be built. Or hoping we have enough F-35's."

"Sir, if I many go back to the F-35 for a moment—its defenders have pointed out that it was all new technology, the cutting edge at the time, and thus we had to be ready for unforeseen problems. And they point out that we could only get an accurate price-tag for the warplanes once we started building them."

"Yet, Brian, they manage to deliver their latest commercial aircraft with the latest technology to the airline companies without too much trouble. Enough is enough. Problems in design and development need to be addressed before you try to sell the product. The airline companies don't put up with it, so why should we? If the manufacturers can keep their promises to the airline companies, why can't they keep their promises to the government?"

"And this government is going to make that very clear to them?" Brian persisted.

You bet your corporate ass I will, thought Clayton. He had some time before Congress was reinstated and begin to undermine his efforts. *At least I may get the sons of bitches to crap their pants, even if only for a few months.*

"We need binding contracts… that work in the public interest." Clayton smiled at Brain. *Suck on that one.* "Yes, we do need some high-tech/high-cost equipment, but we also need to consider low-tech/low-cost as well. We need to push ourselves and the manufacturers to create a variety of cost-effective options." *Even if we only used it as leverage against the military-industrial complex, it should give us some good results.* He smiled to himself over his own simplistic stereotyping. He knew military procurement wasn't simple or easy, but that was no excuse to write blank cheques and let the 'dumb-ass public' pay till they were sucked dry.

"Another answer to defence spending is simply not to buy everything. Why must we build every generation of a particular weapon system? For example, we had the Patriot missile defence system, with its first generation, second generation, third, and so on. Why can't we go from the first generation to the third generation?

"If we designed our first generation with the capacity to be upgraded until such time as the third generation proved itself, consider the benefits." Clayton gave them a wide smile, taking in the camera. "Just because an F-18 isn't stealth capable doesn't mean that in ten years' time we couldn't attach an ultralong-range air-to-air/ground missile under its belly, connected to some kind of over-the-horizon targeting system." The grin spread a little. "Or strap two barrel bombs to its belly to take out a Toyota hatchback."

"But wouldn't other nations try to exploit any potential window of opportunity?"

"Brian, you're not listening. There won't be a window of opportunity. And even if some thought we had a vulnerability, no nation is going to attack the US while we have a viable nuclear arsenal. Why is Iran so committed to keeping its long-term nuclear program? Here's a hint: it's not because they're running out of oil." Clayton's eyes flickered for a second as he saw Jonathan and Abb.

"Sir, if I may... We need these high end systems. Precision missiles are not there simply so we can drop them and forget about them. They are used to reduce civilian casualties. We can't go back to using dumb bombs." Brian was convinced he was correct.

"We could end up being accused of war crimes." Amanda supported her colleague.

"During the Trump years, Senator Rubio once asked the incoming Secretary of State, Rex Tillerson, 'Is Vladimir Putin a war criminal?'

"The response Tillerson gave was 'I would not use that term.'

"Now, if the systematic slaughter in Aleppo... the deliberate targeting of hospitals-- was not a war crime, then our use of dumb bombs in or near built-up or civilian areas cannot be placed in question.

"If Russia's use of dumb bombs is without sin, then American use of dumb bombs is also without sin."

Amanda could not keep the shock and confusion from her voice. "Sir, are you advocating—"

"I am not advocating anything. I am merely pointing out the obvious. "Such as the fact that it is well past time that we had a top to bottom overhaul of the defence department . . . to stream-line and improve efficiency. Perhaps even put an end to the close military-industrial relationship... impose genuine completion... that is, if department heads want to remain employed in the department of defence.

"Now, I must take my leave, till later. Thank you for coming." Clayton was out the door the second the pleasantries were over.

"What's the mess now?"

"The FBI... Well, not them. Director Shaw has asked for an emergency meeting."

Texas

The bald, fat-bellied man turned off the TV with an angry snap. "The son of a bitch. That damned stinking son of a bitch. First he declares martial law. Now he wants to take away our guns." He turned to the other two men in the room. "I told ya, didn't I tell ya?"

"Yeah, Bobby, we heard."

"Then are we going to do it or not?" Bobby stared at the young man with acne running down his face. The kid had agreed with everything but then suddenly wanted to back out—only to recommit later, in a roundabout fashion. Bobby knew he had to push the kid until the job was done, especially now, when they were so close.

"Yeah, sure." The skinny, acne-faced young man nodded in mock agreement. "And we can send a rocket to the moon while we're at it. Come on."

"Joey, it has to be done. We have to defend our rights, man," Bobby insisted.

"Sure, sure. Look, why can't we just stick to things we know? We know guns, not this stuff."

"We got to make the Gestapo listen, man. Only when we got the power will they listen."

"So we are just gonna cook up something like that in the backyard?" "All we need from you is to get the stuff in; that's up to you and yours.

Got it?" Bobby smiled and grabbed another beer.

"Sure, sure. Me and mine can get the stuff into the States, but have you got a dude who can cook it up?"

"Just get the stuff in. We'll do the rest."

"Yeah, we'll see. Okay, all good to go. My shift starts in forty." Joey stood on unsteady legs, grabbed his jacket and walked out of the small apartment.

The third man turned to Bobby. "You think Joey can pull it off?" "He's got the contacts, man. He can get damn near anything over the border. Naw, I ain't worried about him. It's Him I'm worried about." "Come on. Bobby, he's cool. You saw the way Alex wasted those two pigs. He didn't blink an eyelid."

Bobby sneered. "That's what I mean. The snake-eyed bastard gives me the creeps. He didn't have to waste those cops; he set us up, man. Why do you think he had us go to Florida?"

After several meetings, Alex had asked them to meet him in Florida. Which had been strange enough, but his insisting that they travel by bus and pay for the tickets in cash had raised suspicions. Those were confirmed when they met him at the agreed place and time, only for the man to gun down the two police officers in cold blood.

"Come on, Bobby, he was establishing old-style street cred, my man." "Shit, he dropped us in it."

"And he dropped himself in it, man. Don't you get it? No-way he's a pig. We're in this together. We can do him for murder, and he can do us for accessory, which is the same thing, man."

"He's a psycho and a damn commie bastard to boot."

"But he'll deliver, because he's a Russian and those bastards are all into money now."

"He's a psycho."

"You don't like him 'cause he looks like a black-ass Mex." "I don't like him 'cause he's a psycho and a black-ass Mex."

"Yeah, but after he delivers, we won't need him—know what I mean?"

Washington

"Ladies, gentlemen, be seated. How bad is it?" Clayton did not bother with the formalities.

FBI Director Shaw began the briefing. "Not good, sir. Governor Parker and Governor Soulban and a number of influential community members are seriously involved in a conspiracy to leave the Union. We need to act immediately. We have them on wiretaps. The president of Mexico has strung their representatives along beautifully. And we have these representatives talking to the governors and their people on over three hours of incriminating recordings. It's an open-and-shut case, sir."

"Are they planning to use force?" Clayton inquired.

"That is irrelevant, sir, even if they were to call for some referendum on leaving the Union their actions are treasonable."

"We still need more," Clayton objected.

"But sir, the evidence is unassailable." Shaw sounded offended.

"It's not enough. We need more to avoid a fight with the locals. We need something to keep the peace until they see the evidence, until we can prove this betrayal in a court of law."

"I don't know what else we can do, sir. And we have to act now or else risk the situation escalating out of control."

"I will not risk two or more States going up in a fireball. Imagine what the anarchists will put up on their websites." Clayton shuddered at the thought of two States engulfed in fire. "We need some kind of insurance." "Sir, with respect, we need to act now and deal with the aftermath as best we can. Things go bad we can always send in some extra federal forces." Shaw offered it as a suggestion, but he was far from convinced it would achieve anything.

"After the event—" Clayton glanced up, with an idea forming. "We need to send in our people before it all falls apart. What if General MacAdams was to send our soldiers from overseas to Texas and New Mexico?"

"On what pretext, sir? It might look a little suspicious if we landed… say, an Army division in their backyard."

Ethan Campbell leaned forward. "Not if the National Guard and Army reserves had been sent out of the State beforehand. Sir, if the Army reserve units were immediately deployed to all the hot spots across the country, then it wouldn't seem so suspicious if we sent the overseas units to 'reinforce' whatever National Guard may have remained behind."

"Yes, that might work—if we deploy the reserves in small units and keep them too occupied to worry about what's going on back home." Clayton gave them a winning smile, yet it was more directed at Ethan. *The boy's got a head on his shoulders.*

Abb Cole noticed where Clayton was looking and wondered.

With that detail dealt with, they went over the general state of affairs. "I think that will do for now." Everyone rose to leave, but Clayton stopped Director Shaw. "Arnold, a moment, please." Director Shaw waited in his seat as the others filed out. "I feel that I need to be kept more fully informed."

"Yes sir, I can deliver a daily briefing."

"No, your work is far too important to have you interrupt it every day just to brief me. Is someone else available?"

"Assistant Director Doug Langley. He's in charge of day-to-day matters to do with the rioting. Good man—"

"No, someone without a mountain of work on his desk at the moment. Is there someone who is in-between assignments?"

"I suppose Assistant Director Drywood. He's just tidying up the loose ends with Congress." Shaw looked at Clayton as if to ask if the man met with his approval.

"Fine. Set it up, will you?"

"Yes, Mr. President," Shaw stated without enthusiasm. Drywood was not his preferred choice. The man was a little too independent a thinker for his taste.

"2-year old boy may have fatally shot his father."
2015/08/20
"2-year-old accidentally shoots, kills his mom in Idaho Wal-Mart."
2014/12/30

"'Guns don't kill people, people kill people.' "Then those homicidal 2 year-olds should be locked up and the key thrown away, right?"

Grant Friday

"Give those murderous two-year-olds life without parole, right? Am I right or am I right? Just throw the book at them, teach 'em a lesson, I say. We have to crack down on these hardened criminals."

From comedian Jamie Rock's reply to statements made by Republican front-runner for the governorship of Texas calling for more guns in the home to allow parents to protect their children

Chapter 6

DEATH PENALTY

"Thank you for your time, Mr. President."

"My pleasure, Kate, Ryan," Clayton soberly addressed the young woman and the equally handsome man seated next to her. Obviously another double act, but now they had upgrading the calibre. Both were experienced and hard-nosed street fighters.

"Now, I want to get to the hot issue on our viewers' mind," Kate began with an earnest smile. "The death penalty for anyone convicted of selling drugs."

"Of course," Clayton replied, wondering if their concern was due to the fact that that most of their viewers were of the Hollywood/ liberal persuasion. Probably worried their suppliers might give up the business.

Kate continued, "The public is deeply concerned over this issue. I must ask, are you actually suggesting we hang drug dealers even if they are selling only twenty-five dollars' worth of illegal drugs? Many are saying that it's… well… it's inconceivable to execute someone for such a minor offence. Especially, sir, when so many States have legalized marijuana for personal use. Do we really want to hang someone for something that is legal in the neighbouring State?"

"Kate, it's not about twenty-five dollars' worth of cocaine, heroin, or marijuana. It's about dealers selling poison to our children. It's about the many hundreds of deaths from overdoses each year. It's about the tens of thousands of lives ruined. It is about the shattered families. And marijuana use is still a federal offence… for good reason… The cost to our young is simply too high."

"And the economic cost?" Ryan jumped in.

"Absolutely, we need to consider the expense and its impact on lives. We have tens of thousands who spend years, decades living in the gutter… spending everything they have to pay for their habit, committing crimes to feed their habit. We simply cannot keep going the way we are.

"Nor does it end there. The casual users with their so -called 'party drugs' can still waste thousands of dollars a year that could go into paying for their home, a new car, that new TV they have always wanted. And thus they could be feeding our desperate economy rather than a drug cartel." Clayton was speaking smoothly, without rancour. He had used that very excuse when he had first address the media on the issue and was not about to back away from it now.

"People forget how much the nation's drug habit costs. The latest estimate puts the cost of illegal drugs at close to forty billion a year. Just think what that money could do for our struggling economy, to say nothing about struggling families. How many children are going to school hungry because their parents are drug addicts?"

"Yet the point remains, Mr. President. No one overdoses on marijuana, and it doesn't really ruin lives. While cigarettes and alcohol do kill people… thousands each year." Kate smiled her best plastic smile. "Many have asked why marijuana should be banned when cigarettes and alcohol are legal. Why not act against the cancer sticks and alcohol that do so much damage?"

"Come now, Kate." Clayton sighed and shook his head. "Why do people still come up with that ridiculously old and tired excuse? Back then no one knew the dangers of smoking. Indeed, if they had known, they might well have made it illegal. As for alcohol, it seems you never heard of Prohibition."

"Which didn't work."

"And legalizing alcohol after Prohibition has been a disaster, as you have so eloquently pointed out. How many millions do we spend on alcohol abuse?" *Choke on that reply.* Clayton was getting annoyed once more by their stubbornness. "If so many Americans didn't make money selling alcohol to their fellow citizens, we should consider placing serious restrictions on how much should be sold and when—if not outlawing it again." He gave them a small grin.

"But Mr. President." Kate gave an audible sigh, as if exasperated by his seeming petulance. "For many Americans marijuana use is such a trivial offense, compared with crack cocaine or hard drugs."

"Kate, this is not about marijuana. Americans are hooked on far too many drugs, both legal and illegal. And these drugs are doing real harm, to the users and innocent people. Just look at the number of car accidents where alcohol and marijuana are involved. We need to confront the drug epidemic destroying thousands of lives."

"Yet many would argue that it should be their choice." Ryan responded. "This week alone Woody Samuelson made a strong case that most people can control their usage, and therefore it should be legalized so it can be better managed."

"Yes, there are those who can indeed handle their drug use—especially movie stars like Mr. Samuelson. He and his rich, privileged friends in Hollywood can always go into a five-star rehab-resort, come out after a refreshing month or two, and make another movie.

"Except, what about the thousands who cannot handle their drug abuse and do not have millions to enjoy a Hollywood resort?

"To those who say, 'Why should I be denied my drugs because others can't handle their drug use?' my reply is just as direct: 'Why should others suffer because you're a selfish bastard?'"

He then looked Kate straight in the eye. "Do you approve of babies being born into this world addicted to crack cocaine?"

"Isn't that an argument for us to concentrate on the hard drugs?" she shot back. "Why risk alienating the public by going after soft drugs that are as accepted as tobacco and alcohol?"

"Because a few moments ago you reminded us just how harmful tobacco and alcohol are. This is exactly the sort of thing that truly saddens me. A few moments ago, Kate, you asked why we have not outlawed cigarettes when they cause so much harm. And in the next breath here you are arguing for the legalizing of a drug that medical experts now believe inflicts much more long-term psychological and physical harm than cigarettes." *And I bet you don't even see the hypocrisy of it.*

"Well, that is up for debate. Many say marijuana is safe."

"And why is that? Is it because the media have failed us once more? Failed to provide the factual details to enable people to make an informed decision instead of listening to those who want to make a profit from selling drugs, or are users themselves?"

"Sir, we provided extensive information—"

"Really? Shall we test that theory? Do certain plants produce toxic chemicals in their leaves, Ryan?"

"What, I… what has that go to do—"

"To prevent animals from eating their leaves, certain plants produce toxins, poisons. So Ryan, are tobacco and marijuana leaves toxic?"

"Well, they obviously have some effect." *Shit, shit,* shit, *don't fall into the trap… too late.* The truth was, like most, Ryan didn't know with any accuracy the makeup of the marijuana leaf.

"So if tobacco is the cause of so many deaths and does such much harm, why do you believe marijuana is perfectly safe?" Clayton's smile grew as he addressed Ryan.

"Well, like most things there are a number of differing factors Involved." Ryan was decidedly unsure where he was going. But felt he should make no clear statement. What was the difference between cigarettes and weed?

"So you hold that it's not the toxins in the tobacco leaf, but rather the herbicide sprayed onto the leaf that causes cancer?"

"No, of course not." They would castrate him if he accused the tobacco companies of poisoning the public. "It's simply that people..." *No, don't go there.*

"Ryan, is it true that many in the medical profession such as the staff at the Seattle Children's Hospital—which I visited three months ago— accept that marijuana is responsible for inflicting or worsening paranoia and depression in children who have been treated with medical cannabis?"

Ryan could only stare back, his face blank with utter defeat.

"Kate, is it true or false that there is 'growing evidence' that cannabis is linked to eight forms of cancer... throat cancer being the most notable?" She squirmed in her seat. "Well, I can't say with any absolute authority." "It's not that clear cut. Certain studies can be debated." Ryan knew he had to go carefully. *Bastards making us look like fools.*

"Yes, especially by those with a vested interest in clouding the issue. A pity the medical community does not share that confusion. It is now accepted that one in six users of marijuana will became addicted." Clayton slid the knife in and twisted the blade with a pleasant smile.

"Kate, is it fact or fiction that cannabis is now twice as potent as it was in the sixties? And if so, does that mean it's that much easier to get hooked and that much harder to get clean?"

She gave up. "Mr. President, you know experts agree that selective breeding has increased the chemical THC in the cannabis plant."

"So it is true that over 60 per cent of Americans in drug treatment programs, which include children aged twelve to seventeen, need treatment for marijuana, Kate?

"Now before we go any further I would like to make a correction. Alcohol does not kill. And cigarettes do not kill. The accumulated effects of alcohol and cigarettes do kill over time.

"Now, what do you think is the result of the accumulated effects of marijuana?" he asked the bewildered reporters.

"With respect, sir, all that information is easily available—" Ryan began their defence.

"You are absolutely correct. You have all that information at your fingertips. And yet…" Clayton paused. "And yet, you still allow cannabis supporters to tell everyone that cannabis is safe. Even though it's addictive enough to send people into rehab, you allow supporters to go on TV and declare it to be *perfectly safe*?" He sneered. "Let me tell you, getting addicted to anything is not my idea of its being perfectly safe. And you… the media have allowed people to say that kind of *shit*?"

The word was a hammer blow to both reporters. A president of the United States simply did not use such language in public. They were further unbalanced by its implied contempt. "Indeed, you defend their 'right' to spread such propaganda. Is it any wonder that the media have lost all credibility?" He smiled ever so gently, as if he was only half disappointed.

"I am not one to indulge in conspiracies, but I must say, I can almost believe the one about the media being in league with liberal elements of society that want to legalize cannabis so that they can use it as their Trojan horse to legalize cocaine and heroin. Laughable, isn't it?" He was asking Ryan, but in reality he was addressing the audience.

"But you are right to criticize your government's stance. We do need to do more, much more, to fight the abuse of tobacco and alcohol. In fact, I'm glad you've brought this up, Kate. Yes, I think the media can indeed do so much more." Clayton smiled innocently at the presenter.

"The media?" she squeaked.

"Yes, just think what the media can achieve with daily information segments before and after the news. Each day you could present the latest statistics, with graphic pictures of mouth cancers one day and the next day pictures of lung cancers. Yes indeed… just imagine TV, radio, and even the Internet all doing their part." He smiled at the two reporters. "I will be more than delighted to endorse a media information campaign. Let's make it a regular event, shall we? We'll bring this up in all our follow-up interviews, Kate."

"I'm not sure I understand… Are you planning to have the government begin an antismoking campaign?"

"No, I mean the media can engage in a campaign against smoking and alcohol. The media as an independent, neutral body can present the facts, each and every day."

"But, sir, we can't." Kate was shocked. *He can't be serious, it's just . . . It's just ridiculous. That's not our job.*

"And why not, may I ask? You can keep it totally apolitical. It'll be just the media doing its civil duty. Reaching out to the youth of America and showing them the dangers of smoking and of excessive use of alcohol. Just imagine the benefits of five-minute segments in peak time each day, with media and television stars all warning about the dangers of smoking and excess alcohol." Clayton paused as if he had been struck with yet another great idea.

"Indeed, let us not stop there. The media can begin a nationwide campaign to ban the sale of cigarettes during daytime. Cigarettes… and perhaps even alcohol… should only be purchased between eleven in the evening and five in the morning. You can mount a petition and get the public to sign up. You will have my total support, Kate."

Ryan glanced at Kate. *Did he just flush her career down the toilet? They'll never let her in the same room with this guy. Shit, the cigarette companies are going to have a heart attack.*

Sorry, babe; looks like you're screwed.

"It'll never work, sir," Kate said with an edge of desperation. "You'll just drive it all underground. Criminal gangs would—"

"Do nothing, Kate. It'll still be legal, just a little harder to get hold of during the day."

"They will buy in bulk," she stammered.

"Easily dealt with, using one plastic card that the public could show to the seller, thus limiting all sales to one packet a day . . . or a bottle or two a night." He smiled at her. "Now let's get back to the matter at hand, Kate." Clayton's smile had grown even wider as he addressed the presenter, as if he had no idea of the mess he had landed her in if the idea was taken up.

"This is not simply about marijuana. This is about the deaths, the ruined lives, and the economic cost to our society from all illegal drugs. The billions wasted on drug prevention and rehabilitation. This is about taking the war on drugs seriously for the first time."

"Excuse me, sir. Did you say we haven't taken the war on drugs seriously?" Ryan looked startled.

"You tell me, Ryan. If you're caught selling a packet of drugs, what is the likelihood that you'll get jail time or a suspended sentence for your first offence?"

"The three-strikes rule will get you life, even for selling marijuana, Mr. President," Ryan pointed out. "That's pretty serious to me."

"To you, to Kate, and to me it is serious and very real. Unfortunately, to some it simply doesn't enter into their thinking. Remember, for years petty criminals have watched others getting away with only a slap on the wrist. Doesn't that create a state of denial?" Clayton shook his head as if disappointed over some great wrong. "Too many live in denial. They need to be shown, indeed, shocked into reality. Some need to see the consequences of their illegal activities day after day after day before it registers." *And what a dumb-ass fool must you be to be caught selling dope three times in a row? Prison's probably the best place for the idiot; at least that's one moron who won't be contaminating the gene pool.*

"As with so many issues facing America, the response is always too little too late. How many decades will we wait with our hands in our pockets until the problem becomes so big that the public's only response is to surrender and run away from the problem?

"When the drug problem was small, did we have drug dealers automatically being sentenced to ten years hard labour? Were they lectured by guards on how they had lost all rights of citizenship when they sold drugs?"

Both reporters nearly choked at the force of his reply, then glanced at each other.

"So we need to hang people to get their attention, to get them out of their 'state of denial'?" Kate shuddered at the very idea.

Clayton looked her straight in the eyes. "You sound as if you approve of drug dealers selling drugs to our children?"

Ryan did choke on that one.

"Mr. President," she snapped at him in protest.

"You do?" Clayton inquired innocently.

"No, of course not. What I mean is that some have argued that the war on drugs has been lost, and we should legalize them, as they have done in Europe. And then concentrate on rehabilitation programs. There are many who point to Portugal, where the number of deaths from drug overdose has gone down and drug-related crime has hit an all-time low."

"But has it really worked, Kate? Is Portugal drug-free?" Clayton glared right into her eyes. "You refer to one survey. Yet according to others, the legalization has also increased its use. As far back as 1997, as I recall, a survey in the Netherlands showed that usage amongst eighteen-to-twenty-year-olds went up from 15 per cent to 44 per cent when marijuana was legalized. I wouldn't call that a victory.

"As for your Portugal, Kate, marijuana use went up 37 per cent amongst eighteen to twenty-four-year-olds when it was legalized. Would you call that a victory?" Clayton glared from one to the other. "Experts have pointed to a fundamental fact; it is well known that availability and acceptability only increase drug use. We would simply be filling the pockets of drug peddlers." *And state coffers—gambling, alcohol, drugs… as long as the States get their cut, who cares about the consequences?* Clayton reflected, shifting in his seat.

Kate would not surrender so easily. "Yet others have argued that legalizing drugs has reduced the harm—"

"Then present the facts, Kate. Show the studies, show the results… tell the truth. And tell them about the real issue."

"The real issue?" Kate parroted in confusion.

"Yes, my dear, the real issue. Was I misinformed when I was told that the earlier you start taking drugs, the harder it is to get off them? 'Start 'em young, and hook 'em for life,'" Clayton whispered softly. "Well, is that true?" He paused as if to give both a chance to respond.

"Some have suggested… the possibility," Ryan blurted. "Although I can't confirm…"

"If we legalize drugs, would we be condemning ourselves to spending billions each decade as we deal with each new generation of addicts as they go through the horrors of drug rehab? Legalizing it hasn't eradicated drug use in Europe. Indeed, one may well ask if it hasn't simply hidden the problem.

"Do we want to perpetuate drug abuse, or do we want to *really* take the war to the drug dealers?"

"Sir, I'm not sure I understand." Ryan seemed totally lost by now.

"If it's legal, is there any real incentive to deal with it, Ryan? Are they sweeping it all under the rug and hope no one complains? Well, I suppose that is one way to deal with the cost . . . Do they have four-star drug resorts for the rich, and the gutter for the rest?"

"Many have suggested that we could use the savings realized from cutting back on crime prevention," Kate responded swiftly, now on solid ground—or so she thought.

"Glad to hear there will be no more murders, rapes, or robberies. I'm so happy to hear that all crime will vanish once marijuana is legalized. Going by that logic, we really should legalize heroin, crack, and every hard drug out there. Hell, Kate, if we decriminalized murder and rape, just imagine how our crime statistics would fall." He smiled even more brightly at Kate.

"Let me remind everyone, over the years we've been cutting policing to the bone, so do we take the few dollars left in the police budget to feed into, what would be, an ineffective rehab program?" *Kick them while they're down; that way maybe they'll stay down.* Clayton's frustration was growing.

"And hanging someone for twenty-five dollars' worth of marijuana is the answer?" Kate repeated.

God, this woman is fixated, Clayton thought even as his smile grew even wider. "The death penalty will send a clear message to the dealers that either you stop or you'll hang—and hopefully send a clear message to our youth that drugs are not safe."

"Yet you have been a long-time opponent of the death penalty for murder. How can you reconcile this contradiction?" *Get out of that one.* Kate tried to hide her smile.

"Yes, I have been opposed to the death penalty for murder for many years and still am." He paused and took a long breath. "People must understand that there are two fundamental differences, Kate. First, people kill... murder... for all sorts of reasons, from love to hate, from anger to vengeance. From vanity to jealousy, and every emotion we have. All of which makes rational thought difficult.

"We all know that emotions can override our logical fear of death—especially when we know state executions are avoided like the plague.

"While, with drugs it's for one reason only: money and more money. It's about profit and loss. Profit is all the money you make selling this poison, as opposed to a light sentence for your first drug offence.

"Now, with the death penalty, it's a choice between making twenty-five dollars or the hangman's noose. That will stop a lot of people from selling drugs."

"And the second?" Ryan wondered aloud.

"The second is why I personally oppose the death penalty for murder. We need to get the right man. We cannot hang an innocent man for a crime he did not commit, which has been the case with a number of murder convictions in the past.

"With drug dealers it will be a different story. With drug dealers we will set up special law enforcement teams, perhaps three or four in each city, to catch drug dealers and only drug dealers. These units would be made up of specially selected officers who will secretly film their actions, obtaining audio evidence. Eyewitness testimony. If necessary, we can have three undercover officers each going and buying drugs from the dealer individually, one after the other. So that there will be no doubt of the dealer's guilt. We will have the drugs he sold; we will have the money the officers gave for the drugs." Clayton looked from one to the other.

"Yet Senator Walker has been quoted as saying that the death penalty for murder has not been effective in reducing the murder rate, so why would it be effective for drug dealers?" Kate was now looking for any tiny hole in his argument.

"I am pleased that my learned colleague, a true Republican, has seen the light and now opposes the death penalty for murder."

"That doesn't answer the question about its effectiveness as a deterrent." Clayton slowly breathed out. "I repeat, because too many simply do not consider the consequences. And is that really a surprise? It takes decades to execute someone for murder. By the time the execution is carried out we have all but forgotten about the crime, concentrating instead on the lawyer's cries for compassion. We forget the woman who was raped and strangled; we forget about the child beaten to death with a hammer. We hear only the cries for mercy from the lawyer—but not the cries of that woman, that child as they beg for mercy.

"And, more critically, there is the way we do it, all in secret. As if we were ashamed of it. A hundred years ago it was done in public, in the open, a clear warning to one and all. Now we act like such timid creatures, as if we had become afraid of taking the tough stand, of making the hard choices. A nation, a people cannot be timid, be afraid and be great at the same time. We need to aim high."

"And yet we are going after the little fish, not the drug lords," Ryan pressed.

"Oh, no. We will go after the big fish. Yes, we start small, out of necessity. But once the street dealers have seen a few fellow dealers hanged, things will change. Imagine being a drug dealer and watching all the TV stations stop their regular broadcast to show a dealer walking up the scaffolding, show them putting the hood over his head and the noose around his neck. Then the screen goes blank and you hear that thump as the trapdoor opens. Two minutes later the picture is back, showing the man's feet dangling in the air. After seeing a few such demonstrations, wouldn't you squeal to save your life?

"The dealer will get one chance to provide the police with his supplier. Then it will be the supplier's turn to squeal. Thus, we will work our way up the ladder to the drug lords.

"This is not about some drug dealer selling twenty-five dollars' worth of drugs; this is about targeting everyone in the drug trade, from the street corners all the way up to the drug lords in the only manner that will bring them down. Squeal or hang."

"Mr. President. The death penalty hasn't stopped dealers in countries that already have the death sentence. In all honestly, from the heart… can you be certain that it will work?"

"Yes, Kate I can. And I'll tell you why. A long time ago I read a very interesting article. In it, an American was on a business trip in Saudi Arabia. He was being driven to his appointment, and he happened to notice a number of cars left abandoned on the side of the road.

"He asked his driver about the vehicles. The man responded that the cars had broken down and the owners had simply abandoned them. Well, he then asked, weren't they afraid someone would steal the cars? The driver gave a little laugh and said of course not. The penalty for stealing in Saudi Arabia is to have your hand cut off. So naturally no one was going to steal those cars.

"They believe—they *know* they will lose a hand if they steal." Clayton looked from one to the other.

"The problem we have is that too many delude themselves, too many live in a state of denial. Ryan, how many addicts told themselves they would never get hooked? That they were too smart or too sophisticated, that only dummies get hooked.

"Equally, how many dealers believe they'll never get caught? Why? Because no one has shown them they are wrong. We will show them they are wrong. If that means watching hangings carried out day after day, then that is what we need to do.

"The Saudis believe that they will pay for their crimes. Americans have to believe that they will pay for their crimes as well. For far too many Americans it's 'I can get away with it, so why not?' Well, that has to end. As I said, it's time we got serious."

That silenced the pair for a second or two. Then Kate spoke up for the defence. "And what do you say to those who argue that the death penalty is cruel, harsh, and inhumane?"

"That is an opinion, an individual's point of view. I could just as easily espouse that putting people in prison is cruel, harsh, and inhumane. Indeed, many experts in that field would argue that if we want to rehabilitate convicts, we need an entirely different approach, a system where we concentrate on rehabilitation and not incarceration, on re-education and not on punishment."

"Do you support this view, Mr. President?" Kate was a little bewildered by now.

"You tell me. Imagine a criminal sneaks into your home and brutally rapes your twelve-year-old daughter and then bashes in the skull of your five-year-old son, leaving him a vegetable for life. He is caught and sentenced to five years in a Norwegian-style rehabilitation facility, a kind of 'camp med' in the middle of a lovely forest with his own cabin, equipped with TV and radio. And he has the keys to the cabin, so he can go in and out whenever he wants.

"Now, on his release, will you shake hands and say everything is forgiven?" Clayton looked Kate squarely in the eye. "Come now, Kate, he's done his time, right? You can forgive him, right? He's paid his debt to society.

"So what if he raped your daughter and bashed in the head of your son? Be fair; he's done his time in a rehabilitation resort. You can shake hands, right?"

"I… uh… that is to say—" She shuddered. "Well, that *is* a hypothetical question, Mr. President. But do you support rehabilitation over incarceration?" She desperately tried to shift the focus. But she thought she had him. Politicians, when worked into a corner would normally waffle on and make fools of them-selves in the process.

"I support both, Kate."

"Sorry?"

"A criminal should be punished for his crimes and then rehabilitated. As an example, I would say if a man is sentenced to ten years, then for the first seven years he should pay for his crime in a strict penal institution— and here we need to take back the prisons from the convicts and establish a more 'boot camp' style system. A system that is both fair but very, very strict.

"Now, after the seventh year in his sentence, if he has shown the correct attitude, he goes to a purpose-built rehabilitation centre, which provides education and training courses. Prisoners could be trained as electricians, carpenters, or cooks… even earn college degrees. We should do everything we can so that they can become productive members of the community.

"And rehabilitation should not stop once the person has left prison. We would need to support halfway houses and offer temporary jobs to provide stability.

"At the moment the whole system is a giant joke. A sad joke. We have so many first-time offenders going to jail in some false hope of rehabilitation, and instead they come out as hardened criminals. We need separate prisons for first-time offenders that have direct links to proper rehabilitation centres and effective programs.

"Yes, we need to punish those who have violated people in the most horrible ways, but equally we need to uplift those who can be saved, give their life meaning, hope, a sense of value . . ."

"And the sanctity, the value of human life? How does that square with the death penalty?" Ryan stepped in. "The churches have long argued that—"

"Oh, please. What do we teach in our schools?" The president scoffed.

"What?" Ryan looked puzzled.

"Come now, it's not a trick question. What do we teach in school?" "I'm not sure I know what you mean."

"We teach evolution in schools. Not creationism. As a nation we do not have God in our schools. Therefore, as a nation, we do not believe that a person has an immortal soul; as a people we do not believe we are made in God's image. We are not of the divine.

"In our schools we teach our children science, that our DNA is nearly identical to that of chimps. So Ryan, how identical are we to chimps? Is it 90 per cent, 95 per cent, 97 per cent? According to science just how identical are we to chimps?" Clayton snapped at Ryan. *And in Africa they eat chimps; that should tell you something.*

Kate swallowed. *Ryan looks as if he wants to plead for help. The bastard's actually enjoying himself, making us look like fools.*

"Schools teach that humans and apes had a common ancestor. Given all that, what makes us special? Gives us this divine sanctity of life?

"Enough, Ryan, do not waste my time arguing about the valve of human live, not when our schools argue that we are nothing but animals that can make interesting noises. Do not talk about the sanctity of life when so many Americans want a secular state... free of God.

"We slaughter up to thirty thousand Americans a year because we love guns more than human life. And here you are talking about the value of human life."

Both Kate and Ryan, indeed the entire room were stunned into such silence that it was beyond their minds to conceive of any new questions. No politician had so bluntly stated the obvious.

Clayton looked into the camera. "Let us go to the heart of the issue, shall we? We have three choices. The first is to vacillate and do next to nothing, exactly what we are doing now.

"The second is to surrender, give up, and legalize soft drugs. The benefits are notable, we are told. They will tell you that the money spent on drug enforcement can go into health care and drug rehabilitation. Ignoring reality, what little we may save, Congress will simply put into the pockets of the health insurance companies.

"Worse, they will expect drug users to voluntarily enter rehabilitation. Now, why should they? If it's legal, so why shouldn't they enjoy whatever drugs are out there?

"It's only when the drugs are illegal that you have a reason to stop. In truth, we will simply be creating a permanent underclass of drug users, some of whom will migrate to hard drugs.

"And what do we do with hard drugs? Legalize them as well? Legalizing soft drugs won't get rid of the hard stuff. Criminals will only redouble their efforts. If they can't sell marijuana to adults, then will they sell crack, ice, heroin, and marijuana to our young?

"What is your answer to that? Have the government sanction the legal sale of heroin or crack-cocaine to adults and later to your children?

"'Never happen,' I am certain my critics will argue. Just as I am sure they will tell you that criminals would never sell whatever poison they can to our children. Is anyone gullible enough to believe that?" He asked the camera lens.

"We need to eradicate the *acceptance* of drugs; otherwise we'll just go from one epidemic to the next, no matter how good any rehab programme may be. If it's not Ice today, then it'll be a new drug tomorrow.

"The third option is to take the war on drugs seriously. For the first time we take drugs seriously. Special teams of drug enforcement agents assigned to target drug dealers. Once caught red-handed, they either squeal and hand over their supplier or face a military court. If they choose the courts and are found guilty, they will be publicly executed within six months; none of this insane twenty years on death row."

"Sir, the military can't judge civilians; I am sure you know that."

"As I have explained, this will be offered up to the people in a referendum. They can change the law, if they wish. If the public wishes, we can set up legislation enabling the military courts to prosecute drug dealers for the next five years. Then we evaluate the results."

"But why the military?"

"You think our civilian courts are squeaky clean? We have no dirty Judges? Let's be honest, our legal system is more joke than deterrent. We have gotten to the point where gangs rule prisons, happily selling drugs there. How many lawyers do we have with their snouts filled with cocaine and their troughs filled with drug money?"

That should silence the lawyers a little. Clayton grinned at the idea. Numerous judges and lawyers would hesitate to take issue with him, fearing that they would be branded as drug lawyers or dirty judges. After all, the general public believed that defence lawyers had only one objective, to make money and more money rather than any real commitment to justice… with good reason.

"Our military courts have not been exposed to the corrupting influences of drug money. With the fear of the death penalty we can attack drug dealers at every level. Yes, we begin with street dealers, but we work up to the middlemen and finally the drug lords. Money and threats from a drug lord to keep quiet won't work on a street dealer when he fells a noose around his neck.

"Up until now the drug dealers feel safe, but when that changes, everything changes." Clayton paused as if in thought, as if judging his next words carefully. Then he addressed the camera:

"A final word. Do not think I am against rehabilitation I see its value. But, I know, it needs to be properly funded and managed. Addicts have to be able to come in for treatment without any fear of prosecution. They need to be helped with proper treatment… and that is what we should do.

"Yet all that is merely the beginning. I could go on for hours about the need for real jobs, ongoing counselling, group therapy, halfway houses… and even relocation to the other side of the country—if that is what it takes to get them away from any bad influence.

"And it doesn't end there, we must remember that. Although many young use drugs for a thrill; some have deep-rooted social or mental health concerns that we also have to address. We should cover all these areas with a serious commitment in time and resources.

"Plus, a far greater commitment to a nationwide, multi-year education programme targeting our youth, warning them of the dangers of drugs. Now, you got all that?" Clayton asked the two reporters.

Kate and Ryan almost cringed; they feared he might ask them yet more questions, as if they were schoolchildren facing their headmaster. Their heads were already beginning to swim.

"So are the American people prepared to put in the billions needed? The real money needed to succeed? Because I can tell you the government doesn't have the tax dollars.

"We can't pay for what we have got… I remind everyone that for decades we have been cutting the numbers of our military personnel to cover the cost of our toys, just as we have been cutting the budget for police and community health." Clayton looked from Kate to Ryan with challenging eyes, daring them to question his words. "We are drowning in debt, people."

"Well, can't we take a page out of the States that have legalized marijuana, sir? They are collecting millions in sales tax that could cover some of the cost . . ." Ryan inquired, more on automatic than anything else. He had been taken utterly by surprise at the depth and fury of the debate. He had seen the other interviews and was impressed with Clayton's background knowledge, but had expected the president to have reached some limit by now. Instead he had blasted them with a passion.

"I agree totally, those States willing to sell drugs can fund their own health care. For that reason I will be ordering all federal funds for health care to States that have legalized marijuana to cease."

"Sir?" Kate gasped.

Ryan snapped up straight in his chair. "You're cutting funding—you can't, can you?"

"The States want to make money on marijuana, for now that's fine. They want to fund their budgets by selling drugs, so be it, but it will be without federal money to pay for their health costs. I see no reason why federal money should be used to pay for illness and diseases… the cancers and depression… that these States have brought down upon themselves."

"But you can't blame marijuana for everything."

"Nor do we know how many other diseases the drug may be inflicting. As I pointed out, the government simply doesn't have the money. So it's not going to pay for State-induced drug illness."

"That is so unfair…," Kate began; *what about those that have done nothing wrong?*

"No, what is unfair is hardworking, honest people being asked to cover the health cost of people deliberately abusing their bodies.

"I am so tired of hearing the same old pathetic excuses that we need to offer them compassion and sympathy. And yes, where we can help we should, absolutely.

"But equally, no one put a gun to the head of drug dealers or drug users and told them to sell or use drugs, or we'd blow their brains out. It is past time people took responsibility for their actions and stopped making excuses.

"Let me wrap this up. This is not about some Robin Hood giving twenty-five dollars' worth of marijuana to the poor. This is about the brutal murders of many Mexicans, Americans, and Colombians and the drug addicts dying with needles in their arms. The tens of thousands of ruined lives. People are dying; that is not a fantasy. And it is the pushers selling twenty-five dollars' worth of drugs as much as the drug lords that are responsible.

"Now, any further questions?"

Watching the interview from a corner of the room Abb turned to Jonathan. "So what do you think?"

"He nailed them." *But you know that, so why ask the question?*

"Come, walk with me to my office." Both men turned and walked out the door and down the long corridor.

"As you know, the president does not have a wife," Abb stated as they negotiated the twists and turns on the way to Abb's office.

Jonathan knew it was a rhetorical question. Everyone knew about Clayton's private life.

"And I've noticed that the president has been very impressed with you. I think he likes you. Which is why I think it would be helpful if you both developed a more intimate relationship."

"Sorry?"

"The president… or rather Clayton Prescott has needs, as we all do." "I don't quite know what you mean."

"I think you do. He needs someone to confide in. He needs to talk and let out his feelings. I may not be able to go into classified areas with my wife, but she has been a godsend. And I was hoping you would be willing to let him… well, unload on you. But this is strictly up to you.

"Look, tomorrow he will be giving a short speech at one of those stupid town hall meetings. Just go will him and be around; if he wants to talk, just listen. You'll be doing him a real service."

One of Abb's staff put his head around the door. "Sir, the president would like to see you in his office."

Abb glanced at the clock on the wall. "Damn, the two o'clock. I'm on my way." It was still a little early. Clayton probably had something to talk about before the meeting started.

Abb arrived to see a seated president watching one of the TV screens in the empty room. The meeting was yet to start.

"So what did you think of the interview?" Clayton touched the controls of the remote.

"The interview went well, I thought. Neither really laid a glove on you, while you gave Kate one hell of a bloody nose." Abb offered his evaluation in a soft, hesitant voice. "Although I doubt you'll get the support you need, even if they know you're right. Maybe if you exempted marijuana, the public might actually support you on the rest."

"What complete and utter hypocrisy." Clayton whispered aloud. Abb waited for more. Instead Clayton remained seated in silence, his elbows resting on the desk with fingertips pressed together as if to form a roof. Abb waited and waited just that bit longer; then he glanced at the door, trying to decide whether to leave and return when the meeting began.

"Some time ago"—the voice was distant, as if Clayton were not really speaking to Abb—"years now, a magazine decided to ban some pop star from its cover. She had a tendency to appear on stage a little lacking in attire, and it seems they wanted a more positive role model.

"Anyway, the next day chat shows were debating the merits. What interested me was that one of them brought up the fact that banning whatever only makes the young want it all the more.

"And off course children will often do the exact opposite of what they are told, that's no surprise. But was it simply that?

"That was when it hit me. They were blaming the child for the failure of the adult. They don't want their children exposed to pornography, yet the Internet is full of it. They don't want their precious children to take drugs, but the streets are full of drugs.

"If there was no pornography and no drugs, if people adhered to an accepted dress code, then there would be no need to ban it."

"The child mimics the adult." Abb whispered his understanding, after a fashion.

"More like the adult remains the spoilt child… We're all to blame but we're not honest enough to admit it."

Americans have a polarized view of drugs.
It is either a criminal matter or a health issue.
When in fact it is both.

Earnest Black

Chapter 7

GOOD HEALTH IS MADNESS.

The presidential limo headed back towards the White House under a blackened sky. Fortunately today it was from the threatening storm clouds.

"The audience seemed more open to my position on the drugs issue, don't you think?" Clayton addressed Abb Cole on the car's new encrypted communications array.

"You were talking to a select group of nutcase conservatives, sir. They will praise you on drug control and damn you on gun control. Maybe you should tone it down just a little?" Abb all but begged. The president's constant campaigning on drugs and guns, along with the need for health reform, were beginning to become unsettling.

Clayton's behaviour was starting to worry Abb. He just did not see the reasoning, this near compulsion the president had. Was it a compulsion? A need to leave something behind… *now that he's had a taste of mortality.* The horror of Congress would be enough to make most men feel the need to leave some kind of legacy behind, something to mark their existence.

If only he didn't seem to be stirring up a hornet's nest, if he didn't seem so extreme. That was the danger—that he might push the establishment too much, push the public too much. The gun lobby was already raving mad, talking about starting another revolution. The health insurance industry had started screaming that the commies were under the bed once more. It was something straight out of the sixties, with their warning of big government sticking its nose into a person's personal medical records. All part of some government conspiracy… yet another one. God, the crap they were coming up with.

But it had been Clayton's reply that had him almost pulling his hair out in shock and disbelief. It had been so Machiavellian in scope and brutal in delivery. Within minutes of the health lobby raising their objections, Clayton had invited several of the foremost critics to debate the federal health insurance scheme.

Abb cringed at the memory. As they arrived at the White House, Clayton presented each of them with a conical tinfoil skullcap in front of the cameras.

"So the government's microwave mind control can't take over your thoughts." He laughed as he ushered them into the conference room, chatting happily as he did so. It just seemed to be a giant joke.

But his guests were all momentarily struck dumb. The tinfoil took the shape of dunce's caps. Anyone who actually wore one would look ridiculous. Abb could see that they had not expected such intolerable behaviour. He could just imagine their thoughts. This was unheard of; they were people of importance being publicly ridiculed by the president.

Abb had fallen into a near panic, but far worse was to come. Prescott, the university lecturer and debater with a near-encyclopaedic memory, had calmly and brutally trotted out detail after shameful detail.

When they had spoken of improvements in the industry, he had countered by asking; "So hospitals no longer have taxis leave confused, uninsured, patients on the roadside still in their hospital gowns?"

The dignified white haired Dr. Tenwood-Green jumped to their defence. "Those allegations were never substantiated."

"No," Clayton happily replied, "just caught on cameras at the free medical clinics where they were dumped."

When Clayton's opponents for public approval of his health scheme argued that the ever-rising costs were not all that bad and would eventually stabilize, he pointed out that his answer came from a toilet, where he had once found an old magazine with its edges twisted and torn. Inside the pages was an old survey conducted in 2012 which showed that even back then the US had the highest medical costs in twenty-two of the twenty-three advanced countries.

Back then the average cost for an angiogram in the US was $798, while in Canada it was $35.

A medical MRI cost $1080 in the US but only $281 in France.

Five years later a MRI cost Australians 215, in the US it had gone up to 1,119.

To remove an Appendix for Australians it was 3,814 compared to US citizens who paid 15,930.

"So how much do Americans pay for their angiogram, MRI's nowadays, Doctor? Has the cost gone down? How much do Australians, British and Canadians pay when they go for their angiograms?"

"Well, I can't say with any detail."

"No, of course not. You wouldn't want to tell the public that they now pay up to nine times more than their Canadian cousins, now would you?

"You are certainly the last person one should ask about medical services, Doctor." Clayton had then glared at the camera. "We wouldn't want people to know what a grubby fraud the medical profession has become."

"Sir, that is totally—"

"Omission is as fraudulent as providing misinformation. Omission is lying, sir—letting the public believe they are getting the best health care at the best price while you silently fleece them like sheep without a care for their well-being… isn't that fraud?" a smiling Prescott had asked the group. "The medical profession is committed to the public's well-being," Dr.

Tenwood-Green declared.

"Tell that to the fifty million Americans who can't afford health care. Tell that to the thousands that are once more losing their homes to pay for their medical expenses.

Tell that to the thousands dying prematurely due to our poor medical care.

Tell that to American women who are dying at three times the rate to their Canadian cousins during child birth.

Tell that to the Australians with their universal health care, the British with their universal health care, and the Europeans and the Japanese with their superior health care… so they can all laugh in your face.

"They provide affordable health care to *all* their people—they're not losing their homes or dying prematurely because of lousy health care." Clayton snared straight in Dr. Tenwood-Green's face with heated passion.

"It was the Republicans' changes under Trump—" Dr. Tenwood-Green began.

"Enough, sir. Few working-class Americans still believe your scandalous untruths. Why else do you think so many Americans no longer wish to vaccinate their children against measles? Is it because they see you in the pockets of the drug and insurance companies?"

"That is rather unfair, sir," Dr. Tenwood-Green protested. "The public needs to realize it costs tens of millions to develop a new drug. Drugs are by necessity expensive."

"So the patenting rights, the many years where a pharmaceutical company has exclusive rights to sell its drugs, aren't enough?" Clayton fumed in indignation. *How can they possibly argue that after all these years?*

"There are also a number of external factors to consider." For whatever reason, either loyalty or reward, the doctor fought on for the pharmaceutical industry. "We must understand that it takes years to develop the drugs at a massive cost. For any company to remain viable, it must show a return—"

"A profit." Clayton hissed his disapproval.

"Well, they need to make a small return for their investment." "Really? In my youth I travelled to a number of countries. One of those was Australia, and thus I came into contact with their PBS… the Pharmaceutical Benefit Scheme. Basically, their government negotiates over the cost of each drug and buys it in bulk… cutting the price massively.

"In another country, the New Zealand government puts out a tender for the drugs they want. They buy at the cheapest price offered—while the US government buys the drug at whatever price the pharmaceutical companies want, thanks to… the men and women of Congress.

"An Australian may pay twenty dollars for what costs an American two hundred or three hundred dollars. Even better for them, when Aussies become aged pensioners, they automatically receive whatever drugs they need at just under seven dollars a packet—no matter the actual cost."

Clayton shook his head in disgust. "Why, sir? Why has your profession not supported any reduction scheme here in the US? Is it because the economics of our system are simply too tempting?" Clayton's face was a stormy as his voice.

The good doctor opened his mouth to protest most vigorously. Clayton gave him no opportunity to speak. "Now, can you understand the public's point of view, sir? Do you see why more and more Americans look upon you with contempt, distrust, and loathing? And they have every right to do so. If the medical profession gave a damn, it would have run screaming to hammer down the doors of Congress and presented its own proposal for a decent health care system.

"If you truly cared, you would have demanded universal, good quality, low-cost health care for all Americans decades ago. You would have had a working group travel the world to see how Britain, Germany, France, and Japan provide their health coverage and then pick the best elements to truly create a world-class health care system. But no, that was asking too much.

"It is your decades of betrayal that condemn you, sir. For far too many you are seen as Judas taking your thirty pieces of silver to keep silent about the horror that the insurance companies have made of American health."

"That is totally incorrect. For example, doctors working in hospitals do not set policy. The medical profession has always worked within the accepted guidelines for the betterment of the public."

"And yet more and more people believe that doctors do more than remain silent, that they actively collude in lying and misinforming the American people. The years of silence over addiction to legally prescribed painkillers being one of the more obvious cases. That resulted in many Americans believing that doctors were in league with the drug companies and the… former Congress"—a shadow of pain crossed Clayton's face—"to get Americans hooked on painkillers so the drug companies will have an endless demand for their product."

"Those wild rumours were never taken seriously. There was never any proof—"

"Yet, how low is your credibility when so many now believe you work hand in glove with drug companies to get Americans hooked on legal drugs? And people were getting hooked—"

"Sir, many drugs have side effects… but the good they do cannot be denied. It is not that certain medical drugs are deliberately addictive. Rather it is a case of improper management by those using the drugs that is the real issue of concern. The public must understand that the medical profession's highest priority is the well-being of the public."

"Then why is it that in the last ten years more and more people see you as selfish, greedy, and manipulative? Tell me, sir, how many now call your Hippocratic Oath the 'hypocrite's oath'? Be careful, sir; you and the medical profession may find yourselves on the wrong side of history, and the backlash may be far worse than you imagine." Clayton all but glared at the doctor with frank contempt.

"Do you know what my greatest concern is for this country?" Clayton demanded as he leaned back in his chair. "America's future health costs. Already we are fast approaching the point where health care may reach 24 per cent of our GDP. Imagine our economy trying to function when it's paying 30, 35 per cent of our GDP to GPs, surgeons, and insurance companies.

Imagine a surgeon charging a quarter million for an operation. That can-not be allowed to happen, sir, and I will do everything in my power to prevent it."

"That is a preposterous scenario," Dr. Tenwood- Green jumped in. "It will never happen. The people would never allow it, sir."

"How are they going to stop it?" Clayton cryptically replied, as if he knew something the rest of them did not.

By God, that had been brutal enough, Abb had told himself. But that had been just the warm-up. The following thirty minutes had been an absolute barrage of fury focused by contempt to cover the health industry in utter condemnation. Abb was sure that the delegates were a few inches shorter when they left.

Abb had to give the man credit: no president had set their critics and the media on the run like Prescott had. He was an outright butcher. Abb had waited for the backlash. Yet, instead of the public being outraged at his strange behaviour, they had rallied around him. It seemed as if the crazier his behaviour, the more vicious his attackers, the greater the public support for him.

To drive Abb ever crazier, Prescott had come out the next morning to assure the public that "not all medicos are the lackeys of the obscenely blotted and self-serving medical insurance companies." Abb shook his head in dismay at the sheer audacity of that one. Prescott had used the media's own weapons of fear and suspicion against them, outplaying them at their own game. But how long could it last, and what then?

And just why was he doing this? Was there some reasoning behind his… erratic behaviour? It just seemed so insane. That was worrying him.

"We'll see, Abb. Stop worrying and relax. We have a big day tomorrow." Clayton heard Abb groan and smiled.

"That's what I'm worried about. Can't we delay the speech for a few days to go over the details?" Abb hoped he could convince the president to delay his announcement.

"We don't have the time, Abb. We have to keep moving while we have the momentum. Trust me, this is necessary. See you at the White house." Clayton stretched out in the car before he turned to an equally unhappy man seated beside him.

"You have doubts too, Jonathan?"

"No sir. From what little I've heard in your discussions, it's what the country needs, a new direction. We need to get the economy moving; everyone keeps saying that." *But how the hell are we going to achieve that?* Jonathan knew the country was bankrupt in every sense of the word. The government could barely pay its employees; how could they magically restart the engine?

"Then why the glum face?"

"It's nothing really—"

"Out with it, man." Clayton used his most fatherly voice.

"Sir, I just—I accept your reasoning. It's just hard to accept hanging someone for a few dollars. Why not life imprisonment for drug dealers, if I may ask?"

"The shock value, Jonathan. In a way it's all about the shock value. It focuses people's minds on what's important. Theoretically, what else have you got? We have nothing else that can have any real effect. We tried the 'three strikes and you're out' policy, which achieved next to nothing." Clayton smiled a sad little smile, one that spoke of sorrow and regret. "It's almost as if you need shock therapy to get a response on any issue these days."

"It's just hard to accept, ending a life so casually." Jonathan showed his sadness in the deep lines around his eyes.

"Oh, please. Don't give me that. We terminate half a million foetuses in abortion clinics each year."

"Sir, that is different; they are not alive."

"Prove it."

"Sir?"

"Prove it, Jonathan."

"Sir, they have no heartbeat, no brain activity."

"Oh, Jonathan, Jonathan, and you went to such fine schools. Tell me, what is an amoeba?"

"Sir?"

"An amoeba?

"Uh, I'm not sure. You are talking about the protozoan?"

"Yes, an amoeba, what the biologists call a single-celled life form. It catches its own food, reproduces itself, all without any brain wave activity or heartbeat.

"The entire scientific community, Jonathan, including the medical community, accept that an amoeba is a living, if not breathing, creature. Yet that same community considers a multicellular foetus… which is growing every day… to be, what? Unalive?

"Don't you see the hypocrisy? It has to be alive. You don't give birth to four pounds of clay, after which the shaman enters the room to do a rain dance and say the magic words to turn clay into flesh and blood. You can't say that a foetus isn't alive. Something is alive or it is not. It's like that ridiculous cliché: 'I'm not pregnant, I'm only a little bit pregnant.' Talk about bull, Jonathan. It's yet another example of the hypocrisy of the medical so-called 'profession.'

"Okay, I'm not saying that it's independent of its mother. If you want, you can call it a 'dependent life form' or a 'formulating foetal mass'—hell, you can call it a parasite for all I care; you can call it unborn. But don't give me this rubbish that it isn't alive. It may not be independently alive, but it is by our own definition alive. It has to be, unless we want to rewrite basic biology."

Clayton breathed out. "Enough of that; we're getting off the track. The point is, an amoeba, a foetus, a human being—we're all alive in one shape or in some form. So what is the big deal about hanging a few hundred... maybe a thousand drug dealers when we eradicate half a million foetuses each year?" Clayton shrugged as if the matter was of no importance in his eyes.

"Are you thinking of trying to overturn *Roe v. Wade*?"

"Oh no, Jonathan. I won't touch any Supreme Court ruling. But spare me the double standards. Where is the real difference between an abortion and an execution but in the minds of the hypocrites?"

"A lot of people would argue that that's quite a stretch."

"Because that's what they want to believe, Jonathan. Let them prove me wrong. Look, I understand, we need abortions to clean up our mess... when women get pregnant. I accept that. I know I would be wasting my breath if I were to argue that we should be responsible for our actions... as if people would actually do so. But I just wish the hypocrisy would end, for our children if nothing else."

"Sir?" Jonathan blinked.

"Just thinking out loud, John."

"How can children have faith in us when we engage in hypocrisy?" Jonathan made an educated assumption.

"Yes." Clayton grinned at Jonathan. "Children aren't stupid. They understand the truth, that abortion is a declaration of failure. It declares that we are everything we say we are not. Declares that women are sluts, men are pigs." Clayton smiled at Jonathan. "My good sir, if we were truly such noble beings, there would be only a handful of necessary abortions carried out each year." Clayton's steady gaze locked onto Jonathan's eyes with calm certainty.

Jonathan took the leap. "So what we really need to do is to create a new category, a separate title for a foetus. Say, a proto-organic mass with insufficient foetal matter to sustain independent or separate cohesion once extricated from its established biosphere. That way the kids can trust us again."

"Now you're just skating on the edge of absurdity," Clayton stammered. "Aren't I?" Jonathan grinned

Clayton gave a burp of a chuckle. Then he smiled and nodded with a tight little laugh. Some of the tension that had been building up drained out of him.

They were silent for a few seconds that seemed to drag on for far longer. "It's the hypocrisy of it, Jonathan, damn it all. No wonder half the world wants to bomb America; we do nothing but engage in hypocrisy. Here we are engaged in the righteous castigation of everyone and anyone we think unworthy. But do we look at ourselves and see the hypocrisy of our words and deeds? That's what really galls me. As the president, it all falls on me to validate our smug self-righteousness to one and all." Clayton looked out the window.

It all falls on me… Jonathan silently considered Clayton's words and began to understand the president a bit more.

"Sir… may I point out that the world is equally full of hypocrisy. The Russians, the Chinese, the Muslim world… hell, the Europeans. Find me a politici…" Jonathan cut off the end of the word as it emerged for his lips. "Anyway, the world is full of it."

"And that exonerates us?" Clayton's tired eyes turned upon the young man.

"No, it can't. I'm just saying not to take on more than what's your due." They had not travelled five miles when the head of Prescott's security detail broke the silence.

"Sorry, Mr. President, but we need to make a small detour. We have protestors marching on the White House."

"Again?" Jonathan snapped in frustration, this is getting to be too much.

"At least it's peaceful," Agent Mercer offered.

"On a cold day like this, it would be." Prescott grunted softly, to remain silent for a few seconds. "Agent Mercer, could you have the kitchen staff start boiling water and set up a stand on the White House lawn? We'll serve up some coffee and sandwiches."

"*Sir?*" Agent Mercer gulped then closed his mouth.

"As long as it is peaceful, I have no problems with people protesting. We can all share coffee and sandwiches and have a sing-a-long."

History never did record Agent Mercer's reply. Peter Shepherd, however, director of the Secret Service's presidential detail, did need a little time to get his blood pressure under control before walking alongside the president to the front lawn. "Mr. President, again, I must ask you to reconsider meeting these people." He kept step with the shorter man.

"I understand your concerns, but really, they were hardly expecting to be allowed entrance onto the White House lawn or to see me in person, so I doubt they've brought their assault rifles, grenade launchers, and submachine guns." *Like good, responsible citizens; God save America.* Clayton sighed.

"Sir, the risk is unacceptable. The Secret Service is charged with your safety, and taking this kind of unnecessary risk places too great a stress on my agents."

Clayton Prescott slowed in his walk. "I do understand the risk involved." He turned to face Director Shepherd. "At the first opportunity arrange a meeting with all your senior people and yourself. We need to talk."

"Yes sir. But right now——"

"I'll stay behind the men with the body armour," Clayton promised. "Not that I can do much else; this thing you had me wear weights a tonne." Clayton then glanced at the director. "And at the first sign of trouble you can personally escort me back to the White House."

"Later then." Director Shepherd hoped there would be a later. Still, the president was right. This was so totally unexpected that no hostile party could have prepared for it.

He took up station beside the president with a grim face, ready to do grave injury to anyone who got too close. He kept one eye on the line of people and the other watching the president of the United States serving up hot cups of coffee to a procession of stunned protestors.

"Burk, the guy coming up, blue coat, white shirt," he whispered into his sleeve.

"Andrew Johnson, nominal leader of this collection of nut-jobs," replied the small, all-knowing voice in his ear. "He's a major pain for the corporations, a real anti-capitalist. But no serious criminal record per se, spends too much time being arrested at protest marches to do anything else." Burk had linked to the database holding the names and faces of all known radicals, extremists, zealots, fanatics, and idealists that were not red, white, and blue through and through, along with a longer list that were.

"Andy Johnson, correct?" The president smiled as he handed over a cup of coffee to the protestor.

Who hesitated in disbelief. Even now his prejudice against the system made it hard to believe the Man himself was actually out in the weather handing out coffee.

"Uh . . . yes, Mr. President." His mouth opened in a gasp.

"I thought I recognized you. So tell me, what are you protesting about today?" Clayton grinned at the man's stare.

Andy's mouth opened wider for a second as he collected his thoughts. *What are we protesting about? There have been so many lately.* "Uh… well, uh, isn't it obvious? We're raising our voices against the sheer number of unemployed people that are denied any future in this land of the free."

The man behind Andy spoke up. "Yeah, that's right. We want jobs." "I see, and you think that by coming here you will be able to obtain employment?"

"Senator Holt said all this stuff about guns and drugs is just a smokescreen to avoid doing something to get us jobs," the second man continued.

"Really, Andy, I am… surprised and disappointed. You really have dropped your standards. An upstanding radical like yourself falling for such mundane rhetoric. Really, I would have expected better." Clayton shook his head as if addressing a pupil who had performed below his best.

Clayton stepped back and raised his arms, calling to the crowd, "Ladies and gentlemen, people, a moment if you please. You have all come to the White House to ask the president for jobs. Well, you are right to do so. Tomorrow at noon I will be offering you a future with jobs. We… that is, *America* needs a radical new outlook. It is time for a new direction, a new approach. And I can promise you come tomorrow I will be offering you salvation."

The stunned look on everyone's face was a treasure that Clayton would secretly enjoy for many years to come.

City of Archangelsk, Russia

The news broadcast showed more rioting, police dragging away protestors. The air thick with tear gas and smoke, jets of water from the police water tankers, lines of black armoured police. A rather normal, everyday event, save for the blood on the pavement as several more protestors lay bleeding. The scream of sirens as ambulances and police vans took yet more of the critically injured or dead to nearby hospitals. No matter how low the temperature dropped, the fires would see to it that it would be a hot night in Paris as it was in Brussels.

The fresh-faced announcer spoke of how the unrest in American was continuing to spread to other parts of the world.

The man named Aloth felt no emotion for the suffering shown on the line of TV screens in the warm shop. He simply turned away and began walking towards his apartment, a two -room hole. But it was suitable for his needs. After removing his coat, he checked the old battered phone. It had three messages. He pressed the new message button.

"Aloth, ring me tomorrow—it's Anna. You know the number." He grinned a little.

"Hello, Aloth, Misha here. I just go in, hope to catch up with you at the regular place... say around nine? I have three bottles of vodka all ready, one with your name on it, and one for Sasha."

Aloth's smile froze. His finger hovered over the button. After eighteen months of driving trucks for the Russians, he had finally gotten "the call." He had little time, but had enough. He would need to rearrange his schedule. Fortunately he had worked numerous shifts for his fellow drivers, so getting whatever route he wanted and time needed for the mission would not be too difficult. Once he had the route from Misha, if . . . if . . .

He quickly packed a bag with the usual items for the following day, just in case he had to leave early.

He had to contact Sasha immediately. Fortunately, the man should be back by now. Both drove trucks crossing much of Russia. They had both started this journey together and might well end it together.

He thought of the small farm where they had first met and wondered if the time had come. He let out a small grunt. It had been a long road. Even before the farm, both had been veterans, unlike the other two virgin recruits who trained with them at the farm, yet their commanders had insisted they go; the training had be brutal and harsh. Designed as it was to select the best and most committed. It came as no surprise that they were both selected. The surprise came with their mission briefing; they had expected combat, not this.

To travel into the heart of Russia and stayed unnoticed. Find jobs in or near the city of Archangelsk where they could justify travelling over long distances. To ensure that when the call arrived, they could move without drawing unwanted attention from the authorities. Yet for all his speculation, the mystery remained. What could it be that required them to go to such lengths?

He left the apartment without looking back.

After a quick bus trip to another apartment block, he was knocking on Sasha's door. A minute later the clean-shaven face of Sasha confronted him. "What?"

"Misha called and asked if we would like to share some vodka. He has a bottle for each of us."

Sasha's eyes lit up; the meaning of Aloth's words had not escaped him— three bottles...

"That maniac, I haven't seen him in ages, and then up he pops from nowhere, just like him. Let's go." Sasha spoke for any hidden listening devices in his apartment. It was unlikely, but they had been drilled to perfection. The importance of the mission demanded nothing less.

They met up with Misha at a nearby nightclub. Over the noise, no one heard Misha as he gave Aloth part of the route he would need to take. Aloth then made a few calls to some of his fellow drivers. By the third call he had the route he wanted. Once satisfied, the three men spent the night, to all appearances, drinking heavily.

Only in a dark unseen corner did the three men huddle together to silently offer up a prayer to their God. With a final hug, they went their separate ways.

That night Sasha phoned the answering service to call in sick.

The next morning Aloth was in his truck, on the road and well ahead of schedule, for he needed to take a short detour through the dirty side streets to a tired-looking warehouse.

Waiting at the warehouse doors, Sasha quickly rolled them both open and just as quickly closed them once the truck was inside. Without a word they swiftly lifted two large wooden containers and several smaller cartons and boxes onto the back of the truck.

Some of the boxes contained items that, although illegal, were vital to the mission. The remaining boxes also contained illegal items but were simply camouflage.

As part of their cover they had engaged in some minor smuggling. Enough, they hoped, to convince the authorities, if they were caught with the illegal items in the truck, that they were part of an insignificant smuggling ring and not planning an attack. Indeed, their work for the smuggling ring had actually offered them a degree of protection, as the criminal organization paid off the local police to look the other way.

With Sasha in the back of the truck, they pulled out of the warehouse to begin their journey.

Observing the warehouse from the corner of a nearby building, Misha saw the truck leave. He then waited a few moments to satisfy himself that no one was following the truck. This was the critical moment. If the Russians were aware of them, then they would be following the heavy vehicle. But no one was driving down the dirty street.

Satisfied, Misha rushed down the side street and climbed into his old and equally battered car. Carefully he pushed the gears into place and followed at some distance behind the truck, watching and hoping not to see anyone else following the truck.

In the truck, Aloth drove at a slow, steady rate. Just slow enough to ensure any vehicle behind him would want to overtake the truck unless they had an interest in staying behind the heavy vehicle.

After the first half hour, and no mobile phone call from Misha, he began to relax enough to increase speed. They still had a schedule to meet, if not the one his employers wanted.

He stopped twice along the way. At both places two men swiftly climbed into the back of the truck, watched by Misha from afar.

They continued on for the day and towards the night, careful to adhere to all the road rules. They had to be careful, now that they had finally begun the mission of their lives. They had been promised true greatness if it was achieved. They would stab at the very heart of the beast.

Chapter 8

ISRAEL AND PALESTINE: A LOVE AFFAIR

Damn it, you never see him alone anymore, Ann Hornwood thought as she entered the room already filled with five senior members of the White House staff and a school of toadies. She was feeling less than warm-hearted and charitable today. Worse, he looked tired. What else could she expect, after the last three days?

"Ann, come, sit down. Now, what has got you so worried?" Clayton beamed a bright smile to the entire room.

"Sir, it's the Israelis. A few individuals I know have discreetly brought to my attention that the Israelis are concerned about our funding. No surprise, really, given as we are planning to cut back on some overseas aid. But that column in the *New Age* calling on us to cut Israelis' military aid by half has them worried." She looked embarrassed. "Anyway, the Israeli ambassador has been quietly talking to a number of senior members of the Jewish lobby. And it may have had some success, sir, the lobbyists have met privately with what's left of the Republican leadership."

"They're fully entitled to do so," Clayton admitted.

"Yes sir. Only with the current uproar over questionable campaign contributions from the last elections, it wouldn't look good for us… conservatives or liberals. Sir, we can't have anything that hints of a back-room deal, not when we are asking the public to make sacrifices. It wouldn't go over well."

"Oh, for the love of—" Brandon Keel was clearly frustrated. "How much more of this crap are we supposed to take? Why the hell can't we just tell the Israelis where to go?"

"A rather rhetorical question when you consider the millions of votes involved." Gene Austin grinned in sympathy. "And we need them, sometimes."

Like a bullet in the back of the head, Brandon thought. "And so we get the Israeli–Palestinian headache in return. Something we definitely don't need."

Austin nodded in agreement. "That's one headache we've haven't found an aspirin for."

Clayton addressed the room. "Even so, America must stop this endless refusal to act. We can't wait till hell freezes over before the two parties come to an agreement."

"Absolutely, Mr. President, we need an independent policy from the Israelis. Enough is enough, no more of this tail-wagging-the-dog stuff." Brandon saw his opportunity. "Why should the US take the heat simply because the Israelis won't give an inch? We are making too many enemies because of them."

"Let's not go overboard, Brandon," Gene grumbled aloud; the kid was such a bleeding heart. "The Palestinians are hardly innocent. And they had their chance. Chairman Arafat threw away their best chance at Camp David decades ago."

"That's open to debate, Gene; some say it was the Israelis. Anyway, as the president said, we can't wait fifty years before they agree to… more talks."

"What do you propose, Brandon?" President Prescott inquired.

"We start off with the obvious, sir," Brandon plunged in. "We have long advocated a 'two-state solution.' If Israel hands over all the West Bank and Gaza Strip, we have a good chance at a real peace."

Gene Austin observed drily, "The Israelis won't go for that."

"I'm glad to hear that Israel makes America's foreign policy decisions, sir," Brandon snapped back. "Look, if the Israelis won't give the Palestinians the West Bank, then they need to give compensation—say, two acres of Israeli land for every acre of the West Bank they keep, and it has to be good land with water. Plus, the Israelis pay double the going price for any buildings or orchards on any occupied land they will keep… or have already destroyed.

"Before you say anything, Gene, it has to be that way. Only by overcompensating can we take the high ground. We need to make the Arab world believe it's a good deal for the Palestinians, or else we are wasting our time. We need to throw in as many sweeteners as we can… even a land bridge between the Gaza strip and the West Bank."

"Wake up, Brandon. You could give 'em Jerusalem and two-thirds of Israel, and it still wouldn't be enough." Gene snapped at the man.

"Mr. Secretary, if we can get the Arab countries to see the benefits for the Palestinians, then we can get the Muslim world off our back. Can't you see that?"

"And can't you see that the Arabs don't give a damn about the Palestinians? Listen, time after time I've heard them go on and on about how 'the Palestinians are our brothers, you Westerners do not understand, the poor Palestinians are our brothers.' Well, you have a damn good look at how they treat their Palestinian 'brothers' in Lebanon. Do you know they deny the Palestinians some forty professions? Oh, they can carry bricks, but they can't practise medicine, can't practice law, can't—"

"Oh, come on, Gene, where is the surprise in that?" Ann spoke up. "Refugees always get the short end of the stick in the Middle East. When Syria came apart and the Syrian refugees flooded into Jordan, they weren't allowed to work. They had to beg or work illegally. Don't ask for compassion from an Arab. That's just the way it is."

Gene Austin turned to Ann. "'That's just the way it is'? That's your answer, Ann? You think that's all there is to it? Nothing more? Think about it. Say you're a fully qualified lawyer, but I tell you the government won't let you practise law. You say 'why?' and I say 'isn't it obvious? You're a woman.'

"Or you, Brandon—let's say you are an award-winning architect, but I come up to you and say you can't practice your profession. You say 'why?' and I say 'it's it obvious? You're black.' Now, do you think you'd want to stay in this wonderful country or pack your bags and go off to the Promised Land?

"Why else did they squeeze the Palestinians in those filthy refugee camps and let them rot? To made them want to go back... knowing the Israelis wouldn't let them. They shit and piss on the Palestinians while telling us how much they love their 'brothers.' Get real. The Palestinians are their excuse for hating the Jew boys. They are the justification they want to wipe the Jew boys from the face of the earth. We've tried waving the carrot in front of this mule's face for years, and it hasn't worked."

"So your suggestion is the stick? More Israeli attacks, more violence? More land theft? Where has that gotten us?" Brandon faced Gene with conviction. "It won't be easy, but a new approach with genuine understanding may get results. Isn't it worth a try?"

"And it will get you nowhere. We've been trying the carrot for decades without success. They'll take what we give and then renege on their promises, blaming it all on the extremists." Gene Austin was far from convinced.

"You don't know that for certain," Brandon insisted.

"Of course I know that for certain. How many times in the past have we been burned, damn it?" Gene glared at Brandon.

"There are Palestinians, Arabs who want real peace, if we are willing to compromise," Brandon insisted with the passion of the zealot.

"Will you stop dreaming for just long enough to have a hard, honest look at the Middle East?" Gene Austin fired back.

"Have you? Look at the monumental changes that have taken place in just the last two decades." Brandon's voice shook with fervour.

"Have you?" Gene responded with equal zeal. "Each year another disaster, more upheaval, and another piece of the Middle East becomes a war-zone or falls to fundamentalist Islam."

"Because America keeps burying its head in the sand, refusing to take a hard, honest look at the Mideast and come up with a valid policy—some strategy that will work. If we had helped, really helped to nurture their aspirations decades ago, it could've translated into possible opportunities we need to counter the Islamists." Brandon turned to the president, hoping his slight change of tack would give him the president's approval. "Mr. President, if we had shown good faith with the Palestinians, we could have been seen as neutral."

"Damn it," Gene Austin interjected, "I just told you the Arabs don't give a damn about the Palestinians. It's all hot air and pretence. The Palestinians are their excuse to vilify the Jews."

"And the Israelis are the innocent victims in all this? They don't knock down Palestinian homes and then steal their land? And if they protest, they aren't shot like mongrel dogs. That's all perfectly acceptable?" Brandon fired back with equal passion.

"Oh, yes. That's right, you subscribe to the belief that putting a bomb in a school bus is a legitimate means of protest." *What does it take to get through to this guy?* There was nothing they could say or do that would change anything. Hate was bred into their bone from the first day of school.

As a young man he had been part of a US delegation on a fact-finding mission to the Middle East. At a Palestinian school he had heard the teacher lecture his young class about the "occupiers," the "oppressors," and the legitimacy of their struggle against the "invader." As if no Jew had existed in Palestine prior to 1945. He'd found it sickening. Here was a teacher preaching hate to children instead of enlightenment. How could they come to any arrangement when so many were committed to blind hate?

Abb spoke from his seat. "Gentlemen, I think we can all agree that we need a consensus that—"

Austin all but bellowed, "There is no consensus that can be reached." "Not with stone-headed conservative fossils," Brandon softly hissed. "At least we don't surrender like a bunch of limp-wristed liberals eager to make any excuse for murderers and terrorists," Austin snapped at the younger man. "Your kind love to blame the Israelis for everything, when there's only one thing wrong with the state of Israel. There are simply too many Jew boys in Jew land; end of story. You can go ahead and kiss the Arabs' ass all day long, but it won't change a blessed thing. For the Muslims the problem is that there are just too many goddamned Jew boys in Jew land. That won't change no matter what you say. I'll—"

Then the enormity of his outburst struck home. "I'm sorry, Mr. President. I apologize for my inappropriate expression." Austin took a deep breath in frustration. "I'll have my resignation on your desk by tomorrow morning."

"You will do no such thing. You are right, as are you, Brandon. The sad truth is that you are both correct, unfortunately. Worse, you have provided me with the proof of just how intractable a problem we face." Clayton became silent for several seconds. "That said, we desperately need to present our own peace plan. I can live with the Palestinians having all the West Bank and Gaza Strip." Clayton sighed, looking at Brandon. "And, I suppose, if the Israelis won't go for that then it's a land exchange. And yes, Brandon, all homes, buildings, and orchards must be remunerated at double the current price. What else? Your sweetener—I suppose a land bridge connecting the West Bank with the Gaza Strip is acceptable."

"Sir, isn't that a bit much?" Gene Austin was worried.

"Hardly; the Israelis can have as many tunnels under or bridges over the corridor as they want."

"Jerusalem, sir?" Brandon added.

"As for Jerusalem, if the Israelis won't give the old half to the Palestinians, then they'll give total control of all Muslim holy sites to the Palestinians. If a site is holy to both, then both must have equal control." "And the Palestinian refugees, sir, currently dwelling in Lebanon and

Jordan?" Brandon persisted, in wild hope.

"Palestinians born in Israel would naturally have a right of return." "Can't we just let them all go back?"

"Brandon, if you're born in Canada, you're a Canadian; if you're born in America, you're an American, no matter where your parents were born. You're born in Lebanon, you're Lebanese even if the no-good government will deny you your legitimate right of citizenship.

"Equally, no one can illegally, or even legally, cross a border and then declare himself to be a citizen of the country without the approval of the government. All nations have the right to protect their borders. Even we, supposedly, have the right." *Not that you could tell lately.*

"I know it's harsh. But perhaps we could convince Lebanon and other nations to ease up on those of Palestinian ancestry to the point where most would be happy to remain in the country of their birth rather than go to an uncertain future." Clayton looked from Brandon to Gene. "If we can lift the pressure, who knows? Perhaps the numbers will be so small that the Israelis will grant their request."

Gene Austin shook his head. "Sir, that is all well and good, noble even. But it won't change a thing on the ground. The issue of Israeli security needs to be addressed. They won't give an inch unless they get security; otherwise you're pissing into the wind."

"Here's an idea, maybe if the Israelis stopped targeting Palestinians?" Brandon stood firm in his belief.

"It's called self-defence," Austin commented; "we've killed enough terrorists with our drones. This will never work unless the Palestinians want peace."

"How would we know unless we try?" Brandon insisted. "If we can talk to the moderate leaders… on both sides… we may achieve some good results."

"That has been tried before." Austin fumed, *Damn it, we're just going around in circles.*

Clayton looked from one man to the other. "Agreed, we have offered them the carrot many times in the past. So let's use the carrot-and-stick approach this time."

"And what will the stick be, sir?" Austin studied the president. "Now that is the question. Any ideas?" Clayton looked around the room.

Most returned his questioning eyes with blank, stony looks.

"Gene, Brandon, I want you both to work on this. Within a week, people, America will present its own blueprint for peace between the Israelis and the Palestinians. And one that will squarely lay the blame on the ones who reject it."

"Sir, I have my doubts." Gene Austin was not about to rubber-stamp anything.

"Gene, I know the Muslim world may never truly accept the existence of the Jewish state. But this is about us being seen as fair and just, actually practising what we keep preaching to the world. We will present a fair and very just peace offering.

"People, I don't expect the Palestinians or the Israelis to jump for joy. But what matters is that the US will accept what is fair and just. That the people in the streets in Jordan, Lebanon, and even Iran see the US, if not as a friend, then not as the enemy. We want a fair and just peace between both groups and will be willing to do the right thing. Well, I need to get moving. Thank you all."

The crowded room began to empty out.

Watching the staff leave, Abb Cole turned to President Prescott and quietly whispered, "I know this is a stressful time. But you seem to be rather forgiving of Gene."

"Didn't you hear the reality beneath his words?" Clayton responded just as quietly. "We're talking about four and a half million Israelis surrounded by a hundred million Arabs, with their imams preaching jihad. Wouldn't you be scared?"

"That's why you picked Gene?" Abb inquired in a mild tone. Clayton nodded. "He won't sell out the Israelis." "Any more than Brandon would the Palestinians."

Clayton turned to look at Abb with probing eyes. "I always took you for a greater supporter of Israel."

"When Israel was the victim of naked aggression by the Arabs, I was. Now that they're as intolerant as the Muslims in my book, they've lost a lot of their legitimacy.

"And you, which side do you favour?" Abb asked the president.

"I'm a politician. I hold no position or view that has not been pre-approved by the polls."

Abb grunted as he turned away with a small grin on his face. Brandon had hung back as the others left; now his hand rested on the doorknob. He turned to face the two men. "Sir, do you have a moment?" "Go ahead, Brandon." Clayton grinned at the man's slight discomfort. "Sir, I have been thinking about your gun initiative, and it's a good start."

"Why, thank you, Brandon. And?" Clayton said with surprisingly little sarcasm.

"Sir, with all due respect, it isn't enough. The real problem is the gun manufacturers. As long as they can keep on making more guns than we need, the carnage will never end. We don't need more guns. And with this virus threat hanging over the manufacturing plants—it's a perfect opportunity."

"I am well aware of that." Clayton sighed. "In a better world, I suppose, we could've limited gun manufacturing to law enforcement, the military… and maybe for export for ten year or so." *With that and locking up our guns, who knows, we might have actually achieved something worthwhile… even if it took decades.*

"Sir, you can't deny the public their legitimate right to bear arms," Abb stammered, nearly catatonic with shock.

"Oh, come on, Abb. This country is drowning in guns. The illegal guns confiscated by the police could easily be refitted and sold to legitimate gun dealers. That alone would keep us in guns for decades—and could cut the cost of guns by half." Clayton waved Abb's concerns away.

Abb disagreed. "I think the price would skyrocket, sir."

"The price would go up only if there was an insane demand, mostly from gun nuts. Be honest, just how many guns does a person need? Hell, if we were to impose a limit of five guns per person, we could close down the bloody industry for the rest of this century." Clayton paused to think.

"Sir… such a scenario would in all likelihood create long delays." Abb was not certain that it would, but it was possible. "Last week, we had an incident where a husband and his wife were attacked by the woman's ex-husband with a knife in a mall in Texas. The husband later complained that if he had not been waiting for a gun licence, he could have defended himself."

"And if the ex-husband had gone into that mall with an assault rifle? How many innocent bystanders could he have killed? Worse, far worse, imagine if everyone in the mall had a gun. Can you imagine the number of people killed in the cross fire if everyone pulled out a gun?

"Damn it, Abb, a man with a knife can kill one or two people; a man with a gun can kill one or two dozen. It's clear that guns are the damned problem. Hasn't Europe's tiny death toll proven that? Hasn't the Australian government's gun buy-back scheme proven that?" Clayton knew that the number of Australians killed by guns plummeted after the Australian government had initiated a national buy-back scheme. "No matter how many lies the Republicans screech at the top of their lungs, they can't hide the truth. The fewer guns we have, the fewer dead we have in our morgues; that is a fact."

"But with proper education and gun regulations we can reduce—" "Gun restrictions haven't worked, Abb. Gun regulations are simply not tough enough, especially with the gun lobby working day and night to water them down. You know that. The terrorist shooting of those fourteen people in San Bernardino, California, in 2015 proved it.

"California has some of the toughest regulations, but it still wasn't enough… Gun regulations are a joke, Abb." *When you can legally buy assault-style weapons, how the hell can you call that tough gun control?* "There is only one real answer." Clayton clenched his jaw. "But sadly, we live in a country filled with sad, timid little people who have very little respect for human life."

Abb countered, "That is unfair. Sir, many people honestly believe they need guns to defend themselves."

"You're a bit of a shooter, I'm told?" Clayton grinned at Abb.

"That is beside the point, Mr. President. There are millions of law-abiding citizens—"

"Screw them, Abb. I am so sick of those selfish bastards whining about their rights. You tell me, damn it, you tell me honestly, in your heart of hearts. Tell me that the changes I have proposed would deny one law-abiding citizen his gun? Yet there they are, screaming that I will take away their guns, a 'damned Commie' for trying to save the lives of a thousand children each year. And I'm a commie. They murder our children and I'm the criminal?

"It's time and well past for you to decide which side you are on, Abb. So you tell me, here and now, what's more important to you, your precious guns or the life of your daughter? Just how much blood do you want on your hands?

"The Republicans can wallow in their filth and lies. But this isn't about the Constitution, it isn't about people's rights, and it isn't even about guns. It's about the gun *makers* and their all-important profits. It's well past time you realized that."

Brandon began, "Then sir, why don't we just—"

"Because," Clayton snapped, burning with frustration, "the gun merchants have millions of mindless drones and that they can feed a steady diet of paranoia and fear. And that means they are more powerful than the president of the United States, Brandon, and don't you ever forget it." *If only people would open their eyes.*

"This is about a billion-dollar industry that cannot allow even the tiniest changes. After all, if guns were properly controlled, they wouldn't get into the hands of criminals, children, or those with mental health issues… And if that were to happen we might reduce the slaughter.

And that, sir, is a real big problem for them. A really big problem as people might start to think that having more regulations isn't such a bad idea—regulations like limiting the numbers of guns a person can have and the types of weapons. If that happened, then the number of deaths would go down, and we can't have that. Why do you ask? Because, my friends, we might impose more regulations that could cut into profits." Clayton half grumbled to himself. "And we can't have that, now can we? This is America, where profits matter, but lives don't… at least not to Congress and the death merchants." Clayton took a slow breath and released it. "Well, enough of that; we can't dwell on guns all day. We have other matters to attend to."

"Yes sir." Brandon took his leave. But as his hand gripped the doorknob, he had a thought. *Then why are you bothering if you believe we can't achieve anything?* That was how it sounded to him. Brandon was perplexed. Clayton wasn't the type to waste time and energy on a hopeless course.

The grim but new roads of new Russia

Aloth glanced into his rear-view mirror as the small car carrying Misha overtook his truck. Aloth grunted with approval; all was going to plan. By Misha taking the lead it signalled that the man felt confident no one was following the truck. Now Aloth would stay just far enough back to see if anyone was following Misha.

If not, then Misha would lead him to the staging point, wherever that was, to begin their mission in earnest.

Finally they could strike back. It had been a long and frustrating wait. But he had been told that from the beginning. He had to stay silent, let everyone think he was a tired man who wanted nothing to do with war and Jihad. Content to adopt a Russian name to avoid prejudice from the locals and keep his head down—and make a little profit from a few less-than-legitimate deals.

After a good two hours, with no signs of pursuit they turned onto a small, winding road leading into the backwoods and finally a small farmhouse with a large, battered shed.

Aloth squeezed the truck in behind the shed. As he climbed out of the cab, he saw Misha walk towards a man he had not seen before.

The two men eyed each other. "I am Misha."

"Yuri." The man nodded slightly. "You have something for me?" Misha took a bottle from a small bag slung over his shoulder. A single bottle of vodka, half emptied. "We have another two boxes of the filth in the truck." He snarled; he hated transporting the alcohol back to his homeland, just as much as he enjoyed pouring it down the drain when he arrived home.

"You are not how I pictured you," the man told Misha.

"Just dyed my hair a little and put on a pair of contact lenses, my friend. And no beard, I am sad to say."

Yuri grinned. The disguise was perfect. It was so obviously a pretence that it worked beautifully. The FSB and other Russian intelligence agencies would simply see a spoilt young Saudi indulging in obviously questionable behaviour. Yes, Yuri could see it, a fool pretending to be a gangster by transporting Russian alcohol into the Muslim homeland. They would laugh at the spoilt child with too much money trying to be a gangster with a few local thugs.

They walked over to where Aloth waited.

"Aloth, this is Yuri." Misha introduced the man.

"Welcome to paradise." Yuri offered his hand, and Aloth shook, noting that the man had calluses and a strong handshake.

"Rest and eat; tomorrow we begin," Misha told Aloth.

"The boxes?" Aloth asked Misha.

"Yes, we need to air out the uniforms and clean the weapons first." Misha nodded to cover his mistake.

Together they carried three of the smaller boxes into the farmhouse. They opened them and dragged out the uniforms and weapons. After hanging up the uniforms and cleaning the weapons, they sat down and ate. Once finished, the eight men sat around the small kitchen table, waiting while Misha pulled out a map of a Russian military installation.

Aloth studied the Russian base in detail, observing how the base was arranged around a series of large flat parade grounds with lines of barracks facing the small open squares. A large headquarters building sat in one corner facing a large parade ground, with the officers' quarters nearby. Large areas were fenced off, some holding rows of military vehicles. Numerous separate buildings dotted the camp.

One good-sized road led into the camp. Three smaller roads led out of the camp, undoubtedly heading towards firing ranges and training areas in the surrounding country-side.

"This is a map of a Russian training base less than ninety miles from here," Misha began, noticing the look Aloth gave him. *Yes, I know you know it looks like an army base. Be patient, will you?* "In a storage vault they have up to ten small nuclear devices."

"We are going after an atomic bomb?" Sasha marvelled in disbelief. "To do so, we will need to take control of the guardhouse." Misha pointed to a square building next to the main road leading into the camp. "Once we have secured it, we leave three men to guard the gate. From there we need to secure their headquarters. At night they normally have no more than three men on duty: one duty officer, a sergeant, and a driver. Once their headquarters is ours, we can go for their vault." Misha indicated a small area near one corner of the base, easily overlooked if he had not drawn the men's attention to the thick bunker-like building and the high wire fence surrounding it.

Aloth studied the map. "Should we waste time on taking over their headquarters and risk possible discovery?" The headquarters building and the storage bunker were some distance apart.

"The storage vault doors are hard-wired to the camp headquarters, with another line straight to Moscow. Opening the doors activates the alarm. That is why we need to take control of their headquarters, both to prevent the alarm from being raised throughout the camp and to ease Moscow's concerns when they inquire. If we cannot neutralize the alarm, we will be facing their rapid reaction force of thirty men."

"Can we cut the line to Moscow from the headquarters building?" Aloth had a sinking feeling that it would not be that easy.

"No. It is a direct line buried underground; it cannot be cut. We need their communications room to assure Moscow that a team has been sent to investigate and report back that it was a false alarm."

"And should they not believe us? How much time will we have before Moscow contacts the camp commander? Or would they simply contact this 'rapid reaction force'?" There were too many unknowns. What kind of backup systems did they have? What were their protocols, procedures? "Would they order an immediate lockdown of the base?"

"That is unlikely to happen."

"If it does?"

Misha's response was silence.

That much, Aloth thought. "They will have roving patrols checking the perimeter if nothing else."

"Yes, but if we arrive exactly as planned, we should have enough time to get in and out before the first patrol circles the base and returns to the guardhouse."

"How do we approach the guardhouse without arousing suspicion?" They would be fools to use his truck or civilian cars. Aloth wanted more detail, much more.

"I have two ex-military sedans in the shed that I have resprayed and made presentable," Yuri informed the others. "They should pass inspection at night."

"How do we take the guardhouse?" That detail concerned Aloth considerably. If so much as one guard raise the alarm they were finished before they had started. There would be anywhere from seven to a dozen guards just in the guardhouse. Then there were these roving patrols; the Russians were not famous for their timekeeping.

"We will have help."

Ah, the cryptic response that will ease all our fears. Aloth's mood grew steadily blacker.

Back in the White House

The tall, iron-haired colonel stood at attention before the president. Although he did not show it, he felt a little uncomfortable. The fact that he was wearing civilian clothes instead of his uniform did not sit well on the wiry man. Nor did it help that he had been brought into the White House through the back door, as if he was a thief being hired for a heist.

"Please, do sit down, Colonel."

"Thank you, sir."

Clayton scanned the file marked *Lieutenant Colonel Karl Alexander Talbot.* It was an impressive file on an officer who had performed a considerable number of highly classified missions. He had been top of his class and qualified in numerous training programs in the Special Forces community. "Now, has General MacAdams fully briefed you on the current situation concerning Texas and New Mexico?" he asked, still reading.

"Yes sir."

"Then we can dispense with the preliminaries, Colonel Talbot." He looked up. "I want you and your Special Forces teams deployed to Texas and New Mexico, ready to deal with any serious outbreak of violence that may culminate in injuries or deaths. I am talking about a serious outbreak that the locals can't deal with."

"You believe there is more going on than what I've been briefed on, sir." It wasn't a question.

"Maybe this is exactly what they say it is—a bunch of bonehead politicians and fools thinking they can legally secede from the Union."

"'Legally,' sir?" The colonel showed his opinion on their position by the frigid tone.

"The States joined the Union, so technically that implies they can leave. I'm not a lawyer. We'll let the courts decide. But I do not accept that a handful of politicians and privileged individuals actually believe they can get Texas, New Medico, Arizona, and maybe California to leave the Union without some kind of serious muscle."

"With respect, I have served with military units in Texas and have never seen any sign of disloyalty, Mr. President." Colonel Talbot felt he had to vouch for the men of Texas.

"There has to be more, Colonel. Maybe they thought the Mexican Army would actually cross over into the US to support them. But that is too far-fetched for me. There must be something we've overlooked. That is why you and your troops are to be quietly deployed to those states. You will wear standard equipment and avoid any attention. I want you there as backup if something unexpected pops its head. It might be the state Guard units or some crackpot lunatics; I simply don't know.

"But we have to consider the possibility that there is more going on than we know. And it may be necessary to take immediate action without waiting for clearance from up the line.

"That is why I asked you here, to make it clear that you will personally be in charge, with my full authority to act. Your country needs your services more than ever before. Your job is to monitor the situation down there. If the local authorities, the FBI, or the Army units we're sending come up against something too big for them to handle, then you're to deal with it before it get out of hand, quietly if possible. The quieter the better: I would prefer not to have the regular Army units involved in case they are used to compound our problems."

"No pictures of American soldiers firing on American citizens, sir." "Damn right. Deal with any unforeseen violence, planned or unplanned, swiftly and effectively before it comes back to haunt us. If there is no upheaval, if there is no threat to this nation, then enjoy the sunshine, get a tan, and then go home to your family."

"Understood, sir."
Where do criminals get their guns from?
From the public.
So why has the public given them guns?

Harold Blunt

Chapter 9

"You can not buy loyalty. Something you Americans never seem to learn."

A friend

The rustic farmhouse in rural Russia

Misha grunted in good humour as he dragged the grey uniform shirt over his shoulder.

"What do you find so amusing, my friend?" Yuri's words held as much warmth as his stone-cold face conveyed.

"Oh, just thinking of a famous British secret agent and how he would have invaded the camp all by himself. Only the infidels could believe such nonsense." He laughed as he adjusted the Russian army tie and the poorly fitting army jacket.

The man called Yuri—this was indeed his real name, but in his heart of hearts his true name was Mohammed—looked at Misha with a hint of confusion.

"Something I said to someone not long ago."

Once they had dressed, they gathered in the spare room of the farmhouse, and Misha addressed the other men. "My friends, Allah willing, we will deliver a blow to the great enemy from which it will never be able to overcome. Praise Allah, this will herald a new world that will free our oppressed brothers throughout the Islamic world and bring the glory of Islam to all of Allah's children.

"Finally, we will be able to bring the peace and freedom that our brothers have been so long denied," Misha declared with absolute conviction. "The enemies of Islam will no longer interfere in our affairs. They will not conspire

148

to take our holy sites, steal our brother's land, destroy his home, and say it is just and right. Tomorrow, brothers, it all changes. Islam will take its rightful place as the true guiding light of the world. Pray with me for the destruction and death of our enemy."

Afterwards the eight men inspected each other's appearance, giving microscopic attention to every detail; no mistakes could be allowed. Once satisfied, they walked into the shed and dragged away the sheets covering the two military vehicles, Aloth started the engine, turned on the lights of the first car, and drove it out of the shed.

In minutes they were on their way into the night, the two sedans leading with Aloth's dilapidated truck following just behind. The country road was roughly sealed and as unwelcoming as the night skies. The thin tree branches stuck out like skeletal fingers eager to scratch and claw. The cold was biting with true hate. Such an inviting country; Misha shivered.

The mini-convoy rumbled along until they reached an equally uninviting turnoff leading towards the military facility.

"Damn the Russians and their bloody roads," Misha hissed as a pothole rammed his spine into his skull. "Truly a tourist paradise. Russians must love being miserable." By now he was in the blackest of moods, more than willing to stereotype all Russians as sadists.

"This is the true 'mother Russia,' not Moscow," Aloth replied, quoting from his inherited wisdom.

After another fifteen minutes of slow travel they were a short distance from the camp's outer perimeter.

"This will do." Aloth pulled the car off the road. He jumped out and switched on his torchlight, before waving to the man driving the truck to park the heavy vehicle as far as he could within the trees. It was the best he could find; hopefully it would remain unnoticed.

Aloth had argued that they should leave one man to guard the truck but had been overruled by Misha, who assured him the truck would be safe enough; the road was deserted at this time of night. And if some drunken fool did find it sitting beside the road, what then? By the time any Russian returned with help to empty the truck, they would be back. Aloth had grumbled silently to himself but finally accepted there was little chance of discovery, and they would need all the manpower they could muster.

The driver jumped into the second car. Before the door had closed, they were driving down the rough road until they reached the squat guardhouse with its waiting security detachment.

Aloth brought the car to a stop and stepped out to open the rear door for Yuri. Then he gave Yuri, in his lieutenant colonel's uniform, a smart salute. Yuri with his harsh Caucasian features looked like the perfect Russian officer.

Yuri sternly glanced around, trying his best to appear assertive, commanding, and arrogant as he imagined all senior officers in the military to be.

The two young Russian guards manning the gate jumped to attention. Aloth turned to the young guards, both of whom looked almost too young to shave.

"Lieutenant Colonel Vorishnov will be conducting a surprise readiness inspection. Where is your duty officer?" Aloth barked loudly.

"In the guardhouse, sir." One spoke up in a youthful, if timid, voice. "Notify him to report here immediately," Aloth barked louder. "No delays."

"Yes sir." The guard turned to head towards the guardhouse and thus never saw Aloth or Yuri each pull out a silenced pistol and fire.

Two bullets in the chest from Aloth's silenced pistol struck the boy facing them, a third into the head ended it. Two from Yuri struck the other boy from behind. He took a step closer to the prostrate boy and fired another directly into the back of his skull.

Even as the guards collapsed, they heard the soft reports of silenced gunfire from within the guardhouse.

Both men rushed to the door of the guardhouse, hoping desperately that the guards had not been alerted.

They entered the small office that led into the guardhouse itself and found a tall figure in the uniform of a Russian lieutenant standing within the doorframe.

The Russian lieutenant spoke in a soft voice: "Did you bring the vodka?'"

"Don't fire, it's him. —No, just 'four bottles of red wine.'" Misha had raced up behind the two killers to prevent any deadly mistakes. "Where are the rest of the guards?"

"Dealt with; they are in the other room." Lieutenant Sergei Neboatov of the Russian Army turned aside to allow the others to enter the guardhouse.

"Quickly get the bodies into the storage room." Yuri had no time for pleasantries or traitors. He did not believe he was betraying the country of his birth. After all, he knew he was obeying a higher calling when he had converted to Islam.

Turning around he headed back to the car. With Aloth grabbing hold of the feet of a dead guard, Yuri dragged the soldier through the door into the guardhouse, then down the two rows of steel frame bunk beds that lined the large room towards the small storage room at the rear. Yuri barely took notice of the bodies still lying on their beds, every member of the guard detail had been shot in the head.

Once the bodies were jammed into the tiny storage room, they emerged from the guardhouse. Leaving three of their number to replace the guards, Aloth and the others crawled back into their cars. A few moments later the cars were slowly driving down the main road within the camp before turning down a series of narrow roads. The headlights of the small convoy passed over wooden barracks and unimpressive, depressingly low buildings.

Checking his watch yet again, Misha was caught by surprise when the car stopped in front of the camp headquarters.

Lieutenant Sergei Neboatov stepped out of the car and kept the door open for Yuri, still in his role of Lieutenant Colonel Vorishnov.

Once inside, they found the duty sergeant and driver seated behind a long desk. Both jumped to attention.

"Sergeant, in a moment you are to contact Colonel Kurpov. And—" Lieutenant Neboatov never finished as Yuri walked to the left side of both men, swiftly drew his silenced pistol, and shot both in the head. Blood and grey brain matter splattered the nearby wall. No sooner had the two Russians collapsed onto the floor than they were dragged into a small side room, leaving a trail of blood along the floor.

Lieutenant Neboatov ignored the mess and crossed to a large block-shaped safe. As the duty officer, he held the keys to access the safe. From within he extracted the spare set of keys to the base commander's office. He stood up and walked down the corridor to the commander's office, with Misha close behind. The Russian used the spare set of keys to gain entrance and then proceeded towards a small wall safe.

Inside was everything they needed to acquire the nuclear devices they so hungered for.

"We are fortunate the buffoon is such a forgetful drunk. Half the time he does not even remember his own name." Sergei sneered in contempt. "Or care to follow the required security procedures. The drunken bastard just leaves everything lying around."

Standing behind Neboatov, Misha felt a twinge of guilt as he watched the old lieutenant work the combination of the safe. He had not wanted to tell falsehoods to the old imam back in Afghanistan, even if it had been a small one.

They had indeed received very valuable intelligence from the Pakistanis but only of a limited nature.

Mostly they had provided the door to a Russian Lieutenant, twice overlooked for promotion, with a bad conduct report from a belligerent commanding officer against his record—and a few whispered suspicions that he was less than reliable when it came to the state.

Thus, ironically, they had fanned the twin fires of anger and hate that had consumed the man, to where there was nothing left but a desire for revenge against the state.

Still, it had been wise not to bring up the lieutenant's involvement to the old imam. The less anyone knew of the truth, the better it was for the mission. And if all went well, the Russian might continue to be useful in the future.

Misha grinned to himself. And there was an extra, delicious benefit to be had. If the details of the mission did come out, then having the Pakistanis take the major share of the blame would not be such a bad thing. As the Chechen had said, they were lying dogs without honour or loyalty and thus worthy only of contempt.

On opening the safe they swiftly collected the keys and various codes needed.

Leaving Yuri and another to secure the building, they hurried to their cars. Soon Aloth and Misha were driving down the small road till they reached the storage area. They stopped in front of the twin gate, to allow Lieutenant Sergei Neboatov to approach and call out to the two guards within the small fenced-off compound.

"Open up, surprise inspection."

Both guards recognised the Lieutenant and thus had little reason to suspect anything was wrong. Especially as surprise inspections had become the norm of late. Fear and uncertainty were everywhere these days. In this new new-Russia suspicion of everything and everyone choked every aspect of life.

Thus they ignored security procedures to swiftly open the gates and stood at attention.

Both watched the two cars drive up to the double doors of the large concrete bunker and thus never saw the lieutenant turn without breaking stride and fire his silenced pistol.

From there it was a simple matter to open the massive, reinforced double doors with the correct keys and then the vaults with the correct codes.

"Hurry, we must arm at least two devices," Misha told Neboatov in a hushed whisper.

"It will take too much time," Neboatov declared as he turned to face Misha.

"We need at least two armed and ready, to ensure the success of the mission," Misha insisted.

"We will be wasting time that we do not have if we are discovered." Neboatov was equally insistent.

"If we are discovered, will it matter? We cannot outrun the Russians," Aloth growled from the back. He was annoyed that they had been unable to brief the Russian beforehand as to their intentions.

"Stop arguing and just do it; we are wasting time talking. Moscow will follow procedure, so that should give us enough time." Misha hoped he was right. With luck Moscow would not become concerned as long as they had Yuri at the base headquarters to ease Moscow's concerns. They had the time, and it was necessary, Misha told himself yet again, more in hope than in conviction with each second that passed.

"Arm the first two; Aloth and Sasha will move the other two into the car," Misha told Neboatov. The mission required four nuclear weapons, but only two needed to be armed immediately. The other two, the weapons that would change the world, could wait.

Misha indicated for Sasha to help Aloth move the suitcase-size nuclear devices to their car. The two men swiftly transferred one from the bunker into the boot of the lead car. Both men then returned to the bunker to carry another device into the backseat of the lead car.

By the time they had entered the bunker for the third time, the first device was well under way to being armed, with Misha watching and learning the procedure from Neboatov.

Finally, the device was armed, and Neboatov had begun to work on the second when the silence of the camp was shattered.

Sirens went off, screaming their alert throughout the camp.

Lights slowly blinked into life throughout the camp.

Within the bunker Aloth turned and looked at Misha with a look of total defeat.

The White House

"So Brandon, Gene—what have you got for me?" Clayton addressed the two men as they entered the Oval Office.

"Sir, we have the preliminary ready. We've put in all the points we went over the other day." Brandon Keel handed Clayton a thin folder that outlined in detail all the points they had gone over two days ago. "Land swaps, compensation, and a land corridor from the West Bank to the Gaza strip. Palestinians born in Israel having the right of return, even their offspring being allowed to visit… with government approval. That's all fine. We have the carrot, but the stick remains the problem."

Gene Austin shook his head. "All we've got is the threat of cutting aid, we haven't got much else to use as leverage. UN sanctions won't work to any real degree. We think they're more likely to harden Israeli attitudes. What we need is something that will really make them stand up and take notice. We know you want this done within the week—but for the life of me we can't see anything that will really work."

"Okay, so what is it that each side wants more than anything?" Clayton asked both men.

"For the majority of Israelis, I'd say security, sir," Austin offered. Keel shrugged. "Palestinians, a homeland, but we knew that from day one."

"Security and land?" Clayton whispered, and both nodded in consent. "Apart from the hard-liners, who want all the land they can get, most

Israelis want security." Gene Austin hammered his point home.

Keel cleared his throat. "The same here—land and I suppose some security would be it for the Palestinians."

"So, it's pretty much about land and secure borders," Clayton whispered to himself. "That is brilliant." Clayton grinned at both men.

"Sir?" Austin looked at Clayton in confusion.

"You're both geniuses. We offer the Palestinians the land they want, and we offer the Israelis security by threatening to take it away." Clayton grinned at both men. "We offer them the carrot and the stick, and it will be the land."

The other two glanced at each other, each wondering if the other man knew what Clayton was taking about.

"Any act of aggression will result in the loss of the one thing they both value, land. If the Palestinians fire rockets into Israeli, they will be required to hand over five square acres of Palestine to Israel. If an Israeli assassinates a Hamas leader, then they will hand over five square acres of Israel to the Palestinians."

"Sir, Hamas won't agree," Austin replied. "They want to destroy Israel, not live in peace."

"And you think the hard-line Israelis would agree?" Keel shot back. "We go over their heads by presenting it to the world—presenting it to the UN. We can have it backed up by a binding UN commitment from member nations. The US and Europe will guarantee Israeli compliance, while Russia, China, and the Arab world will enforce compliance by the Palestinians." Clayton seemed pleased with the idea.

"And the Russians and Arabs will actually enforce compliance?" Austin asked. "I wouldn't put any money on that."

"That's a fair question," Keel added.

"'You wouldn't put money on it,' you said." Clayton glared at Austin with the look of victory.

"Yes sir." Austin glanced at Keel, who looked just as confused. "What if failure to enforce compliance will require the responsible governments to pay a million dollars a day to the victim?"

Austin smiled. "So if the Palestinians open fire on Israel, and they don't choke up the land, then China, Russia and the Arab world will each choke up a million a day to the Israelis?"

"It'll never work, sir," Keel said, shaking his head. "The governments won't go for it."

"You're undoubtedly correct. But that'll be up to them. I want to present a fair, just deal to the world and then sell it to the people on the streets. We have had a massive public relations problem with many in the Arab world for decades. Too many think we're blindly loyal to Israel. We need to be seen as fair and impartial."

They think we're blindly loyal? Brandon almost sneered. *After decades of blindly catering to the Israelis, they just* think *we are blindly loyal?*

"And finally, after a few years of peace and stability, who knows, maybe both could engage in some mutually beneficial programs. Who knows, in time we could promote the idea that they should combine both states into an economic free trade union. That'll help both sides with their economy. A few years later they could hold referendums on joint projects—water development, that sort of thing. Joined economically, they could go further, a shared passport, even a shared currency if they wanted." Clayton kept thinking off the top of his head.

"Gentlemen, we need to present a real opportunity for peace. If the world does not accept it, so be it. But it's time that America is seen standing up and calling for a fair, just, and lasting peace between all nations, creeds, and faiths. We—the world can't keep going the way we are going. We have to try for a genuine peace. It can't hurt." *At least this time the blame will go to those that deserve it, and it won't be America this time.* Clayton felt like smiling in satisfaction for the first time in days.

Chapter 10

You don't want me to take government handouts? Then pay me a real wage.

—Sign on the toilet wall

Russian Military Base

Aloth turned and looked at Misha and then ran towards the bunker doors.

"No, no." Aloth saw tiny lights appearing from windows. Then more lights showed signs of unwelcome activity throughout the camp.

Several freezing and frigid seconds later came the first tentative shots, distant rifle fire sounding deep within the darkness. A minute later they heard the rattle of light machine gun fire. The flashes of tracer fire were followed by an explosion that was repeated by an even louder detonation than the first. All of which was coming from the west, towards the rear of the camp, well away from the main gate, the camp headquarters, and the nuclear storage bunkers.

"What is going on?" Aloth looked at Misha in total confusion. Who were the Russians shooting at? Were there two Russian patrols engaging in a firefight? Or was it something else?

"We have to get moving. Keep watch; you see anyone approach, call out."

"But… we can't get out. The main gate—"

"Will still be open, Aloth." *I hope.* Misha wanted to believe it was true. He knew they had no other option.

He went over to the device that Neboatov had armed and with Sasha he carried it to the second car. He then raced back into the bunker. "Set the last one to detonate in… fifteen minutes."

"What? That is not enough time to get away," Neboatov protested. "We cannot let the Russians see how many devices are missing and report the number to Moscow." The heart of the plan was to cover up the number of devices liberated by engulfing the base in a nuclear fireball. "Anyway, these are not some multi-megaton bombs."

"But if we are delayed—stopped for even a few minutes—we could be caught in the blast radius," Sergei persisted. If they were caught in the blast, then the mission would fail.

Sasha stepped forward. "I will stay behind; just lock the doors. I will wait until the Russians have broken in and then detonate the device at the last moment."

"No, we need you to fly out one of the devices," Misha said in a rush. "Fly? Ah, yes." Sasha suddenly understood. "Well, Yuri can fly a plane as well as I; he was bragging about it for most of last night." He grinned.

"And he is not here, but I am. You need as much time as I can give you." Misha looked at the man, and finally he nodded. It was for the best, he thought. He needed Aloth to drive the truck since all the papers were in his name, while he needed only one pilot to fly the plane if the plane's actual crew turned out to be a problem. It was irrelevant whether the pilot was Sasha or Yuri. In truth Sasha had been a fortunate backup in case Yuri was unexpectedly incapacitated.

They hung back, allowing Lieutenant Sergei Neboatov to finish arming the second device and show Sasha how to detonate it.

Even in the cold of night they sweated as they waited, desperate to be on their way. Time dragged as never before. The firing grew and then faded— and then erupted in even greater intensity. *Come on, hurry up,* Misha silently shouted at Sergei.

"Done." Sergei Neboatov backed away from the bomb.

The men hurried to the storage bunker doors. As they closed the massive doors, Aloth stared into Sasha's eyes; not a word was spoken.

A few moments later the two cars were speeding down the narrow road. In the front passenger seat Misha opened the small box he had put into the car when they had first arrived back at the farmhouse. He pulled out the small radio from within and switched it on. To his relief he heard a voice calling over the radio.

"The gate is open, the gate remains open. All praise be to Him. The gate is open."

"The main gate is still in our control; head straight for the base entrance." Misha yelled.

"And the others?" Aloth yelled, thinking of Yuri, even as he knew the answer.

"They were to head for the gate at the first sign of trouble, but they are on their own. The mission is all that matters; success will liberate millions of our brothers." But Misha desperately hoped that Yuri had managed to get the duty vehicle working and then headed for the gate. He was important to the mission, though perhaps not exactly in the way he might have thought.

"What is going on?" Aloth shouted as he struggled with the wheel. He saw the fire fight that was growing with each minute in intensity.

"We have friends who are creating a diversion." Misha twisted around to see the increase in rifle fire. "And hopefully they will be able to hold the gates open for us. This has been planned for. Go, do not stop for anything." *As if I was planning to stop for tea.* Aloth hoped Misha actually did know what was happening in a world that had become as dark and bleak as his own soul.

Fortunately, Misha had indeed been briefed on many aspects of the operation. Pride burned in his veins every time he remembered the honour they had bestowed on him.

He knew that when planning the operation Ahmed and the others leading the battle for the new caliphate had always expected something to go wrong and had taken steps to safeguard the mission.

This had been their safeguard. Somewhere between forty and ninety of the Turk's and the Chechen's men were attacking the rear of the camp to create a diversion, while a smaller force were sent to reinforce those holding open the main gate. Their team leaders were under strict orders about whom they were to target… Or else it was going to get very ugly for Misha and the others.

Explosions ripped through the area where the Russians parked their vehicles, destroying some and damaging many others to foil any Russian pursuit.

Misha grinned at the sight of the fireballs. They would draw away even more Russians from the main gate and its defenders. So far the plan was working; for all their training, the Russian elite forces had been caught totally by surprise, their reaction slow and confused.

The cars sped towards the gate, racing through intersections before taking a sharp turn.

We're going to make it. Aloth was convinced Allah was watching over them. But then it began to go wrong. A set of blinding headlights flared into Aloth's eyes. The screech of rubber could be heard as a truck came out of a side road.

Aloth turned the steering wheel just in time. The Russian army truck struck the edge of the car's bumper bar, with a sad cry of torn metal.

They continued down the badly lit road until they could see the main gate—just as another military truck rolled across the road.

"No!" Aloth spat as the six-wheel truck half blocked the route out of the camp. Dark shadows raced about the truck.

"Go around," Misha screamed as he ducked down. "Use another route." "You find one," Aloth retorted, knowing they had only one chance at escape. He put his foot on the accelerator and swerved off the road. He aimed between the wooden barracks and the truck, where there was plenty of room. But standing in-between was a solid-looking light pole.

Too close, he hissed to himself as the car caught the edge of the pole. The collision deflected the car back towards the road. With a savage growl, he gripped the steering wheel and desperately realigned the wheels to scrape the car along one edge of the half lowered tailgate, that protruded out like a blade from the truck.

A few wild shots rang out. One struck the edge of the windscreen, more from luck than design. Most of the soldiers were still aiming their weapons towards the guardhouse. That had saved them for the moment.

Aloth squeezed the steering wheel as if he could physically push the car even faster. Instead the passenger side window shattered. A moment later the side mirror exploded.

By then he was passing the gate and on the road leading out of the camp. To his amazement the second car followed.

"Piss on you, no," he hissed. From out of the darkness a vehicle turned on its lights and advanced down the road towards them.

"It is ours, *inshallah*. The men will block the road, to stop pursuit." Misha hoped that he was correct and then offered up a silent prayer of gratitude when the vehicle passed them.

The two cars raced down the road, nearly passing the dark shape of Aloth's truck.

Fortunately, Aloth had been watching the sides of the road and had braked just in time. Misha jumped out and ran for the truck. He scrambled into the cabin and followed the cars. Driving like madmen, they continued down the dark but reasonably straight road.

Aloth glanced down at the old-style gauges and then realized he had not checked the mileage when they had escaped the camp and thus was unable to tell how far they had travelled from the camp.

We should be far enough away, he hoped even as they continued their mad rush. Just as he breathed a sigh of relief, a giant fireball erupted, lighting up the night sky behind them.

Aloth offered up a silent prayer for Sasha. And now of all times, he wondered what the man's real name had been.

They continued on for several miles before stopping along the shoulder of the road. Misha jumped out of the truck and sprinted to the lead car. Together with Aloth he lifted one of the unarmed devices into the back of the truck and then opened one of the two large crates. Inside they found a large but innocent-looking refrigerator. The refrigerator needed to be large as the interior had been heavily reinforced. They placed the device into the purpose made metal refrigerator, closed the lid, and then nailed the box shut.

Even before they dropped down from the truck several vehicles had already pulled up next to them. Their Chechen and Turkish guardian angels swiftly jumped out to form a tight perimeter around the vehicles.

Only then did they realize that Sergei Neboatov lay slumped across the wheel of the second car. Blood filled his mouth, staining his teeth red. Misha and Aloth quickly pulled him out of the car and placed him in the care of a Chechen who knew something of patching up wounds

Both men then aided the Chechen fighters to extract the second large crate with its refrigerator from the truck to insert the second nuclear device inside. Once the wooden box was nailed shut, the fighters moved the second device into one of the civilian vehicles, a small truck that looked surprisingly top-heavy.

Other Chechen fighters pulled the armed and ready nuclear weapon from the battered military car and placed it in a dark grey Toyota utility.

To Misha's relief he found Yuri had managed to escape with the other fighters.

"Yuri, you must see to the safe delivery of one of the devices, do you understand?" Misha demanded.

Yuri nodded his blunt head. "Of course, I will do whatever is necessary."

"Good." Misha took out a map of the local area. With a torch he showed Yuri where they were. "I know you have been making deliveries to several airfields for your second employer."

Yuri nodded, suddenly understanding why he had been introduced to the smuggling gang by one of their number so long ago.

"You will make another such delivery. But this time you will escort the load all the way to its destination. Friends will be waiting when you arrive. They will take you and the device to a safe location."

Yuri almost grinned. Several of his "cargoes" had crossed Russia to reach the Balkans. This time the load would undoubtedly go to an Islamic caliphate stronghold or safe-house to wait for the right moment. Once more he was impressed by the planning. What he had assumed to be merely a cover was now of vital importance.

Misha went on, "It is best that you go with only two others. Good luck, my friend." They clasped each other's upper arms. "Take this." He handed Yuri a mobile phone. "They will contact you on landing. Go with Allah." "Just succeed with your mission, my friend." Yuri nodded and then walked to the small top-heavy truck.

Misha watched him climb into the truck and then walked over to where several fighters stood in a tight knot, addressing a brute of a man with greying hair, a sour mouth that was missing several teeth, and eyes that were slivers of malice.

"Your real mission begins now, Commander." Misha's acknowledgement of the man's rank surprised the brute for a second, just long enough for the man to realize who was in charge of the mission. "Nothing must stop you from delivering the device to its intended target," Misha told him.

The fighters looked at their commander, who simply grunted and gestured them back to their vehicles. "The device is armed," Misha told the hulking commander. "I will show you how to detonate it."

The man nodded. "I have two men with some experience. What of the target?"

"It is the infidel city of Mezen. Get the device into the centre or as close as you can to the city, and then detonate it."

"It will be glorious." The brute's eyes flared open at the thought. Misha gave a curt nod. Then he led the commander to the dark grey

Toyota utility and showed his men how to detonate the weapon, with considerable help from the manual Sergei had used back at the camp.

Once satisfied that the men understood how to detonate the device, Misha walked to where Sergei rested against a tree, his life's blood slowly seeping out of him, even with the tightly wrapped shirt keeping the wound closed.

"Sergei." Misha knelt down beside the man. "Sergei, listen to me." "I can't go on…"

"No, but you must live. You must live long enough to tell the Russians that the terrorists plan to attack the city of Mezen and then Moscow. You hear me? Mezen, then Moscow, repeat it."

"Mezen and Moscow… But how do I explain how—?"

"You were captured and escaped, being shot in your escape from the terrorists. But you overheard them planning to attack Mezen and Moscow. Do you understand?" Misha heard movement at his back and then saw Aloth standing over him.

"Yes, Mezen and Moscow," Sergei murmured.

"Yes, hold on. Do not die; you must warn the Russians," Misha pressed on.

"Misha, the others are ready to move." Aloth spoke with a cold voice, seeing the fighters climbing into their vehicles.

Misha gripped Sergei gently by the shoulder. "Pray to Allah to give you the strength. You must not give in until you have done this last service." Sergei Neboatov nodded. "Allah will reward you." Slowly, reluctantly, he released the man and walked away.

Aloth and Misha jumped into Aloth's truck and drove some distance before turning off onto a side road leading away from the convoy of vehicles heading towards Mezen.

"You scarified our brothers." Aloth spoke as he drove them down the dark road.

"They were always meant to be a diversion. So yes, but who knows, they may succeed in incinerating Mezen." Misha admitted without guilty.

They drove further away from Mezen and then turned towards the Russian coast. Hours later they reached a small cove and an even smaller village. Turning left, they drove the truck to a collection of three large shed. Misha jumped out and opened the door of the third shed, watched over by an old man holding a large torch.

"You have the money?" the ancient mariner bent over with age inquired.

"We have it. Is all in readiness?" Misha asked.

"The boat is ready," the old smuggler told the Saudi.

Misha looked out to the small harbour and the wide ocean. In two hours Aloth and he would take the boat and their cargo out to sea and rendezvous with a ship that would take them to the New World and their destiny. The thought made him smile.

White House Briefing Room

Clayton walked out onto the podium, determination carved into every line and wrinkle of his face.

The assembled media cringed inwardly. They had become proficient at examining the signs and portents in miniscule detail. And the signs were not favourable this dark day, making a few shiver in concern. If the winds blew in the wrong direction, then the media could take yet another battering, followed by castigation and then castration for some.

A few members of the media, male and female, had already been assigned to a number of less than noteworthy assignments. Others had been consigned to the bowels of some circle of media hell. Already, many were careful when talking to Kate or Brain after the powers above had unleashed their fury and several lightning bolts upon the unfortunate pair.

"Thank you all for coming. I may not be brief, but I will be to the point. "The economy is a mess. We must act immediately to create jobs and save the economy. The question is how. How do we compete with the low wages in many parts of the world? Well, I know what corporate America will say. We could cut corporate taxes even more and the 'trickle-down effect' will happen. Except it hasn't. In fact, when President Bush gave them a tax holiday the result was that some CEOs gave themselves a pay raise and cut thousands of jobs from their companies. Now, is that really the answer?

"Alternatively, they will argue we should slash wages and benefits even more. How about that for an answer?" Clayton paused as he took a deep breath.

"As far back as the seventies people working in the meat packing industry were making as much as eighty thousand a year, as were those in the steel and rubber-tyre industries. Now people in the same industries could be making as little as fifty thousand a year. And as a result they are barely able to pay their bills—just like the millions of Americans, right now, working two jobs and still unable to pay all their bills."

Clayton then raised his hand as if to signal a stop. "But don't worry about that because once the economy picks up, their wages will start to rise. Right?" He snapped, "That's what corporate America has been telling us for decades even as their executive salaries continued skyrocketing—from million-dollar paycheques to multimillion-dollar paycheques.

"After the global financial crisis they assured us that the economy would pick up, and then we'd have wage growth. Well, did we have real on-going growth in wages? Oh, we have had short term hiccups... little spurts of growth.

But did we reduce poverty, reduce inequality? Or do we, once more, have people working—actively employed—whose income is so small that the government needs to subsidize their pay with food stamps or some form of tax relief payments?

"Think about that, we have people who, although they are paying state and local taxes, are paying no income tax because their wages are so low.

"Now, some have argued that these people should just get an education, a college degree, which will hopefully get them a better-paying job. Okay, that sounds fine, but do we really need another five million doctors or another ten million accountants? A hundred million programmers?

"And who will work in the meatpacking industry? Will we have men and women with doctorates, university degrees in packing meat? A four-year university degree for environmental waste removal so we can pay people a hundred thousand to collect our garbage?" He badgered the media. "No? Then who will? Do we import millions of foreign illegals to sweep our streets, harvest our food? Or do we have further automation and have robots pick *all* our crops? Great idea if we want to *really* increase unemployment.

"Clearly that is not the answer. So what is the answer? Wild-eyed optimism? Just need the opportunity to succeed." Clayton shook his head, dismissing the idea.

"Oh, I know many Americans believe in opportunity: you work hard, and you'll find your pot of gold. But in reality, we have very limited opportunities in this day and age. The days of new mountains to climb, new lands to conquer are past us. We are a developed economy; only a tiny fraction of us will be involved with the next great idea, the next great thing that will save the economy. That is, if it comes.

"And there is the catch. Will there be any more great ideas, another Internet? Yes, we will make many new discoveries. But will they provide a hundred million Americans with great, wonderful new jobs? We simply do not know."

Clayton looked around the room from one face to the next. "What we do know is that renowned economists now accept that poverty wages are a drag on the economy. For the economy to function, people need to have a decent living wage that gives them a level of expendable income. Enough to pay for their new TV, car, Internet connections, holiday trips… enough to pay for their children's education and for health care." He sounded frustrated, as if he were lecturing a roomful of dull-witted failing students.

"That is why we cannot continue down this path, we need a radical new outlook. It is time for a new approach. My fellow Americans, today we start down a new path for America, or else we go down the path of ruin. Here and now this government will be committed to cutting the cost of living for those most in need, the poor, and low- and middle-income groups. That will be our mantra—the goal of my presidency.

"And the best way to do that is for the government to go into business. The government will make money, not by printing it but by earning it. There are a number of ways the government can do so.

"One is a government-owned but privately run solar power scheme. The government buys and installs solar panels to place onto the rooftops of low- to middle-income earners in America. The earning from the electricity will then be divided. Half will go back to the government to defray installation and maintenance costs while the other half goes to the homeowner. In time the scheme will turn the government a tidy profit, while saving the homeowners hundreds a year in power bills.

"If the project goes well we can consider other opportunities, such as funding and supporting solar-powered electric or hybrid cars for the less fortunate. The idea would be for them to use these cars to get to and from work, from home to the mall and back. These small, low-cost roundabout cars could save their owners thousands of dollars a year in gasoline expenses.

"Along with these and other projects, the federal government will create a Federal Health Insurance scheme. Again, it will be government-owned but run as a profit-making venture, with lower costs and a high moral compass. Now you undoubtedly have many questions, but time is limited. So we'll limit it to a few questions for now; you'll be fully briefed in time."

Clayton could almost hear the groans of disbelief. He had done it once again: caught them all flat-footed, with no real idea what to ask.

Gordon Andress of the *National* jumped to their defence. "Mr. President, many will say that the government just can't manage a free-enterprise endeavour, that it has no experience and is simply ill-equipped." "The schemes will not be run or managed by the government. There will be no giant government bureaucracy involved. 'Government-owned but privately run' is the key. And to ease your concerns, if one should fail, it will be closed down just like any other private enterprise. We will not be balling it out."

Andress followed up, "A government scheme was rejected some time back. Why do you think yours will work?"

"A good point, but again, it'll work because it will be privately run by an independent board, not a government department drowning in bureaucrats or politicians."

"But where are you going to get the money to pay for everything? Will you raise taxes? Cut spending?" Andress responded to Clayton's argument.

"Neither and both," Clayton declared flippantly.

"Could you clarify that, Mr. President?" Andress pressed on.

"Once a new Congress has been sworn in, we will raise taxes and cut spending. We have no choice but to pay off our debt. No Representative or Senator can do anything else and still uphold his or her oath of office." At that point Clayton paused, as if to take a breath.

"And right here, right now I call on every American to make it clear to the new Congress that we cannot go back to business as usual… No more refusing to pass budgets, playing political games. Make them sign a contract if you must, but they must pass the budget and accept tax reform on closing loopholes, or they must resign, end of story."

"So tax money will go to fund your solar scheme and this health insurance?" Gordon Andress begged for an answer.

"No, no tax money. At first we too wondered where we would find the funding, and we came up with a few ideas. But then it became obvious: we would simply ask the wealthy to donate. Years ago, the billionaire Warren Buffett castigated the wealthy. He spoke out about how he was paying less tax than his secretary.

"The following day one of the less charitably-minded amongst us said that Mr. Buffet could always donate to the Treasury. I think that suggestion was a marvellous idea. The Treasury will set up a website where it will present a list of the top 10 per cent of the wealthiest Americans, along with how much they are estimated to be worth and how much they will donate to the government fund. I trust that will satisfy any doubts that you may have.

"This way the people will see that the wealthy do care about our great country and are not the parasites that run to a tax haven at the mere mention of raising taxes." Clayton saw a hand rise from the crowd, he nodded to the man.

"And if they do not donate, sir?" Andrew Johnson, the socially conscious, the anti-capitalist all but jumped out of his seat.

"I have every confidence in their love and commitment to this nation."

"They haven't done it in the past. And a lot of the wealthy have packed their bags—"

"We have a long tradition of the wealthy donating, just not to the government, because, quite rightly, they would fear that the government would try to make it a regular event. And let's be honest, would you donate money to see it misspent, wasted by the government?" He had seen too many Senators and members of Congress attach riders and other provisions to bills that had made him sick with disgust at such waste. Hell, why would anyone give a cent to a body they knew to be as corrupt and self-serving as Congress? He certainly wouldn't.

"That is why this will be a one-off event… and the revenue will go into these moneymaking ventures. The money will be professionally spent and accounted for and not used to create another government bureaucracy or fatten the wallet of some Congressman's friend." His blunt accusation had its desired effect. He saw them look at each other in concern; they knew that if they pushed him too far, he could retaliate with a vengeance. They all knew that much of the media had sold their soul to corporate America decades ago. *Never bite the hand that feeds you* flashed across their minds.

"Yes," Andress continued the exchange, "that's all good and well. But I can't help thinking that some may be less than inclined to donate."

"Well, there were alternate suggestions. One was to follow the 'trickle-down' logic." Clayton smiled his best boyish smile, as if a little embarrassed by his disclosure. "As we know, the rich have long argued that as they get richer, their wealth will trickle down to the rest of America.

"And further, public companies argue that if we cut their taxes they would bring in overseas cash they hold off shore, thus promoting growth by investing that money into the economy…"

"With respect, sir." Andress jumped up. "That does not match the facts. The Bush and Trump tax holidays saw the bulk of the repatriated money go to share buybacks, pay rises for senior management or the shareholders.

"Little was spent on helping the economy through training or serious Research and Development.

"Why should we believe they will increase employment this time around? Especially… when the department of labour predicts that we will loss near twice as many jobs to automation than we did last year."

Thank you, Gordon. I think I'm going to have to put you on my Christmas card list. "Once Congress returns, we will enact a new law. If the top 10 per cent and multi-nationals cannot… clearly… show that they are creating a quarter million new export-oriented jobs each year, then they will have to face a tax of 71 per cent with all exemptions and write-offs removed… That revenue would be sufficient to begin the schemes I have outlined.

"Naturally, if they can show that they are indeed creating those jobs, then they can continue to pay something like the 17 per cent in taxes that some now pay."

"That could still take months, Mr. President." Andress was still taking the lead. "You have been going on about how vital it is to save every cent, move faster and faster to cut our debt."

Forget the Christmas card list I want you on my team. "That's true, yet we still need the Congress to enact new laws—or if the people prefer, I suppose we could hold a nationwide referendum immediately. That, I suppose, would make any new laws enforceable. And Congress could only override the referendum if they took it back to the people in another national referendum." *Oh yes, we're in the groove now.* "But I am sure we won't have to go down that route."

"And that is how the government will make money?" Andress sounded as if he was warming to the idea.

"Yes, and other ventures."

"For example, sir?"

"For example, Gordon, there is talk of banks needing another bailout. If so, I say bring it on. I'll give them the money, but there will be a few strings attached. They borrow, fine. But they pay interest at triple the going rate. The government has to borrow at 2 per cent, so the banks will pay 6 per cent; if we pay 3 per cent, they will pay 9 per cent."

"And if they can't pay the money back?" Andress whistled under his breath.

"We do it the way the banks have always done it, Gordon. If they can't pay up, we just seize the home, or in this case the bank and the executives' golden parachutes." Clayton could feel the collective shiver run down the spines of bank CEOs all across America.

"If Bank of A was to ask for fifty billion dollars, it would have to provide the federal government with some form of guarantee. This way, should the bank fold, the government will have first bite at all the bank's properties and such. This will, of course, include shares belonging to the CEO and board members, including options or bonds and the like.

"And we can add more: As long as the government has even one share of ownership in the bank, it can veto any pay raises and block any bonuses. Any proposed bonuses will go instead to the government's coffers until all government shares have been sold.

"Furthermore, we can stipulate that the bank will be at risk of fines and additional penalties should it renege on any conditions of the agreement.

All of this will assure the public that their money will work for them and not simply pull Wall Street out of a mess of its own making."

Andress frowned, smelling a rat. "And this will all be locked in? The government won't change its tune?"

"It's up to the people. If they want the Congress to enact legislation, or if they want a referendum ensuing that the government can bail out a bank only with the public's approval, then call for it, and I will back you a hundred per cent.

"Equally, the people can demand we write new laws that make the original Glass-Steagall Act of 1933 look pathetically weak." The act had separated the banks, splitting the savings and deposit banks from the investment banks that many believed had caused the Great Depression.

"We'll continue to guard the old savings and deposit banks so they can provide money for our physical infrastructure. But we can, *also*, enshrine laws where Investment banks and their boards are open to legal action for fraudulent behaviour if the banks are deemed to have acted in a predatory way or have engaged in questionable behaviour."

Clayton felt as if he should give the media a two-hour lecture but stopped himself. What was the point? People were too lazy or selfish to learn, so they had to suffer and suffer again because they simply wouldn't learn. And then they had the nerve to complain when the inevitable happened, as if they actually deserved sympathy.

Gemma Matthews from the *Post* raised her hand. "Mr. President, can we go back to this Health Insurance Scheme? One of the arguments against government insurance is that it will have an unfair advantage."

Clayton nodded. "It most certainly will have, Gemma."

The room went silent. They'd never have expected him to openly admit to such a thing.

"It will be allowed to make *only* a 2 per cent profit. Any moneys that are realized beyond that will go back to those buying the insurance. Our insurance scheme will be to help its customers, not to stuff the shareholders' pockets."

"But that's… not capitalistic."

"On the contrary. The government will provide a needed service and make a profit, capitalism at its best. It just won't be greedy. Now, if the other insurance companies want to do likewise, that is their choice. I won't demand that they cut profits."

"What will you do with the 2 per cent profit the scheme will make, Mr. President?" Matthews was getting a sick feeling.

"One per cent would go to government coffers; the other one per cent will be held in case of blowouts and to improve benefits."

He gave them his best smile. "My fellow Americans, we are a developed economy—indeed, an overdeveloped one. And thus, economic growth through conventional means is limited or nearly over. Even the worst economist will admit that growth in America is now mostly achieved by the acquisition of assets as opposed to any natural growth in the market.

"In the past, if a company wanted to grow, either it bought another company, thus reducing competition, or it expanded to overseas markets and often moved overseas for the cheap labour. We have gone nearly as far as we can go with the current system. We need new directions, new approaches—a new vision for the future—or we stagnate.

"Isn't it better that the government works for some of its money rather than simply collecting taxes? Instead of being an occasional obstacle, it becomes a true ally for growth. This is my proposal: a government that actually works for its money while endeavouring to cut the cost of living for those most in need. But for that to happen, I need you to make it clear to the new Congress and Senate that that is what you want.

"And should you have any doubts over the new Congress's commitment, then you must demand for a national referendum, a referendum that will cement this vision into law. Only then will we take the steps needed to save our country." Clayton raised a hand. "Thank you all for your time."

They all stood up, caught, wanting more but not sure what to ask. "My staff will arrange for more interviews shortly. Right now I have a few matters that need attending." Clayton thanked them again and then left the room, to find a rather concerned Abb with a more cordial Jonathan waiting to brief him.

"Your smiling disposition does not bode well, Abb. Is it me?" Clayton asked Abb.

Abb managed to mumble a reply.

"Out with it." Clayton was slightly annoyed.

"You just signed you death warrant, Mr. President," Abb gaped.

"You agreed," Clayton answered him.

"You insisted. I have always been loyal to the office of the president, no-matter how doubtful. But this is way too much. You're pressing all the wrong buttons. They'll all be against you.

"So far you've gotten away with it because you actually sound like you've making sense, and you kicked the media's backside so hard, they have been afraid to take you on. Not anymore; the big guys will go after you now—as if any of them would donate even a cent." They didn't get rich by playing nice or showing compassion. Abb looked at Clayton with sympathy. They're going to gut you like a fish, if I can't get you to back off." *What's wrong with the man?*

Clayton turned to the other man. "Do you agree, Jonathan?" "Sir, it's not my place."

"Come, come. Be honest." Clayton grinned.

"It was brilliant, sheer brilliance, sir." Jonathan smiled from ear to ear.

"What?" Abb sputtered.

"Sir, for the first time we are playing them at their own game. In the past they have used the argument of the 'trickle-down effect' and gotten away with it because there is absolutely no way we can prove that wealth from the rich doesn't trickle down to the poor." Not that it did; Jonathan was certain of that. If it was trickling down, then how come the poor were getting poorer, while the rich were getting richer?

"But now you've done it to them. There is no way they can absolutely prove that *they* are creating a quarter million jobs. We know it'll always be up to the economy anyway." You wouldn't see the corporations hiring a quarter million employees in an economic downturn. He grinned with laughter in his eyes. "So if we push hard enough you can make them scared, really scared. Maybe scared enough that they'll donate now rather than face a 71 per cent tax."

Jonathan saw the look of disbelief from Abb. "You can't be serious." Abb scoffed softly. *Damn it, don't encourage the man,* he wanted to scream at Jonathan. *We need to limit the damage this has done; it may have already wrecked any chance of Prescott being elected to the White House.* "You really think a little fright like this will work?"

"Yes sir, I do, because for the first time we have our own terror weapon to use against them. Just as they have used fear, suspicion, and doubt to get what they have wanted, now we too can use fear. Fear that they will be slapped with a 71 per cent tax."

Jonathan turned to Clayton with his grin spreading wide across his face. "Sir, you've got them by the balls; it's just a matter of how hard you want to squeeze. And now is the perfect time: the public is hurting, and they want blood, sir. You just need them to know you're serious." Jonathan almost felt like cringing as Abb's face darkened. He could understand the chief of staff's concern. Clayton's policies could undermine the president's chance of being elected to office.

But didn't Abb see that this could also give the president what he needed to win any election? The public had lost faith in the system, and here was a man who stood up to take on the system. It could give him the election, no matter how much the establishment wanted him gone. Hell, the more they opposed him, the more the public would rally around him. They were hungry and angry, and for the first time in a long while they had blood in their eye.

Yes it was a risk, but the potential benefits were unimaginable.

"Finally." Clayton smiled at Jonathan.

"You agree with him?" Abb was stunned. "If you do impose that kind of tax, it won't be hundreds leaving; they'll leave America in their tens of thousands."

Clayton turned to Abb with a grin. "I'd almost impose the tax just to achieve that."

"You're losing me." Abb was wide-eyed with shock. *He's totally lost it.* "Abb, America does not need fat old CEOs fiddling the books so they can create yet another financial bubble. In many ways they are the problem."

Clayton looked down the corridor to check that they would not be overheard. "I need a private word with you before the FBI briefing, Abb." He then turned to the younger man. "We will need a bit of privacy, Jonathan. If you could tell Assistant Director Drywood that we will be a few minutes later than expected?"

"Yes, sir." Jonathan sped off to warn the FBI official.

"I am about to ask you to do something you may not be all that happy with."

Abb Cole looked at the president, truly looked at the man for the first time. *Shit . . .*

Twenty minutes later both men entered the Oval Office where Assistant Director Andrew Drywood waited.

"Have a seat and tell me the latest," Clayton said to him.

Drywood sat down, organized his notes, and handed a file to the president. "There is some good news, sir. As you can see, the rioting has stabilized; it's not getting worse. But we still have more than twenty large or small breakouts of violence or social unrest."

He had learned that the president did not so much care about the details of his verbal reports. His written reports provided all the graphs and details. Rather the president wanted his opinion on the feel, the mood on the street.

"Of the riots, most were small protests that were quickly dispersed… that is, when they did become violent. One gathering of around one hundred thousand got violent towards the end, thanks to a couple thousand troublemakers, but with the military presence to support the police, it was swiftly contained. The organizers apologized to the governor; he had previously given them permission. Satisfied with the apology, he came out the following day and led the march in support for better wages." He glanced up from the page he was using to check his facts.

"Excellent, that's what I want to hear."

"Further, sir, more local authorities are beginning to feel they can better manage the situation, especially as the protestors are mostly complying with the restrictions. But the situation remains delicate. Just about anything could set off another wave of riots. We really need to tread gently."

"And how does the military situation stand?" Clayton showed his concern over sending in the military.

"We now have over eight hundred and seventy-five thousand military personnel on the streets. Doing an excellent job, I'm told. In fact, it appears that they are having some effect on low-level street crime. They have even been involved in a couple of arrests."

Abb noted, "I saw that on TV last night; got us some good press." He seemed pleased, Drywood noticed. Although the chief of staff did look a little shaken; *guess someone took the wind out of his sails.*

"Yes, sir." Drywood stated matter-of-factly. "It's more media hype than anything real, but it is giving the public the idea that they and their homes are safer." He shuffled his files and looked up at the president. "And equally, the relative calm could also be a result of the government providing shelter for the homeless."

"And the weather, how is it affecting the situation?" Clayton enquired. "The last day or so has been keeping more people indoors, although it is expected to warm up in a couple of days; that may get more people out onto the streets."

"Pity," Abb grumbled; *the colder the better.*

Not for the homeless, asshole, thought Drywood. "The bad news is the escalation in violent attacks on individuals and companies. Thirty-nine threats of violence and attacks on wealthy and influential citizens, with sixty-eight attacks on corporations, most of which we suspect were carried out by the anarchists.

"But the main issue is the targeted assassinations, sir. We have had eleven killings in the last three days—senior NRA members or high flying CEOs."

"You only suspect the anarchists?" Abb glared at the FBI Agent, as Drywood handed both men a list of individuals and buildings that had been attacked.

"We have no concrete evidence at this stage, sir."

"Do you need it?" Abb could only just contain himself.

"We are not in Russia or China, sir. Further, the neo-Nazis are being closely looked at in one case, that of the murder of Markus Randal."

"And just what would the neo-Nazis have against Markus Randal?" Abb demanded. Randal was a well-known figure in Virginia.

"He had recently accused two neo-Nazis groups of fuelling the upswing in gun violence. There was clear evidence that he was trying to deflect the outrage over the gun massacre in Virginia . . . the one where nineteen children were massacred by those two teenagers." He deliberately threw that in Abb's face. "Also, he was not directly under threat from any of the anarchist websites."

"Who was this Markus?" Clayton glanced at Abb then at Drywood. "Markus Randal, age fifty-nine, was the head of the Rifle Association in Virginia. He was answering the front door and was shot twice in the face. The shooter was obviously trying to be ironic." "How so?" Clayton seemed interested.

"He put two slugs in Mr. Randal's mouth, four days after Randal had attended a Rifle Association meeting and stated that he would never surrender his guns, as he needed them to defend his 'voice for freedom' and speak out against the 'Nazi-thugs' responsible for the Virginia massacre." There was a note of smugness in Drywood's tone. "He was laying it on pretty thick, by all accounts."

"You don't seem to be overly sympathetic," Abb noted.

"Oh, I have deep sympathy, sir—"

"It's just that you don't think very highly of the man," Clayton whispered. "Correct?"

"With respect, sir, at best he was talking nonsensical trash; at worst he could've got people killed."

"What?" Abb stuttered as if he had swallowed an especially sour lemon and was choking on it.

"Sorry, sir. But he was talking rubbish." Drywood shook his head. "Everybody talks about having guns in the home to defend themselves even when the argument is singularly flawed."

"I find that to be debatable. If a man is suitably armed, I am certain a person can defend his home." Abb almost sneered as he said it.

Drywood shrugged. "Sir, it doesn't matter much if you have or haven't got a gun, not when the criminal has the element of surprise. A criminal isn't going to knock on your door and give you five minutes' warning to get your gun.

"Why do you think law enforcement goes into a suspect's home fast and with guns drawn, other than to use speed and surprise as an advantage?

"The fact is, if people were seriously concerned about home invasions, then you'd be facing a gun barrel every time you knocked on your neighbour's front door." *And when the local cops roll up to your neighbour's front door, he can explain why he was threatening you with a weapon.* "As the president said, it's more fearmongering by the NRA than reality."

Abb shook his head. "I disagree; a good solid door will give you plenty of time to get to your weapon."

"With all due respect, sir"—*You're a damned asshole*—"it also gives you time to run out the back door. Or lock yourself in a safe room and press down on a security alarm button."

"And if they come in the middle of the night?"

Jesus, what a dick . Drywood might as well have tried to talk sense to a stubborn mule. "Sir, wouldn't you be asleep? But there is a solution to that. I saw a movie once, in which this killer had to move house, so he went to this apartment and the first thing he did was find the most uncomfortable chair in sight and place it in the corner of the room where he could see the room and doors. That was where he would sleep so no one could sneak up on him."

"That's a movie."

"Exactly, sir, but if you're seriously concerned about a home invasion, then wouldn't you need to be on guard twenty-four/seven? Like sentry duty in the army." Drywood breathed in as he locked eyes with Abb. *Can you believe this crap?*

Are you going to have your wife stay up half the night to guard the front door, while your oldest son guards the back door? Shit—you want every fucking kindergarten, school, college, and university to have wall to wall guards? Every post office, every bank staffing a five-man SWAT team? When you're driving home you're going to have armed men in the backseat to stop some addict from approaching the side window and blowing your stupid brains out? When you're holding your dick in a toilet and some low-life shoves a gun in your face, what are you going to do? Piss on him?

Drywood soldiered on: "It's all hypotheticals and hot air—just like 'the only thing that can stop a bad guy with a gun is a good guy with a gun.' With all the police and all the military on the streets right now, have we stopped all the bad guys?

"Look at the 2017, Las Vegas mass shooting by Paddock from the 32nd floor of the Mandalay Hotel, who stopped him? Was it a Hotel employee; 'a good guy with a gun' or the police?

"Remember than incident that happened some years ago when a sheriff's deputy in Texas was shot in the back as he was filling up his patrol car? He was 'a good guy with a gun,' so how come he didn't stop his own shooting?

"If you're a 'bad guy' with a gun, you will always have the advantage over the 'good guy' with a gun; because nine times out of ten you'll have the element of surprise."

"That is not a vote of confidence," Clayton pointed out.

"Sir, the best way to stop a bad guy using a gun is to stop the guy from getting a gun in the first place," Drywood stated in a flat voice, holding firm control of his temper. He had seen too many mangled bodies to be sympathetic with fools and gun supporters. "The real issue, as you pointed out, is the number of guns in America."

Isn't it goddamned obvious? Or maybe I'm getting too old and need to retire. Yeah, let somebody else mop up the blood; wonder if this dick would volunteer?

"We just need to increase punishment, longer prison sentences," Abb chimed in.

"We have millions of Americans already in jail," Clayton said with a shrug. "Prison hasn't worked so far."

"Then we need a new deterrent," Abb declared.

"Yes sir," Drywood answered, "and what would you suggest?" *If caught with an illegal firearm in your hand you will lose your hand? Thank you, Mr. President, for that little bed time story.*

Abb sat in silence.

"It's just too easy to get hold of a gun," Drywood declared. "And that's for both criminals and law-abiding citizens."

"I don't follow." Abb's eyebrows crushed inwards in confusion.

"Too many citizens become overconfident. Carrying a weapon makes them feel safe, so they're more likely to walk down a dark alleyway, cutting across the park at night. They're not putting good locks on doors or installing an alarm system because they have an assault rifle in the house. They'll buy the gun but won't take the training for their own safety . . ."

"We don't allow the selling of assault rifles. They are semi-auto and used mostly for hunting." Abb told the FBI man with a hint of real anger in his voice.

That startled Drywood; he might have gone a little too far.

Clayton asked, "Is that why gun magazines have photos of US soldiers and police SWAT teams, to show the differences between their military weapons and your 'semi-auto hunting rifles'?" He scoffed for effect. He had seen enough gun magazines preaching the similarities between military and civilian weapons to make Abb's argument laughable. "Abb, why keep 'hunting rifles' for home defence if they aren't considered to be in the same league as military or police firearms?"

"Many do use those so-called 'assault rifles' for hunting," Abb declared. "Do they use bolt action or thirty-round magazines?" Clayton asked him.

"Sir?" Abb gave Clayton a blank look.

"A bolt action rifle is for hunting; a thirty-round magazine is for killing lots of people.

"When my father went hunting," he continued, glaring at Abb, "it was with a bolt-action rifle. He prided himself that he used one shot for one kill. He never felt so impotent that he needed a thirty-round magazine to bring down a deer. He was a real hunter—not some sissy pretender in a camo jumpsuit thinking that a gun will make him a real man.

"Andrew, for the record, what difference does law enforcement see between full-auto and semi-auto?'"

"Most don't see any real difference. Personally, anything that has a magazine should be classed as an assault rifle. I've seen what they can do."

"That is your view," Abb retorted.

"Actually that would be history's point of view, Abb." Clayton sounded as if he was giving another lecture back in his old university. "Recall that our soldiers were carrying the M1 Garand in World War Two, which was semi-auto with an eight-round clip.

"In the early days of the Vietnam War, our soldiers were carrying the M14, a semi-auto with a twenty-round magazine. So just what is the difference between them and a Bushmaster semi-auto rifle, other than a mere technicality?" Clayton paused for a moment. "Indeed, I could argue that only a bolt action rifle should be called non-military."

"Well, going by those criteria, a musket is a military weapon. We used them against the British." *During the War of Independence,* Abb told himself.

"A good point for banning all firearms wouldn't you say?" Clayton gave Abb a small smile.

Abb groaned at the very idea.

Chapter 11

THE KREMLIN

The aide rushed into the palatial bedroom of the president of Russia. "Sir, we have a grave situation." Mikhail Kurpov's voice was edged with concern. That did more to awaken the president than his words. "What?"

"A Spetsnaz training base was infiltrated by a gang of terrorists. We believe they managed to detonate one of the special devices held at the camp."

A shiver ran down the president's spine and settled in his gut like a lump of hot lead. Hurriedly he pulled a robe over his shoulders and followed Mikhail as he walked down the corridor. "What do we know?" The president was already in a cold fury at this outrageous violation.

"A breach of the storage bunker holding the devices set off the security alarm here in Moscow and the base headquarters. The duty officer in Moscow called the base. A man identifying himself as the base duty sergeant responded and reported all was quiet but that the officer in charge had sent a patrol to investigate. They believed it was a faulty alarm and assured us everything seemed secure.

"Fortunately the officer on duty in Moscow knew the real sergeant and was suspicious when he did not recognize the man's voice."

"So, with all our security we were alerted because an officer happened to know the man who should have been on the other end of the line?"

"They apparently followed established protocols. But, yes, that's correct. We raised the alarm from here, and the base went on alert. Reports from the site are somewhat confused. We know there was an exchange of gunfire, and then a nuclear tactical device was detonated."

"How many did we have at the base?"

"Twelve, I believe." Mikhail Kurpov did not hesitate to answer. "What are we doing to track down these weapons? Do we have any idea how many the terrorists have?"

"We do not know that they were after the weapons." *We don't even know if any escaped—much less whether they took any of the weapons,* Mikhail Kurpov wanted to say but thought better of the idea.

"Of course they were after the weapons," the president snapped at his aide.

"It could have been just another terrorist attack." Mikhail Kurpov bit his tongue even as he spoke those words.

"They went to all the trouble of attacking a heavily armed military base instead of a soft target and just happened to find the bunker doors open? And the special devices armed and ready to detonate? Don't be a fool."

"Your orders, sir?"

The president of Russia paused. His instinct was to cover this up. He could instruct the FSB to quietly deal with the situation. Only, how many already knew? The terrorists who planned the attack for starters, and they could be relied upon to tell the world. And then there were the survivors—if there were any. The pesky Americans would have detected the explosion. Could he claim it was an accident? As if nuclear bombs go off by accident inside a hardened bunker. He needed to know more.

"Order a state of emergency. Lock down the entire area. Send in every air and ground unit we have. Search under every rock until you have accounted for every device. And get our people to find out who was responsible and why they were not stopped. I want to know who did this. They are to use all means necessary, understood?"

Mikhail nodded in understanding. The hounds would be unleashed without restraint. Terrorist supporters, terrorist suspects, anyone who might know anything would be taken into basements and "convinced" to talk. "But if all the devices were destroyed in the explosion—"

"Then get me proof. Get me proof. I feel this in my gut. There is more to this than just a stupid suicide attack. I know they went after the weapons."

The Road to Mezen

The brute of a Chechen commander wiped the palms of his hands against his pants. He gazed absently out the window at the empty darkness of the night. Still no sign of any kind of activity from the Russian filth; he silently prayed that it would remain so.

He turned around to look at the man in the backseat.

"Some increased traffic, but more confusion than anything." The man spoke as he continued to listen to one of the two radios in the car. He was listening to a police radio that had been taken from a car belonging to a pair of Russian police officers they had killed to acquire the radio. The commander grinned when he remembered the look on their faces as he shot them, how they had changed from arrogant thugs to cringing cowards.

Well, what else could you expect from bullies who used their uniforms to push people around? Two more dead Russians would do nothing to balance the ledger of blood that this rotting carcass of this soulless country owed him.

Russia's secret war on Chechnya was still festering, even if Russian soldiers did not die. In one way or another the bloodletting continued, even if it was committed mostly by Russian lackeys in his homeland. *No matter; soon, very soon all that will change.* He stretched and watched the darkness.

"Wait, yes. They are receiving orders to establish roadblocks. Where is that damned map?" the man in the backseat demanded as he rummaged about in the rear to find the map of the local area.

As the man spoke, the driver spotted the distant lights of a helicopter following the road towards them. Fear gripped the commander's testicles. *They cannot be stopped, not now,* he pleaded in silence. *Let it not be one of their gunships.* His irrational fear grow. Even the Russians were unlikely to open fire unless they had some knowledge of who was in the ragged convey of vehicles.

Yet the lights came closer, almost lazily, as the copter approached.

Then they watched the fat dragonfly body pass over their heads.

The Chechen commander gave a sigh of relief. The man at the controls was probably another bad or drunk pilot who needed the road to guide him, he concluded. Although the helicopter was not travelling swiftly, it was still going too fast to be scanning the road.

"Keep going," he snarled at the driver when the man gave him a sideways glance.

"Yes, found it." The man in the rear spoke up. "They have been ordered to set up a roadblock here." He circled a spot on the map and gave it to the commander. "If we are lucky, we may pass before they set it up."

With his usual eloquence the commander grunted once; it was unlikely. The convoy sped on down the road. Twenty minutes later the second smaller radio squealed loudly. The man in back glanced down at it. The warning signal was from the scout car, the lead vehicle that was fifteen kilometres ahead of the convoy. The scout car had made contact. But with who, was it the police, state security, or the military? They would find out soon enough.

"Slow down but keep going," the Chechen snarled in anticipation, the thought of revenge surging through his veins.

They drove on until the convoy turned a corner, when they spotted the police roadblock some distance away. Behind the roadblock were the distant predawn lights of civilization.

Up ahead the Chechen commander's scout car, an ugly white tin can of a car, had just cleared the checkpoint when its exhaust spluttered and the engine died less than thirty metres beyond the roadblock. That came as a surprise to the police, especially when the driver jumped out and lifted the hood of the vehicle.

After a quick glance under the hood, the driver called out to a pair of police officers for help.

"Please, friends, I need to be home before the wife thinks that something has happened. I can pay."

The driver smiled as he waved to the two closest officers, while subtly watching the others manning the police roadblock.

His grin widened. To his relief, the other police were already turning their attention to the shaggy, uneven convoy of vehicles coming down the road.

As the two policemen came face to face with the smiling driver, he slipped a thin knife from under his sleeve and inserted the razor-sharp point just below the body armour and into the kidney of the first officer. The Chechen in the passenger side had already walked around behind the officers and threw one arm around the second officer's neck, grabbed the officer's chin with his other hand, and gave it a savage twist. The neck snapped instantly.

Both fighters glanced over to the police roadblock as a few alarmed voices were raised, but the voices were directed towards the oncoming vehicles, as the lead car was not reducing speed to stop. Even as the alarm was sounded, both men grabbed the two officers' firearms and jumped behind their vehicle.

The first two vehicles in the convoy roared down the road and were greeted with a hail of gunfire—which began to choke and stutter as the two fighters behind the roadblock opened fire into the unprotected backs of the Russian police.

Even with screams and cries erupting from amongst them, the lead vehicle's tyre exploded from a well-aimed bullet's impact. The vehicle swerved left and then right, coming to a stop fifty metres in front of the roadblock. The second car swerved and came to a stop next to the first.

An instant later the occupants jumped from the second vehicle and began firing in support of the stricken vehicle.

The next two vehicles roared off the road to attack the roadblock from the left flank. One of them had just enough luck to reach the edge of the roadblock before a bullet stopped the driver. But the driver's sacrifice had achieved its purpose. Attacked on three sides, the police were overwhelmed and easily slaughtered. A few tried to escape into the woods but were shot down in a virtual hail of bullets.

"Clear the road," the bullish commander ordered his second in command. "Get all the police vehicles lined up along the side of the road. Nice and neat… as if they were jerking off as usual." He doubted that it would fool anyone for long. But if the Russian thugs had been unable to radio a warning, then perhaps it would be enough.

"And leave two of our men in police uniforms to wave any passing traffic through," he shouted at his lieutenant's back as the man raced away. It was worth a try.

The Chechen studied his surroundings. He then grabbed one of the passing fighters. "Get all of our working vehicles lined up over there." He pointed to a spot on the other side of the road. "Have the drivers check that each is working. Move; we leave in five minutes." He pushed the man on his way.

They cleared the road just in time for a blue sedan and then a dark grey Toyota utility to speed past.

The Chechen commander crossed the road to where the working vehicles were being assembled. "Do we have enough?" he asked his lieutenant.

The grizzled veteran nodded his ugly head. "If we cram more men into each car, or else we can use some of the Russian security cars." The man left the decision up to his commander.

"Good idea; have the police cars lead the convoy. We can use them to break open the next roadblock." If they were lucky, but he doubted they would have such luck a second time.

The ugly lieutenant grinned and set about organizing the convoy.

Above the Road Leading to the Now Non-Existent Russian Army Base

The two Russian Army helicopters overflew the road in a staggered formation. When the lead helicopter's infrared scope noticed something next to the road that led to the now non-existent army base.

"It could be a body," the co-pilot reported.

"Understood." The pilot's response was neutral at best.

The helicopters were merely the beginning of a swarm of alert helicopters and planes searching an ever-growing area in a desperate effort to find an elusive and unidentified prey.

The pilot wiped his chin with his gloved hand. Less than an hour ago he had been silently complaining and cursing to himself as he was dragged out of bed and told to pull on his boots.

He was still wondering whether all the trouble was worth the effort as he walked into the briefing room.

The briefing had changed all that, but he could not bring himself to believe the words. He almost thought this was some sick joke thought up by command. That was before he had witnessed what was left of the now non-existent Spetsnaz training base. All the complaints had left him. From there he had followed the road leading out of the camp with a silent, boiling rage.

"He may still be alive," the co-pilot continued. The body was showing some heat.

The wheels of the helicopter had barely touched down when the first man of the security detachment on board leaped onto the ground. The rest swiftly followed with guns drawn and pointing out in every direction. They approached the man with some hesitation.

"Alive?" the team leader asked the medic.

The man turned over the body and hissed, studying the wound. "Not for long, if we can't get him to a hospital."

"Lieutenant, can you tell me your name?" The young team leader found that he could identify the man's insignia.

"Lieutenant Sergei Neboatov, I heard them… Mezen, Moscow… bomb… nuclear bombs for Mezen, for Moscow. Escaped capture, tell them the terrorists are going to strike Moscow."

"Lvov!" The young sergeant called over the team's radio operator, already working out the message he would send.

The message the young sergeant sent ignited a burst of activity and messages. One went straight to the waiting president of Russia.

"Moscow, they dare to threaten Moscow?" he shouted at his aides, that were beginning to crowd into his office. "With a nuclear device, they dare?" he demanded as if to even state such a thing was impossible. "We have a nuclear arsenal that makes the Americans, the entire world cringe in fear, and these mongrel dogs would dare threaten us?"

No one threatens Russia, no one. Do not millions in the West wet their pants in fear of Russia's power? Oh, they pretend they believe in socialism, and they oppose the evils of their capitalist government. But he knew the truth: deep down the Americans and Europeans were cowards, terrified of having to stand up to mother Russia's might. Yes, he nodded to himself, he knew the truth.

Which made this all the more insufferable. *We have the power to incinerate the world. And these thugs, these terrorist apes dare to threaten Russia… threaten me.*

"Mr. President, we need to move you to a secure location, if they manage to avoid being captured."

"Yes." He shot up out of his chair, even as his nostrils flared at the idea of running.

"We still have plenty of time." General Anatoli Vorishnov's voice rumbled out of the thick barrel that was his chest, one covered in medals. "Unless they have an ICBM up their ass, they will need days to reach Moscow," the old warrior told the lackeys surrounding the president. "And we need to decide if they plan to attack Moscow now or at a future date."

"What are you talking about?" Mikhail Kurpov demanded from the old warrior.

"The terrorists could try to hold a device over our heads as a threat—"

"You are saying they will not use them?" Mikhail saw a ray of hope. "No. More than likely, they will target Mezen as a demonstration of their power. If they attack Moscow, they have nothing to hold over our heads. Are they madmen drunk on blood, or will there be threats, demands, and sadly… a ransom to pay? We must prepare for both possibilities, Mr. President."

Thirty Miles from Mezen

The two police cars in the Chechen convoy swerved left and right, blocking the road. Up ahead was a wall of police cars and even two armoured vehicles. The rest of the convoy came to a slow stop behind the two captured police cars.

"Set up a defensive position," the Chechen ordered as he stepped out of the car.

"Why not try to break through?" The driver was not known for his towering intellect at the best of times.

"Just do it," the commander snarled, watching the police. The Russian thugs were not making any effort to close with them and engage in battle.

Good, a stand-off; the Russians were concerned we might set off their little tactical device. He grinned in victory. *Splendid, just keep your eyes on us.* He watched his men deploy their cars in a rough makeshift perimeter.

His ugly lieutenant walked over to him. "The Russians want to talk to us."

"If only they were so willing years ago." The brutal looking commander's lip's curled around the words. Then his brothers, wife, and children would still be alive. His family would be whole. His home would not be a crater in a burned-out village deep in the mountains.

The security forces had targeted his father as a suspected Chechen freedom fighter. They had missed his father but not his brothers, children, and wife.

He spat on the ground. What a laugh the Almighty must have had. They had targeted his "terrorist" father but missed, yet they had still killed one of their intended targets. Although his father had not been involved in the struggle, his devout wife and he had indeed been freedom fighters. They had been the ones involved in organizing and plotting several attacks against the Russians and their lackeys.

"Do we talk to them?" the ugly lieutenant asked, more for confirmation than anything else.

"Yes. Let us give them a list of their atrocities and crimes against humanity for them to take back to their masters. Let us make it quite clear why we do this. I have much to say."

Driving away from Mezen

Yuri drove the old top-heavy truck in a style that the Russian police were accustomed to. He wanted nothing to give him away. Still he clenched and unclenched his big hands around the steering wheel. The two passengers sat quietly, one of them asleep; for they knew they were only muscle to help Yuri when or if the time came.

The front wheel dipped, launching a spray of grey water and waking the man next to Yuri, who gave out a soft grunt of surprised interest. "What was that?"

The man beside the window spoke for the first time. "Nothing, you lump of lard." Then he addressed Yuri. "And still no one behind us, or helicopters overhead."

It was getting light enough to see some movement in the sky.

"Keep watching." Yuri knew it was a rather pointless exercise. If they were being followed, there was little they could do about it. But he was at the edge of his composure. *Just a few more hours,* he thought.

They turned off the road onto another more modern road. They stayed on it until they eventually arrived at another turn-off that took them down the highway into the heart of Russia. They drove and drove till they reached their intended destination—a local airfield, made of two commercial-sized airstrips with several hangars for old and tired aircraft of various vintages. Yuri drove the truck next a large shed. Together they swiftly unloaded the truck, placing the regular cargo onto a pair of trolleys. The three men then loaded the large wooden "refrigerator" crate and a few smaller boxes onto a third trolley.

A thickset man with thinning hair emerged from out of the airport office. His hands were grimy and oily but not from working on the aircraft's hydraulics. "Yuri, my friend, I was not expecting you today."

"You know how things can turn up… unexpectedly. And travel is always good, yes?" Yuri forced a grin to appear on the left side of his mouth.

"You have everything?" the heavyset man asked.

Yuri pulled out a thick envelope filled with non-Russian currency.

"Everything is in order," he said, handing over the envelope.

"Yes, I can see." The pilot took the envelope. "Load up; we are three hours from take-off." He pointed to a well patched-up but rather aged-looking ex-military Ilyushin ll transport aircraft.

Yuri nodded. Things worked so much better in the black market. No questions and excellent service; even the planes ran on time.

Straining their muscles they began pushing their load towards the waiting plane. The Ilyushin ll was a favourite of Russian smugglers, as it held many places where they could conceal certain kinds of questionable cargo. The boxes and large containers were swiftly loaded into the massive belly of the transport. They were far from the prying eyes of any customs officials, unless they were on the payroll. *Don't you just love the new Russia? So accommodating . . . with the right incentives*, Yuri mused.

Soon the transport plane would begin its long flight towards the Balkans, and from there they would continue on by road into the heart of darkness. He smiled at the thought. He had always liked the sound of that phrase, and for the first time he felt that he truly meant it. On so many levels, this part of the world was entering the darkest of nights. His grin grew wider.

Thirty Miles from Mezen

The sun was rising. The Chechen turned his face towards its first rays. He welcomed their touch, as if they were touching his skin for the first time in his life.

And in a way it was: for the first time in his life he felt a sense of justice. Today he would punish the Russians for all the deaths they had brought to his family, to his country and people.

He was not an overly religious man, but today, knowing he would die, he felt a release, a sense of freedom. He had faced death many times, but each time he knew he would cheat it. Today he knew he would embrace it willingly. Was this what the holy warriors felt as they drove their bomb-loaded cars against the infidels?

After the loss of his family, he had stopped going to the mosque. He'd done little but bury his family and drink. A short time later he took to travelling. With the travel came a life of petty crime and violent assaults. All of which made him the perfect candidate for this mission, his recruiter had told him. The Russian and Chechen security forces had soon lost any interest in him, especially when his father had gone into hiding, while the police had little to no evidence of his crimes, as his victims were never left alive.

"The radio," a voice called out.

He snapped around so quickly, he nearly stumbled. He raced over to the car. "Is it them?" He had to know.

"Yes." The radio operator nodded and then spoke into the handset "Say again."

"God is merciful and has embraced our mission." The radio transmission lapsed into static.

"It is done." The Chechen screamed with joy and even envy. He laughed as he ordered his men to climb into the vehicles and charge the Russian blockade.

His heart was beating with pride as he saw the mushroom cloud slowly rise into the sky. His plan had worked. Sending the bomb in with just two cars well ahead of his convoy had worked.

He climbed into his car, and with a mad howl of glee, he charged straight into the hail of machine-gun fire.

The Kremlin

The president of Russia sat in his favourite chair for a minute before standing up to walk around the room once more, unable to sit for longer than a few minutes.

"How could they have detonated a nuclear bomb in Mezen when you told me we had them cornered on the road?"

"I do not know." Mikhail Kurpov shook his head. "The ones we had surrounded must have been a diversion. To let another sneak the device—"

"I do not want guesswork."

Another aide came running into the room. "We have just received a message from the terrorists, sir. They have sent a list of demands. The major one is that all Russian forces and allies in Chechnya are to leave within a week, or else they will detonate two more bombs within our cities."

"Mikhail Kurpov, you are to do everything, everything to find those damned weapons, is that understood?" The president did not even question the number of nuclear devices in the hands of the terrorists. He feared that they might well have obtained the entire stockpile.

"Yes, of course."

"Find them, find them, Mikhail." *And when we have the devices back, I will turn their land to ash. With fire and storm I will make their land bleed. I will unleash such destruction as the world has never seen. How dare they strike at our motherland?*

Do the fools truly think we will not find those weapons? We are not the soft, weak-kneed Americans or pampered Europeans afraid to get blood on our hands. We will do what must be done to get our weapons back. And then—they cannot imagine what is waiting for them.

The president of Russia grabbed the sheet of paper from the aide and quickly read the list of demands. "Mikhail, you will need to be… gentle with Chechnya," he almost whispered. The terrorists' warning was clear if anything was to happen to Chechnya.

The White House

Clayton Prescott walked into the briefing room. The senior agents of the Secret Service all stood up as he entered.

"Please, be seated. Ladies and gentlemen, I have asked you all here so we can clear the air over some recent events. I am fully aware that your job it to protect the president of the United States and that you do not regard your profession lightly.

"Some of you feel that I have taken unnecessary risks, and perhaps I have. But you need to understand; just as your job is to protect the president, my job is to protect the office of the presidency.

"So let me be perfectly clear. I will not take foolish risks, but you need to understand, that given the state of our nation at this time, the office of the presidency must take priority over my own safety.

"Now I don't expect anything to pop up that will put our interests in conflict. But I expect you all to understand the seriousness of our current situation.

"In short, the office of the presidency comes first. There can be no slur placed upon the office. In this moment of crisis there can be no doubt; nothing can be allowed to tarnish the office. I believe you are all professional enough to understand the necessity of that and accept that whatever risks I may take will be for the sake of the office." Clayton then thanked each one and quietly left the briefing room, heading to the Oval Office. He felt a little down, as if he had disappointed the agents in some way.

In a reflective mood he sat behind his desk and was considering his next meeting with the Cabinet when Jonathan came rushing into the office. "Sir, Mr. President... something has just come up."

"Yes, Jonathan."

"There has been—" He seemed lost for words. "A disaster, a catastrophe... a fight, a gunfight... I think the Army calls it a 'fire-fight.'"

"Where, what happened?"

"Texas, sir. People were marching in protest against the treatment of its governor. During the march there was shooting. We don't have many details, but there have been several fatalities. And the Army may have been involved in the shootings."

"Get me the details." Clayton sat in his chair, refusing to turn on the TV in case it was more bad news. Wondering what he could have done differently, he barely noticed as a stone-faced Ethan Campbell, his National Security Adviser, entered the Oval Office.

"Sir." His dark face looked somehow pale, devoid of colour. "We have a report... an alert warning. One of our satellites detected a large flash in a remote area of Russia. It was in a wooded area with a small population. It is possible, but we are only guessing right now, that it may have been a small nuclear detonation. The satellite was nearly out of range so we haven't much to go on. We will have confirmation shortly.

"But I have been told their alert status has not been raised, so we can assume they do not consider us to be the aggressors in this—if it was a nuclear release. Thank God."

The president of the United States simply stared at the far wall. "Sir, do you want to make a statement to the press? They'll learn of this soon enough." Ethan inquired.

Clayton remained silent.

"Sir, Mr. President?"

"No press release. I want you to get me the Russian ambassador. If it was a nuclear detonation we need to offer our condolences, our sympathy for any losses, and our assurance that we will offer whatever assistance we can. We'll wait for them to… inform the public." *When does the madness end? Are we truly lower than the lowest of beasts that we would even consider releasing this nuclear horror upon ourselves?*

Let it just be a mistake, God, let it be some stupid glitch.

Chapter 12

In defence of their huge wages CEOs often quote:

"If you only pay peanuts, you only get monkeys."

So what does that make the low wage earners? Chimps
or chumps.

—Harold Blunt

"We have Senator Holt and Senator Walker with us tonight." Glen Fox smiled with that perfect set of teeth that looked as expensive as the thousands spent on his suit.

"Thank you both for coming in tonight." He smiled again.

"My pleasure, Glen." Holt began.

"Happy to be here." Senator Walker shifted in his seat.

"Now, I would like to go back to your comments made earlier today. Do you actually consider the indictments of the governors of Texas and New Mexico to be criminal abuse of the president's authority?"

"Absolutely." Senator Walker sounded indignant. "This is a blatant attack on our freedoms. He's acting like a tyrant, and he's unleashed the military upon the American people. It's a violation of the Constitution, and he can't be allowed to get away with this."

"Then you do not hold to his accusation that these men were engaged in inappropriate behaviour... even treason?" Fox engaged in a little theatre. Prescott had made no accusations; rather, it had been the Justice Department that had laid charges against the men.

"What crime did they commit?" Senator Walker retorted. "We have no evidence of a crime being committed, apart from government accusations. They were not responsible for the deaths of some eleven Americans...

killed by the military that is under the president's command. He has to be stopped."

"Exactly. Who knows what he'll do next?" Senator Holt jumped in. "It's not merely the unjustified violence, it's the abuse of power. It's this ban on freedom of association and of movement that has to be stopped and all the other insane ideas.

"This executive abuse of power must end." Senator Holt sat ramrod-straight in his chair as he paraphrased one of his favourite ultra-conservative colleagues of old. That old Republican had brought the government close to collapse more than once in his career.

"He has gone too far. Just look at this naked attack on the people's right to bear arms." Senator Walker continued. "The people have rejected gun control."

"Yes, we'll get back to that in a moment, sir." Glen Fox sounded sincere. "But first, you're in total agreement that this talk about the two governors being involved in some scheme to leave the Union is without any substance?" Fox even looked shocked.

"Totally unproven, both men are known to be amongst some of the strongest opponents of the presid… the acting president's policies." *Well, they were now,* Holt told himself. "Glen, everyone knows that this gun registration plan of his is simply the first step in a gun confiscation scheme. Without doubt, once the guns are registered, he'll try to take them. Equally, both governors were opposed to this insane Federal Health Insurance scheme of his."

"Senator Holt is correct, Glen," Walker insisted." This Federal Health Insurance plan is totally unneeded. We have plenty of health insurance companies. Haven't we seen what a mess government involvement creates? It must be stopped. Equally, this inexcusable use of military violence in Texas cannot be allowed to stand."

"And more, Glen, the unsubstantiated claims made against these men need to be properly investigated to avoid any suggestion of illegal behaviour." Holt glanced at the other Senator. Neither wanted to actually state that Prescott had ordered the governors' arrest simply to intimidate them; it was enough merely to imply it.

Fox addressed both men. "So clearly the president has no authority to order our men and women in uniform out onto the streets?"

"Absolutely not. We now have the military running riot. To be sure, I can sympathize with our men in uniform being ordered onto the street, but they simply cannot kill American citizens. I would remind everyone that the military cannot be used to enforce or execute the law on US soil."

"So how do you propose to bring an end to all this unrest?" Glen shone his pearl whites at the two elder statesmen.

Holt did his best not to sound as if he had memorized his statement. "Unless the acting president takes immediate steps to redress our grievances, we will have no choice but to bring impeachment proceedings against him. He needs to accept that the *existing* legislature must be involved in all decision making affecting the country until a new House and Senate have been sworn in. We call upon the acting president to heed our call for the sake of the nation and to immediately return all military units to their barracks."

Senator Walker added, "Along with halting all these polices he is trying to implement unilaterally."

"Well, that's understandable." Glen Fox smiled his famous smile. "And we'll be right back after this short commercial break."

They relaxed into their seats until they were given the signal that they were about to go back on air.

"We are back with Senators Walker and Holt, discussing the events in the capital of Texas where soldiers have been accused of opening fire on American civilians." Fox stopped short, as a small voice spoke into his earpiece.

"A moment, please..." He paused in shock. "We have president Clayton Prescott on the line." He actually glanced into the camera with a look of surprise and even disbelief.

"What?" Senator Holt stammered.

"Gentlemen." A voice broke the silence. "I was listening to this interesting repartee and thought I could perhaps offer some unpolished insight. Now, you were debating—"

"The totally unjustified accusations"— Walker jumped in before Clayton could finish—"and criminal treatment of the governors of New Mexico and Texas, and the killing of Americans by the US Army. Mr. Acting President, how can you justify such criminal behaviour?"

The man was in a rush, Fox thought.

Silence was the only reply.

Fox finally spoke up. "Mr. President, are you there?" "Yes, Glen. I was just waiting for you."

"I'm not sure I understand." Glen Fox was confused.

"Of course." Clayton's words were spoken lightly, with an air of amusement. "Tell me, Senator Walker, do you believe in the principle of innocent until proven guilty?"

"Of course I do. It is a fundamental principle of our great country."

"Yet, in your eyes, the government and the military are guilty until they have proven their innocence. That, sir, is unacceptable. This totally unsubstantiated attack against the government serves you poorly, sir.

"Unlike the government and the military, both governors and the others that were indicted will face an open civilian court of law. With proper counsel they will be allowed to confront all the evidence against them. As opposed to this trial by television you and your colleagues are mounting against the military. Yes, some soldiers opened fire according to some reports. Other reports suggest they did so only after the local police were fired upon by protestors. Need I remind you that three of the dead were police officers?"

Senator Walker replied in a thick, annoyed voice, "Equally, there have been claims from some of the protestors that they were engaged in a peaceful protest when fired upon without provocation by the military." He sounded indignant that anyone would dare challenge him. "Whichever, the point remains that the military has no place being on the streets of our great nation, acting like some army of occupation."

"Tell that to Theodore Roosevelt when he had the US Army train its guns on the police and company thugs in defence of striking unionists, Senator." Clayton's voice was again light and friendly, the voice of a lecturer enlightening one of his more challenged pupils. "Let us be clear, the military can be used for certain specific circumstances within the US. Need I remind you that US Marines were sent in to quell the L.A. riots so many years ago?"

"That was… uh, those were different circumstances. This is simply unacceptable."

"Would you prefer this continuing violence, Senator? Do you want to bring America to its knees?"

"Of course not, but if the army acted inappropriately?" Senator Walker appeared to be convinced of his argument.

"I will not condemn our men and women in uniform until wrongdoing has been proven. Equally, should there be any inappropriate behaviour, then I will take full responsibility for their actions."

"Am I to understand that you will take responsibility for the army's action?" Glen Fox jumped in with a glint of victory.

"You just heard me say so. But first let us go on the principle of 'innocent until proven guilty,' shall we?" Clayton responded coldly, with a hint of disdain.

"Exactly, 'innocent till proven guilty,'" Senator Walker snapped. "The acting president cannot go around attacking our political leadership just because he disapproves of their politics."

"A moment, if you please, gentlemen," Clayton interjected. "'Acting president,' Senator?"

"I mean, sir, you have not been elected to the post. You have no mandate. At best you are a temporary president until elections can be held. I will remind you that you were not the vice president elevated to the presidency. This is an unprecedented situation that needs to be rectified." "I see. Tell me, sir, do you support the Constitution?" Clayton's voice was smooth with no hint of abrasiveness.

"Of course I do, absolutely. It is the single greatest document there is." Walker seemed to sit straighter in his chair.

"Then why are you trying to undermine it? I have been sworn into office in accordance with the Constitution, Senator. Therefore I am the president of the United States—unless you wish to alter the Constitution? Is that your plan?"

"Uh... I simply meant—"

"That you wish to reinterpret the Constitution or alter it at your convenience, Senator?" Clayton was now aiming for the man's throat.

"Of course not," the Senator barked in disbelief.

"Secondly, I made no accusations against either governor, Senator. As you are fully aware, it was the US Department of Justice. So are you accusing the Justice Department of overstepping its authority?"

"You're saying you have no involvement?" Holt's voice rang out with uneasy surprise.

"Do you really want to accuse the men and women of the Justice Department of criminal conspiracy?" Clayton hissed. "Really, Senator, I understand the need to sell the message, but must you really overdo it—and worse, attack these young men and women who serve our country in hopes of scoring a few political points? Must we create endless conspiracies and conjure enemies in every shadow?

"Yes, Justice charged them with my approval. And I would do so again, I remind your audience that these men have been accused of attempting to convince a foreign nation to take possession of parts of the United States...

This was not some referendum held by the people on the future of Texas." Clayton paused for a moment then continued.

"I am quite happy to work with the remaining House members and Senators. Indeed, I would say we *must* come together. Far too many Americans are eager to make wild, unfounded accusations. We, the government, in this time of crisis should not give them any more ammunition for their fantasies."

"That all sounds very correct and proper, sir," Holt answered. "But the fact remains that we have dead Americans."

"And the cause of their deaths will be investigated by the proper authorities—or are you about to accuse the FBI of being involved in yet another midnight conspiracy, Senator?"

"Really sir, I take offence at your tone. This is not a question of far-fetched conspiracies but rather the legitimist concerns of the people—"

"Gentlemen," Fox jumped in, "let us move on to another hot topic of discussion, the concern of many Americans over the gun debate." *The damned fool keeps shooting himself in the foot.*

"Yes," Walker declared, "this wilful and illegitimate attempt to take away people's guns is a clear violation of the Constitution—which you purport to defend. And we will not stand for it. We demand that you drop this covert buy-back scheme and do so publicly."

Silence was Clayton's response that grew longer as they waited for his reply.

"Mr. President—Are you there?"

"Yes, Mr. Fox, I was merely waiting on you."

"I'm sorry… you want me to interject something?"

"I was waiting to see if you wanted to respond. Still… Senator, just where did you get this nonsense that registering people's guns will get them confiscated? As I pointed out, sir, I cannot do so without changing the Constitution. I can only do with your permission. Are you saying that *you* will support a gun buy-back scheme, Senator?"

"Of course not," Walker sputtered, "but in the future—"

"In the future pigs may fly, That does not mean I will attach wings to them. If I contemplated doing so, it would be with the consent and approval of Congress, the Senate, and the American people. Now, are you planning to change the Constitution so you can take the people's guns away, Senator? Are you signalling your future intentions?"

"This is absurd. You are twisting everything I've said." Walker ground his teeth in frustration.

"I'm just returning the favour, Senator, treating you to a taste of your own debating tactics." Clayton sighed softly. "Let us be clear. All I propose is to deny criminals easy access to more guns by securing and registering the people's guns.

"Can we not work together to achieve such a result? And Senator, if you feel that the Constitution is insufficient, Congress is insufficient, and the Supreme Court is insufficient to the task, then offer additional safeguards. If you do not have faith in the Constitution or in Congress, then write a law to further protect the rights of law-abiding citizens, along with safeguards for their well-being. Is that really too much to ask?" *For you to do your job,* Clayton went on silently.

"That's all well and good." Senator Holt bristled at the idea that Clayton could actually be making sense. "But it will not stop the illegal guns coming in from Mexico, sir. Locking away our guns gives criminals the advantage."

"Senator, Senator." Clayton sighed. "You know full well that Mexican criminals and American criminals get their guns from American gun factories. Ask the FBI if you don't believe me; support the truth for once."

"I will not...," Walker began with anger in each word.

"May I suggest that you take a good hard look at Europe? Europe has very much the same porous borders as we do, with hundreds of thousands of undocumented refugees escaping Africa and the Middle East. Yet, Senator, where are the thirty thousand Europeans killed by legal and illegal guns? For all their open borders, they do not have a thousand dead children due to guns coming from Africa.

"Why?" Clayton hammered away. "Could it be that the handful of guns smuggled into Europe are not the problem? Rather it is America's ridiculous lack of domestic regulations that are the problem, our refusal to take guns seriously."

Now Holt jumped in, hoping to add his weight to the debate. "You are avoiding the real issue..."

Clayton almost kept the sarcasm out of his tone. "That, unlike America, without spending billions on securing its borders, Europe doesn't have a massive influx of military style weapons?"

"No, no . . . that's not what I mean. That—" Senator Holt stopped to begin again. "We need to get the economy up and running by cutting the budget and not waste time on some smoke-and-mirror issues you have raised to hide your failure to act."

"'Smoke and mirrors' Senator?" There was a moment of hesitation by the president.

"What else would you call the death penalty for drug dealers, the gun confiscation plan, and worse, this ridiculous Federal Health Insurance? Don't we have enough insurance companies? Haven't you learned anything from that last disaster when the government tried to interfere with health care?"

"Senator, the Federal Health Insurance scheme is to rectify the failure of both government and the marketplace in reducing costs," Clayton answered with some impatience.

"Then you accept that the Democrats' Affordable Health Care Act was a disaster?" Holt thought he was finally getting somewhere.

"As great as the Republican 'replacement.' How is it going by the way?" Clayton snorted and then chuckled in contempt. "I totally accept that the Republicans have done an outstanding job of sabotaging health care for the poor at every stage."

"That is a bald-faced lie. They were trying to save the public from a socialist health care system."

"Along with denying millions of Americans any level of decent health care, Senator. But let's stop this misinformation campaign. The Federal Health Insurance scheme will have only one purpose, and that is to reduce costs. The FHI will go into competition, genuine competition with the insurance companies—and if it provides better service and reduces costs, what's wrong with that?"

"Nothing, if it were true, but you have no evidence to support your claim, it will probably only raise the price of health through administration costs. This is just a despicable, underhanded act to support your socialist agenda."

"One minute it's 'smoke and mirrors,' and the next its some kind of 'socialist agenda'? Must we really politicize every issue, Senator? These issues are too vital to our national interest. Consider the damage we inflict on this country by not working together."

Was he pleading with Holt? Glen Fox thought he had heard a faint note of desperation in his voice.

"Don't try to avoid the issue," Senator Holt snapped at Clayton. "We need to make major cuts in expenditure."

Clayton sighed. "When Congress is reinstated, I will happily push for cuts in wasteful expenditure."

"So you say, but in the meantime you want to create two giant bureaucracies, enlarging the federal government even more. We need to cut the budget and reduce the size of government." Holt believed he was on solid ground.

"Really, Senator, why do you continue to spout such discredited views? It's not the size of government that should be the issue. What matters is how efficient it is.

"The modern governments of today cannot be the fossils of yesterday. They must be imaginative in reducing waste, in supporting safe and sustainable production. The government does not have to be a roadblock; it can be a springboard."

"And you will achieve this by putting a few solar panels on rooftops and setting up some third-rate health insurance scheme?"

"They can be the proof of a new era in government commitment to this country—an era of service to the community's needs and a more responsible and efficient government." Clayton paused, to draw them in.

"Think of the billions in waste we could save. There is so much the government can achieve, has achieved. I would remind people that it was the government that created the technology that built the Internet." *Although that hasn't stopped the Internet companies from complaining about government "interference" while the tech companies engage in some of the most elaborate tax avoidance schemes going.*

"Gentlemen, any sane economist will tell you improving the government's performance can be one of the best ways to reduce the size of government, not by cutting vital services but by improving them." *Just why am I wasting my breath stating the bloody obvious?* Clayton wondered. *Can they really be this blind?*

"The government can do a lot if it gets out of the business of doing nothing." *More to the point, if Congress gets out of the business of undermining good governance,* Clayton wanted to shout but felt it would be imprudent.

"Consider what an efficient government could achieve, especially if its aim was to make a profit. The government pours billions into universities, which make wonderful discoveries, some of which are patented. Yet just how much does the government get back from these discoveries? An efficient government, a new age government would provide excellent education so that it could profit from any discoveries."

"And just how does the welfare state create innovation, efficiency?" Senator Holt demanded with the stubbornness that had worn down many over the years. "How does wasting billions of taxpayers' dollars on pipe dreams ease the burden on those most in need?"

Silence was the reply that once again dragged on.

"Mr. President, are you there?" Fox almost sighed; this was becoming a habit.

"Yes, Glen." They heard Clayton sigh in reply. "Senator, you oppose the welfare state, you support small government?"

"Absolutely." Walker added his voice to the debate. "Splendid, then you will both join with me to cut waste?" "Absolutely." Both were a little caught by surprise but pleased.

"Then I look forward to having a broad dialogue with you to cut waste—"

"We do not need a dialogue." Walker felt they had the measure of the man now. "We know what needs to be done. We must cut spending on welfare and services to help the middle class grow."

"Indeed." *And we'll ignore the homeless, the poor, the millions in desperate need.* Clayton's heart sank. "I can see your point." They just don't give a damn.

The men on the TV gave each other a small smile of success.

"Well, we can certainly cut the size of the IRS by removing loopholes and tax avoidance schemes that require so much manpower to police." *Choke on that, you bitches,* Clayton fumed in silent anger. He knew he was playing them now, but their refusal to even consider his offer was frustrating.

The bright faces on TV suddenly paled.

"Talk, this is all talk. We need to cut spending and red tape; that's the best way to force the creation of small government." Senator Holt all but shouted his insistence, saying anything that came to mind as they tried to digest what Clayton had just advocated.

"Gentlemen, we all recognize 'small government' and 'reducing red tape' as code for less government regulation, and less regulation means more corporate pollution, more poisoning of our water, land and air. Many hate red tape, but we need it.

"We must face reality," Clayton boldly declared. "We need 'good' red tape unless Americans want BP to dump another million tonnes of crude into the Gulf of Mexico. Or unless we want to allow another American city to poison its citizens by polluting their drinking water with lead. How many more dead streams and rivers do you want to create, Senator?

"It may be all right for someone living on the fortieth floor of a New York apartment to drink sparkling bottled water at a hundred dollars a glass. But what about those who must drink out of the tap?" Clayton paused as if he had sighed in regret. "Do we really want our food, air, and water poisoned so some multinational can make another billion-dollar profit?" Clayton asked the audience.

"So your answer is a giant, bloated, unproductive government?" Holt responded with the traditional line.

"I have no problem with small government, Senator. Provided Congress enacts the toughest regulations possible that can be easily and automatically enforced, with massive criminal fines and punishments. That's the only way corporate America will respect the environment and the people's health… which Congress seems more than happy to ignore. We must all keep in mind that if we have a government that is too weak, then it cannot carry out its functions. To quote Andrew Becket;

'The weaker the government, the greater the abuse inflicted upon the weak and those unable to defend themselves.'

You would do well to remember that." Clayton scolded them as if they were naughty schoolboys.

"Is that how you intend to justify increasing the size of government?" Holt brushed aside every word Clayton had so far uttered. "Do you deny that this gun registration scheme will only increase the size of government?" "Probably in the short term, but in the long term it can cut government expenditure in dealing with the costs associated with gun violence. The hospital costs alone would be worth it."

"More talk, promises that will never be kept." Senator Holt repeated himself with some concern that Clayton could win over the audience. "I want to know, what will you offer to reduce expenditure that we can all agree upon?"

"I can assure everyone that I am in full agreement with the reduction in wasteful expenditure, Senator."

"Then declare your plans here and now." Holt turned up the heat. "This is hardly the time or place. Right now we need to concentrate on getting this country back on its feet."

"No, this is the right time. Tell the American people where you will cut expenditure." Holt hoped he could get Clayton to commit himself.

"Seriously Senator, must I remind you of the procedures involved? I do not dictate expenditures or write the laws. We have a consultative process, as you are fully aware." There was an angry edge to his words as if frustrated by Holt's stubbornness.

"The public have a right to know your views on this matter. I would remind you, sir, as you did not declare your position prior to taking the presidency; many have no idea what you stand for. This is the opportunity to tell the people. You must have some idea of what cuts you would like to make. You don't have to present anything detailed."

There was a momentary pause, when Holt thought he had won.

"Very well, Senator, since you insist," Clayton replied.

Fox felt a twitch; he was a good judge of men. That was why he preferred the company of men.

And the pitch in Clayton's tone had changed suddenly—for the worse, he thought.

"We can cut military spending if all nuclear states reduce their nuclear arsenal by 20 per cent, saving billions.

"Also, we can cut farm support to multi-billion dollar agribusinesses while still giving help to small family-owned farms."

Senator Holt jumped in before Fox had a chance to speak. "Wait one minute, sir. We can't just undermine our defence; that's insane."

"Really, Senator. Our security would not be threatened by a reduction of 20 per cent by *all* states, not just us but Russia, China, India, Pakistan, Britain, and France. Just consider the benefits, the millions we would save in maintenance costs alone. Then there is the added bonus that we could use the reduction of our stockpiles to encourage other states not to go down the nuclear arms route." Clayton's voice no longer held that small note of congeniality.

"You want to disarm America?" Holt sounded affronted.

"Senator, do you require a hearing aid?" Clayton's voice sound concerned for the man's health.

"What?"

"I asked if you were deaf, Senator. I can only assume you're deaf since I said a 20 per cent reduction. That will still leave us with thousands of warheads. Then we have the elephant in the room: the trillions the government gives to the pharmaceutical companies in handouts—"

"Don't talk nonsense," Holt barked. "We don't give money to the pharmaceutical companies."

"Funny, I'm sure you were there when legislation was passed prohibiting the government, the largest buyer of drugs, from bargaining with the drug companies over the price of the drugs. Just how many billions did that bit of legislation cost the taxpayers, Senator? How many billions could we have cut from the budget if the government had been allowed to bargain with drug companies over the cost of their drugs?" Clayton's accusation dripped from each word.

"Developing a new drug costs the American pharmaceutical companies many millions in research," Holt replied. "It's only right that we encourage development of new drugs, which have saved millions of lives."

"And wasn't it fortuitous that you and your friends in Congress were there to handsomely compensate your friends in the drug industry . . .

"While Europeans can pay one dollar a pill, we in the good old USA get to pay one hundred a pill. Well done, Senator." Clayton's silky voice filled the room.

"They still need to spend millions in research," Holt persisted.

"Funny, I always thought we patented drugs to ensure a healthy return on their investments. Or are you saying that the companies are not satisfied with the billions they are currently making each year, Senator?" *How many times do you have to repeat yourself before they listen?* He remembered his argument with the white-haired Dr. Tenwood-Green.

"Now," Clayton continued, "we go to the biggest measure: tax reform, to remove all the loopholes for the wealthy, which will add billions to the budget."

"There, you see," Senator Walker erupted. "More attacks against the wealthy, the very people who have built this country. You talk of unifying the country, yet here you are attacking the very people who have built this country. Do you want to start a class war?"

"It's a bit late. The wealthy have been engaged in class warfare against the poor for centuries. Must I remind you of the two thousand years of brutal oppression by the ruling classes? Or should I simply remind you of the early days of the motorcar industry in America with its bloody battles between owners and employees? I must say, your lack of knowledge on this matter is… disappointing."

"None of this changes the facts that the country is in ruins," Senator Holt resumed, "and all you are doing is fiddling with gun confiscations and some insane socialist health care instead of getting the country on its feet. We need to reduce the interference of the government and cut the size of a bloated bureaucracy. My party has long argued that—"

"That the rich should avoid paying their dues?" Clayton cut him off. "Unlike you, the public knows that it often the wealthy that create new industries, which in turn create jobs. Not that you would believe that." "Oh, no, Senator. I agree, the wealthy have created millions of jobs."

Clayton's agreement caught everyone by surprise. "They have been creating millions of jobs in China, Asia, and Africa, just not here in America. My fellow Americans, where do you think China got its seed money from? Where did they get the money to build all those new factories years ago? Think about it: if you had ten billion, would you invest in America and get a 2 per cent return or invest in China and get a 10 per cent return? The mega-rich are indeed investing in new jobs—all over the world, but not in America."

"That is a scandalous lie," insisted Senator Walker; "everyone knows that corporate America is one of our largest creators of jobs."

"So where are the jobs, Senator? During the global financial crisis, the top 1 per cent doubled their wealth. Just how many new jobs did their wealth create back then? How many factories are your wealthy friends building right now?

"It's the economy not the rich that create jobs in the US."

"Mr. President, that is more than enough." Senator Walker went on the offensive. "You know it's not as simple as building a few factories. The economy is complex, with many forces and demands."

"Here's a question for your audience, Glen. Who exactly has been trying to create, to stimulate job growth? Who do you see trying to stimulate the economy, the capitalists of Wall Street or your government?"

There was a moment of silence.

"And we are back to empty promises and lies," Senator Holt resumed. "As if this federal health scheme isn't some socialist attempt to nationalize health care; as if your registration programme isn't about the confiscation of guns."

"Senator Holt, for the last time, there is no plan to confiscation any firearms."

"Prove it. Prove that no one will have their guns stolen." Holt was becoming more red-faced by the moment.

"Senator, I have already stated the facts."

"But you cannot guarantee that a future government won't use the gun register to steal the American people's guns." Again Holt ignored everything Clayton had already stated on the subject.

"What more can I offer? What else is there…? Very well," Clayton growled. "Tomorrow I will announce that the government will open negotiations with German and Italian gun companies to buy in bulk, and thus, if all goes well, the government will sell their weapons at half the going price in the USA.

"To all gun owners: within three months you will be able to buy the finest precision-made guns from Germany, the finest handcrafted Italian guns, at around half the current price."

"You can't," Holt exploded.

"Why not?" Clayton fired back.

"We can't," Holt repeated, in a near panic.

"And why not? Isn't that the proof you wanted to prove that this government isn't anti-guns?"

Holt looked from Walker to Fox and then back again. The TV audience was given the rare sight of two powerful senators and an even more powerful TV announcer looking confused and stumped.

"We have to consider the… all the possible ramifications," Holt stammered.

"Seriously, Senator, what possible ramifications are there? It's a simple purchase of goods by the government to be resold to the public. I'm sure even you can manage it."

"We have to consider the… quality, and the—possible economic ramifications." Holt was getting a little flustered by now.

"What 'economic ramifications' do you mean?" Clayton's voice sneered. "Are you worried about the possible loss of profits for the American gun industry?"

"We have to take a number of factors into consideration, consider the jobs we could lose," Holt babbled.

"I thought you would be delighted, Senator. If I can sell a product at a cheaper price, what's wrong with that?" Clayton sounded shocked. "Well, we can see where you stand when it comes to cheaper fire arms." Clayton allowed a moment for Holt's reply to be exposed as the nonsense it was. "But what will millions of Americans think of the benefits of cheaper firearms? Indeed… thank you for the idea, Senator." Clayton's silky hiss sent yet another shiver down their spines.

Now, what was Prescott up to? Walker glanced at Holt. This was turning into a disaster.

"It just hit me that I've been thinking small. Why should we limit ourselves to firearms? When the Federal Health Insurance scheme is up and running, I will instruct it to open negotiations with foreign pharmaceutical companies. By negotiating the price and buying in bulk, the scheme can buy drugs cheaply and then pass them on to the federal government at a massive discount, saving the federal government and thus the taxpayers billions. Do you hear me, *sir*?" At the final word they visibly paled. But it was more from the shock of what his words conveyed. This was a nightmare come true.

"None of this will work." Holt was almost pleading. "Private enterprise is what has built this country."

"And is now destroying the nation we love. Our great land was built on competition, not on monopolies and cartels. If we are to regain our true stature, we need to stand up and reintroduce competition, not crumple beneath the weight of giant monopolies. We need to stand up against the power of the monopoly, a threat as great as Communism was in its day. Indeed, one could argue they are one and the same.

"And it is now abundantly clear to me that only the government can supply the balance—can reintroduce competition. Only the government has the power to stand up to the cartels and monopolies, to fight for the people's rights to a decent standard of living."

Clayton cleared his throat. "I phoned in hoping that we could reach a broad agreement, to overcome our minor disputes and to work together. You know, 'If you're not part of the solution, then you're part of the problem.' That's why I believed it was so important that we come together, to find solutions.

"And what is your response, gentlemen? To stay in bed with the death merchants, the drug pimps, the cartels? Or stand against the very people who elected you to your office? Quite frankly, I am tired of this continuous opposition from the dregs of a once-noble Congress and Senate.

"Even worse, I am very disappointed with you, Glen." Fox was startled. "What?"

"I paused a number of times to give you the opportunity to correct these... individuals. To stand up and demand that they tell the truth, not shout their lies. But not, you allowed them to lie and lie and lie. I should have expected nothing better from these privileged fat cats who have systematically undermined our nation for decades but I held higher hopes from you."

"How dare you?" Holt bellowed. "I am as patriotic as anyone... I have always stood for the ordinary citizen!"

"That is a slanderous accusation," Walker chimed in. "We have always worked for our fellow citizens—"

"Really? How much are you worth, Senator Holt? Is it eight or nine hundred million? You, Senator Walker, what is your family's worth? Two or is it three billion? And you represent the 'common' man? Don't make me laugh. You haven't represented anyone but the wealthy for decades."

"I don't see how that affects anything, sir," Glen Fox protested. "And just how much do you make a year, Glen? Is it fifty thousand or a couple million? Your pay-packet doesn't influence you?"

Clayton lowered his voice. "My fellow Americans, I am sick of the lies. I expected no better from these men of wealth—although I hoped the media might have taken to heart what I've asked of them. But no, their allegiance has always been to the money.

"Well the days of the cartels and monopolies must end. Millions of Americans are out of work, lining up to get food stamps, and all your 'representatives' can do is defend big business..."

"I will not stand for such accusations," barked Senator Holt.

"It's time for a real change," Clayton ploughed on. "I say it's time for real democracy in our land. Thus I encourage every loyal American to demand that a nationwide referendum be held, at the time of the next congressional elections. This referendum will give the people the power to dissolve the House and Senate for up to two years."

That truly silenced the senators.

"Removing the House and Congress this will allow an interim body to repair our nation's capital. This interim body—let's call it a presidential cabinet or council—will be mandated to fix the system itself... to deal with such matters as the filibuster, pork barrelling, and the Gerrymander. It will put limits and conditions on lobbying by special interest groups. It will ban the legalized corruption that is endemic in our government.

"It will enact laws that will allow *all* Americans, including all Democrats"—he couldn't use the word *nigger* in a public forum—"to vote without interference.

"It will deal with all the violations Congress has visited upon the people's rights. There will be no more leaving government positions vacant for an indefinite time. When a president nominates a candidate for a given office, the Congress will have three months to endorse or reject the nominee. If the Congress refuses to act in the appointed time, then the nominee is automatically appointed." Clayton knew he had well over two hundred government positions vacant due to the former Congress's refusal to carry out its duties.

"We'll fix government so that it will work for all Americans once more and not just the oligarchs.

"My fellow Americans, it is time to save our government… even if we have to dissolve it."

You could have heard a cockroach scuttling across the floor.

Chapter 13

I don't think Obama was a Muslim.

But with his total failure over Ukraine and Syria, Putin owed him the Order of Lenin.

—Brandon Keel

Inside the Oval Office

"Mr. President." FBI Director Arnold Shaw looked straight at Prescott, ignoring the presence of General MacAdams and the rest of the Joint Chiefs. "The situation has escalated to all-out war. The murder of the newly selected Senator and the naked threats against a number of nominees has proven that, beyond doubt.

"These attacks and the shooting of nine bankers and senior NRA members within the last two days have raised the violence to an entirely new level. It's no longer an upsurge of social unrest; it's a planned, organized attack on the government and society."

"We have shootings every day of the week, Director." General MacAdams glanced at Shaw with mild disapproval. "I would remind you that we have so many guns on the street, it could have been any nut-job." "The assassination of Senator Meriweather was with a single shot from a Special Forces–type sniper rifle. We believe the sniper was some 850

metres away." Shaw pointed out.

"That's quite a shot." Clayton agreed with the director.

"Not so much nowadays, sir," General MacAdams told the president. "They recently brought out a computer aiming system you can attach to a rifle. With that, any hapless idiot can become a competent shooter. Any competent shooter becomes a world-class sniper."

The general looked Shaw in the eyes. "Eight hundred and fifty metres, a thousand metres—better get used to it, Director. Soon anyone with a grievance will be able to reach out and pop your head like a zit at a thousand metres." *Hope the politicians have plenty of body armour, not that it'll help.*

"If the system is still new, can you track the individuals involved?" Clayton asked the general.

"As I understand it, a large number were stolen from a storehouse recently." The general shook his head in defeat. "There is quite a massive black market for that kind of tech."

"Whatever for?" Clayton wondered aloud with sarcasm dripping from each word. "Just wonderful, is there anything in this country that we can secure?" Clayton asked aloud.

The men replied with stone faced silence.

"Simply marvellous; do continue with your good news." Clayton nodded to Director Shaw.

"Yes sir, the latest two NRA members shot were similarly targeted with long-range rifles, as if they were being hunted." Shaw deliberately avoided looking at MacAdams. "The NRA is furious over this. They want action or they are threatening to take action themselves."

"Now they want gun control?" Clayton looked at Director Shaw as if genuinely surprised.

"They are concerned for their senior members, sir."

"Just not their rank and file," Clayton sniped. "Just how organized are they?"

"Uh… the attack on the Senator-designate was planned in detail. They had five instantaneous riots, drawing away law enforcement. Allowing a small group of terrorists to enter the building where the governor was officially endorsing Mr. Kelly. The terrorists broke in, and after a swift altercation, they told both to resign. The attackers threatened to hang both if they didn't."

MacAdams spoke up. "I don't think it was that serious, Director. From what I've been told, a crowd of protesters got into a scuffle with the governor and the nominee. There was a lot of shouting and name calling and some pushing. Yes, there were threats made, unacceptable threats as that, but hardly a hard-core anarchist attack."

"The situation is getting far more serious than you seem to think, General. We have several senatorial designees being threatened against accepting their nominations. Along with half a dozen governors who have received death threats unless they select individuals who pass the anarchists' criteria. They need to be heads of charities, human rights lawyers, or social justice activists. They want bleeding-heart liberals with social agendas."

"I see; no politicians wanted," Clayton declared. "Inexcusable, I agree. But hardly a slide into all-out anarchy, I would think. I understand that the street-level violence has almost plateaued." The president seemed relaxed by the latest news reports.

"That's because the street violence was mostly for show, sir. At the time we believed the anarchists were simply indulging in violence and mindless destruction; we now know differently. Although some houses were owned, a number were unoccupied homes; even the small shops and local buildings that were torched were mostly empty." There were a lot of empty house in America.

"That explains, to some extent, the lack of public outrage. Most people weren't losing their homes. But now the anarchists have shown their true agenda: they are now looting large shopping centres, attacking banks and other industries—and targeting prominent individuals for assassination. This is a far cry from just burning down empty houses and trashing cars. This is class warfare. Sir, the local FBI branches are already being hammered with demands from local authorities."

"I was unaware the FBI answered to local officials," Clayton commented.

"Of course we don't, sir. But we need a serious course of action, a stronger response. And we need the army to stop coddling the protestors." He glanced at the seated general. "It's almost as if they were encouraging the violence. The other day the army was running festivals with games for children and… singing."

"Which may well be the explanation for the slowing down of street violence, wouldn't you say, Director?" General MacAdams was not impressed with the implications.

"Sir, a stronger response is needed. It's time to consider more extreme measures." Shaw sounded determined.

"No, we do not," Clayton answered. "We will do nothing to give the anarchists legitimacy, is that understood, Director? The military is doing an excellent job; I can't praise them highly enough. They are keeping the majority of the marches peaceful, and if that means supplying hot sausages and burgers with a Coke on the side, all the better. This is not the time to aggravate the situation." He was losing patience with Shaw's attitude.

"Sir, they… senior figures in the community are concerned for their safety."

"Too bad they didn't consider that years ago. A little homespun charity would have gone a long way. Still, if they want more protection, they can hire more private security. They had been more than happy with that arrangement, so why change now?" To Clayton it seemed that far too many of the wealthy were happier to pay for their own security rather than put their hands in their pockets to help pay for the extra police the country so desperately needed.

Still, personal protection was so superior to the generic service the police offered.

"I will not use 'extreme measures,' Director. Thank you for your time." *You want to resign, feel free. Hopefully I can find someone with some smarts. The damned zoo must have at least one monkey they can give me.*

The director made his excuses and left. General MacAdams had turned to the president. "Mr. President, your support is appreciated. But we are concerned that we are lacking a coherent strategy. If the current level of violence were to escalate once more, there could be serious consequences."

"Why do you think people need guns, General?" Clayton asked. "To defend themselves, sir."

"Wrong, normally they need them to kill niggers, the homeless, the poor, and their children. But today they need 'em to kill American soldiers, General. Remember that; you're all part of an insidious conspiracy to take over the government."

The general snorted in contempt at the mere idea.

"Trust me, General, there are plenty of redneck trash eager to prove themselves right. And I will not allow traitors to murder American soldiers while calling themselves patriots. We need to ride it out; if we start applying any kind of pressure, this could blow up in our faces."

Clayton studied the general's face and concluded that he wasn't convinced. "General, I am aware that there have been presidents who were too afraid to act, timid creatures unable or unwilling to employ the power of the presidency when needed. And thus they have cost America greatly. Yet, ironically, this is the one of the few instances when taking strong measures is actually counterproductive. I assure you it is not fear that prevents me from being more forceful. Rather, we must have the courage to believe we can overcome these difficulties in the long run."

A Corridor inside the White House.

"And that's why I was late," Jonathan insisted.

"You really expect me to believe that?" Brandon Keel answered as they walked down the long corridor.

"Yes, because I like making up ridiculous stories about wine bottles, angry waiters, and whipped cream. You can give me the benefit of the doubt, you know."

"Never happen."

"Not today, that's for sure."

"How could he?" Keel spat out as he shook his head.

"Who?" Jonathan glanced over to Brandon.

"I thought he was anti-gun." Brandon growled in frustration, feeling betrayed. "How could Prescott support the gun industry? It's a disaster." "I'm not so sure," Jonathan responded as they continued down the corridor. "When you think about it, by buying guns from overseas and selling them at a reduced price, we will be cutting the profits of the gun manufacturers in the US. And without the millions they give to the gun groups they won't have the same influence."

"But we'll still have a mountain of guns out on the streets," Keel protested.

"Yeah, but in a way the president's already answered that. If we are smart, this could actually be a brilliant move. The guns the government sells can all be registered into his federal database. And over time that may convince the public that the government isn't out to confiscate their guns." "I don't know that sounds almost too devious—even diabolical."

Especially when you consider the way the president blow up last night.

"Yeah, well… that doesn't mean we can't take advantage of the situation. Come on, this could work to our advantage."

"I don't know. You really think this could achieve something worthwhile?" There was a glimmer of hope in Keel's voice.

"No money equates to little or nil political leverage." He grinned at Keel. They both knew how the Washington political system worked.

"It just seems as if he's out of control," Keel conceded.

"Yeah, I know. That worried me at first. But then I thought—you know, we can still work with this."

"Okay, but what if he loses it totally, blows up again?" What if the pressure was getting to him? The thought of an out of control president was not something he wanted to contemplate.

"There is that, but he still made sense even if he seems a little unsteady. I think we're only just beginning to see the real man." *Do we really know the man?* Jonathan wondered as both men walk in silence. "Who knows? This could be the very thing we need to take on the gun industry."

"I don't know, there are a lot of jobs involved." Keel scratched his ear.

Jobs always seemed to dictate policy.

"Screw them. Do they care how much blood is on their hands? I don't know who's worse, the drug pushers or the death merchants. We should just hang the lot."

Keel smiled. "You've been listening to the president again."

"Crazy or not, he actually makes sense. For all the wild outbursts, he's still got it together." Jonathan hoped so, at least. "Anyway, what's the latest from Russia?" He wanted to change the subject.

"Martial law continues, more crackdowns on the opposition. The 'Tsar' rules with an iron fist."

"Well, that's one bastard they'll have to carry out feet first." Jonathan nodded to himself. "So how many are confirmed dead?"

"Twenty-eight hundred confirmed dead, but they have a very long way to go… especially when you'll never find the body. The real figure may never be acknowledged."

"Is there anything on the terrorists?" Jonathan felt sick in his stomach. "No, still blaming the Islamists. No one's taking the credit. Truth is, no one outside of Russia really knows. Heard some chatter that the 'Tsar'

himself had done it to stay in power."

"He wouldn't. No one could be that ruthless—"

"Yeah, right," Keel replied in a heavily sarcastic voice; clearly he thought differently. "Look, I can't go into it." There were security clearances to be considered, even within the White House. "Look, I'll put it this way; there are some journalists—and even a good number of Russians—who believe that a series of terrorist bombings in Russia, prior to 'Tsar' Pootin's election, were actually carried out by operatives of their old KGB secret police and not the Chechen fighters."

"How did they work that out?"

"Some KGB, re-named FSB agents were caught setting a bomb in an apartment block, using the same military-grade explosives that were used in the other bombings. But it was covered up as some training exercise…

as if they actually needed to conduct exercises with real explosives in the middle of an undeclared war." Keel scoffed at the absurdity.

"But why would they do something like that?" Jonathan asked, frankly puzzled.

"The powers in Russia knew they couldn't get their man Pootin into power unless they had a war, so they provided Russia with one."

"Hang on… if some portion of the Russian public believed he was responsible, then how did he get voted in?" Jonathan was having trouble believing what he had heard.

"The Russian mentality, the state comes first. Don't look so shocked." Keel snorted. "It's a question of where your loyalties lie."

"I never thought about it like that. Lucky we're not that close-minded." "We're worse," Keel cut in. "You know, the president does make sense. Remember that interview he gave a few days back? How so many Americans will believe anything negative about the USA no matter what?" "They do have some grounds for suspicion, Brandon," Jonathan stated flatly. "The CIA and NSA haven't exactly covered themselves in glory these last few decades."

"You mean those hackers from last year? The ones that dumped classified documents onto the Web? All they did was prove we were following the rules."

"There were others, before them, that Snowden guy who exposed NSA meta-data collection inside the US."

"Come on, that was a setup." Keel waved the allegation away.

"The NSA wasn't collecting the public's meta-data?" Jonathan looked at Keel, again slack-jawed in disbelief.

"What? No, that's not what I meant." He saw the look Jonathan gave him. "You really believe that asshole had decided to tell the world about NSA data collecting because he was a conscientious objector and wasn't recruited by that old spook in the Kremlin?"

"Wait, wait. You're saying Snowden was a Russian agent?"

"Just because he was born in the US doesn't mean he wasn't a Russian asset. Look, think about it. What do you know about the guy and his work for the NSA?"

"Uh… I think he was employed as an NSA consultant for three months, on a short term contract." Jonathan tried to remember what he knew about Snowden's story.

"Okay… okay, let's go with that." Brandon allowed himself a wry grin. "And in that time he had this epiphany of conscience, right? So just when exactly did he have the time for this epiphany? Was it before or after getting the clearance to read the tonnes of classified files that he illegally acquired?" He scoffed in contempt at the idea.

"Maybe he had the clearance to read a few files," Jonathan ventured, "and that convinced him to become a whistle-blower."

"So a three month consultant gets clearance to read classified files. Just when did he get clearance, if he was just a computer nerd?" Keel retorted.

"Yeah, okay." Jonathan was caught for a moment. "But didn't Snowden later come out and say he was some kind of hard-core CIA operative or something like that? So he may have had prior exposure to the NSA?"

"So now you're telling me he wasn't a consultant but a CIA spook? And they loan out their spies on three-month contracts to rival agencies to have a good snoop around? And a rival agency would be happy with that? The NSA must really trust the CIA. And just when did the CIA admit Snowden was theirs?"

"Don't mess—" *Wait, is he messing with my head?* Jonathan suddenly realized that he simply did not know enough about all the details. The CIA would hardly admit to anything under most circumstances.

"Yeah, I am messing with you, but that's my point: you don't know half the facts… Hell, I've been leading you around by the nose." Keel stopped walking. "Look, a lot of idiots believe Snowden was a hero, others a traitor. And like you, the truth is they don't know. Because only Snowden and the Russians know what he told them.

"Forget the crap on the Internet for a minute. What did he tell the Russians in the back room? That's the sting in the tail. Say he was CIA, then that makes him a traitor, pure and simple, because he would have spilled his guts, told 'em everything he knew about American intelligence." He grinned. In a way the president was right when he criticized the media. *If you don't know the full details, then you're just a bag of hot air.*

"And, say, he was just an innocent contractor, why didn't he go to the media?" Keel paused as if collecting his thoughts. "Amazing, isn't it, that he had the spy-craft needed to download all those files without raising any suspicion, followed by a quick trip to Hong Kong. Then he jumped over into China, where we can presume he gave them a copy, and then another flight straight to Russia, all nice and smooth just as if it had all been organized. Now, why go to Russia? How did he know Russia wouldn't hand him over to the US?"

Brandon turned to face Jonathan. "Not that I'd believe anything he'd say—his word isn't worth shit. We know that for a fact; he swore a sacred oath to this country and broke it. He sold out his country, and God knows how many people were killed because of him."

"Hang on, even our government admitted no informer was killed by his leaking."

"That was because we scrambled to get them to safety. But how many lives could we have saved if those assets were still in play and providing us with intel? How many terrorist attacks could we have prevented? You ever thought about that? Worse, ten years later, how many of them could have become agents of influence? Maybe directing or influencing their national policy. Just look how much Pootin benefited by having Trump as his personal bitch."

Go easy, Jonathan told himself. "But you don't have any proof that the Russians were in it with him. You sure you're just not pissed off by all the Russian hacking on the US?"

"Isn't that the proof you want?" Keel replied. "Wouldn't they have bent over backwards to recruit Snowden? Come on, Junior, think. As they say in the movies, 'Who benefits?' Who benefited when Snowden exposed US spying on the German chancellor? Was it the American public or Russia… in Russia's efforts to split up NATO? Just how does exposing American spying on allies marry up with his concerns to protect American privacy?

"When WikiLeaks get those top secret documents about America bugging the Japanese government, who benefited? Who would benefit from any wedge between Japan and America? Was it the American public or Pootin who benefited? Russia used Snowden to humiliate America so just how did that benefit the public? Everyone spies… it's the amount of harm that you inflict on the other side that distinguishes friend from foe. That's why Snowden was a traitor. I may not have approved, but I could have accepted his argument that he did it for America if he had limited himself to exposing US monitoring of its citizens. But he didn't.

"Look, remember that time when we complained about Chinese hacking of our civilian companies and getting personal details on government employees—what response did one of them give? 'What's your problem, Uncle Sam is the biggest hacker of all.' Just how did Snowden help us protect our commercial services from Chinese spying?

"The only real winner was Pootin.

"Funny isn't it, Snowden wanted to expose NSA spying, so he goes to one of the most media repressive regimes going. You don't see any irony in that?" The murder of some twenty journalists and human rights lawyers in Putin's Russia, plus the systematic eradication of an independent media, proved that.

"Look, Snowden and WikiLeaks both hammer America, but how often did you see them condemning Russia and China's systematic violations of their people's basic rights?

"You ever seen them hammer Russia over Syria? Ukraine? How about Russian media repression… going all the way up to outright anti-Western propaganda?"

Jonathan considered Keel's words, it was accepted, even amongst elements of the media that the Russians were actively trying to split up NATO. They were known to fund a number of anti-Western, anti-NATO individuals, groups, and political parties that would serve Russia's interests within Europe itself. What was surprising was how little Russia's activities in the West were reported on by the all-knowing and "neutral" press.

For a moment he wondered if Clayton had been a little too close to the mark when he questioned the media's loyalty. *God, I hope I'm not getting paranoid.*

"You tell me, Junior, what did Snowden get out of it, a cabin in Siberia, maybe? Now what did 'Tsar Pootin' get out of it? A few cracks in NATO's wall and some personal revenge. Remember, 'Tsar Pootin' was pissed that America wasn't taking Russia seriously. We weren't treating Russia as an equal partner. Correct?"

Jonathan shrugged. "But they aren't. Russia is America's equal only in nuclear warheads." He conceded the obvious. Jonathan knew Russia was an economic basket case; only fossil fuel money was keeping it afloat and even that revenue wasn't what it used to be. "Come on, even before the crash it was a mess… With a population of a 140 million its GDP was smaller than Canada's own.

"And if the demographers are right it'll lose a third of its population by the end of the century… A *THIRD*… down to a hundred million… some great super-power. The guy couldn't be that out of touch with reality?"

Jonathan was surprised to hear Brandon chuckle. "You know, at first I thought they had used those NSA files to secretly get the big sissy, Obama, to back off from bombing Assad's regime in Syria after the dick had used his chemical weapons on his own people. Back then I still wanted to believe the sissy had balls. What a joke… I was just as bad as Pootin, denying reality. I wanted to believe the jellyfish could grow a backbone. He screwed the Iraqis, the Syrians. And, as if I needed more proof, he screwed the Ukrainians. It took me a long time to admit he was never black; he was yellow . . . all yellow. Reality is often ignored, Junior. People really do believe what they want to believe—and screw reality."

"Don't you think you're being a little harsh? After all, he really didn't have any viable options. Did he?"

"Obama had them, and with Syria he had a damn good one. If he had acted fast… in the first two years he could have told Israel to get off its ass and open up the Golan Heights for the Free Syrian Army. Sent five, seven thousand US army trainers to turn the Heights into a giant training camp, re-supply centre, make it into the opposition's command and control hub… And not one American boot on Syrian soil.

"Instead, the sissy waited years before he decided to act, by which time Islamic State and the other Islamist groups owned half of Syria. If Obama had acted right away—but no, he just had to wait and wait, while pissing himself."

Jonathan shrugged again. "That is standard foreign policy; always too little, always too late."

"That's not an excuse, God damn it. How many Syrian children died while he was cracking jokes? If he had helped bring an end to the fighting within three or four years, how different would history have turned out? Prevented all the death, destruction, the refugee flood into Europe… You have Islamic State spreading terrorism all over the world, all because of Obama. Look at all the years of misery because of his inaction. Sometimes doing nothing is worse than doing something."

"But he kept on saying they didn't know who to support—how the rebels were 'doctors, farmers, and pharmacists' who didn't have a chance in hell against the Syrian regular army. I'm sure I remember him saying that." "So?" Keel snapped. "Who the hell did he think fought the War of Independence? A bunch of twenty-year veterans of the Indian wars? He thought that the boys who fought in WWII had all served ten years in the regular army beforehand? That we had entire Marine divisions made up of twenty-year veterans of the Banana Wars earlier that century?

"And eventually the big sissy changed his tune years later, didn't he? Only by then it was too late; by then the Islamists had too much power and influence." Both knew that after sitting on the fence for years Obama had finally given approval to train Syrian rebels to battle the Islamic State. "The handful of rebels he did train weren't enough, so the loser finally got in bed with the Kurds. That pissed off Turkey so much they got in bed with Russia."

"To be fair," Jonathan pointed out, "they all had their own agendas… Turkey, Iran, Lebanon, Russia. I mean honestly, who the hell can we trust in the Middle East?

And why bring the Israelis into the picture?" He knew the Golan Heights were captured territories occupied by the Israelis.

Keel smiled the smile of sweet victory. "The Heights would have given us control, real control without interference. By having our soldiers train them, we could have cherry-picked the best and brightest for special training, picked the right people for leadership roles. Trained not just the soldiers but the people you needed to fill Obama's 'vacuum.'" *And filtered out the religious nut jobs.*

"Look, Obama kept on saying he didn't know who to support. Well, the answer was simply, you help the people who come to you for help. Look, if you're training them you have some influence—especially if you get hold of the guys with enough brains to stretch mentally and challenge their way of thinking. The Heights could have been a magnet for all the anti-Assad forces. We would have provided training, weapons, logistics… even better, we could have picked a handful we could trust to use shoulder-fired surface-to -air missiles. We could've kept a tight rein on the weapons— given out only ten or twenty missiles, and for them to get a replacement missile they'd have to return the missile's launch tube.

"Anyone with a brain knew that the Free Syrian Army needed safe sanctuaries… just as they knew that the resistance forces needed real support, not that fairy-light bullshit the spineless jellyfish was spouting. It's like the pinheads in the Pentagon never learned a single thing from 'Nam." He cursed, knowing full well that during the Vietnam War the VC/NVA had safe havens in Cambodia where they could go to rest, rearm and prepare for the next battle.

"And the cherry on the cake," he went on. "We could have done it right by turning them into real soldiers. We could have trained entire companies at once, train them to operate in even larger groups."

"And politically, would the Israelis have gone along?" Jonathan decided to address his concerns over Israeli involvement.

"If they were smart, they would have begged us. Think about it, they would have been seen as friends to the people of Syria. On top of that, Israel could have said, if the Free Syrian Army frees Syria and turns it into a non-Islamic democracy, then Israel would hand over the Golan Heights. Just think of the goodwill and political ramifications of such an act upon a liberal Syria! We would have won on so many fronts… political, ideologically.

"Instead, the sissy all but handed Syria to Pootin. For all the talk about peace and political solutions, when the sissy left office, what had he achieved? You know, he screwed up supporting the rebels so badly that I thought he wanted them to fail… hoping that would silence his critics."

"Come on, you're joking, right?" Jonathan came back, shocked again. "Just look at that crap he came up with. The rebels could fight ISIS, but they were to leave Assad alone. Shit, everyone knew Assad was the real problem."

"Well, what about the Ukraine? What could he have done without escalating matters?"

"Could have given Ukraine one or two hundred drones. Twenty armed with air-to-ground missiles to take out any Russian missile sites; the rest could have been armed with anti-armour missiles—and again without a single pair of American boots on the ground. The biggest problem would have been training the Ukrainian pilots."

"A lot of people feared the consequences if we had escalated the situation."

"Crap. Russia and the US have been butting heads for decades, and how many times have we gone to war? We don't 'accidentally' go to war just because we've had an 'incident.' When we supplied those surface-to-air Stinger missiles to the Afghan resistance during Russia's occupation of Afghanistan, did Russia bomb America? When Turkey shot down the Russian bomber in 2015, did Russia bomb Turkey in retaliation?

"Think it out, what could Russia have done if we had given the Ukraine a few drones? Sent in its own fighter jets, its army, exposing its lies of non-interference to the world? Force the Europeans to grow a spine and impose real sanctions?"

"Even so, Obama was afraid of being dragged into the conflict," Jonathan persisted.

"Look, if Obama had been dragged too far into a conflict, it would have been because *he* was too weak and pathetic to stop himself. Damn it, he was the president, the commander-in-chief. That means he had all the power he needed to extract the US army any time he wanted; remember, we're damn good at cutting and running.

"Look, I don't think Obama was a Muslim. But with his total support for Pootin over Ukraine and Syria and his sucking up to the Cuban and Vietnamese communist regimes, he deserved the 'Order of Lenin.' Maybe it's because his father was a Kenyan and not an African American, so he didn't think it was a big deal. But African Americans had fought, bled, and died in the Civil War for freedom and democracy, and there he was selling them out. What was so bloody hard about providing Ukraine with a few drones? About helping train liberal Syrians? Why is it so hard to stand up for human rights?"

"That's harsh, maybe even unfair." When considering some of the men who had sat in the Chair—shit, Nixon, Bush... and then the Trump disaster— was he really that bad? President Caine was the first one worth the effort to vote into office for decades, and look what they'd done to him. "You do realize that the power of the presidency has limitations. He couldn't just wave a magic wand. And he did promise to get America out of Iraq."

"And that means sacrificing everything we fought for? Look, I think he was compassionate… not necessarily all that honest, but he did want to do good. Even so, that doesn't mean a thing if he achieved nothing or made things worse. Look, he left a mountain of shit in the president's chair for that clown to clean up.

"Look, I'm no fan of Bush Junior, but at least he cleaned up his own mess.

"By the time Obama had entered the White House, Iraq had quietened down. Militarily we had won; between the US military 'surge' and the Sunni 'awakening' we had won, no matter how much Obama's lackeys wanted to rewrite history. The violence had died down. Al-Qaeda in Iraq was all but finished." Not that you'd believe that if you listened to the liberal media. "We had victory in our grasp and then that thug al-Maliki and Obama through it all away.

"You know the history, as the last American soldier was coming home, Iraqi president al-Maliki ordered the arrest of the Sunni vice president for running death squads. Then he let the Shiite militias run rampant, murdering any Sunni they wanted… Alienating the Sunnis and Kurds, opening the door of Islamic State… throwing away the best chance we had to establish democratic principles in Iraq, while Obama sat on his hands."

Could we have? Jonathan wondered. *Iran, Iraq, Syria, Afghanistan, Egypt… don't they all have the same obstacle? Islam. At the end of the day, isn't that the real problem? You can lead a horse to water, but that doesn't mean he'll drink. I don't know… maybe… maybe in another hundred years.* "So what could he have done to convince al-Maliki to make friends?" Jonathan had his doubts.

"Assured him we would support him. Look, al-Maliki was reported to have been afraid of a coup," Keel stated with solid conviction. "So did Obama offer to keep an armoured brigade in Iraq, not just to train the Iraqi army but as a praetorian guard to protect al-Maliki from any coup? That, plus convincing al-Maliki that he could go down in history as a giant… the father of a new Middle East if he offered the hand of friendship.

"Look… why should we endure bullies and tyrants when we could have helped at no cost to ourselves? Obama had no moral conscience, for all his fancy talk."

Jonathan gave Keel a sad smile. "You know, you really have something against him."

"Yeah, I suppose I have. But damn it, Obama offered us hope, and he turned into a bag of hot air. That was what was so frustrating. All the others, Bush, Clinton, they were politicians; no one expected anything for them, but damn it he had promised 'yes, we can.'

"If only he had a backbone. That was the most painful part. Obama could have achieved greatness. He could have been a giant, another Abraham Lincoln. If he'd had what it took to make the hard choices, if he'd had the fire to lead America instead of wallowing in indecision. It would have been hard, bloody hard, but that was the path to glory; the harder the battle, the greater the victory.

"He failed the crucible of leadership, both foreign and domestic. For all his talk of a re-set with the world, he humiliated us in the eyes of the world, he humiliated us… After the Gulf War, we were regarded as a military superpower; by the time he left office, the Russians, the Chinese, the world were laughing at us. Maybe… maybe he was a closet Muslim."

Jonathan kept his own silent counsel. He knew Keel's great-great-grandfather had died fighting in the 2rd Kansas Coloured during the American Civil War; his great-grandfather had served in WWII and his grandfather in 'Nam. His family's history had shaped him as much as his politics. He was a militant liberal. Jonathan smiled to himself. God, a fighting liberal; what next?

Then he spoke up. "I hear what you're saying. But remember, everyone argued that they saw no military solution."

"Bullshit, don't give me that. When I hear some spineless weasel say, 'I see no military solution,' I want to puke. What they are really saying is 'There is only a military solution, but we haven't got the balls to use it.'"

Jonathan stared at him. "Come on."

"No, I'm telling it straight. Just where was the negotiated solution to the conflict in Sri Lanka? The truth is, unless you win militarily, most conflicts just drag on and on. Remember Colombia and the FARC guerrillas? That went on for decades.

"The Balkans achieved peace through the barrel of a gun.

"Pootin got his way in Syria by using a military solution. Look, real negotiations began when Russia and Iran had won military supremacy in Syria. They put boots on the ground. While Obama sat and twiddled his thumbs, he really earned his 'Order of Lenin' that day.

"Putin was a damn sight more a patriot than Obama ever was. "Look, political solutions work when enough military pressure forces one or both sides to the negotiating table. Or when both sides realize they can't win militarily. It's when you run out of steam—that's when you start negotiating, or when you're losing.

"Here's reality for you, if you have the power and the will, then a military solution trumps the negotiated solution, no matter what the politicians tell you. All you need is to be ruthless and have the manpower. Look at 'Nam in 1975. The twenty-two North Vietnam Army divisions that invaded South Vietnam proved that." Brandon pinched the bridge of his nose.

"Look, Jon, I'm not even talking about boots on the ground. The Syrians were prepared to fight; that was the greatest betrayal. We didn't start the Syrian uprising; we didn't cause the uprising. It was the people. Why couldn't we have helped the people of Syria?"

"Maybe military assistance was viable," Jonathan noted. "But why should it always be the US? Where was Europe? After the Paris attacks in 2016, what did they do? The French president eventually declared 'war' and sent a few extra planes to bomb Syria. Did they send even one combat brigade of the French Foreign Legion?" Jonathan was frankly unhappy with Keel's view.

"I'm not saying everything should be on America's shoulders." "Then you agree that Europe, the Western world failed? Europe sold out the Ukraine, Georgia, and all the other bits of Europe that Russia swallowed because they didn't have the balls. Hell, how many cock-sucking Europeans made excuses for Russia's naked aggression against Ukraine? Plenty of them argued that Russia felt threatened—the big superpower with thousands of nukes felt threatened by tiny Georgia. Then 'warmongering' Ukraine was a threat, so Russia 'had to' undermine it for its own defence. They're so full of shit.

"Brandon, how many European cocksuckers supported Putin's Syrian involvement?" Jonathan looked him squarely in the eyes. "You can't blame Obama for the pissants of Europe, afraid of their own shadow, hiding behind fortress Europe." Not that it was much of a fortress when millions of refugees came flooding in. They had soon regretted doing nothing, pissants.

"Hell, how many of 'em argued that dictators like Saddam and Assad should be left in power to stop Islamic fundamentalism?" Jonathan hammered away. "Love to hear them say that if they actually lived under Assad… should give 'em a one-way ticket to North Korea." Smug intellectual ass-wipes sitting safely in the West, thought Jonathan with contempt.

"Look, they piss me off as well," Keel snapped and then dropped his voice. "But what the hell do we stand for if we can't even help people fighting for their own freedom?" He spoke with growing bitterness. "And he was supposed to be the leader of the free world."

"And when has any American president been the leader of the Middle East?" Jonathan shot back. "Just look at all our 'allies' in the Middle-East, and name one you can trust. Pakistan told us they were our best friend ever—true allies to the very end, even as they armed and trained the Taliban to kill American soldiers. You can trust Afghans as long as you don't turn your back on them. At least that way they won't shoot you in the back." They had sure as hell shot enough American soldiers in the back.

"Even now," he went on, "you think America can trust the Iraqi government to support real democracy? Not while it's in bed with Iran. Saudi Arabia is acknowledged as the biggest funder of fundamentalist Islam… spelt terrorism… in the world. You know they provided the seed money for Islamic State in Syria. Or are you going to tell me it was the Bank of London?

"Iran is one of the main supporters of terrorist groups.

"The Turkeys of Turkey won't lift a finger to help us unless it helps them. Remember how they 'helped' us by killing Kurds who were fighting the Islamic State? That was real helpful. Hell, the moment they got an Islamic government, they started cracking down on freedom of speech, on democracy. How much Turkish blood has the government got on its hands? It doesn't end there; each Egyptian government is as two-faced as the last. They all have their own agendas.

"The way I see it we have no friends in the Middle East, and that includes Israel. We have no allies worth a damn. About the only people I have time for are the Kurds." Jonathan had long held sympathy for them, denied a land of their own. While the Muslim world ranted and raved about their Palestinian brothers' enslavement under the Israel jackboot, not a word of sympathy from them for their 'brother' Kurds. In that Prescott, was right: who isn't a hypocrite?

"And are our Western allies any better?" Jonathan hammered away. "You want to tell me the Germans, French, Japanese don't spy on us? They don't act in their own interest? When I was a kid, I still remember when several Senators laid into a Sony player with sledgehammers. You remember why? Because Sony had sold high-tech propeller blades to the Russians so they could use them on their subs, making it that much harder for us to track them.

Just after World War Two the Brits sold a few of their new jet engines to the Russians. Copies of those engines were in MiG fighter jets that shot down American pilots in the Korean War.

"Honestly, I can count the number of America's real friends on one hand… and I'd still have fingers left over." Jonathan grinned, it really was a dog-eat-dog world. "You know, it does seem as if we both lack a certain level of trust."

"That's 'cause we get played for suckers too many times." "That goes for our president?"

Keel stopped short at that, not simply because he had no wish to be disloyal but because there were times when he was uncertain about Prescott. The man could be confusing, going from one extreme to another. Granted his obvious intellect, still, something else lay hidden under the surface. But what? Was it merely animal cunning, or was it something you didn't want to be in the same room with?

"Don't know," he reluctantly admitted. "I do know we get played far too often. The public may not believe it, but we're too soft, too honest, nowhere near as devious as the Iranians, Chinese, or Russians."

"Brandon." Jonathan raised his hands in surrender. "Look, I accept that the Russians and the Chinese are two-faced bastards. But let's not go overboard. I mean… do you really believe they nuked one of their own cities? Especially since I've heard the Russians are scared shitless that there may be loose nukes floating around. That's not a good scenario for them." Jonathan looked and sounded concerned. In reality he wanted some reassurance that it was not as bad as he thought it was.

Keel nodded once. He had already received classified reports from several Intelligence agencies and knew the Russians were running around trying to find "rogue" nukes. But were they really rogue? "Yeah, it could cause problems for them. But it would depend on where they went off. Say one went off in Moscow, then yeah, they're the victims. On the other hand, if a nuke went off in Berlin or Washington at a critical moment—now who would take the blame and, as in the movies, who would benefit? Sure, the terrorists would get a win, but Russia could really benefit if it brought about NATO's collapse."

Jonathan's head was spinning. "I'm so glad I don't have your job." "Is Prescott holding another interview?" Keel asked.

"What do you expect?" Jonathan glanced down at his wristwatch. "We've got about ten minutes before the next one."

"The polls... what do they say?" Keel's expertise did not range into that area.

"Shit... damned if they know themselves; it's a bit early. Depends on how the interviews go, I think... hope."

They parted ways, after which Brandon Keel walked to his office, where he turned on the television. He wanted to see how the president would handle the latest interview.

Brandon smiled as he saw the president leaning forward, almost hunched over and on the edge of his seat. God, the man looked like some bird of prey ready to swoop. Not his usual, relaxed pose. Guess they really pissed him off last night.

"I accept that, Mr. President. But many callers have asked about your reasoning, sir," the interviewer pointed out in her cultured voice.

"Ingrid, as they say; 'If you're not part of the solution, then you're part of the problem.' And last night the remaining members of the Senate showed me where the problem lay.

"Senators Holt and Walker called upon me to reduce expenditures and cut the size of government. I responded with what I considered sensible options, and they threw them back in my face. Understand me, I am not against small government; indeed, I am prepared to support small government with the reforms I have outlined. But the size of government is quite simply not the real issue."

"You believe we need an efficient government and one that makes money... even if it has never managed to do so."

"And why hasn't it? Perhaps it's because Senators and Representatives have spent most of their time promoting themselves rather than working for this nation. The simple fact is that we need to fix the fundamentals that have been eroded over the years by a wilful Congress."

"And dissolving the House and Senate is the answer?"

"When they are the problem, then yes. How many decades, centuries, has Congress had to deal with such matters as filibusters and rampant pork-barrelling? How long has true representation been hampered by gerrymandering? How long has lobbying by special interest groups run riot, unhindered by sane limits and conditions?

"Imagine Abraham Lincoln and his Cabinet freed from the shackles of Congress for two years, to reform Congress, to establish an independent, politically neutral tax plan to fix our budget problems. To restructure the government bureaucracy... our Congressional members have often complained about the size of government, yet have they cut the size of their own staff? Do you remember the last time Congress had an efficiency drive to reduce wasteful spending within government bodies?"

Clayton paused. "Well?" he sternly asked.

Shit, shit, shit. I hate my job. I used to so love my job. "I don't have the exact details at hand, sir."

"Yes. Well, imagine if heads of government departments were looking forward to a pay *cut* if there were no improvement in efficiency and customer satisfaction." And wouldn't that open the ugliest can of worms? Clayton's smile widened. Especially in departments that had repeated cuts in their budgets by Congress.

"Yet, is dissolving Congress really the answer?" Ingrid asked. "Senators Holt and Walker have publicly stated that doing so would be an attack on democracy… on its principles, on the very foundation of democracy."

"And just what principles are they talking about? You interviewed them, Ingrid, so just what is their foundation of democracy?"

She blinked. *What did he say?* "They… the balance of power between the legislative and the executive . . . it would give the executive branch all the power of government."

"Yes, that would be their narrow definition of democracy… a contest, a struggle for one's own interests. So narrow and nondescript. So tell me, Ingrid, do you agree that such a definition is a true representation of democracy?" He looked squarely at the young woman.

"Of course…" She paused, suddenly realizing just what he had asked. After a moment's silence, she gave a timid response. "Having a Congress is important. But I would say electing candidates of your choice in free and open elections is true democracy." She so wanted to bite down on her tongue, furious that he had so nearly made a fool out of her.

"That is such a standard description, and so superficial that it barely qualifies in this day and age." He barely gave her a nod of approval—nearly cancelled by his look of mild disapproval as if he were listening to a less than adequate student.

"I'm sorry?" She was stumped by his words. "How can free elections not be the first principle of a democracy?"

"Come now, Ingrid, is that really the best we can do? Scholars have written numerous books on the subject, and we are reduced to time-worn clichés? Need I remind you that Hitler and Putin were elected to office?"

"They were… well… Putin's later elections were hardly open." "Russia would disagree. Indeed, Iran would argue it holds free elections, even if the candidates are vetted by their Supreme Islamic body." *Only good little Muslims need apply.*

"Sir, are you saying free and open elections aren't enough?"

"They should be, but are they? Can we not better encapsulate this core belief that we so vigorously claim as our birth-right?" He persisted; it hadn't been a rhetorical question.

A moment's silence, and then she ventured, "Perhaps if you were kind enough to elaborate, sir? What would be your definition of democracy?" "At its core… at its most basic level, are we not dealing with power? May I suggest that democracy is the people having the power to remove that which holds power over them? Remove the individuals, remove the insti—"

"I'm sorry, sir," she jumped in, "but isn't that the same as free and open elections? Electing a new candidate into office?"

"The power to remove the individuals, what about removing the *institutions . . .,*" he repeated. "Now, that is far different from voting someone into office, Ingrid.

"Voting a person or institution out of power does not mean that it must be automatically refilled. It could be eliminated or replaced with an entirely new institution, a new organization and structure. Thus, if the public is not pleased with Congress—or the presidency—why keep it?" he asked Ingrid, who was now visibly stunned.

"True democracy should allow us to replace or to remove those in power and the institutions of power, as some have done in the past, using a rather blunt form of change." Clayton looked at her with inquiring eyes.

Shit.

"Revolution, Ingrid, where one form of entrenched government is thrown out and replaced with a totally different form of government. Now, let me be clear. I oppose violent revolution, and we have no need for violence when we have the vote.

"What is the point of removing a group of individuals when we leave the same power structure in place that created the dysfunction in the first instance? I put it to you that democracy is about the majority having the power to remove individuals and institutions that have power over them… and may I add that includes the media when they fail us."

"But how would we deal with the budget… the business of government?" "It could all be handled by a president and an elected Cabinet of twenty or so individuals for a maximum of two years. Then Congress can be reinstated… with the public's approval, of course." He then grinned rather sheepishly. "Efficient government for two years… just think of all the money we'd save."

"With respect, I think many people, not just politicians"—*the few that are left*—"would argue that you are talking about removing the checks-and-balances that Congress offers…"

"You mean the stagnation, the near-perpetual deadlock? To the great satisfaction of the wealthy who just keep on raking in all the wealth while Congress sits on its hands?

"As for your fears, Ingrid, are you telling me that in all America we can't find one honest Abe? Find thirty honest men and women who will act for the good of the country? Really, Ingrid, can we not find a handful of American who aren't egotistical, self-serving, vainglorious politicians? Who will for two years focus on reshaping the House and Senate so they work? Imagine a law that forces Congress to work together or face removal with no option for re-election. How many would get off their high horse and work for America?

"Now, as for the business of running government, such as the budget. We could have world-renowned, independent economists plan the budget for the two years. That could only help the budget." He grinned and turned to the camera. "Imagine qualified people actually doing the books; wouldn't that be a first?"

"So, you're saying that Senators Holt and Walker have no reason to be concerned about any possible abuse of power, a takeover of the state?" He gave a sharp snort that resembled a laugh. "It's a bit late, I'm afraid.

We've already had your 'coup,' Ingrid." "Sorry?" she blurted.

"Come now, it happened back in the 'eighties." "I… I'm not sure I understand. What coup?"

"Why, the one where corporate America staged a successful campaign to achieve unassailable control of the government—all without guns, just by employing money." Clayton grinned with those large teeth as if he were a piranha ready to attack. "It always amuses me how the NRA goes on and on about how they need guns to prevent a government takeover, when the takeover has already occurred. If it weren't so sad, their argument would be laughable."

"Are you serious? Mr. President, the people choose who will be elected." "Miss Benitez, really. It's long acknowledged that America is one of the most legally corrupt countries in the world. Owned and operated by the rich."

That should set of some fireworks. Clayton's smile widened. "Sorry? Did you say 'corrupt'?" She was shocked, not by the words—

many honest people would agree with him—but by actually saying it. *No politician admits to being bribed.* "You can't be serious!"

"Of course I am. Why do secretaries pay higher taxes than their billionaire bosses? Is it because secretaries can't buy politicians?" Thank you, Mister Buffett, who had pointed out this reality in his own business.

"My proposal to engage with overseas pharmaceutical companies and buy drugs in bulk, thus saving Americans billions, has already been ridiculed by Congress. Why? Is it because American pharmaceutical companies have ordered them to do so? Let us stop the lies. As long as politicians need money for elections, we will always have legalized corruption."

He paused for a moment. "And that is America's Achilles heel. If this state of affairs doesn't change, countless Americans will completely lose faith in government . . . and then our nation is truly lost." Clayton's voice seemed to be carrying a mountain of weight. "That is yet another reason we could do with the dissolution of Congress. By doing so, we can get private donations out of elections."

"But the cost of a modern campaign is enormous. Are you suggesting that the public should fund their campaigns?" *There you go; bite on that and see if you don't choke on it.* She smiled ever so innocently.

"Yes, the media has a lot to answer for," came Clayton's cryptic response. She blinked, not in surprise but in fear. Too many of her fellow journalists had regretted crossing swords with the man. His ability to run rings around a discussion was getting people worried. "I think you'll find that there is a long tradition of the media exposing corruption." She was not certain that this was the right direction to take.

"That is an excellent deflection, my dear. But I was pointing to a double standard in the media. You all go on and on about 'the people's right to know,' and indeed, you are more than happy to expose any salacious scandals. Yet election time comes around, and politicians want to present their views and positions to the public. What do you say? 'Sure... as long as you pay for it.'

"Scandals you'll splash all over the airwaves, but rely on you to help inform the public on something as important as the policies of those who will govern our nation? We can forget that."

God, no. He's talking about free advertisement. The twisted bastard is trying to get us to pay for their crappy lies...

"Ingrid, we wouldn't need to spend billions on elections if the media actual believed in its civil duty to inform the public—as some have argued. Should they not give each candidate a certain amount of free air time? And it should not end there, they insist. We should do the same with the newspapers, where for instance the centre page could be a pull-out section, where the newspaper asks the candidates ten questions each. The candidates would declare their positions on a topic and explain why they hold to those views. And the next day it could be another ten new questions from the public."

"Free air time… even for negative campaign ads?" She was grasping at straws by now.

"It would be their airtime. But for me personally, the more negative their ads, the less time they should get." Clayton was smiling happily.

She smiled back, but through gritted teeth, desperate by now to change the course of the discussion. "But even if airtime were free, that's only part of their campaign costs. How would you fund the rest?"

"There are obvious options. Many Americans already donate considerable amounts, so why shouldn't they donate to a futures fund?" *Like the money the rich spend on their art collects.* "Thus when election time comes around, the candidates get the accrued interest, and only the interest, for their campaign with no strings attached—and no campaign donations to influence candidates. That and the media doing their job should be enough.

"Another option is a direct tax. If the public is satisfied with the performance of their politicians then they can permit, say a one-half percent campaign tax. On the flip side, if the public isn't happy with government performance, then they can cut the campaign tax for the following elections. That, I think, would be an encouragement for good governance."

Clayton's grin spread. "My personal preference would be for the government to fund political campaigns from government profits. Such as the solar energy scheme, the Federal Health Insurance scheme and other moneymaking ventures. In short, the better run and profitable our government becomes, then the bigger the campaign cheques it can give to those seeking to join Congress."

"Will there be enough?—if you are going to limit the profits government can make." Ingrid went with the flow.

"There is that possibility. But as I stated previously, the more efficient the government becomes, the greater the profits."

"Sir, I can't help pointing out that many would think you are asking too much of the government. We all know that traditionally, government…

historically, government has never tried to generate its own wealth. It has always been the private sector that has done so. What has changed that you think government can earn money?" *Why the hell should it?*

"That's because it has never been tried. And given the poor performance of the private sector in building infrastructure for this country, the government may actually do better."

"Are you saying capitalism has failed?" It sounded that way to her.

"What is capitalism?" he whispered.

Oh, shit. Not again; no more.

Clayton turned to the camera. "What is real capitalism if not real competition? Once we had hundreds of meatpacking houses, and now we have less than a dozen. Once we had numerous small to medium shops; now we have an ever-shrinking number of giant multinational corporations."

He looked her straight in the eye. "What is the future for the US and Europe when the majority of business are cartels and monopolies? The answer is stagnation and rot. And the government is a perfect example of that. When has government, including the institutions of the House and Senate, faced competition?

"It's time we changed all that. Capitalism needs competition, and government needs it as well."

Clayton glanced at his watch. "Well, we have five minutes left, so I thought we should go over the Surgeon General's latest report concerning excess sugar. And especially about have much poison is in each bottle of soft drinks."

Shit, damn, shit, she silently screamed between clenched teeth, while trying to keep her smile in place as she freaked out.

"Now, I noticed that the media are apparently not overly concerned, in fact seem to be dismissive of the harm that so much sugar is doing to our children…" Clayton continued on for his five minutes.

Much to Ingrid Benitez's regret, the sugar industry was not going to be happy with her network. Maybe they could find an excuse to cut it out.

"Well, I think that about does it for now." Clayton stood and said his goodbyes.

He entered the corridor to find Abb waiting for him.

"Sir." Abb looked sick. "There has been a massacre in New York. It's going viral on the Internet."

New York City

FBI Deputy Director Drywood watched the buildings pass by… 720, 734, 740… The FBI vehicle stopped, and he stepped out. He pulled the collar of his coat tighter as he took a good look around at all the tall buildings.

Park Avenue, Manhattan. *God, it looks as ugly as it is soulless,* he thought. The front of the building still had a police guard, who immediately reported his arrival to the detective in charge when he identified himself. In this case the detective was a tall, heavyset woman with iron-grey hair who emerged from the building and walked toward him. "Detective Ursula Brenton." She extended her hand. He took it. "FBI Deputy Director Drywood."

"Deputy Director?" Her large paw squeezed, threatening to crush his hand.

"At ease. The FBI isn't trying to take over the investigation. I'm just an observer. The president's got the FBI monitoring anything that might be connected to the anarchists. I happened to be at the local office getting some background on events." Which he knew was often a waste of time. Was he getting desperate to go out in the field or just getting tired of being in the Washington office? *God, the last thing I need is cabin fever.* "So you just tell me this has nothing to do with them, and I can stop sniffing around and go back to Washington."

She closed her eyes for a second. "I almost wish I could say it wasn't them. It wouldn't be so worrying."

"How so?"

"The hit was damned professional, way too professional. If it was them, this country has got real problems." If this was the anarchists, then they were capable of mounting serious attacks.

"And if it wasn't them?"

"Hopefully, organized crime… they could be getting back at a banker for screwing up laundering their money."

"And using the slaughter to hide the hit." He nodded. "Now that would be cute."

She shrugged once. "At least it would be a one off." She sounded very sceptical, with only a tiny hint of hope.

"Talk me through it."

"You've seen the video on the Internet?" she asked bluntly.

"Saw it on the way over."

"What wasn't on it was how they got control of the building, it has the very latest in high-tech security, yet they hacked into it . . . that is, we think they hacked into it. All we really know is that they took control of the security system and the fire alarms, isolating both. Then a group of men dressed as firefighters came into the building. They went from room to room. They had helmets and gas masks so our witness can't give us much of a description.

"Anyway they told the staff and servants to stay in their rooms while they escorted the apartment owners down to the lobby. We figure they brought them down in ones or twos to the lobby. Where they secured them with plastic ties and—" She took a sharp breath. "And then cut their throats from ear to ear in front of the vid cam. When they had finished, they dragged the bodies into a side room, presumably so they could have room for the next couple."

"How many?"

"Seventeen owners and their spouses confirmed dead." The detective handed Drywood a sheet of paper with the names of the dead. He groaned, although he did not know any on the list, he recognized a few names from the latest *Forbes* 2000 list.

"So the question is, was it an inside job?" he asked her. If it was any of the staff with a grudge, that would give them a solid list of suspects to start with. If it wasn't an inside job, then the list got a lot longer.

"We'll have to wait and see what the tech boys come up with."

They walked into the lobby, where she guided Drywood to the far wall, where painted onto the wall in bright red were the words, *Come the revolution.*

"Original."

"But bloody . . . very bloody." The carpet was now a sticky mess of dark red. "If it's them, they're escalating. This was pure brutality."

"It gets you the bigger headline."

When you have the power to stop an atrocity and do nothing aren't your hands covered in as much blood as the ones who commit the atrocity? (Thomas Hardy)

Congress, a special interest group for special interests. (Thomas Hardy)

Chapter 14

Democracy has not failed us.
We failed democracy.
Capitalism has not failed us.
We failed capitalism.

—Thomas Hardy

The White House

The men and women were ushered into the meeting room by Abb Cole at his amicable best. His warm smile hid the battle that was to come.

"Saul, it's nice to see you again." Abb smiled and greeted the powerful Washington lobbyist as he entered the room.

"Abb." Saul Grant's large hand all but crushed Abb's.

"Trevor, glad you could make it, take a seat. And thanks again for coming so quickly. I know how valuable time is for each of you." They seated themselves with minimal fanfare, showing their displeasure.

"Now, let's get going. As you have all seen, the president was less than gracious in his conversation with Senators Holt and Walker."

"What the hell were you thinking, Abb?" Grant spoke in a harsh tone. "How could you let him say all that crap?"

"He didn't clear it with me, Saul. He just called up the station and told them he wanted to talk to the announcer. I couldn't stop him. I wasn't even with him when he called."

"Well he's going to have to retract it, all of it." Trevor Dominican shot back.

"Good luck on that." Despite the blunt words, Abb sounded apologetic. "You didn't see how angry he was. I don't think it's going to be possible to get him to see reason—for now."

"Well, make him see, unless he wants to see his political throat being cut." Saul snapped at Abb.

"Threats or attempts at intimidation won't work on the man. You've seen how irrational he's been behaving lately." Abb himself was not impressed or intimidated by threats.

"Well, make him realize how close to the edge he is skating," Grant pressed on.

"I knew he was losing it when he handed out tinfoil caps to those medicos," Dominican said, certain that he knew Clayton's innermost thoughts. "He's lost it."

"Irrelevant, Trevor," Grant said dismissively. "Abb, you need to get him under control."

"Damn it, Saul. He's already skating on the edge. You know he was planning to leave politics after the death of his wife and children." Abb's voice rose in frustration. "Then the attack on Congress cost him some of his closest friends, and then those idiots spit in his face in front of the whole country. Do you really think he's worried about his political future right now?"

"He hasn't got one, not after that interview… dissolving Congress of all things." Grant obviously had no sympathy for Clayton's situation.

"That's my point, Saul… he doesn't care. As far as he's concerned, he has no future, so why should he care if he takes us and the whole house down?"

"Well, that's not going to happen," Grant told the room.

"Who's going to stop him?" Abb bit back. "The House or the Senate? They can't do anything significant till the elections. So who? You? Do you really think the police or military will back you up? Do I have to remind you about that little incident in Detroit, when the commander of the 2rd Division had his men open up all those empty warehouses for the homeless? And what happened afterwards? Your pit-bull senators made all the noise under the sun, and Prescott went on air and praised the officer. Remind me, what did the polls say?" Grant's face fell. "Yeah, Prescott's little speech about how the military was the real defender of American freedom and not a bunch of 'self-serving politicians' or 'greedy lobbyists' sent his popularity through the roof.

"Wake up, all of you. He's pissed, and the American people are pissed. If he decides to nationalize every large company and hand them over to the workers, do you think you'll have any way of stopping him? Hell, the army would be there to open the door for the workers—and if you try to stop them, you'll be lucky the Marines don't tear you apart."

"Communist—"

"Screw the commie crap, Trevor. That only works for the numbnuts in the NRA. The public is royally pissed. Hell, if Prescott wanted to burn the Constitution, this minute, there would be a stampede to see who'd give him the lighter first. You need to get on the public's good side. Get Holt and Walker to back off. Give Prescott time to cool down. Then when things have settled, I can get him to see reason. That is if none of you do anything stupid and shove your foot in your mouth."

Abb took in a deep breath. "People, this has been a traumatic time for all of us. We have lost a lot of fine people." There were nods and muttered agreements. But he could see past the pretence. They couldn't care less about the dead. They were more interested in getting what they had come for. "Now, I believe I can convince the president that it's in his best interest to tone down some of the rhetoric. But naturally I have to give him some justification for a more conciliatory position, a way to publicly save face."

"So what exactly are you suggesting?" Dominican asked.

"Maybe if the president was to be seen doing something to reduce unemployment."

"Tell him to cut taxes," Grant commented flippantly.

"Don't be an asshole," Abb growled. "Saul, this is not a time to pay games. He isn't playing. Grow up here and now, or kiss your ass goodbye."

"Okay, so you have a plan?"

"The president has already made a few statements about a solar panel scheme. I think I can get him to ease off if he gets enough support for the scheme."

"Another pipe-dream?" Grant asked.

"Does it matter? I don't think a hundred thousand solar panels are too much to ask for if it placates the president, do you?"

"There is a problem with your plan," the woman to Saul's right said. "I understand the essential difficulty you have with the idea. If you donate now, why haven't you done so before? Well, you can present it as the new face of corporate America, the new kinder, gentler corporate face.

"I believe that this can calm the waters, and then I can make him see reason. From there, with a bit of time, I can get him to adopt a more positive stance towards industry… in exchange for future support."

"So he drops his attacks, and we support him in the next election?" Grant stated without much conviction. Not that they had any real interest in supporting the man. But they had to play the game. In truth they would happily support his opposite number in the next election if they got what they wanted.

"Well, we all know how things work in DC. At the end of the day he knows he needs you to get the money and endorsements moving. I just need the time to calm him down." Abb tried to sound hopeful.

The woman spoke up once more. "And just why should we support a man so intent on soiling our good character?"

"Get off your high horse, Matilda. We all know each other. We all know how the system works."

"Then why on earth did you let him did it? It's your job to protect him from himself." Although she really meant it was Abb's job to look after their interests as well as those of the president. They were the elite, after all. They guided the ship of state over rough seas.

"Come on, how was I supposed to stop him? Look, we need time to mitigate the damage and calm things downs before the next election, because if he feels he's finished—well, he could take a lot of you down with him. So we are going to lessen the chaos and ease his concerns. That's why I convinced him I should talk with you to find an accommodation."

"And how much will this cost?" Grant sounded truly upset that he would have to open his chequebook once more.

"Just start the donations, Saul. Have everyone donate, everyone—the marijuana industry, the doctors, the gunmakers, the drug companies, Wall Street... even Hollywood. Especially Hollywood. You tell them to donate till they bleed and then donate more. You can make a big deal out of it: how you all feel the public's pain, how you toss and turn all night... your hearts bleed buckets. That way you get good publicity, and you get the president off your backs. Once you start, the others will follow or look like tight-asses."

"So you want us to get the ball rolling?"

"No Trevor, I want you to kiss ass. Get over it."

"Okay, so let's get into the details." Grant saw the light.

"Of course." Abb smiled. *Bloodsuckers. Even when we're agreed, they still want to negotiate till they squeeze your nuts dry.*

Private conference room in the White House

Maggie "Ryan" Castello stood before the president and waited as he read the folder. Called to the White house on a moment's notice, she had not expected this behaviour. A car had picked her up and was prepared to take her back.

Clayton sat in his chair and continued reading the report as she stood waiting. *If he thinks this kind of tactic will work on intimidating me, he can think again.*

"The FBI report is far from charitable. Half your former colleagues had less than flattering things to say about you." He glanced up at her. "Do sit down."

"Only half, sir?" She sat on the richly padded leather chair.

"The other half preferred words like… 'the biggest self-serving bitch in history.' 'Psycho broad.' 'Back-stabbing slut with genitalia hanging—'" He stopped and chuckled. "Yes, well." He tried not to break out into laughter.

Her face clouded over. "Well, I'm glad you find it so amusing." "They do come up with some interesting expletives."

"Mr. President, if you have called me over just to insult me, I have better things to do."

"Better than being insulted by me, really? I'm almost offended. Anyway, I do apologise, this is not the way the white house normally conducts job interviews, but I am desperately short for time. Although, I must say, going over you . . . FBI résumé again was a delight. Now, the question is… are you man enough for the job."

"I'm a woman, so that makes me twice the man."

"With an overblown ego to match any two men, you certainly have that."

"Mr. President, just—"

"There is a school of sharks out in one of the conference rooms eager to tear me apart. I want a barracuda, a mean, nasty little barracuda, all teeth and a nasty disposition, who will not back down, who won't be pushed around. Are you a barracuda?"

"I have never apologized for my conduct or actions, sir." "The solar panel initiative, you have heard of it?"

"Some kind of proposal for the government to put solar panels on rooftops." *Like anyone really believes it.* "Something like that."

"You don't seem overly impressed."

"With the government's great track record on getting things done right?" Her sarcasm was biting. "No, I don't give it much credence. Besides, private industry would do a better job."

"It's doing a lousy job," Clayton replied. "Otherwise we wouldn't be having this conversation. I want to provide solar panels to the poor, the very people who can't afford them."

"You… You're joking." Her jaw actually dropped a fraction in disbelief. "I asked you to come all this way to make a joke?"

"But . . ." *He can't be serious.* "But if they can't pay for the panels, the scheme will fall flat on its face once the government money runs out." She deftly changed course to hide her confusion.

"The money will come from the electricity the panels generate. If you had been listening, you'd know half will go to each household to spend as they wish. The other half goes to the government for manufacture, installation, and maintenance."

"You're serious?"

"And I want you to run it. And make it a success within six months." "What? Sir—do you have any idea what you're asking? Six months to get it started… that is a tough ask."

"Not get it started but rolled out and on rooftops to the point where the public will totally support the project."

"It can't be done," she said in the flattest voice possible.

"Has to be."

"It can't. Forget the infrastructure, sir, just selecting the best people will take months. Then negotiating the pay and conditions for these highly qualified individuals will take even more time." She was almost pleading.

"Top rate will be seventy-five thousand. Just tell them they are doing it for their country."

Her cheeks inflated; she looked remarkably like a puffer fish. Then she barked a laugh as she realized how insane this was. "I'm tempted, just to see the looks on their faces." Not that she really thought they would actually accept the offer. It was insane.

"Will you be my barracuda?"

"You are asking a lot, Mr. President. Getting it up and running at all will be tough, especially as some certainly won't like it." She knew of several sectors that would not be happy.

"That is why I need the meanest, ugliest, foulest-tongued barracuda I can find."

"You are doing an excellent job of selling this, sir."

"If you can't take the heat, you're no good to me—and you will be taking a lot of heat."

"Can I rely on your support?"

"I will bend like a reed in the wind, turning in a dozen different directions. I will be anything but supportive of your 'failures.' All I can guarantee you is that I will do everything I can to give you as much time as I can."

"I will need to have a free hand."

"As long as you give me what I want, I don't care who you have to kill to get it done."

"And what do I get out of this?" She wanted to know why she should take on this insane job. It wasn't the money, the material gains. She wanted to know the reason why.

"You get to be my barracuda, and you get to prove all your contemporaries wrong."

"How so, sir?"

"That you actually have a shred of decency." He grinned as if he had just heard a private joke. "But mostly you get to prove that you have the biggest ego in the room."

God damn. She suppressed a small pearl of a laugh. "This could blow my career."

"We both know you made your money by the time you reached thirty-five on Wall Street. And since then you have been a—" He glanced down at the report. "'A sadistic bitch with self-destructive tendencies.'" He grinned, showing those large teeth.

"You are present-day America in a nutshell, Miss Castello. So if you manage to save a bit of America, who knows? You may end up saving a bit of yourself. And you can get to prove me wrong."

"How so?"

"By proving there is at least one businessperson who still has some loyalty to this country."

"How can I reject such flattery?" She stood up.

"If this is what you call flattery, I'd like to know what passes for business mating rituals," Clayton responded with flat calm.

She actually grinned. *This is insane.* "I hope you're not squeamish when it comes to the sight of blood. It'll get bloody."

"I'll remember to bring a bucket and mop."

"You know, we're not all bad—businesspeople, that is." "Just as well I give you the chance to prove it then." "You really have a low opinion of us."

"I have a higher opinion of sharks, rats, cockroaches. At least they only do what's necessary to survive. Tell me how many of your colleagues have acted in the best interests of America? Paid all the taxes they should… donated even a few dollars to saving this country?"

She opened her mouth but then shook her head, and with a little less cockiness she turned to leave the room. *Man, he knows how to go for the jugular.* Clayton Prescott was not the man she had expected to find. She turned back to look straight into his eyes. "Why me, really? Apart from my endearing ego?"

"You were born and spent seven years in Italy being raised by a pair of traditional parents working in a small business who actually believed in an honest work ethic. That is before you immigrated to the US." "You really do have a low opinion of American business."

"See, we understand each other so well already. Get back to me when you have something." Clayton smiled a sad, pathetic little smile as he watched her leave. *So I'm reduced to this, having it out with a "psycho broad" to get my jollies.*

Clayton began reading the latest reports on the economy when the intercom buzzed. "Yes." He turned his attention to the voice.

"Sir, Ann is here to see you."

"Send her in, please."

Ann Hornwood walked in and immediately began going through the events of the last few days. Both liked to study how the media were reacting, how they were shaping the opinion polls.

"We have more good news, sir. The levelling-off in over-all violence is on most front pages. That should reflect well."

"And they managed to get garbage collection running again." Ann had been disappointed to learn that several cities had stopped collecting garbage in some districts for fear of violence.

"How is the military being received in the less well-off communities?" Clayton asked.

"The ghettos? Quite well, by all accounts, especially when the media shows them bringing in hot food and providing some accommodations— and establishing, I am told, good security for the homeless and the few rags they own. Looks like they are being far better received than the police."

"Feed them instead of beat them—who would have thought that would work?" Clayton shook his head in despair. "Okay, give me the bad." He hated this part.

"The assassination of the new Senator and threats to the senatorial candidates have had a very negative effect. A number of candidates have already withdrawn from consideration."

"Yes, Director Shaw brought that to my attention with all due haste." "Well, the anarchists did declare they would 'put on trial' any 'fat cat'

who runs for the office."

"They have certainty made their point, a little too forcefully." Clayton rubbed the bridge of his nose. They had all seen the warnings posted on the Internet. The American flag on fire, the faces of several candidates mounted on dummies hanging from the ends of ropes, with signs dangling from them saying, "Death to the rich and traitors of America."

"Well, the killings have put a certain section of the community on edge," Ann admitted sourly.

"I've told Director Shaw to hire more private security if the anarchists come calling. They can afford it."

That held her attention for a few moments. He was obviously not in a good "space."

Ann pulled a sheet of paper from her folder. "I have a few suggestions on how to best handle the 'loyal' opposition when they start trying to blame us."

"You think they will?"

"For failing to adequately protect the rich and privileged? You can bet on it."

"We have tens of millions in poverty, thousands without shelter or decent food, being hurt or killed. We have anarchy and unrest in the streets. But we are failing the public only when a handful of the privileged end up dead?"

"There are legitimate concerns by some that they are being targeted." "Who would have thought? After the way they have so generously helped their less fortunate fellow citizens for generations." He sounded grimly amused as he continued to read from his notes.

"Sir, there is a growing number of individuals leaving the US." "Rats leaving the sinking ship, Ann?" "I wouldn't quite put it like that, sir."

"I would, Ann—and there is nothing we can do. The police have complained for decades that they are overstretched." He looked up from his reading, took off his reading glasses, and sighed. "Out with it."

"Sir, a number of media have asked the same question, and even some of the staff."

"Go on."

"What if the trickle turns into a flood? What if the rich and especially the CEOs leave in real numbers… desert the US out of concern—"

"That the public doesn't love 'em anymore?"

"Sir, please, I'm serious. The violence is real, and the truth is that, although on average a few wealthy individuals head overseas each year . . .

the situation could escalate. The threat of senior business figures leaving the US is real." So far it had been wealthy individuals who could cut and run—especially Hollywood stars telling people they were going on holidays in Europe or doing an overseas movie, as opposed to CEOs who had to work in the US.

"Get your people together. Get all the senior staff you can find. I am going to explain the facts of life."

"Sir?" Her jaw dropped slightly. *Oh, shit. Here it comes,* she thought to herself. With that she began racing around the White House to collect everyone she could.

Some twenty minutes later Clayton Prescott stood in a very overcrowded room, facing a rather bewildered audience. "Ann just asked me a question. What happens if a large number of corporate CEOs pack up and leave? Well, we can all give thanks, that is what should happen.

"America doesn't need fat, comfortably slow, and utterly useless old farts sitting on their chairs waiting for their big payday to hold us back." Clayton could almost smile at their bewilderment.

"People, I will keep saying this until it sinks in: America needs young, energetic entrepreneurs, men and women with new ideas to create new business—much more than we need a bunch of fossils shuffling paper money around. Just how many of these old fossils come up with new ideas, new concepts?

"Name the CEO who created the Internet.

"Name the CEO who designed Microsoft.

"Name the CEO who came up with Google.

"Consider the story of IBM and Microsoft. If the board at IBM had purchase Mr. Gates's software for their computers, how many billions would the company be worth today? They screwed up.

"Who was responsible for the BP spill in the Gulf of America? Was it an entrepreneur or the management of BP?

"Who was responsible for the housing bubble, junk bonds, the GFC? "Who loaned billions to families they knew could never repay their loans? Entrepreneurs or bank executives?

"I am not saying that some entrepreneur *will* create the next great new idea, the next Internet. But we certainly do not need the fools that cultivate an environment that engenders an endless circle of boom and bust." Clayton's eyes swept the room. "Once, I too held them in high regard, but their continuous failures, their continuous undermining of America's economy— their weakening of America instead of strengthening it—can no longer be ignored. Just look at their tax avoidance as the perfect example of where their loyalties lay.

"Once, we could've trusted banks to provide capital to build homes and small businesses, to build up this country. Now we see them destroying the very foundations of our country brick by brick.

"The time has come for us to give this country a sustainable economy. And if that means we don't end up making a bunch of CEOs billionaires, well, life is tough.

"So stop fretting about them. Worry about what you should be worrying about: making a more stable and secure country. That is the real role of government. Our job is to defend America from its enemies both foreign and *domestic*. And that is what we will do. If any of you don't have the guts for it, then pack your bags.

"Now I want real questions here and now."

Ann froze. She understood all too well what was coming: this was a test. If they didn't stand up to him here and now, she knew the whole lot would be out the door within weeks. He wanted his instructions to be obeyed, but equally he wanted people who could think, along with the backbone to stand up to him.

She spoke up, her heart in her throat. "And if they walk, who replaces them?"

"You think there aren't fifty Young Turks, up-and-comers, eager to climb the ladder, willing to spend years building up a company and do a better job if they want to make a name for themselves… and for only a fraction of what a big-shot CEO would demand." He looked around, glaring into each pair of eyes as if daring them to challenge him. "And that's why it's a good idea not to have the old fossils around. How can someone connect with the general public when he lives in a multi-million dollar ivory tower?"

"But sir," said a young communications staffer, "their replacements won't have the same level of experience."

"During the GFC the carmakers had to get a bailout, even with all their experienced executives. The banks had to get a bailout, even with all their highly paid ultra-experienced executives. And now—look at the mess they've made of things. How many people lost their jobs because of these uber-paid, ultra-experienced executives?" Clayton answered her question.

"Get it through your heads; they are the cause of half of America's problems." He hissed through nearly closed lips. "The more the CEOs get paid, the more this country goes from good to bad." He hammered his point home.

He then smiled that wide, toothy grin. "Now, we can't stop corporate America from handing in their passports. But they can forget about coming back another day or doing business with any American company. When Congress is back, I will demand that we change the rules. Former American citizens, as well as companies who make their money here but live or have their headquarters elsewhere to avoid taxes, will face a triple tax on all profits made inside the US. Further, I will call upon all developed nations"—he paused for shock effect—"to establish a universal corporate tax code so that we'll all have the same level of corporate tax… 35 per cent or maybe 40 per cent. Thus nation-states will benefit, not the multi-national corporations. I will make it impossible for corporations to play one country off another." He almost raised his voice as his passion grew.

"But if the developed nations don't agree" Clayton heard one small voice crying out against his maelstrom.

"Then America will cut its corporate tax rate to 1 per cent. The developed world will then have a choice: either agree to a universal corporate tax rate or else compete against us at 1 per cent . . . and once their populations hear that corporate taxes will go down to 1 per cent, every European government will be overthrown.

"More: after that I will go before the G20 nations and make a deal that we will all impose sanctions on any nation that is a tax haven. We will grind every tax haven into the ground." He turned to an open-mouthed and somewhat dizzy Ann. "And then we get serious."

Ann shivered. *He's gone stark, raving mad.*

"We will make CEOs and board members accountable for the sins of the company. We will change the law and make the individuals at the top, not the company, criminally accountable. And if that isn't enough, then we get serious on inflicting real… *real* pain." The fury of his words lashed the crowd till they almost huddled in fear. He turned to Ann. "I trust that answers your question."

Ann tried to smile, to hide her thoughts. *He's lost it, he has truly lost it. He's gone off the deep end. He can't do this. Worse, by the end of the week the whole of DC will know all about his little tirade or at least a version of it.*

The Freighter Northern Winter, *One Day's Sail from Port*

Misha sat facing Aloth in the cramped galley, eating a small meal, watching the News on an even smaller TV screen. Misha had smiled when he first saw the ugly protests and violence on the streets of America. But the violence was not growing. Worse, there were signs that officials were finding ways to bring the rioting under control.

"…as you can see, the church leaders of Chicago, with help from the local council, have turned several churches into temporary shelters. They are offering places to sleep, and with an Army-supplied field kitchen, they are providing free meals, Gordon. This is Mick Demires, Chicago; back to you at the news desk." The man's face dissolved, replaced by another.

"Now we have the latest from Washington. It has just been confirmed that the Israeli ambassador to the US has again spoken to the president to register Israel's opposition to the US Palestinian/Israeli peace plan.

"The Israelis are firmly opposed to the US plan, which envisions handing over the entire West Bank and Gaza Strip for a Palestinian homeland."

Aloth glanced at Misha. "This changes nothing. We are fighting for an Islamic world, not just for the liberation of a piece of Palestine. Our actions may even force more concessions from the oppressors." Misha doubted his words for a moment but then decided he was right. Fear of a second attack would make the Americans humble, too timid to refuse their demands.

"Even so, we still need confirmation," Aloth insisted. "There may be some changes. We need to know that High Command wants us to continue as planned."

"Of course." Misha tried to keep his voice free of sarcasm. *"High Command" indeed; does he think we're part of some great military organization?* Yet the Chechen still thought in military terms; he took orders as if he was in a military structure.

"We are due to make contact shortly." Misha went to his small cabin to wait for a few hours. Finally he switched on the satellite phone, dialled, and waited.

"Yes," came the response.

"Ah… Alex." He stopped himself just in time, it would not do to call the man Ahmed. "We are ahead of schedule and will be able to deliver a day earlier than planned." He hesitated in fear that Aloth might have been right. "Have there been any changes we need to be aware of?"

"Is there a problem?" hissed the voice at the other end.

"No."

"Good. I will send you the location. Remember; turn on the transmitter once you're on the other side of the border."

"I understand." Misha sounded relieved.

"You will be informed of any changes."

Once Misha had received the encrypted email identifying the location of the meeting, he left his cabin, to walk down the corridor with uncertain steps, scolding himself. *Don't concern yourself with petty details; the plan goes ahead as per schedule.*

But the concern that the mission might be changed or even aborted stayed with him for the rest of the day and into the night. The following morning found him unwilling to eat. This was the first time he had held doubts. Only the sight of land on the horizon began to calm his nerves. Only when the ship was smoothly towed to its assigned berth and secured in place did he truly feel comfortable.

With Aloth at his side, Misha watched the large cargo containers being haphazardly unloaded onto the docks.

Fortunately, the Mexican border authorities were more concerned with cargo leaving Mexico than entering it. Thus the container holding their "refrigerator" was not closely inspected, as they had expected. Nor were their passports and documentation, even though these had been meticulously altered from genuine passports, their European owners dead and buried in deep graves.

Again Misha smiled at the depth of skill and planning. *We will succeed in this great endeavour*, he fervently hoped.

His daydream was followed by an ugly night spent in the small hotel named as the meeting place, frequented by several prostitutes of the local area—hollow-eyed women who had lost everything, along with their husbands, to the economic collapse. They sickened Misha for they should have been in their homes attending to their family's needs. But when they were this close to the Great Satan, what else could you expect?

Praise be to Allah, there were no prostitutes in Islam, he told himself with utter conviction.

The following morning the pair began waiting for their contact, eating a slow breakfast of something that smelled questionable to Misha. Untroubled, Aloth assured him it was acceptable to Muslims. He had tasted similar back in Russia. Some Russian pig had even told him that tacos had originated in South America. Although the red peppers were surprisingly mild, he decided.

Before eight o'clock an acne -faced youth, with an arrogant walk and contemptuous eyes, found them sitting at the small table in the bar.

Misha took his eyes from the cool drink while Aloth studied the man in his tight jeans and cowboy boots, surprised by his arrogance.

"I was told to deliver a package for an old friend of Chuck's, Is that you?" The youth actually turned the chair around and straddled it, as if he were some latter-day cowboy from the childish Western fantasies that the Americans so loved. He casually picked up the menu.

Misha almost laughed into the boy's face. But this was not the time or place.

"Sorry, we are just waiting for a friend of our own." "Alex?" the boy asked.

Misha nodded and took another sip of his cold drink.

"Follow the instructions to the letter. Deliver it at the location and at the time. Don't be late or early." The youth dropped the menu on the table and left.

With considerable nonchalance, Misha slipped the small note tucked inside the menu into the palm of his hand. "We'd best get moving," he said taking a final sip of his drink.

They followed their established practise. Misha went to his room, to watch through the window as Aloth began to slowly walk down the street, for all appearances shopping. In reality he was allowing Misha to see whether he was being followed.

When Aloth turned a corner and was out of sight, Misha left the hotel and cruised up and down the street, until he passed the corner where Aloth waited, seemingly inspecting a pair of shoes. Aloth surreptitiously watched as Misha walked further down the street, watching for any one trailing Misha.

Only when they had satisfied themselves that neither was being followed did they take a taxi to a local rental service. There they paid for a week's hire, collected the keys to a small truck, and left. A short drive to the port followed, to collect their cargo. Once their cargo was loaded into the truck, they began another short trip, this time to a rundown section of the city.

They traversed ever shrinking-roads into an ever-growing slum. Mexico was suffering with each passing day, another victim of the Americans' oppression. *Will their evil never end?* Misha now felt comfortable blaming everything on the Americans. It made their coming actions that much more justifiable to him.

By late morning they arrived at their destination, a rundown building, and backed into the small workshop garage. Once inside, they pulled the old, battered roller-door closed. The inside seemed more like a half-deserted toolshed than a repair shop. To compound the insult, the balding middle-aged man who greeted them was sweating so freely that he looked barely able to lift a tyre gauge, much less change a tyre.

Together with Aloth, Misha dragged out the wooden crate, dumped it onto a waiting trolley, and pushed the unsteady trolley to the rear of the garage. As instructed, they pushed aside several barrels to uncover loose sheets of galvanized iron. Behind the sheets was the neighbouring wall, another tin shed even worse off than the garage.

They squeezed into the other building to find a small, ugly, ramshackle truck. Waiting for them was a youngish man seated at a small table eating a large roll filled with ham and cheese. A few words were exchanged before the container was loaded into the rear of the truck, and the three men climbed into the cab to take to the road, heading for one of the major border towns.

By early afternoon they had arrived at an unimpressive-looking red brick house located well away from the town centre. They parked the truck by the side before slowly sliding the wooden container through the large side door of the house. Inside they found the young man with acne slouched over a chair, finishing a can of beer.

"So that's the stuff?" The young man examined the container.

"Yes." Misha grudgingly answered.

"I need to have a look."

"You have the lab facility here?" Misha was genuinely shocked. If they had prepared the facility needed to handle their "biological weapon" on this side of the border, then the entire mission had failed. Misha knew Ahmed had convinced the American renegades that they were delivering a virus, not a nuclear weapon.

"I don't want to play with the stuff, the acne-scarred youth hissed in reply.

"It does not work like that; it is a virulent strain, one of the most deadly in the world. The container must only be opened in a proper biohazard facility. You wish to open it, give me our money and we will leave. You can open it when we are long gone." Misha tried to sound as confident as he could.

"Wait a minute, I was told… I thought we were getting chemicals—" "You were misinformed." He looked the acne faced young man straight in the eyes, daring him to challenge his words.

"Shit." The young man ran a hand across his mouth. This wasn't what he had signed up for. Then again, what was the real difference between a chemical weapon and a virus bomb?

"Now, if you wish to open the container, first give us the money and a good head start, and you can open it." Misha decided to reinforce the perceived danger.

The youth shook his head. "That's not going to happen."

"Then I suggest you get us across the border and open the container in a safe environment, unless you want to die choking on your own vomit." "OK, let's go." They carried the wooden container into another room and then down into the basement. The boy switched on the lights and went to the far wall. With the help of the guide, he unscrewed what appeared to be a small gas pipe. When one end was unscrewed, he pushed the pipe to the left till it was vertical.

"OK, give us a hand." The youth showed Misha where to squeeze metal hooks into small slots in the left side of the wall. They pushed, and the wall came out a few centimetres at a time, allowing the section of the wall to be moved aside until a tunnel was exposed.

The young man ducked his head as he entered the tunnel mouth and turned on the lights, which ran the length of the tunnel, exposing the small railway tracks going down the tunnel.

Sitting on the railway lines were two trolleys.

"I'll go on the first; you got the second. Then the container, then your friend," the acne-scarred young man told Misha.

Misha nodded and informed Aloth of his place in line, as Aloth knew only limited English. A short time later he was travelling down the tunnel and under the border of the US. He emerged inside another basement where the young man waited. Ten minutes later all three men climbed the steps into a well-built warehouse, half dragging the container with them.

"OK, load the truck; we got a schedule to keep," Joey instructed the two men. With Aloth and Misha in the passenger seat of the truck, Joey drove them down a seemingly endless series of back roads until they arrived at a high-walled compound with a large house and two large single-room buildings. The gates opened to allow the truck entrance.

"Everything went as planned, Joey?" a balding overweight man asked, standing next to the door of the large house.

"Yeah, told you. No problem, Bobby, my man. Only I want to have words with you. They were supposed to bring over some chemicals, not this." His jerked his thumb towards the back of the truck and its load.

"Later man." Bobby told Joey in a harsh tone. Then he gestured to the newcomers. "In here." He pointed to the closer of the two single-room buildings. They moved the container into the large room. Its windows and walls already sealed with plastic sheets. Two long tables occupied the centre of the room, surrounded by what looked like medical equipment and numerous instruments.

What resembled a large urn and even stranger equipment ran along one wall.

Misha hissed in despair. The equipment was obviously expensive and definitely not homemade junk. These were not simply ignorant thugs.

"You want to open the container in here?" Misha inquired.

"It's all set up," Bobby replied coldly.

"You consider this crude equipment satisfactory?" Misha bluffed as best he could to gain time.

"It's more than adequate for the task." A tall woman entered the room, well dressed and escorted by two men. Both were equally well attired as opposed to the cowboy with acne and the fat man.

"Doc, you ready to go?" Bobby tried not to look at her body and failed. Dr. Joanna Hockey stiffened, annoyed that she had to endure the buffoon's company. Still, a patriot must sometimes do things that were unpleasant for the good of the country.

"Best if you were all to leave. As long as the cargo is not damaged in transit, we will have no difficulty." She marched over to a small table where protective clothing waited.

The woman surprised Misha; she was too smartly dressed to fit in with these cowboys. She was clearly a step above.

Misha thought quickly, they needed time. "We can leave once you have handed over the money."

"Hey, sure." Bobby grinned.

"But before we have any misunderstandings"—Misha raised his hand to show the small device in his palm—"this is a dead man's switch. If I release the pressure on the switch, it will detonate a small charge in the container, releasing the contents."

Bobby turned to face Misha, gritting his teeth at this unexpected complication. "Sure, but I think that we should first check…"

"The money comes first." Misha looked around the room.

"Five minutes." Bobby headed for the door.

Misha tried to hide his concerns. They had not expected this gang of criminals and renegades to be ready to inspect the container immediately. He looked around and his heart sank when he saw the two guards standing close to the woman. They had the air of professionals and undoubtedly were well armed. Their backs to the wall, positioned so that they covered the entire room. No, he was no match for them, and he doubted that Aloth would be able to overcome them.

There was only one hope. He tried to appear confident, waiting calmly while dreading the fat man's return.

Five minutes became ten and then fifteen. His heart began to pound against his chest wall.

Finally the door opened. "Sorry, boys, we got a slight delay. We weren't expecting you to arrive so soon. We need a bit more time."

"How much more time?" Misha tried to keep his voice harsh and uncompromising.

"Half an hour, hour at the most."

"The agreement was for the money on delivery."

"Yeah, sorry." Bobby sneered in frustration. *The black ass got the upper hand, but only for the moment, only for the moment. Once they have the trigger, then we'll see what's what.*

They spent the following half hour staring at each other.

The woman grew more contemptuous of both groups. This was what you get when dealing with this sort. She glanced down at her diamond-encrusted watch. She would give the fools another ten minutes and then leave, to let the hillbillies explain themselves.

Fortune or good luck came to Bobby's rescue as they heard a vehicle drive up the gravel road to the house. Bobby all but raced out as fast as his short legs would allow.

A few short minutes later Bobby returned with another man, who carried a bag over one shoulder. "Chuck, my man, they got you out of bed?" Joey chuckled to the man who had just arrived with the bag.

"Funny," Chuck replied, clearly peeved as he walked up to one of the tables. The newcomer then placed the bag onto the table. "It's all here, but you're welcome to check it."

"I will." On unsteady legs Misha walked over to the table, he felt very exposed with his back to Bobby and the others. But he had to drag this out as much as he could. He began to count the money, trying to take as much time as he could without appearing to take his time. He made small stacks of hundred-dollar bills on the table.

"You finished yet? You're slower than a smelly nigger trying to find a job." Joey jumped off the table he had been sitting on. "You want to leave today, or you plannin' on goin' next week?"

"Patience—" Bobby never finished as a red blossom erupted from his chest.

"Down!" The word was screamed out in Russian. It had the desired effect as both Misha and Aloth dropped immediately to the ground.

Two men jumped through the door, one standing high as the other came in low. The taller combatant was already facing the left side, the other the right side of the room. The one standing erect had already opened fire with his short-barrelled Micro Uzi.

The other man fired his Uzi an instant later.

Caught by surprise, the bodyguards were cut in half by the short bursts. The tall man in the lead had the blackest eyes Misha had ever seen, which refused to blink as he gunned down the bewildered delivery driver. The tall man's partner fired again, hitting Joey once in the chest and another in the throat.

As if by magic a small gun appeared in the woman's hand.

The tall leader's gun barked once more, and three rounds cut a line across the woman's waist.

The two men matched forward to check each body by placing a round into each head.

"Ahmed?" Misha gasped in relief.

"It is Alex; remember to call me Alex here," the tall man demanded, still scanning the room.

"We must bury the bodies." Misha looked around at the blood-sprayed room.

"No, we will be long gone by the time their police find them. And they need to find the bodies; it is the only way they will begin an investigation." They needed to leave enough of a trail to ensure that the Americans knew the threat was real.

Alex took out a slip of paper and handed it to Misha. "This is the location where you are to take the device. You know what to do when you arrive?"

"Yes," Misha said with a nod.

"Good. I will send our messenger to the American authorities. This is David; he will drive you to your destination." Alex motioned the second man to come forward. "Now, wait outside. We need to leave them a trail." Alex spoke calmly as he removed the backpack from David's shoulder and extracted some tools, while looking at the container holding the "refrigerator."

Some thirty minutes later Alex and David emerged from the building.

"All is done. Load the container and go with Allah," Alex said and took his leave.

Misha and the other two men swiftly loaded the container into the rear of the vehicle then climbed into the cabin of the small truck. David pulled on a baseball cap before they headed down the road into the gathering darkness.

Some while later they stopped in a side street in a nearby town where they transferred the container into a van that was registered in David's name. Misha and Aloth made themselves comfortable. It was to be a long drive following the road for countless miles as they crossed much of the dry Arizona country. *Cutting across the American underbelly*, Misha thought, seeing the land of the Great Satan as it slowly withered and died. Witnessing how low they had fallen, he thought with silent glee. They passed though towns and even a city, with its half empty streets filled with dilapidated houses.

The boarded-up houses looked broken and sad. He thought of them as rotting teeth with black and white maggots crawling around the blackened stumps. Misha smiled as they drove down such streets; this was America. The country was in decay and would never rise again. He thought of himself as something of a student of America, he had studied its rise and now its fall. This godless country, the oppressors of so many millions, where greed and selfishness ruled, always taking from those unable to fight back—this country deserved this most suitable reward, a most fitting reward indeed.

Chapter 15

The best way to strengthen your enemies is to weaken oneself.

—Thomas Hardy

"Thank you all for coming, Senator Soccorre, Senator Scott." Clayton shook hands with the last of the newly minted senators that had arrived from their individual States. He then turned his attention to the old hands as they filed into the room, led by Senator Walker with his best smile painted on his face.

"Glad you could make it Senator." Clayton kept a straight face. "Glad to be here, sir." Walker smiled his best imitation smile. "Senator Holt, good of you to come." Clayton nodded to the next senator in line.

"I wouldn't have missed this for the world." Holt also tried on his been smile.

The senators were followed by the remaining leadership of Congress. Their leader was a tall African American who dominated the five men and women physically along with his considerable charismatic charm.

"Congressman Bradbury." Clayton offered the tall African American his hand.

"After all these years?" Bradbury shook his hand with a wide smile. "Sebastian, I hope the short notice wasn't an inconvenience."

"Not at all, Mr. President; we had plenty of time." In fact Congressman Bradbury had barely arrived at all, as he had not been asked to attend.

Clayton had scheduled another meeting for what remained of the congressional leadership. But the congressman had called and politely but firmly insisted that he and the others should attend any meetings with the new senators. Clayton saw no reason to object.

"Please, be seated." Clayton indicated for them to sit around the large oval conference table.

They had just enough room, adding the six congressmen to the five men and two women who had been inducted into the glorious ranks of the Senate. There could have been triple that number, but numerous candidates had politely declined the offer to join them.

Abb quietly found himself a seat in a quiet corner. Like Bradbury he had no need to be present but decided to gate-crash the party anyway.

Once everyone was seated, Clayton looked around the table at all the new and old faces. "I asked you all here to see what we can do to establish some form of long-term economic sustainability." Most gave him puzzled looks. "I fear we have done little to nothing in preparing our country for a sustainable long-term future and avoiding the next economic downturn."

"What can we realistically do?" Bradbury inquired.

"That is what we have to look into. I propose the creation of an independent committee that will look at our options. Its mandate is to find effective methods to encourage productivity during the next downturn. Build some form of insurance into the system, along with long-term strategies for the economy. People, we simply cannot continue with this endless cycle of boom and bust that so confounds our nation… especially with the threats we are likely to face in the future."

"That sounds like some commie five-year plan," Senator Holt snapped. "I suppose that would explain why China is once more kicking our ass, even with all its own difficulties, Senator. You know, with their disciplined, responsible government and long-term planning," Clayton replied flatly. "As opposed to our flying by the seat of our pants. There are serious options we need to investigate, and a neutral party could look into them."

"And this 'neutral' committee won't interfere with the free market? I doubt it." Senator Holt's teeth seemed to enjoy snapping at Clayton. "Doesn't Congress have enough committees?"

"I am talking about going above politics, Senator, for the sake of the country. And may I say, if it's in our nation's best interests, then it's time government did interfere in the free market." There was a tinge of fury in Clayton's voice now, his patience hanging by a thread.

"Perhaps, Mr. President, if you could provide specifics?" Senator Walker felt Holt was pushing too hard, and they had been warned.

"That would be the job of this independent committee—one without favour that would present us with the best options for the future."

"But you would like them to examine some areas?" Congressman Bradbury inquired.

"I do not deny it. But I want it to be non-political." Clayton tried to be open.

"Still," Walker persisted, "I would like to hear your view. It will help us decide."

"Yeah, dazzle us with the vision of the future." Holt was obviously not enamoured with Clayton's proposal.

"No, I think I'd rather hear your thoughts." Clayton looked at Holt.

Holt became suddenly silent and withdrawn.

"All right, anyone? Sebastian?" Clayton looked around the room. "Well, I suppose we could look into giving the Federal Reserve more power. The mess we're in simply because Trump gave the banks free rein must not be repeated." Congressman Bradbury turned to the president. "Maybe we should look into that Glass-Steagall Act you keep going on about?"

"I thought the president wanted them to come grovelling, so they can pay triple the government interest rate," Holt stated flatly.

"I would prefer that the economy did not suffer for the failure of the banks yet again," Clayton informed the Senator.

"Anyone else?" Holt did not really want to know.

Elaine Bell spoke up. "A number of respected economists have recommended creating a series of futures funds for government infrastructure projects." She was one of the new Senators, a youngish New Yorker with red freckles. "Just think what we could do with even the interest from a few hundred billion right now. And I'd recommend a second fund to support research and technological advancement. I sure as hell don't want our research establishments being taken overseas." This new female Senator was full of ideas.

"This all sounds like socialism to me," Senator Holt replied. "The corporate sector has always been sufficient, so why should we change now?" "I don't know"—Clayton took an icy tone in reply—"maybe because the corporate response has been a complete failure. Do I have to remind you who coursed this crash? And who keeps crawling to the government asking for a handout. Do I have to show you the damage corporate America has done to this country?" *Isn't it obvious or do we need to burn down a few more cities before you get the message?* "To reinforce Senator Bell's words, China alone is pouring billions into its own universities and research centres, how much is corporate America pouring into our universities, senator? "We need to prepare for the future with long-term strategies."

"More socialist claptrap." Holt dismissed the thought with a wave of his hand.

"Senator Holt, that's enough," Walker jumped in. "Mr. President, we agreed to come here in the spirit of cooperation. But honestly, I don't see the desperate need for this 'five-year plan' as Senator Holt hinted at. We have a great deal on our plate right now. Why is this so important to you?"

"Because we are at war, Senator."

"What?" Holt spluttered.

"We are at war with China. It's not a shooting war, but have no doubt, we are in an economic war. China is not content simply to be an economic giant. It has every intention of becoming the world's dominant economic superpower, dwarfing us totally. They have a strategy to get there while we flounder and undermine our own economy."

"You're not engaging in a little China bashing, Mr. President?" Holt was pleasantly surprised. He had never been a fan of China. Unlike some, he had a moral objection to China's human rights record.

"Far from it. In fact, I respect what China has achieved but equally fear the outcome should they come to overshadow us." Even if he was engaging in a little China bashing, that didn't make the threat any less real. And if a bit of nationalism could be the spur—the challenge he believed they desperately needed to move Congress and the nation—then so be it.

In his view, the nation needed a positive stimulus such as the American Civil War and Sputnik had supplied. A number of historians had argued that the war between the North and South had industrialized much of the North by compressing half a century of development into four feverish years. And when Russia launched Sputnik, it set off the space race and propelled America to unexpected heights by landing a man on the moon. So if China's behaviour and threat were to focus Congress's attention on the nation's future, so much the better.

"And this committee would confront the challenge?" Congressman Bradbury was not convinced.

"Bit late," noted Holt, both angry and pleased; "it's already knocking on the door." He was angry because they had taken so long to see China for the unconventional threat it was and pleased that Clayton had actually acknowledged it as such.

"A bit late, I grant you," Clayton replied, "but we can still stand up to them."

"With what, sir? Patriot slogans? Rabid nationalism? We're going to bomb them to keep the public's mind off its economic woes?" Bradbury sounded dubious. He did not like to hear the drums of war.

"Trade, Sebastian, followed by more trade." *Although a little patriotism wouldn't hurt,* Clayton admitted privately. *If you can still find some, that is.* "I was thinking in terms of genuine 'fair' trade agreements with all the Americas."

"You mean free trade?" Senator Walker spoke up to correct the president.

"No, Senator, fair trade. Meaning it will actually benefit everyone—the farmers and factory workers, the ordinary people of Latin America. As opposed to providing privileged arrangements for the multinationals." He looked around the table. "We need to build bridges to markets new and old, not sit on our asses."

"Could that work?" Bradbury asked. "We're not exactly well liked in some places down there."

"Any surprise, given our history?" Clayton added. "How can they not have a problem with us? Just look at our treatment of them on trade, from oil to bananas." To Clayton's mind, bananas were a perfect example. "For decades American companies have been paying a few cents per banana to the South American growers and selling the same bananas for a few dollars in North American supermarkets.

"Ripping people off is hardly the way to make friends. If we paid them a fair price, then they might have a more favourable outlook towards the US. And even better, with more money in their pockets, they could buy our goods. This in turn would undermine China's march into Latin America. We make friends, we reinforce democracy, and we benefit economically.

"People, the economic benefits are simply too great to throw away just to protect corporate greed. If we fail… imagine how much more America will suffer. Worse, imagine having China's totalitarian dictatorship throwing its weight around. Can we take the risk that it might decide to use its soft power to influence others into isolating us? Granted, that's strikes many as paranoid, but what guarantees do we have? God forbid we get involved in some insane shooting war simply because China decides to beat its chest over some contested waters—or supports North Korea's ambition to unify the peninsula by military force. I have no desire to provoke China by making it think we are weak." *We're weak enough as it is.*

"And even if China holds to a non-confrontational position, do we really want to slide down to number fifteen on the economic scale of nations?"

Clayton hammered home his point. "We need to examine all our options, which is what I propose. Whether it is fair trade, health care reforms, the size of government, tax reform, whatever. We need to plan for a future that will not become ash."

Holt spoke up. "Then agree to put an end to all this talk of increased taxes."

"Senator, we are here to discuss America's future. Let's not change the topic." *God, what does it take? Is it any wonder China is kicking our ass when we can't agree on anything?*

"Wrong," Holt shot back. "Taxes are a vital part of any debate about the future. We need a policy of reducing taxes to keep America competitive." "Senator, how do you propose to fund your future budgets?" Clayton wanted to shake his head in frustration.

"I propose we would have a sensible budget, cutting waste by putting an end to this ridiculous welfare state."

"Yeah, we can cut spending on education and completely cut all health care for the poor." Senator Bell's soft feminine voice took Holt's attention away from the president.

"Well—" Holt stopped, realizing what she had just declared to the room. "We cannot live beyond our means."

"Unless you're a Republican, right?" she answered him.

"I suppose we could cut back on all that highway development?" Clayton looked at Holt. They knew that President Caine had been pressured by the Republicans to continue the previous president's building of new highways, in an effort to ease unemployment.

"No, we need those new roads to ease congestion." The senior senator was not easily moved.

"And that's why we have to oppose public transport, so we can have even more congestion," Bell continued. "And then we can build even more highways. As long as the highway lobby gets more contracts, everybody, at least in Washington, is happy."

"Whatever you may think, we need quality transport routes," Senator Walker offered, coming to his colleague's aid. "We need the new infrastructure for the new economy. Driverless cars will need roads that—" Senator Bell was bold enough to interrupt. "We could've just upgraded the existing roads, Senator, and fixed the existing infrastructure, instead of springing for Trump's famous 'highways to onward.'" "That was Democrat propaganda."

"So we do have the best high-speed rail system in the world—oh gosh, if only someone had told me." She fluttered her eyelashes with such scornful innocence that a few chuckles were heard around the table.

"All right," Clayton offered with open hands, "how about we cut subsidies to the multimillion-dollar agro companies, while keeping most of the subsides for the small family farms?"

Holt shook his head. "No, food security is vital. We have to be able to feed ourselves."

"As long as you have the money to buy the food, that is." Bell's bright tone underscored her point.

"Change the law that requires the government to buy drugs at whatever price the pharmaceutical companies dictate," Clayton offered.

"No," Holt answered, "pharmaceutical products are vital to the state of this nation's health. They save millions in surgical procedures."

"And cost the government billions, or is that trillions more than they should." Senator Bell's voice softly goaded Holt's growing irritation at the woman.

Clayton made another offer. "I suppose we can reduce spending on military equipment?"

"No," Holt stated more forcefully.

"We can open long-term negotiations with other nuclear powers to reduce the world's stockpiles by 20 per cent and then 40 per cent?" Clayton persisted.

"No." Holt was turning bright red by now.

"Then what do you suggest? We cut what's left of Medicare? Add twenty million people to the rolls of the uninsured?" Clayton hissed. "When exactly will the Republican health care plan provide coverage to every American? Before or after the 2099 elections?"

"We have the best hospitals in the world. And we did not cut—" Walker stopped short. He knew health care had been a mess under his party, costing more and satisfying fewer costumers. *Damn Obama, if that black-ass had just shut up about health, we could had left things as they were. It's not as if all those fifty million uninsured would get sick.*

"How about cutting wages for all government employees?" *Starting with you,* Clayton thought, trying to keep his voice even.

"You can try avoiding the issue," Holt declared, "but at the end of the day, we can only go forward by cutting taxes."

"And just how do we pay our bills, damn it? We have been cutting taxes and government 'interference' since Reagan, and just where has that got us?

"We have cut taxes to the bone. For all the Republican bull, we are one of the lowest tax collecting nations amongst the advanced nations— twenty-seventh amongst the OCED nations. We have cut and cut taxes and allowed unscrupulous corporate tax avoidance for decades, to the point where we can't even pay our existing bills, much less the massive debt, so just how do we pay for our spending, Senator? How about supporting your country for once?" If Holt wanted to be pigheaded, he could return the favour. Besides, proclaiming Holt a fool to these youngest was something:

it offered future possibilities. Clayton smiled at that.

"How dare you question my loyalty to this great nation?" "If there is smoke…," Clayton replied with a mocking grin. "Perhaps we can consider a compromise?" Congressman Bradbury offered. "Let's not be too hasty." He needed to begin stamping his authority onto the debate. His star was now rising. After the terrible event that struck Congress, many new doors had opened, and now was the time to look to the future—his future.

"There can be no compromise." Holt was adamant in refusing to debate a compromise. "President Prescott is fundamentally unable to accept the need for tax cuts. He is simply ideologically opposed to cuts. That's the real problem here, not some vision of the future. And we certainly don't need to increase our bureaucracy and spending with this ridiculous Federal Health Insurance scheme."

"Let's—" Congressman Bradbury began another attempt to engage in reason.

"I thought your party would love a bit of free market competition, Senator." Senator Bell smiled prettily as she cut in. Even her red freckles were a pleasant delight compared to the ugly red on the veteran senator's face.

"We have plenty of insurance companies," Holt assured her with his usual conviction.

"So what is the problem?" Clayton made the obvious point. "One more can only be good for competition."

"You know full well, sir, the reality is—"

"That this federal insurance scheme," came Senator Bell's sweetly piercing voice, "will actually benefit the public instead of the insurance companies and their shareholders, is that what you meant?"

Holt glared bloody murder at her. *This damn woman is getting a little too uppity,* he thought. *Someone may need to clarify her place in the scheme of things.*

"Elaine, there is no need to be so abrasive." Another new member of the Senate addressed her gently.

"Nat, don't be such a wimp, or no one will take you seriously. Then again, no one has so far." She smiled at freshman Senator Coldlock from Kansas with whom she had spent some time during their induction course prior to entering the Senate.

"Senator," Clayton said with authority, "this is not the time to fight me. You have a— Damn it, if you don't want a Federal Health Insurance scheme, then offer me something better. Give me an alternative that will cut health costs and improve service. We all know we can't keep paying more and more for our health coverage."

"We simply need to reduce the size of government, not increase it. That's how we'll reduce costs," Senator Holt stated sagely, as if it were the most obvious thing in the world.

"While reducing government protection and services to the poor and the environment, right?" Young Senator Bell quipped.

"A tax cut will provide impetus to the middle class," Holt declared in his most righteous tone.

"Is that what you call the millions of homeless these days?" Despite herself, Senator Bell was having a fun time. She even gave a laugh of contempt at the elderly statesman.

"It's obvious that you haven't the slightest idea about basic economics," Holt said, as if correcting an inattentive student. "Otherwise you'd know the massive burden that the government places on the economy." *Enough, woman!*

"Yeah, education and health are so wasteful—except when supplied to the rich."

"Senator," Congressman Bradbury offered, attempting the role of mediator, "let us remain on target here. As I understand it, the Federal Health Insurance scheme will be government-owned but completely and totally run as a private company. It will make money."

"Yes, yes. I know, and it will have a 2 per cent ceiling on profits. That's totally unacceptable," Holt said dismissively.

"That's right, mega profits are what it's all about, right?" The new Senator from New York smiled merrily as she cut him off.

"Senator… sorry, I don't recall your name." Holt was very good with names, but this little slapdown should remind her of her status.

"That is quite understandable, for a man of your… advancing years, Senator. Elaine Bell, the Senator from New York. Pleased to meet you; I've heard so very little about you." That was good anyway.

"Uh—" He blinked. *What did she say?* "Well, Senator Bell, in the grownups' world, we let the marketplace decide. We believe in freedom of choice, the people deciding what kind of health care they should have. That, my dear, is why so many people oppose that socialist Obamacare in this country. And I can tell you I fully support their right to a free market with independent choice..." Holt's words died as he saw the look of disgust on Clayton's face.

"What choice?" Clayton looked at the senator with eyes of disgust. "Kindly spare me this endless regurgitation of free-market propaganda. You're not out there selling horse manure to the yokels. The public has no choice; health care is not optional."

"You can't be serious! People can pick whichever doctor they want. Just how much more choice could they want? Unlike the socialist care in Britain where you have to see the doctor they give—"

"Senator, you can choose to buy a TV. You choose to buy a house, a car. No one chooses to get cancer. If I'm sick, what the hell do I do? Do I see a doctor, or do I lie in bed until I recover from cancer or whatever I've got?

"There is no choice. That makes health care a monopoly, not some free-market enterprise. That, Senator, is why the rest of the developed world believes in universal coverage... whether its socialized medicine or not, because they, unlike the ignorant, know there is no choice." Clayton glared at the man in disgust. "If that means a British-style National Health Service or a government-owned insurance scheme for all, then so be it. Must I remind you that those with so-called 'socialist health care' enjoy increased life expectancy?—whilst in dear capitalist America our life expectancy is going downhill...

"Your capitalist health care system does not work for millions of Americans.

"Worse, unlike the socialists, if we are not careful your free market could see us paying 20 or even 30 per cent of our GDP to GPs, surgeons, and insurance companies, crippling our economy."

"That will never happen." Holt scoffed "That is an absolute fantasy." "I have to agree," Congressman Bradbury put in, "it does seem highly unlikely."

"And you know that for a certainty? You believe that prices for health care will go down?" Now Clayton scoffed at their naivety. "You're all thinking about the here and now, and that is not good enough. It's about time we took the future into consideration before we reach it."

"You're not arguing we should put caps on the pay for… some professionals?" Congressman Bradbury was actually shocked.

"I am saying we need to consider the future. The private sector chooses to pay its senior management tens of millions because it can afford to do so. Can America afford to pay doctors, health professionals, and health insurance CEOs that kind of money?"

"That's ridiculous, absurd," Holt protested. "If the cost is too high, the public simply won't… go to—" He stopped far too late.

The young woman from New York laughed at the elder Senator. "No wonder you're in the Senate, with a mind as sharp as mud."

"Very well, let us consider the future." Congressman Bradbury once more tried to take charge. "Can you be certain that this FHI scheme will cut costs?"

"It will reduce costs, even if I have to go to Canada and Mexico on my knees, begging them to accept Americans for procedures at a fraction of their cost in our nation. Right now, if I paid the Canadian Government twice what they charge for their 'communist' angiograms and add a bus ticket for any US patient, I'd still come out ahead on cost.

"If I have to hire hundreds of doctors from all over the world to settle into Canada and Mexico along our border so I can ship busloads of American patients to their clinics, I will, and I'd still be making a killing.

"People, Americans are already going to Asia… Malaysia, India, the Philippines… to have operations; hip replacements I am told are quite common. If I have to, I'll fill planes with patients and fly them to Asia. We'll all save millions."

"But with the risk of complications, it's totally unacceptable," Holt barked. "They are substandard."

"And how many Americans die at the hands of American butchers who call themselves doctors?" Senator Bell snapped at her elderly colleague. *Bloody senile old twit.*

"Actually, that is an excellent reason for the government to get involved. The FHIS could audit the overseas clinics, select the best ones, and then arrange the flights and operations—a full-care package flight. We could save buckets of money and get a better health care outcome." Clayton saw the look of horror on Senator Holt's face. "If I have to fly them to Cuba, I will." Holt continued to stare at Clayton in shock.

"Yes Senator, the peasants of 'commie' Cuba actually get better basic health care than millions of flag-waving American capitalists."

"What's wrong, Senator?" asked Senator Bell, smiling pleasantly if coolly. "You don't look well. In fact, you look… I don't know—'livered'; I think that's what you use to call in the stone-age."

"Socialized health has always been a disaster," Holt managed to stammer.

"In view of the fact that America has never had it, how would you know?" Clayton happily scoffed. "Although I am told Europe swears by it." "The waiting times in their emergency waiting rooms are appalling." "Actually they are doing better than we are, on average," Clayton shot back. *We're the ones going backwards, you idiot.* "But I will give our hospitals their due credit. If a girl with a broken toenail and rich parents enters the emergency room, then she'll always be rushed to the front, even over a girl with a heart attack and poor parents." He knew he was being vindictive, but there was something to be gained. He saw it in the room, heard it in the voices of the others in the room. They were losing patience with Holt, and that meant he was losing respect and authority.

"I will not allow you to slander the hard-working—"

"Yes, yes, you will defend the God-given right of greedy self-serving pricks to be greedy self-serving pricks." Senator Bell nodded at his infant wisdom in such matters.

"That is totally unfair. They are hard-working men and women with legitimate burdens. Just consider the massive cost of becoming a doctor these days. Then there is the massive insurance they need to pay. I would remind you that American doctors pay premiums twice as high as Mexican doctors do."

Abb sighed quietly as he looked up from his folder. This was getting them nowhere. *Why hasn't Clayton just called for a break?*

"And who is at fault, sir?" Senator Bell snapped at Senator Holt, all pretence of cordiality now gone. "What has Congress ever done to reduce educational costs? In my State we've recently introduced a scheme that's showing results. Instead of giving more money to the universities, we take it away if they don't improve performance or show signs of cost cutting."

Congressman Bradbury could smell the way the wind was blowing. "As for insurance, why haven't you just restricted payouts for lawsuits? That'll cut their premiums."

"It couldn't be because the lawyers want their piece of the American medical pie?" inquired a lean-faced new Senator at the end of the table.

"And that is exactly the problem we all face," Clayton answered. "Everyone has his or her hand out, always wanting more and more. And no one cares because they think they can just jack up the prices. But that is no longer the care, is it, Senator Holt?"

"Don't try scare tactics with me, sir. I will not be duped into believing this liberal nonsense. We merely need to cut taxes to fuel the economy."

"And cutting taxes will provide you with the money to build your next fighter jet, Senator? You're going to ask the Chinese for the money to build our next aircraft carrier?" Clayton released his full fury at the man.

"Don't be absurd. We will always have the ability to fund—"

"Oh, for fuc… Wake up." Senator Bell came close to kicking the illustrious Senator Holt under the table. Fortunately they were too far apart. "How, exactly, are you going to fund government when we have fewer and fewer people paying taxes? Open your eyes, Senator. Every decade more Americans are living in poverty, just so the rich can continue to fill their pockets."

"They are the engine of growth that powers our ship of state." Holt trotted out one of his favourite lines.

"Then why is the ship dead in the water while the big rats are running for the lifeboats?" she replied.

"I toadly… Uh, totally reject such claims."

"You would, especially since they are factual," Senator Bell told the room.

"Missy, I have had just about enough from you."

She grinned at him. "Too bad; I'm just getting started."

"Just what is your problem?" Holt had had enough, more than enough. "My problem? *My* problem? My problem is you. You with your fossilized head so far up your ass your mouth is full of shit. Have you actually walked down the garbage-filled streets with their empty homes? No, you just speed past in your bulletproof chauffeur-driven limo. Have you spent even one night sleeping on concrete instead of your nice warm bed?" "How dare you!" Holt's cheeks flushed crimson.

"No, how dare you, you senile, decrepit bag of rotting hot air. I've had it with you and your pathetic one track mind. You… you hide your narrow ideology behind some ridiculously thin veneer of economic conservatism, when it's all about fundamentalist ideology.

"I thought you were in the pockets of big business—just another political sell-out—but I was wrong. You really are a senile old fool drooling over some abstract ideology. You would rather see this country dragged down, see it burned to the ground than put your precious ideology aside.

"Jesus, you're worse than any leftover 'commie.' At least they have the honesty to admit they base their economics on ideological grounds."

"And you sound just like every bleeding heart liberal I've met who has had everything given to them on a silver plate, never worked a day in their lives, never fought for this country, never bled for this country, but oh so eager to criticize and condemn it."

"Lovely speech, Senator. When was the last time you fought for this country? Bled for this country? Oh, yeah, that's right: you never served, did you?

"But you've fought for the people, haven't you? You've written up hundreds of bills fighting for equality, justice, improvement in living standards… struggled hard to raise the minimum wage, right?" She glared as the Senator. "No, wait… haven't you always opposed raising the minimum wage? When, exactly, have you written legislation that benefited the ordinary man or woman instead of letting lobbyists do it for their own benefit?"

"I will not be lectured by some immature child spoiling for a fight," Holt went on the defensive.

"Come on, Senator. Was it five years ago? No? Ten?" She studied his face closely. "More? Fifteen years? Can you even remember your last piece of legislation that benefited the ordinary guy?"

"There have been so many in my long career, I wouldn't have time to name them all."

"You don't know, do you?" She paused, as if wondering. "You know, maybe you are senile. I understand the early signs are repeating yourself and forgetting things. Maybe we should get you checked out at one of your wonderful clinics… see if you're not losing it." She hissed the words.

"I will not stand for these scandalous accusations. I have been a Senator for over thirty years while you haven't even done one winter. Until you can claim even a tenth of my successes, I suggest you remain silent and listen before you embarrass yourself."

"Then name your great works, Senator," Bell said, spreading open hands. "Come on, what was your great achievement? Come on."

"Go easy." Nat Coldlock, the new Senator from Kansas, spoke up. "Why should I? What has he achieved that's been worth a damn?

He's spent his entire career calling for tax cuts while America went further into debt. You know tax cuts aren't the answer. even a first-year economist knows that. But that's all he can parrot." Her eyes bored into Senator Holt's eyes, daring him to challenge her words.

No one, no one had spoken to him like that. No one had ever accused him of selling out his country. Yet Senator Holt found that he was finding it difficult to castigate this child.

"Let's be fair, Elaine, there is plenty of condemnation to go around." Nat glared at her and then turned to the president. "The racist attack on African Americans under the guise of executing drug dealers is the most blatant."

"What?" Senator Bell glared in confusion at Coldlock.

"Don't play dumb. We all know the vast majority of those the president wants to hang will be African Americans."

"I'm dumb all right," Bell sarcastically replied, giving little away in her tone, "because I don't know what the hell you're talking about."

"It's another form of white genocide against the blacks, that's what I'm talking about." The new Senator from Kansas turned to the president.

"You've denied them jobs, denied them education, and now you're targeting them for legalized murder."

"You're saying only black men sell illegal drugs?" Clayton asked innocently.

"Of course not, but they are placed in an impossible position . . . forcing them to take an undesirable course of action."

"I see." A slight pause followed Clayton's words. "You hold to the belief of the liberal intelligentsia that two wrongs make a right?" Clayton stated calmly.

"I... I don't follow." The new Senator sounded slightly confused. *Ah, youth.* Clayton smiled. "According to you, just because you have no job, it's OK to sell drugs. A 'crime' has been committed against you; therefore you can commit a real crime in return."

"If you are being victimized simply because of your colour," Nat began, "is it any wonder that you may make a few bad choices? If you really want to fight drug abuse, then you fight inequality."

Senator Walker broke his silence. "Here we go again; it's always someone else's fault. The typical rhetoric of the liberal bleeding heart, never take responsibility for your actions." *Stupid asshole; how many of them would have a real job if they weren't born bone lazy? They'd rather sit on their black asses and get high all day then go out and sell drugs so they can get high again.* Walker scoffed. "It's not as if they don't have a choice."

"For a few perhaps, Senator, but Senator Coldlock has a point," Congressman Bradbury said. "Mr. President, you have to accept that some will see this as targeting African Americans."

"Are *you* suggesting that only African Americans sell drugs, Congressman?" Clayton almost sounded shocked.

"Come on," Bradbury replied, "we know that's not the case, but we also know the less affluent communities have fewer job opportunities, a lot less opportunity for advancement."

"And whose fault is that?" Clayton shot back. "How many decades has Congress been sitting on its hands? Kept cutting funding for America's ghettoes?

"Senator Coldlock, even before I took one step into the hallowed halls of governance, two police chiefs actually came to me begging for help. They were sick and tired of having their officers' deal with all the social and mental health problems from within the inner cities. Do you understand, Congressman? The police were asking for help because of the decades of neglect by Congress.

"Do I need to remind you of Obama's speeches on this very topic? So you tell me, what has Congress ever done but bury its collective head in the sand?

"You want to help the African Americans?" Clayton opened his hands as if in invitation. "Very well then, here is your chance: you get your illustrious colleagues here—Senators Holt, Walker, and friends—to redress the cuts. Just ask them for the billions they've denied the ghettoes for decades."

"Well, I... I—" The new Senator stammered, his eyes locked onto Clayton's until his eyes wavered and turned away. Telling Clayton what he wanted to know. Kansas was re-evaluating his loyalties. He was seeing Congress in a new, unflattering light.

"Really, Mr. President, you're being overly flippant, to say the least." Congressman Bradbury sounded conciliatory, eager to find common ground. "We need to keep in mind that the police are often confronted with the shortcomings that the communities have themselves created and failed to address."

"Oh, come on," Bell snapped at the senior Congressman. *You two-faced hypocrite.* "You think those communities want to live in poverty, want the cops to go around in armoured tanks and body armour carrying assault rifles 'cause it looks cool?"

"You have totally misread the situation," Bradbury declared.

"Yeah, you think? Who's really to blame when a cop guns down a black man, the cop or the society that tells him to keep the niggers and undesirables... keep the *trash* in their place?" Nat hammered away.

"That is absolute nonsense. How dare you—" Bradbury shot to his feet. "How dare you deliberately deny tens of millions of Americans any chance at progress?" Nat shouted back with equal force. "And then say it's their fault."

"That is enough." Holt interjected. "We need to concentrate on the real issues, the economy and the big-spending government. Once we have the economy growing, then the economic pie will grow enough to provide for all Americans."

"You really don't get it, do you? You really have no idea. Did you hear even a word the president said about wages?" *Can't the senile fool see? Prescott laid it all out for the whole country. The fool just has to open his eyes.*

Clayton finally intervened. "Okay, perhaps we should have a short break and then see what we have in common. This has clearly aired out our thoughts."

The Road Trip to Washington

David, their driver, spoke rarely and far too softly for Misha's taste, but the man could drive; that much Misha had to admit to himself. In truth it was not the silence but the blond hair that annoyed him. The man was clearly an infidel Westerner; how could he be trusted with such a vital mission?

Misha continued to chew on his bone of discontent even as their van crossed another state line. Only when the vehicle began to slow down did he look out the windscreen to see several police cars and officers on foot manning a major roadblock.

David stopped the van behind a short line of vehicles waiting to be given permission to move on. As they waited, they watched one state trooper walk down the line of waiting cars. After a little while the officer reached their van.

"Is something wrong, officer?" David asked in his crisp native language, which upset Misha all the more. Misha looked away with disinterest. He reminded himself not to be overly friendly. He knew Americans were disrespectful of the law in their own country, even as they insisted all others should obey their laws.

"Protesters are blocking the bridge, so you'll have to wait a while until we can clear the road."

"How long do you reckon?"

"Depends. People aren't happy. St Claire is closing down. You're not from around here." The officer had noticed their out of state plates.

"We heard from a friend that there might be a better chance of finding work in the eastern states."

The young officer nodded; he had no wish to deny them hope, even if he thought they had little chance of success.

"When we get the all-clear, you follow the cars around the outskirts of the town. Like I said, everyone's riled over the factory closing down." He looked back towards the town. "They ain't happy at all."

After a seemingly interminable delay, they were given permission to move on.

"Stay out of the centre of town; follow the cars," the officer reminded them as he walked down the line of cars.

David waved and followed the vehicles towards the town. Yet the line of cars began to shrink the further they went. After crossing three streets, the two cars in front turned right, and the car ahead of them turned left.

"Which—?"

"We stick to the outskirts," David said with confidence, following the car that had turned left.

Nearly halfway around the town they began to get worried as they saw people with protest signs.

David turned left and seemed to enter a new world, one filled with angry protesters holding signs and screaming words of hate. David shrugged and set off down the road.

"Take a side street," Misha told David with eyes wide and fearful. As they watched a mass of bodies walk up the street.

David complied by turning into a small side street. This was a mistake: by doing so, they had cut off another group of protestors. A moment later people were slamming their fists and open hands onto the van. Some struck the side panels with their protest signs.

The small number of police was not up to the task of controlling the mob, which now had a target for their anger. One protestor sent a rock flying and cracked the windscreen.

"Drive, before they pull us out of the car!" Misha shouted at David. Another rock went through the partly open side window. The sound of shattered glass was followed by the sickening thud of rock striking against David's temple.

The van swerved left, Misha jumped the short distance between seats to grab the wheel and steered the van down the small side street, the horn blaring as he tried to steady their course.

The old van had two small front seats with a gap between the seats, allowing Aloth to reach forward, drag David from his seat, and lay him on the floor of the van.

Once the driver's seat was vacant, Misha jumped into it. He then gunned the engine, threatening to run down the protestors if they did not move.

A gunshot echoed as Aloth fired his small pistol into the air from the open side window. It had the desired effect as the crowd dispersed, allowing them to speed down the side road. Only when they were well clear did Misha slow down and finally pull to a stop, where he began shaking uncontrollably. Even during the slaughter in the farmhouse, he had not felt so out of control.

Aloth took the steering wheel and began to drive before asking, "How is he?"

"What?" Misha, sitting in the passenger seat, was confused. "David—how bad is his injury?"

Misha turned to look at the man. Even with his eyes glazed over in shock he saw blood flowing freely from the man's temple. Misha bent over and hesitated; then he sucked in his breath and examined David. With slightly trembling hands he checked for the man's pulse. He found none; he tried again with the same result. He laid a hand on the man's chest to feel for a heartbeat, and again he found none.

"He's dead." Misha could not believe his own words.

They stopped in a quiet street under a tree.

"We need to get the windscreen repaired," Aloth stated.

"I can see that." Misha tried not to shake.

They looked at each other. Back home or in Russia they knew how to see to the repairs, but it struck them that they were unsure how to proceed.

True, they could pay in American dollars but would they raise suspicion if they did not use the vehicle's insurance policy to cover the repairs?

Did American law require the vehicle to have insurance to cover the repairs? And the van was in David's name; would they be accused of stealing it?

Did they even have the correct identification papers for the vehicle? Would their papers pass inspection if they had to hand them in to the police until the repairs were finished?

The container... what do we do with it? Fear ran down Misha's spine.

They could not leave it in the vehicle.

Could they afford the risk of keeping it in this small town while the windscreen was replaced?

They were stumped by the uncertainty of everyday life in America.

The Oval Office

"That went well." Abb declared with only a touch of sarcasm. "Think they bought any of it?"

"That it's time to bury the hatchet for the good of the country? Maybe, if Holt gets to bury it in my skull." Clayton smiled his toothy grin. The idea of fair trade, working together for the good of the country . . . such ridiculous pipe dreams.

"Holt was a lost cause from the beginning, but some of the others were more open. What was it with our lovely Senator Bell? She really had her fangs out for Holt."

"You know who her mother was?" Clayton inquired with little humour.

"No."

"Annette Star. I believe Elaine changed her name to Bell as some kind of protest."

Abb shook his head. "Nope, not ringing a bell."

"You won't outside a rather small circle. She was a vaguely notorious radical in some literature circles, wrote a few books condemning capitalism."

"I'm not too sure how that translates to Miss Bell's attitude."

"Her father was unable to find work after losing his job, turned to alcohol and drugs, and then finally committed suicide. In his suicide note he asked forgiveness for not being able to provide for his young daughter and family. I understand Miss Bell's mother always blamed his death on an uncaring government more concerned with profit than people."

"Then Miss Bell's quite the chip off the old block." Abb had a laugh. "Let's hope her enthusiasm for the job continues."

"Let's hope not." Clayton replied.

"You're not happy with her attitude?" Abb's brow crinkled.

"She has every right to go after Holt. After all, he's happy to screw over anyone who's in his way. I just hope it doesn't become part of her. Her prejudice could blind her just as much as it blinds our elderly Senator.

"And we can't afford it—the country can't afford it, damn it. It's not supposed to be about going after the man; it should be about going after the ball. Why is it so hard for them to think about their country?"

"You're asking me? I'm the last person to ask. I'm hardly the deep thinker. Mind, if my old professor was here, I know what he'd say: 'Shit happens.'"

"Deep." Clayton brightened with a smirk. "Enough small talk. What have we got?"

"We have, for starters an FBI briefing with Deputy Director Drywood."
"Let's get it started."

A few minutes later a tired-looking Andrew Drywood came in, his suit pressed and tailored to fit yet seeming to hang off his frame. He started speaking before he'd settled into his chair "We may have a line on those targeting high-profile individuals in New York, Texas, and Hollywood, sir."

"Go on, Andrew." Clayton perked up at his words.

"There is a group of hackers called Anomalous America. I have their web page here." Drywood handed the small tablet to Clayton and the FBI preliminary file to Abb.

"You will notice how they praised the killings in New York and the senatorial candidate. Now, that's nothing different from a hundred other sites, but this one was especially vindictive towards the young movie actress."

"Who?" Abb asked as he opened his folder.

"Amanda Watson, the hottest item in Hollywood at the moment." "Wait a minute." Abb was confused. "What the hell did they have against her?"

As Andrew and Abb spoke, Clayton read the usual socialist arguments against the rich, before continuing on to the section targeting the movie actress. It gave heated accusations of her spending huge amounts on the latest clothing styles, even as millions of Americans were reduced to wearing "rags." She had staged a massive house-warming party, inviting guests from all over the world to attend, while tens of thousands huddled in makeshift shelters.

It went on to attack Hollywood and movie stars in general. Yet the condemning of the movie industry as parasites and lackeys of the rich seemed almost an afterthought. The attack was clearly directed at her rather than at Hollywood in general.

"Well, I would agree the site wasn't her biggest fan." Clayton watched a short video of her, prancing around half-dressed as was the usual Hollywood style of late. "But what makes her dead useful to your investigation?"

"I believe it was more personal than it was political, sir. I think her killer had a more personal motive. And that may narrow down the list of suspects."

"But Director Shaw has his doubts?" Clayton continued his interrogation.
"Sir?"

"You wouldn't be telling me this if the director agreed," Clayton offered by way of explanation.

"He does not disagree that there may be some personal connection, sir. But he feels that our limited manpower can be better spent."

"Yet, there appears to be no more *personal* grievance here that you would find in a sleazy tabloid or a far-left rag," Clayton countered.

"It's not the personal attack so much as the method. The killer used a string from her own guitar to garrotte her. The other deaths were all coldly impersonal—one could say even professional; this was very personal."

Abb, still reading the FBI report, broke in. "You sure it wasn't opportunistic? She was new to fame, didn't have much of a bodyguard. Not the usual dozen or so goons looking after a Hollywood star, that's according to your own report. The anarchists maybe saw an opening and took it?"

"I know it's not much, but at the moment that's all we've got." "So what are you hoping to find?" Clayton's interest was apparent. "Hopefully, we'll find a way into their network and with that into their centre of operations."

"You think they have a command and control... a headquarters?" Abb looked up again.

"Not so much in the conventional sense, but someone has to be picking the targets. Someone has to be organizing their actions. No matter how much they use the Net, there still has to be some kind of organization."

"You hope," Abb added without sarcasm. "It does not have to be an organization in the conventional sense."

Well, surprise, surprise, Drywood thought; *the guy is listening.*

"Okay, keep us updated on your progress. And I want you back as soon as possible. Oh... may I hold on to this tablet till your return?" Clayton held up the small device.

"Yes sir. And I'll get right on it." Drywood left with his notes and files barely tucked away in his bricfcase.

"Do you think it was personal?" Abb looked at Clayton over his glasses. "Oh, I'd say there's a good chance. I don't think you would hogtie someone and garrotte them with their own guitar string unless there was some emotional connection. The question is whether it was one of the anarchists with a grudge or just some nobody with a grudge." Clayton was still absorbed with what he was reading. "Abb, get Brandon and Jonathan to come in. I want them to read this." "Why?"

"To understand, we have a window into the mind of the..." "The enemy?" Abb glanced at the president. "The public," Clayton responded without rancour.

The four men spent the next half hour reading, after Jonathan had slipped out and with his usual efficiency had obtained three more tablets and gone to the web page on their browsers.

"This is just a collection of hate mail." Abb put down the tablet. "It's the reality of our brave new world, Abb. Here is a movie star cracking twenty million a movie, living like royalty and not ashamed of it… flaunting it in fact. Her actions couldn't be more inflammatory: wild parties, spending money like there was no tomorrow.

"In the past we would've shrugged it off but today it's a whole new world. Just look how they have turned on her. They are not happy." Brandon sounded concerned and disappointed at the same time.

"I hear that," Jonathan said. "Listen to this beauty: 'The bitch boasted that she spent 770 dollars on styling her hair, then went on and talked about spending forty-three hundred on meals and drinks in a fancy restaurant. I have to cut the hair of my own kids and work two jobs just to put enough food on the table. She spends more on luxuries in one day than I could spend in a year. They should have roasted the bitch with a blowtorch before cutting her throat.' Unquote." He was clearly a little shocked by the anger.

"I can sympathize with the lady's distress, but you need to realise these people have a rare talent," Abb protested. "They have made something of themselves. They are entitled to that kind of money."

"Here's a reply for you." Jonathan read another of the many quotes of the day. "What's the difference between being offered one million and demanding six million? I'll tell you in one word: greed, pure and selfish greed. In France, if you earn over a million in a year, you pay real taxes; here, the more you earn, the less taxes you pay."

"Supply and demand," Abb began. "If everyone could act, if everyone could play sports at an elite level, then yes, it's a bit much. What you have got here is petty jealousy… envy."

"You can't honestly mean that!" Brandon Keel protested. "You are saying it's not about greed, ego, and prestige? You're telling me an actor or CEO still needs more once they've made fifty million? They can't live well enough on the interest from a hundred million? What exactly does having five billion get you? Immortality, a star on the Walk of Fame?"

"You get what your worth, and good luck to you." Abb shrugged away their concerns.

"With respect, sir, the French are right on the money. That's a smart way to control ridiculous wages growth," Jonathan answered. "Hell, I still remember some Internet company paying a Wall Street accountant 85 million to move over to California and join the company. You're going to tell me they paid that kind of money 'cause some accountant was worth it? Or because the assholes wanted to strut around and say look how much money we spent to get an accountant? They couldn't find a good accountant for a million?"

"How many IT scholarships could they have given to needy kids with that kind of money?" Keel shrugged.

"That isn't their job," Abb informed both men.

"What is their job?" Clayton asked. "Bleed America dry? I've heard endless economists lecture on how the public needs to spend to get the economy moving. And this while Apple kept—what was it?—some forty or fifty billion dollars in offshore accounts. Just how does that benefit the

American economy?" With a shrug, he added, "Just how does having the top 10 percent to horde billions help the American economy?"

"Some donate large sums to charities," Abb countered.

"That's debatable," Keel said. "You've got some of the richest guys in America running charities. One of them builds road and schools in Africa—but tell me how many crumbling roads and bridges he repairs in the US with his charity write-offs on tax?"

"Argue all you want," Abb said, "but in the end it's still all about what the market is willing to pay. Don't blame me if someone is stupid enough to pay a thousand dollars to sit in the front row at a rock concert or two thousand for a private viewing of the latest movie. We live in a free country.

"Look, you think actors are overpaid, then just don't go to the movies. You think the CEOs are overpaid, then don't buy what they sell." His tone was flippant, but his face said he meant it.

"Like a boycott?" Jonathan said. "Boycott all movie outlets until the theatres cut the price by half? That's not so far-fetched, when you think about it. If the theatres were forced to charge half price, then the industry could demand a cut in pay for the actors."

"Same with sports," Keel added. "Some basketball tickets are way overpriced."

"Brandon, that is far-fetched," Abb said. "And aren't we being a little petty, picking on a few actors or sports franchises? Hollywood is only a small part of the economy."

"No, Abb," Clayton said quietly. "Hollywood is the very epicentre of our discord. It's not just the wealth or the massive egos. It's how they shove their lifestyle in people's faces. Acting like they are royalty. Even the Oscars… isn't that all about glamorizing themselves, showing off how they live in a totally different world than ordinary people do?

"And that's the problem facing us all. Think about it, truly think about it; the poor are seeing the vast inequality that is growing decade by decade, they see the injustice and think we don't care for them. And we desperately need them to believe there is justice, that America does care for them."

Keel looked away. How could you believe in something that didn't exist? It wasn't as if lawmakers didn't have the answers to inequality. They just needed to care. Limits on CEO pay, tax concessions… so many options. *God, maybe Clayton is right and we should dissolve Congress.*

"And placing boycotts on movie theatres is the answer?" Abb persisted. "No, but—" Clayton paused. "If it cuts the cost of living by a few dollars, why not try? And who knows? If it works, it could spread to other areas." He allowed himself a half-smile at the idea.

"And the public could begin to see the royally rich sharing in the pain, at least a little." Jonathan understood what was worrying Clayton. The president saw the anger and frustration of millions with no jobs and no future, all ready to lash out and tear down the country.

Abb was unimpressed. "So your answer is to boycott anyone you think is being overpaid."

"We could try…" In fact, the threat might be enough to get them to actually help out. The thought amused Clayton.

"So if your doctor or your surgeon looks to be too expensive, are you going to boycott him?"

"There you go, Abb. I knew you would see it my way."

Abb's eyes widened. *What?* He recalled Clayton's remarks on health care but had not truly taken them to heart. Now as he looked at Clayton's grinning face, he wondered. *Does Cuba take American Express?*

Chapter 16

Ideology is the refuge of scoundrels unable to hold an independent thought.

—Harold Blunt

The two new arrivals to the city of Washington drove down the tree-lined streets with a true sense of relief, even when they had taken the wrong turn-off and gone in circles.

Both men were much more experienced with Russian and military maps than the insanity of the American highway, heading towards extinction. But finally the two warriors of the faith arrived at an innocent-looking house that actually seemed to be leaning to one side. Unfortunately, the rent had already been paid in advance. And they had nowhere else to go.

Fortunately it looked so unsocial that it would hardly attract unwanted visitors.

Suspicious of the FBI devil worshippers, the two men drove around the block before stopping.

"If I am not back in an hour, leave," Aloth told Misha.

Misha nodded, he understood all too well the risks of discovery. Aloth checked the silenced pistol and tucked it under his shirt before going around the corner to study the street. After a half hour of observation, he casually walked down the street. He studied each window, each car, anything suspicious.

Had the young couple sitting on the step of the house some three houses down from their rented property been there a little too long? He saw that the woman was heavily pregnant, it could be staged, but he doubted it. No one walking their dog… that was a good start, he decided. No line repair crews, even better. No workers' van on the street at all, much better.

Nearly one hour later he returned to the van, and they drove around the block to the front of the house. With Aloth guiding him, Misha backed the van up the driveway but stopped short of the opened garage door. Instead of entering the garage, Misha watched as Aloth opened the front door and was swallowed by the shadows.

Only when satisfied that the house was indeed empty did Aloth wave Misha to back up against the garage, before unloading the container holding their "refrigerator." They carried it into the basement and covered it under a pile of worn boxes and other discarded materials.

Then Aloth took the keys to the van and climbed into the vehicle for a long drive around the city.

Neither man was an expert in dealing with nuclear weapons, and although Misha had been assured, prior to the mission, that the device was safe, they still felt that the device could leave a radioactive trail.

Misha knew their leaders were not learned men in the field of science. *Am I not equally ignorant?* he thought as he watched Aloth drive down the street.

Misha's and Aloth's knowledge of radiation came from the story of how the British police had been able to follow the radioactive trail left behind by the Russians who had poisoned the dissident Alexander Litvinenko with radioactive polonium. They both knew they were well out of their depth and so acted accordingly.

Thus, two hours later Aloth was still driving the van around the city in the hope that this would confuse and bewilder any attempt at tracking them down. He circled and criss-crossed his trail for hours, unsure whether he was being clever or foolish.

Eventually he returned to the house on foot. He sat down on the badly upholstered couch. The furnishing looked as bad as the house. He stretched out. "How much money do we have left?"

"We have twenty-seven hundred and forty dollars, enough for us." Misha tried to sound confident.

"We would still have more if we had argued harder over the cost of the windscreen," Aloth insisted once more.

"Illegal immigrants would hardly have argued over the cost," Misha reminded him.

Aloth had solved their dilemma over the confusing issue of insurance and other possible legal requirements by hinting that they were illegal immigrants to the owner of the small repair shop. With Misha's questionable-sounding English and Aloth's lack of English, they had easily passed for illegal migrants.

"Your idea was expensive, but it worked." Then Misha asked, "The van is dealt with?"

"I left it where Ahmed—where *Alex* said we should. Hopefully he is right, and the vultures will pick it clean. But I never want to take another bus in this country." Aloth had been to Germany on a few occasions, and even with no command of the German language, he'd had nowhere near the difficulty. "I would blow up this city just to make their public transport pay."

"Eat something. I will go get the vehicle *Alex* prepared for us." Misha pulled the thick jacket over his shoulders.

"Are we not supposed to collect this other van tomorrow?"

"It will give us more time to secure the device into it. And it will be beneficial if we go over the route a few times." Ahmed had gone to the trouble of providing them with a van that had local plates and papers to avoid suspicion. "The last thing we can afford is to get involved in a stupid accident." He had no desire to make another wrong turn.

The White House

"We still have very little to go on," Ethan Campbell, national security adviser, opened his briefing. "The Russians are still running around like chickens with their heads cut off."

"That's our best professional assessment?" Clayton inquired.

"They seem to have no cohesive plan of action, sir. Large areas of the country are under military rule, virtual lockdown, and there've been mass arrests of anyone who may be related to this, even in the vaguest way imaginable—along with a lot of people just opposed to the government. But the commitment"—he would have preferred the word *brutality* but knew some of the president's inner circle of counsellors would object—"isn't really there. Especially when it comes to Chechnya, I would have expected rougher handling of suspects by their security forces after such an event.

"Instead it's all haphazard, somewhat lacking, and they haven't shown much in the way of concrete results in tracking down any runaway nukes."

"You still hold that this is some kind of deception?" Clayton asked evenly.

"Sir, the Russians hold on to their nukes tighter than their family jewels. To be honest, I can't see how anyone could have just walked in and taken a nuke without being intimately aware of their procedures and protocols. I can only assume the Kremlin is up to something."

"But to bomb one of their own cities?" interjected the new Secretary of State, Colin Blackwell. The former owner of the title had simply resigned— "Too old for this… just too old," he had told Clayton. The world he knew was crumbling all around him; now all he wanted was to be around his grandchildren and hold on to a little piece of sanity.

The former secretary had not been the only one. A number of the White house staff had resigned, and perhaps it was over personal reasons. Except that Clayton had his doubts and wondered whether it had more to do with the feeling that he was not taking the hard measures needed to deal with the violence. As if cracking down with more violence would bring peace and order. Clayton wondered if they even understood what was happening.

"They have done something like this before," Campbell said. *If you can blow up an apartment block today, then why not a city tomorrow?* "And it gives the Kremlin a veil of legitimacy if they push their agenda by using military force."

"You're sure?" Blackwell asked in all honesty.

"I don't deny I feel frustrated over our intelligence services' poor performance, sir." *And our country's past failures.* "But that does not mitigate the facts. If the Chechens had nuked Russia, why hasn't Russia flattened the country in payback? They could have done it even without any nukes.

"The whole scenario just doesn't fit, sir. The more we learn, the less the parts fit. According to reports, some of these terrorists had been roaming all across Russia. The identified 'terrorists' were in Russia supposedly for over two years. It doesn't add up."

"How so?" Blackwell asked.

"Sleeper cells are a good idea, sir. The Russians have them here, but that's not how Islamic terrorists work. They select a target and go for it, not wait years before implementing it. More to the point, how could they know, a year in advance, that they would be in a position to get their hands on a Russian nuke? I mean, you can't see into the future and know you'll have that kind of access."

"Who really knows? Maybe they had a highly placed agent in play," Secretary Blackwell persisted in his dry voice, so dry it seemed to occasionally crackle.

"Not likely. A nation-state, yes. But for a terrorist group, it's unheard of. Just imagine the difficulties this highly placed turncoat would have trying to make contact with a terrorist group without blowing his cover."

Colin Blackwell wanted to offer as many possibilities as he could. "But do we know they were originally sent in for a nuke, or were they sent in to lie dormant until given the word to—I don't know—hit one or more high-value targets? And the nuke came up by chance."

"Actually, that makes a little more sense… if the terrorist leaders were smart enough to send in small groups and then got lucky." But Ethan Campbell shook his head. "Only it doesn't answer the question of how they obtained access. You don't trip over a nuke. That's as unlikely as their managing to accidently arm the bloody thing. You don't flip an on-switch. You've got a better chance of winning the Grand National three times in a row."

He glanced down at his notes and exhaled. "It doesn't end there. You have the operation itself. Consider the training, security, the organizational skills needed to move that many men. The latest Russian reports are talking of up to sixty men, maybe more. We have never seen a terrorist attack of such magnitude in a non-Islamic country."

"So you're saying it has to be something like a nation-state?" Blackwell was not overly sceptical.

Campbell seemed more convinced than before. "All the evidence points to a state… something bigger than a bunch of ragtag terrorists."

"Yet the Russians are still claiming it was the Chechens?" Clayton asked the group to once more confirm what he had been told.

"They have positive ID on several terrorists. That's straight from the Russians," Campbell declared.

The Secretary of State continued, "What interests me is that no group has actually taken responsibility. I mean to say, if Chechen terrorists used a nuclear weapon, why haven't they publicized it? Why leave it to the Russians?" Blackwell was basically agreeing with Ethan Campbell.

"And we are back to where we started," Campbell pointed out: "why isn't Russia grinding Chechnya into the ground?"

"Maybe the Chechens have a second nuke and told Moscow to back off or they'll use it," Blackwell mused out loud. "That would stop any Russian retaliation."

"But they are still in Chechnya." Campbell countered.

"And walking on eggshells… you admitted as much, Ethan." Blackwell cleared his throat. "The Chechens may have no choice but to let the Russians poke around until they come to an agreement."

"I don't know," said the Secretary of Defence; "if I was the Chechens and had a nuke, I'd have already kicked Russia out of Chechnya or used the damned thing."

"And Russia would then turn Chechnya into a sea of ash." Campbell was convinced of that much.

"Unless the Chechens have more than one nuke," Blackwell pointed out, "and we don't know, right? Anyway, I don't see Russia willing to lose Moscow over Chechnya, so they'll want to come to some accord."

"That's if the Chechens do have a number of nukes." Campbell spoke softly.

"Gentlemen, you're making my head spin. Enough with the known knowns, the known unknowns, and the unknown known and known gnomes." Clayton paraphrased a certain former Secretary of Defence over his failings and explanation for his failures in Iraq. "Ethan, do we have anything solid on the inner thinking of their intelligence services or the Kremlin itself?" Which were practically the same thing.

"No sir. We have nothing, given the latest compromise of our intelligence services. The Russians have us over a barrel. It'll take some time to regain what we lost." Campbell made no apologies. It seemed that with each year they discovered yet another patriotic American passing classified information to the Russians.

"Wonderful. But the question remains: what do we do or should we do? I need to know whether to maintain or lower our threat level, gentlemen. We cannot continue on a heightened level indefinitely." Clayton glanced at each person in the room. Fortunately, the violence on the streets gave them ample cover for the extra security, but the violence would not last forever.

"Mr. President, the problem is we don't have enough intel," Campbell said in an almost dispirited tone.

"And that's the problem," Blackwell added. "What exactly are we on alert for if we don't even know if the threat is real? If we had something to go on, other than the possibility of rogue nukes floating around somewhere in Chechnya, the Balkans, or wherever."

The room became quiet as Prescott consider his options. Finally he sighed. "The intelligence services are to redouble their efforts to learn whatever they can. Our air and seaports are to continue to keep their eyes open for anything out of the ordinary crossing the US borders." As if that was going to be easy or possible, especially now with law enforcement stretched way beyond its limits. Clayton wanted to offer some words of comfort, but he simply had nothing left to offer. "If the military has any resources available, then get them engaged. Now, have we got anything someone wants to bring up?"

The others shook their heads or simply replied in the negative.

"Well, I have a few things to attend to." He dismissed them with an open enough smile. He returned to his office and went through a few issues in his diary before taking a break. Abb came in to share the president's afternoon coffee break, a long established habit that the president held to religiously.

"The Europeans aren't too happy that we're pulling out a lot of our troops." Abb sipped his coffee.

"They'll survive."

"Maybe, but they are beginning to worry whether we'll send them back."

"Worried they may have to grow a backbone one day?" *And tell the Russian bear where to go.* "The poor darlings, I do so sympathize."

"They are rather concerned." Abb looked into his coffee cup.

"Well, you just tell them to rest easy; with their massive spending on national defence and their absolute commitment to defending NATO along with their friends and allies, the Russians wouldn't dream of committing any act of aggression."

"Seriously, Clayton…" Both knew Europe's spending on defence was a pale joke when compared to American spending, just as they were kept briefed by Ethan on the far-right and far-left parties that were opposed to a united Europe and a strong NATO.

"I am serious, Abb. Where were they when we needed them? There was so much we could have achieved, Abb—so much if we were willing." The sadness choked his words. "Be honest: did Greece, Italy, Spain, Germany, France, and the rest match our military commitment to Afghanistan after the invasion? If they had, then we would've had enough manpower to guard the Afghan–Paki border and do some serious work at nation building." *Maybe enough to have stopped the Taliban from coming back,* Clayton silently told himself.

"Suppose it wasn't their major concern… what was that old saying? 'out of sight out of mind." Abb sadly shrugged.

"Okay," Clayton grunted, "maybe that was too far away from them. But where were they when Russia took parts of Georgia, Ukraine and the Crimea? All they could do was wet themselves." He turned away for a moment, feeling a sense of shame. He knew full well President Obama could have done more, much more for the Ukraine. But the Ukraine and Crimea were in Europe's backyard; they were neighbours.

"Where was the outrage? Even if Obama wouldn't provide weapons, there was no reason why Europe couldn't have armed Ukraine. It was a sovereign state and had every right to defend itself.

"Europe has become so spineless it just lies back and spreads its legs. Remember the millions of refugees pouring into Europe because they never had the guts to take on the Islamic State of Syria?"

"Well, they didn't have much in the way of options."

"Tell that to Brandon. We had a very interesting debate once over the millions of Syrian refugees. He argued that the Europeans could have used them as the raw material to create a Free Syrian Army of one or two hundred thousand. Europe could've told the refugees that they couldn't stay but that Europe was willing to train and equip them to liberate Syria from Assad . . . Once training they could have been shipped over to Iraq or Israel to be armed and then sneak into Syria... Apparently the CIA had some kind of plan on offer but no-one was interested."

"Assad would have pissed in his drawers if he had heard that one." Abb grinned at the mere thought. "And Putin would've called a foul."

Clayton slowly rose and walked around the room. "There are always options if you are willing to act. Abb, can you imagine what we could achieve if Europe and America were to actually work together? How many problems and conflicts could we have solved by the mere *threat* of intervention on the massive scale we could have mounted?

"Screw the Krauts and the Frogs. When they become equal partners in this alliance... instead of dragging us down . . . then come and see me." Abb wondered, *Is that why you're bringing our troops back? If the Europeans won't defend Europe, why should we defend them?*

"Sir," came Kath's voice over the intercom, "we have Miss Castello on the video link."

"Well, let's not keep her waiting."

The two men walked over to the conference room and sat around the table to face the large screen. The video link was crystal clear, so clear that Clayton could see a sly smile on his barracuda. He grinned in return. "Maggie, you look like the cat that ate the canary."

"Progress is going faster than we have any right to expect, Mr. President. I think we have a workable plan. I have explained to several manufacturers that, as the US government will be putting solar panels on people's rooftops for free, a lot of companies will be going out of business unless they are selling to us. I gave them twenty-four hours to give me their best offer."

"Wait," Abb interjected, a bad feeling in his gut. "I thought this scheme was for the poor and lower-income housing only." *Not for the middle class.*

"Well, there is no reason why we can't expand once we've dealt with the core issue." She grinned, so in a way she was kind of telling the truth.

"Anyway, I will then demand a 20 per cent cut on the cost. Naturally they won't be happy. But I'll explain that we will be buying as many panels as they can manufacture day and night, so they will be able to reduce their cost. Economy of scale, don't you just love it?"

"So we'll be getting a sizable cut in the cost, good." Abb nodded. "Oh, the best is yet to come. The president's idea of doing a whole street set me thinking. We'll cut out the middleman. My people believe that we can go from the manufacturer straight to the rooftop all at once."

"How would that work?"

"We just have the local authorities—the council, the mayor's office— send out a letter to every homeowner in the area. The letter will have a series of basic questions.

"Do they want free solar panels? They say yes or no.

"Do you own your house, or rent?

"How much do you earn?

"If they earn over a certain amount, will they be willing to pay for the installation or maybe a few extra panels?

"If you earn a lot, let's talk.

"But the actual implementation is the best part of the whole scheme. By doing a town or suburb, a whole street all at once, we realize a massive cut in costs."

"We can't subcontract this to the private sector?" Abb asked. "Actually, no, that's a bad choice for a number of reasons, sir. The panels can last for up to thirty years if they are good quality, with a ten-year guarantee. Now, maybe the private companies will still be around in ten years, but how many in twenty or thirty years to replace an old panel?

"Second point, some of the local power and distribution companies may not be able to remain viable, if too many homes turn from importing to exporting electricity. They may find it economically difficult to keep the power lines and substations properly maintained, making the government the best choice to step in and take over."

"You're talking about taking over power companies?" Abb shuddered at the thought.

"That would depend on the power companies, but why not? Isn't that the president's agenda? Government owned, privately run… with only a 2 per cent profit margin to benefit the community." *That last bit will really piss off the shareholders,* she thought as she smiled sweetly at Abb.

Who all but choked on any suitable reply he could devise. "We create a problem, and then we exploit it?" She replied with a smile that vividly conveyed, *Capitalism is wonderful, isn't it? That is, of course, when you're the one doing the screwing.*

"Well, I, for one, think you're overreaching." Abb was not about to give her an easy ride.

"I know it's not government policy, sir. But I would argue that it is better to be ready than unprepared for the worst case. After all, we don't want another Afghanistan, Iraq or Florida on our hands." She shook her short hair. That was government for you, never thinking past the next poll.

"Even better, the government would be in a far better position to help power industrial manufacturing." She continued when she saw the look on Abb's face, it was turning a slightly more bright red.

"I was under the impression that solar still can't provide 'base load.'" Abb had read enough to know that solar panels simply could not provide the constant flow of power that heavy industry needed.

"Sir, that is old news, prehistoric even. We've had the ability in some measure for years, just never the will to act." She knew industry had never put in the serious money and effort needed. "Anyway, I am not talking about powering all of industry's needs. Just giving our industry an edge, by cutting their power bill, even if it is only by 15 per cent, that could give them the edge against their overseas competition.

"Just look at those new semi-automated factories, with whole roofs covered in solar panels . . . we just need to get serious.

"There are parts of America that drown in sunlight. The Mexican–American border alone could be a powerhouse for new American industry.

"Mr. President." She beamed. "I've talked to some experts, and this is such a win–win situation that I can't believe we've ignored the benefits for so long. Not only will the low-income people get a cut in their power costs, but the environment benefits, industry benefit; the only ones not benefiting are the old power companies."

"And they'll happily roll over and die for us," Clayton joked with a dry belly laugh.

"They have no one to blame but themselves, sir. They could have been a part of it instead of opposing it."

"Just another screw-up by corporate America, Miss Castello?" Clayton saw her lip twitch, just a tiny little twitch.

"Anyway, if they get off their asses and adapt, they can still play a part. It's a question of whether they want to be constructive or obstructive." She kept her eyes steady as she watched the president for any sign of what he thought.

"How long before we get started for real?" Clayton asked the question he desperately wanted answered.

"I can't give a real date as such, Mr. President."

"We can't afford to wait. We need to move on this immediately," Clayton persisted.

"Sir, we can't rush this. That is the worst thing we can do. We need to make certain we comply with all state and federal regulations. Ensure all employees are properly trained. We cannot roll this out without knowing what we are doing."

"I understand the difficulties, but I have made it abundantly clear that we have no time to waste."

"Sir, you chose me for a reason," she stated flatly. "Do you want this to work?"

"What is a time frame you are comfortable with?"

"Give me a couple of months to get everything in line, and I promise you that within six months to a year we can get serious. Give me another two years, and we can go with electric cars."

"Electric cars?" Abb stared at the video screen.

"Let's go all the way, Mr. President, it's what you said you wanted. We'll have those solar panels feeding electricity into people's homes so why not little electric cars for day to day?"

"The president was making an observation, Miss Castello. Not enough people are buying the ones already on the market."

"I am aware of the cost, sir. I have a few ideas—"

"Hell, we still have people thinking of them as golf carts." "That's one option."

"Go ahead, Miss Castello," Clayton prompted.

Abb stopped, what did she say?

"We could put it into legislation; anyone getting a licence must use an electric car for their first two years. We could sell it to the parents as a way to stop their kids from wrapping their cars around trees.

"And as they grow older, the female drivers, at least, may well stick with their electric cars for the fuel savings." She grinned. "Girls don't need eight cylinder rockets to pamper their precious egos. So they may see the benefit of using 'golf carts' to go to the Mall and back.

Who knows, the boys may even wake up as well."

"Even when we've seen electric cars outrace and outperform gas-powered cars?" Clayton told Maggie Castello. In his younger days he had spent some time at the speedway track where gasoline and electric cars had competed against each other. The battery-powered cars had the rather nasty habit of outrunning the gas-powered vehicles.

"Yeah, fortunately for us the general public—and parents in particular—are wilfully ignorant of even the most basic facts, Mr. President . . . Most wouldn't even know what the latest generation of battery can do." She tried to keep a straight face, thinking, *You should know you gave the public one hell of a lecture on their ignorance.*

"I don't know." Abb was frankly sceptical. "From what I've seen, there just doesn't seem to be much of a market. We've had the electric car for decades, sir."

The president's little barracuda groaned in disbelief. *God, save me. What is it with this guy? Does he love the taste of his own foot in his mouth?*

"We just need to sell the idea. Really sell it: how they won't have to pay for gasoline. Maybe we have a gasoline tax to subsidize the cost of the electric car for the first couple of years, at least for those with lower incomes."

"Damn it, they'll have a fit." Abb tried not to explode.

"It's really about the mental adjustment," Maggie said; "that's the biggest problem."

"Well, that's a surprise." Abb glanced at Clayton with a knowing look. "Now, what about the elephant in the room, Miss Castello?" Clayton inquired.

"I am well aware of Big Oil's efforts to undermine the electric car, sir, but this time we already have established an electric and hybrid markets, and if we move before they can react, then we have a chance—if the government of the day is committed." *With tax or other inducements*, she added silently.

"Certifiably, I would presume?" Abb took a stab.

"I didn't say it would be easy." Maggie Castello had to agree with Abb's comment.

"Miss Castello," Abb went on, with his final argument, "there has been a lot of talk recently about the hydrogen-powered car. If the development of the hydrogen car is only a few years away, aren't we wasting our efforts?" "Abb." Clayton sighed. "Coal, gasoline, LNG, nuclear, wind, or hydrogen—whatever you use, the individual will have to pay. That's the beauty of free solar. Whether it's for the house or the car, solar is free. It's freedom, freedom from cost.

"With hydrogen, depending on what they come up with, you could still have to fill up your tank, so you don't really benefit; someone still has his hand in your pocket. But not with solar." He grinned at Abb. "If you can manufacture your own hydrogen at home for free... well, then hydrogen cars it is.

"I'm sure you'll do your best, Maggie, and let us know of any new developments."

"I'll be in touch, Mr. President."

"Thank you," Clayton ended the conversation. He then sat back to consider his options.

Abb finally broke the silence. "Sir, I need to talk to you about this boycott idea."

"Go ahead."

"I really think this boycott of theatres is a bad idea. The movie stars have a lot of clout, and they're bound to scream that any cuts in ticket prices will only hurt the people working in the theatres, not them."

"Relax, Abb. Jonathan and even Brandon agreed with you. Truth is, I don't think the people have what it takes." Clayton turned and looked him in the eye. "They're just too self-absorbed to even consider boycotting theatres to get a better deal." He turned around in his chair and stood to stretch his back.

FBI Building, Washington DC

"Boss, the director is on line two."

Andrew Drywood sighed quietly and lifted the receiver. *What the hell does he want now?* Andrew was just about to take his flight to California to push the FBI branch office. If they could find a link between the actress and the anarchists, it could be the break they needed. They had to find some hole to get in behind the anarchists' cyber encryption.

"Director?" Drywood spoke into the handset.

"Andrew, on your way to California, do a stopover in Arizona. Myles O'Bandan wants to have a word."

"Is this connected to my trip to California?"

"Maybe. We have a multiple homicide on the border with Mexico. Something caught his eye. You'll have the file before you're on the plane." Andrew tried not to let his annoyance bleed into his voice. "Yes, sir, will do."

He hung up the handset, grabbed the small case that he kept in his office for emergency trips, and headed for the door. He was divorced, and his daughter was grown and estranged from him, so he was free to travel as he pleased.

Andrew was still slightly annoyed as he sat in the backseat of the FBI car taking him to the airport. He went over the preliminary report once more on the flight, trying to find some link to his case.

He was still going over the case in his head as the plane landed and was met at the small airfield terminal by Agent O'Bandan.

"Myles, good to see you, old man."

"Just 'cause you're so much younger than me. You out of your Pull-Ups yet?" Myles swiftly ushered Andrew towards the parking lot and into the front passenger seat of his old car.

"One case of haemorrhoids, and you make it sound like a death sentence." Andrew managed a grin. "So why am I here? The report came up as a straightforward gang shooting." And why had Myles come to meet him personally at the airport?

"With an innocent passer-by caught in the middle, a Dr. Joanna Hockey, right?"

"Correct." Andrew was having doubts.

"Except that she wasn't just passing by. Going by blood spatter, she was inside, not outside in her car."

"What?" Andrew's eye could burn a hole through Myles' forehead. "The local cops were pressured by certain people—family, so I heard—

who wanted to keep her murder separate."

"I can sympathize. Arizona is pretty much an old boys club." Like Texas it had too much redneck inbreeding for his taste. "But you don't need a deputy director to sort this out. I'd be surprised if they didn't want to hide the fact that one of their own was buying drugs."

"I don't think she was. This is where things start to get interesting. The good doctor was trained as a microbiologist, working in one of the biggest research labs in the state."

And that meant she knew her way around a lab and equipment therein. "Was she their 'chemist'?" Now, if she was part of the gang, the one actually cooking up the product, that would sting.

"Originally that was what I thought, especially since the two investigators assigned to the case have been rumoured to have political connections. No sooner did they get to the crime scene than they were interfering in the forensic process—started covering up some of the equipment, even moving the body before forensics got there.

"That's how I got involved. One of the local crime scene investigators is a bit of a stickler. He didn't like where all this was leading, and he especially didn't like been leaned on. Not when the 'drug lab' didn't look like any drug lab he had ever seen. In short the drug lab wasn't a drug lab."

Andrew turned in the car to face Myles. "What are you trying to tell me?"

"From the little my guy got to see, the equipment looked more like a bio lab. You know, research in bugs and viruses. He's see enough drug labs to know you don't need a third of the equipment or anywhere near the safety precautions they had set up. And he thinks he identified a few pieces of equipment. Stuff you'd use in microbiology, not drug manufacturing."

"You're not thinking… another Congress. You have any evidence?" "The place was stripped bare by the time I could send anyone over." "So all you've got is an eyewitness who thinks he saw . . . What exactly?

Some strange equipment and suspicious behaviour by the local cops?" Myles defended his position. "That is more than enough to raise some concern. But there's a bit more, mostly from the make-up of the victims." "The report said one, Joey Kenndale, was linked to a major drug and illegal immigrant ring." Drywood had noted that the rest had not been identified.

"We got IDs just in. Two we've identified as ex-National Guard, with no criminal records but fully paid-up members of the local State Guard. They were armed, so they were involved in some way. But I would guess they were just muscle." O'Bandan handed over two sets of files showing photos and their personal details.

"You've identified the last two?"

"That is where it gets even weirder. They have a long history—a Joe 'Bobby' Kennedy and a Freddy 'Chuck' Madigan, both hardcore 'mountain men' militia. Both are white supremacist rednecks just waiting for the day when the UN invades America."

"Shit, not that crap again?" Drywood shook his head in disbelief. The United Nations couldn't even tie their own shoelaces, so how the hell were they supposed to invade America? And why would they be dumb enough to try?

Although if they were smart and neutered all the goddamned stupid redneck dickheads, that wouldn't be such a bad idea.

"Pair of shit-for-brains, I know. But the question remains, why would this bunch come together? Unless they were working to bring in something big and ugly… say, like some killer virus."

Andrew's small smile vanished and the hard face of a professional investigator returned. "You're talking conspiracy."

"It is what it is. Take a step back and look at the big picture. Start with Congress and then consider the orchestrated riots, the targeted killings in New York, California, all the assassinations… Now tell me all that was the work of a bunch of hippy radicals and crazy anarchists. The people responsible had skills, they had training."

"Again with the military; you've seen too many movies." Just about every second criminal in movies was ex-special forces or a Navy SEAL. The armed services must be pumping out five million special forces a year. The bloody shit that was on TV these days. His two brothers had been Marines most of their adult lives, and neither had done time in jail.

"More like an understanding of law enforcement and local knowledge, what you'd find in those local home and State Guards. Some of them have a lot of former law enforcement and local people in them, along with the kind of nerds you need to hack into high level security systems."

"You're talking about the—"

"Yeah." O'Bandan nodded. "It would be a lot easier for New Mexico, Arizona, and Texas to leave the Union if the country was a mess, especially if it was scrambling to deal with a lethal virus."

That explained all this cloak-and-dagger from Myles. "I knew there was a reason I never sent you any get well cards." But could this really be some conspiracy, some insane attempt to allow a few States to leave the Union? Drywood slowly turned around to take in the scenery.

Only, the scenario just didn't seem to fit, something just didn't jell to Andrew.

Why aim for the hard targets in their New York high-rise apartments and walled communities? If all they wanted to do was to cause chaos, why not stick to soft targets in the poor suburbs? Easier and safer, Andrew thought. And why not target the African Americans to raise the race card?

And that was the real issue, he realized. Those redneck mountain men would never support any US State joining Mexico.

Did that explain the shoot- out? The mountain men had one agenda, while the Doc and the Arizona establishment had another?

Had Myles get it wrong? He admitted he had his own doubts.

Was it two groups then? Two different groups with clashing agendas, settled in the traditional method—a shoot-out with the winner taking the prize. *Shit, we're missing too many pieces of the puzzle. There just isn't enough to go on; we need more, and we need solid evidence.*

"Myles, get a team over to that farmhouse. Do it quietly, but go over everything. Don't miss anything. I'll be in California for the next few days. Contact me directly if you find something."

A Secure Room in the White House

It was not called the panic room, no matter what a few smartass kids had hinted about the room. And it certainly was not the Situation Room, but the men who sat around the small table gave the room a degree of serious deliberation that unsettled Ethan Campbell. Still, he refused to show any concern as he watched FBI Director Arnold Shaw read the single-sheet printout yet again.

"Is this credible?" the director asked the deputy head of the NSA. "The intercept was made at the location given, by the individuals as stated in the file."

"So it's credible." He repeated more to give himself time to think. "And on this 'package,' is there anything more?"

"Given the source of the communiqué and the possibility of rogue nuclear bombs having gone missing in Russia, we have only one conclusion," the man from NSA answered.

"We don't know that to be factual," Shaw told the man. "The FBI doesn't go on guesswork. And may I add that it seems more than remarkable that you got this detailed a communication when you have so brilliantly failed in the past."

"We have been working long and hard to redress past… oversights." The NSA official spoke in his usual clipped voice.

"No one's leaking your classified data this week?"

"Gentlemen, please," Campbell asked both men. He knew there was little love lost between them, but they needed to focus. "What do we tell the president?"

"We tell him that some Muslim terrorists may have sneaked a bomb onto US soil," the NSA man offered.

"Because of some intel traffic stating that 'the package has been delivered'? We need some kind of evidence, which we haven't got. Equally, we need to have some strategy available to the president, some ideas to offer. Do we?"

Director Shaw looked around the table. "And we already have a heightened threat level. What more can we do until we have something concrete to offer?"

"So we wait for more intel?" Campbell said. He looked across to the director of the CIA seated heavily in his chair.

The DCI gazed at the faces around the table, one by one. "We haven't gotten any hard intel on any nuke, real or imaginary, inside the US." He did not really want to admit that, just as he hated the reason why. America was relying more and more on SIGINT—the interception of wireless communications—instead of human-obtained intelligence.

That meant, recently, less and less money for the CIA. Indeed, both the CIA and the FBI were annoyed that the NSA was getting the lion's share from Washington.

But the real tragedy was that the CIA was becoming even more limited in acquiring human intelligence. And one day that was going to come back and bite them on the ass, he thought. *If it hasn't done so already.*

Director Shaw addressed the other men. "So we have nothing but a message that could, in all probability, be an attempt to mislead us or the Russians. Hell, I would say if the 'package' had been delivered, it would be up Moscow's ass. Do we have anything solid that it's heading our way?"

"No." The others slowly shook their heads.

"Then we leave it till we have something?" Director Shaw asked the others.

"Can't you commit additional resources to this?" Campbell inquired in a flat voice.

"What resources? The FBI is stretched; we have too much on our plate. I can't do anything unless you want to bring this to the president's attention." He studied Campbell.

Who shook his head. "The president has enough on his own plate. We just have to keep digging. Find something that'll prove we are worrying about nothing." He hoped.

And the message did have a smell to it. It had been just a little too easy for the NSA to get a hold of.

Chapter 17

"I see no military solution."

Code for:

"the only solution is a military one, but we're not about to use it."

—Harold Blunt

The military solution is often the only solution that will get people to accept a political solution.

—Harold Blunt

The FBI Director's Office, Washington DC

The TV showed the elder statesmen and the three new inductees into the GOP holding grim faces with straight backs as they stood on the white steps of the Capital building ready to defend the building and the nation against the gathering hordes. Today the hordes were a small group of senior citizens with small placards held aloft in the cold breeze.

"It is clear that our great nation is facing a terrible crisis." Senator Holt addressed the assembled media with the practiced outrage that often convinced even himself. "Every day there are more attacks on the public, on people's property. Recently these terrorists have escalated to the assassination of public officials.

"And while America burns, what does the president offer? He makes more assurances that the terrorists will be brought to trial.

"'If we can just calm down and reach an understanding,' then all will be well. As if 'accommodating' terrorists is the answer to our problems.

"Well, my fellow Americans, I do not believe so. Rather we need to understand the underlying cause. I would ask you all, is this simply a matter of law and order, as the president would have you believe, or something far more serious that our nation must either confront and deal with or fall into disrepair?

"I believe we face a fundamental crisis that stems from being overly generous. The problem we face is this 'age of entitlement'—which, I believe, the president blindly supports: the unrealistic demands placed before this nation by the selfish, the self-centred, and the 'me generation,' with their belief that they are entitled to have everything they want and they are entitled to have it now.

"Unfortunately, these spoilt children have spawned the anarchists who even as we speak are committing acts of terrorism that undermine our ordered society." The Senator pressed his message upon the media herd at the steps of the Capitol, like some old-time orator offering his wisdom to the people.

"With my colleagues, we will push for America to take the correct course, away from this self-destructive direction, and pilot our great ship of state to safe shores. And we call upon all Americans to demand that the president act in accordance with our laws. We have people living in fear." He spoke with genuine anger, furious with Prescott. In a matter of days Prescott's little tirade to his staff over CEOs fleeing the US had been widely leaked. The fact that Prescott had not gone public had scared a lot of people even more. In no time Industry was donating like crazy. Hollywood had already donated close to thirteen million; even the marijuana industry was pissing itself.

To make it worse, even Walker and his 'colleagues' were treading carefully, the bunch of snivelling ass-lickers. *No one's got the guts to stand up for themselves anymore.*

They had to stop Prescott now before he ruined the country.

"Right on," a voice to their left screamed. "Especially the filthy rich, right? Screw the rich! High time we burned the temple of greed, burned Wall Street . . ."

"Down with the capitalist oppressors," cried the leader of the small band of protestors to the left of the senators and media, waving their placards high in the morning air, like ancient samurai warriors about to charge the Emperor's enemies.

Andrew Johnson smiled. Oh, how he loved these early-morning rituals, and now to be able to actually reach the very steps of the halls of the oppressors. *Glory, oh glory be to you on high.* Raising his placard, he led the charge of sixty- and seventy-year-olds against the handful of officers and security guards. If he was lucky, pictures of the Pigs beating up retirees would run on the six o'clock news. This was going even better than he had planned.

Blah, blah, blah, Director Arnold Shaw thought as he turned down the volume. *Can't they talk like real people?* He hated politicians, almost as much as he hated politics. But that was the game, the way to advancement, to get something done.

He worked through some files he had left from the previous day. He was reading the preliminary report on yet another attack, a fire-bombing on a Republican office, when his intercom buzzed.

"Yes," he snapped.

"Sir, Jan Mahoney and Ted McArthur are coming up to see you." His secretary replied.

'Up' was from the communications section of the FBI headquarters building. Jan Mahoney was in charge of the FBI's extensive communications facilities. Ted was a specialist, which meant something notable was up for them to come running to him.

Both entered in a near rush. "Sir, we . . . we may have a problem." Jan Mahoney handed him a single sheet of paper. "We are analysing the voice message as we speak but this came in to us direct."

To the president of the United States

> By now you have discovered that we have transported a
> nuclear device into your country. To avoid detonation of this
> device you will comply with the following instructions. Any
> deviation will result in catastrophic destruction of a major
> city along the western coast.

Shaw stopped reading at that point. "What is this, a joke?" "It's authentic." Jan told the director with cold eyes.

"'Authentic?' We get a dozen crank calls." He stopped himself. Mahoney would not have brought this up to him if it had been a prank call. There would have been verification. But still, this just couldn't be real.

"Sir, the message came with all the confirmation of authenticity needed. Not only that, if you read further down, you'll see they provided the serial number on the Russian nuke."

His eyes skimmed down the sheet of paper. "That doesn't mean a thing. We know one nuke was set off inside the Russian base, another in Mezen, and that's all we know. We don't know if any others were taken, and we certainly don't have the serial numbers."

"Did anybody bother to ask the Russians for those numbers?" she asked in a flat voice.

He looked at her, his mouth open to respond. Then he closed it with a quick snap and breathed out, once. "The Russians keep saying the bombs were 'crude' homemade devices—you know, made in a toolshed, using stolen uranium… some such nonsense. No, this is just an attempt to rattle our cage. We have no evidence to even hint that a nuclear bomb has entered the States."

"No evidence doesn't mean the threat isn't real, sir. The message made it clear we have only twenty-four hours to respond. Shouldn't we consider our options?" Jan Mahoney felt she was wasting her time but also felt she had to try.

"Such as?" Shaw grumbled.

"Take the message and the instructions seriously. After all, in twenty-four hours the 'messenger of God' will be at the 'infidel's' gate. They couldn't have made it any easier." She stared straight at the director. The director grunted and looked down to read the rest of the message.

> Our messenger of Allah will be waiting outside the infidel gates of the White House at exactly midday wearing a red beret. The messenger will not be armed in any way but a transmitter will be strapped to the messenger's chest and be connected to a dead man's switch. Any attempt to remove the transmitter will result in the messenger activating the dead-man's trigger which in turn will result in the detonation of the nuclear device.
>
> You may inspect the transmitter to satisfy yourselves that it is not an explosive device.

Once you are satisfied, you will have the messenger
escorted directly to the Oval Office where the messenger
will deliver our list of demands to you in person.

"Jan, this just proves that this is an attempt to rattle our cage. Come on, you don't really expect a Chechen terrorist to just show up on our front doorstep! No, if some nut does show up, security can handle him. We have enough to do." They were already stretched to the breaking point, he reminded himself. "Just inform the Secret Service that they may find another nut on the president's lawn."

"But..." Jan began.

"Yes?" Shaw's brow rose in mild irritation.

"What if they take him into custody without knowing what's expected of them? And worse, what if the Secret Service mistake this 'dead man's switch' for a bomb and shoot?"

"Jan, do you really expect this 'messenger of Allah' to show up?" She was stumped at Shaw's question. It was just too crazy for words.

And they did not have any evidence to prove there was a bomb sitting somewhere on the West Coast.

"Can we get the other agencies involved? They may have some overseas connections that can verify or discredit the authenticity of the message." They had to be able to come up with something.

"You think they will take this seriously?" Shaw's irritation grew. "It can't hurt." Jan tried to prod the director in the right direction. "Okay, see what the other agencies have to offer."

Jan Mahoney went back to her office and frittered away the day. Even after her shift, her unease remained as she drove across town to her small apartment. The coming evening and a hasty meal brought no relief; she constantly checked the time as the minute hand dragged across the face of the clock.

She looked around her room, still uncertain of what to do. She could hardly go back to work even if her seniority allowed her the front door. After all, what could she do? Sit at her desk and wait?

She went and made herself a coffee, sat down on her couch, and switched on the TV.

Perhaps one of the news channels had something. Instead she got an interview with Clayton Prescott. He seemed to be on the TV a lot these days. The interviewer was wrapping up a question.

"…Now, sir, to go on, how do you respond to Senator Holt's accusations from earlier today?"

"It always amazes me that we have people complaining about the very thing they have always wanted. The Senator has fought for what these people wanted… demanded… this 'age of entitlement' that he has condemned. These 'spoilt children' are the Senator's children.

"The Senator has approved laws enshrining these 'spoilt children's' rights but has never asked for anything back—no responsibility, no obligations to the state. Has he ever called for the public to support the community? Donate a few hours to a charity? Has he called for a social conscience compact to bring all Americans together? Or even promote the little things… called on Silicon Valley to offer a thousand IT scholarships a year to children in struggling communities? Asked medical professionals to donate some of their time to free clinics?"

"You're saying Senator Holt is partly responsible for the people's 'sense of entitlement'?"

"He has carried out the public's will, we need to remember that, Candice. But I believe you're ignoring the real question. The fundamental issue is whether the unrest comes from this 'sense of entitlement' or out of a sense of injustice?"

"You're saying the rioting is about envy and jealousy?" She trod carefully, not wanting to fall into the trap of trying to answer his questions.

"Hardly. I would say they are suffering and believe that no one wants to help them. I would remind you that more and more people are living in abject poverty. People are suffering."

"You almost sound as if you approve of their actions."

"You are once more ignoring the fundamental question. It is not whether I approve of their actions or not. Rather, do they consider themselves the perpetrators or the victims? That is where we must start the debate. Do they believe they are 'spoilt' or victimized? Indeed, how many consider the anarchists to be fighting for justice, believing they are freedom fighters?"

"I would think the answer is obvious." "Is it, Candice? Are you certain?"

Oh God, no, please. She had feared that he might engage in another theoretical debate. When he indulged in his flights of fancy, she had felt uncomfortable for her colleagues doing their interviews. She had prepared by watching all Prescott's interviews, but at times she felt as if he was trying to make journalists feel inadequate. Not that she felt inadequate or wasn't keeping up; it was just his tone.

"They are committing violent acts. They are murdering people; how can they be anything else but terrorists?"

"Are you sure? Remember, 'one man's terrorist is another man's freedom fighter,'" Clayton responded calmly.

"But there can be no doubt; just look at all the killings and the violence." She was incredulous.

"Yet to some, such actions are necessary, even justified. Indeed, some believe they have no choice. That is where the true battle lies, in showing them the truth," Clayton responded.

"So how do you… show them the truth?" She could hardly believe he had an answer to such a question.

"We start by addressing the basic issue, Candice. What is the difference between a freedom fighter and a terrorist? We have to present a clear definition and not endless opinions."

"But we have clear definitions."

"Do we?" Clayton smiled pleasantly. "Yes, we have definitions. But clearly they are not up to the task. Again, for too many 'one man's terrorist is another man's freedom fighter.'"

"But isn't it generally accepted that a terrorist is someone who commits a criminal or violent act in pursuit of their ideological or religious beliefs?" Candice put it strongly. "Isn't that obvious enough?"

"Tell that to the British government," Came Clayton's dismissive reply.

"Sorry? Candice blinked.

"In 2016 the British Government declared National Action… a well-known racist group… a terrorist organisation. They were declared a terrorist group not for what they had done but what for they had advocated, promoted. Now, I repeat, not for any terrorist acts… no for any specific act of violence, but rather for their advocating for violence.

"Now, I am more than happy to charge some-one for the crime of promoting violence, when they are guilty of such… But, here we have a government declaring a group a terrorist organisation simply for its beliefs, abhorrent as they may be." *It should have been the British media and not the government that had taken the racist assholes on*, Clayton concluded.

"Even more disturbing, I have heard Intellectuals in the West argue that US drone strikes should be classed as terrorist attacks.

"On top of all that freedom fighters commit violent acts as well. "Do you see how easy it is for terrorists to argue they are fighting for a noble cause and thus are freedom fighters, when we prove to be such utter failures?"

"Then—" She was stumped. "How do we prove them wrong? And would they accept the argument anyway?"

"Now that is the real question. We need to present a definition that everyone can agree upon—no matter your ideological or religious views, no matter which side of the argument you are on." Clayton sighed softly. "Granted, there are many descriptions, but clearly they are insufficient in this day and age."

"What would be your interpretation?" *You egotistical ass; think you're so smart.*

"I am only one person," Clayton replied in a humble voice; "we need to build a solid consensus."

"But you must have some idea." Wiggle out of that one. She thought she had him cornered.

"I believe it should be debated by legal minds who could present a straightforward, unquestionable definition that all can agree upon."

"Sir, this is a vital issue, at the moment, as you have pointed out. Surely you can offer a valid viewpoint to start the debate."

"Well…" He leaned back in his chair.

Got you, she thought with glee.

"I suppose… well, I support the definition that a freedom fighter is someone who commits a criminal or violent act against the *state* that has denied the individual his or her basic human rights—the right of assembly, free speech, freedom of association, or other basic human rights." Clayton stopped for a moment. She could see his eyes wander off into the distance as he collected his thoughts.

"For example, if an American were to place a bomb in a bus filled with American citizens, well he's a terrorist, because the state has not taken away his rights, and he has attacked innocent civilians.

"On the other hand a Chinese or a North Korean citizen who places a bomb in a bus filled with government officials could argue that he is fighting an oppressive regime because they do not allow him his basic rights.

"A freedom fighter must be able to argue he is a *victim* of the *state*, being oppressed, where he has had his basic rights taken away, were he has been illegally arrested, imprisoned, tortured, or what have you. And thus we come to the anarchists in our country, and the question whether they are freedom fighters or terrorists."

"Well, by your definition they're terrorists." That sounds obvious. "True, the state is not oppressing them. Unfortunately, a few have argued that institutionalized poverty, inequality created by the *state's* denial of support, is a denial of their basic rights."

"That's totally unfair. The government can only do so much." Her eyes widened as she realized what he had done. Then again, what if government had done a better job?

"Correct, but you need to convince them and the public of that. Only then will the legitimacy of their violent acts be brought into question." He sighed.

Candice tried to figure out just how she had been wrong-footed and why he had gone through this tortuous process. *Was he screwing with me? Or was he giving America another lecture without making it sound like one?* She hated being used, hated being manipulated.

"So how would Israel and the Palestinians fit into your equation?" she probed. "Should we really be supporting the Israeli state when it denies the Palestinians their freedom of movement in the West Bank, along with a long list of violations against their human rights?"

"Yes, Israel is a tricky one."

She was stunned. "You accept that Israel is violating the Palestinians' basic human rights?"

"Will you accept that Palestinians are murdering Israeli citizens? So who is the innocent party?"

She brought up a long-standing justification. "The Palestinians have argued that because every Israeli will serve in the military and can be recalled, all of them are legitimate targets."

"So an eighty-year- old widow living in a retirement village is a legitimate target if killed by a rocket? A five-month-old baby whose family may migrate to Canada before he can talk is a legitimate target? Further, what about the Israelis who oppose expansion of Jewish settlements in the occupied territories? What about those who refuse military service?

"Hell, going by the Palestinian argument, Israelis can kill any Palestinian simply because he's a Palestinian and might become a terrorist. What utter rubbish.

"Candice, I can point to dozens of Israeli violations. You can point to dozens of Palestinian violations. We can argue about who is responsible, who started this or that. But in the end we must stop fabricating excuses, stop allowing groups to justify the unjustifiable. Rather, we need to begin anew with a clear vision to confront terrorism. And truly defining it is the first step."

"I have one final question, sir. For the record, are you truly thinking of taking away the passports of the rich if they attempt to desert the US to avoid paying their taxes, as some senior sources in your administration have been quoted?"

"Candice, the government will never take away the passports of American citizens. If someone surrenders their passport, that will be their choice. As for the issue of taxes, let me be perfectly clear. If the people demand, in a referendum, that we take action against those who wish to avoid paying their taxes, then the president and Congress are duty-bound to act."

She blinked. *Did I walk into that?* "Thank you for your time, Mr. President." She gritted her teeth behind her porcelain smile.

The Farmhouse in Arizona

Special Agent O'Bandan had decided to take a more personal approach to the investigation, a more subtle one. The forensic team and their equipment had been loaded into the back of a nondescript truck and then driven to the farmhouse. He had followed a half hour later in his own car.

He grinned sheepishly. The plan was so James Bond, but he felt he could do without questions from the locals about whether something was going on down on the farm.

Now he waited. A glance at his watch told him it was near midday. He was getting hungry. That was no surprise; he had not eaten since early morning.

He looked around. The countryside was refreshing in a dry, burned-out way. He took out his pack of cigarettes and looked at them in despair. He had been trying to stop for over six years.

"Agent O'Bandan, O'Bandan, sir, sir." The voice rang out as if the owner had found the fountain of truth.

What's up with him? "Calm down, Brenson, don't have an aneurysm on me."

"Sir, we got a major spike." Brenson seemed to think that would explain everything.

"Spike of what?" He lowered his gaze and saw what was in the man's right hand. He was not a tech-nerd, but he knew it was one of those newfangled Geiger-counters. *Oh, shit.*

"The radiation count is extreme, sir. A highly radioactive source was in the building. We need to get the right equipment to examine——."

"Is it dangerous?" The cigarette suddenly tasked like ash in his mouth. "It's not high enough to be lethal to us, but there had to be some high-grade radioactive material in there. We have to declare a priority alert." He inhaled deeply. "I'm pretty sure it's weapons grade."

"I… Okay, understood." O'Bandan spat out the cigarette. He almost wanted to try another to see if it would settle him down, but the taste lingered.

Instead he ran to his car, where he opened the driver side door and reached for the encrypted phone. He called Drywood's direct number and hoped the assistant director would not leave him hanging. As he waited, he considered calling the FBI branch office, but that would only take even more time to go through the different levels. He shuddered at the sudden thought. He was all too familiar with the bureaucratic morass that could easily delay getting a proper search under way.

"Go ahead," came a voice on the secure line, responding to his call. "Andrew, we got a radiation count, a heavy radiation spike that my guy says is weapons grade." He looked to Brenson who nodded back. "This is serious, I've got Brenson here to give you the readings—"

"Forget it. I'll call Washington. Log and pack everything you've got. Go straight back to the office, and send all the data straight to Washington. I'll try to get them moving."

"Right, good man." He exhaled. Drywood wasn't laughing in his face. He could not have asked for more.

Assistant Director Drywood hung up and took a breath to calm his nerves before he picked up the handset. He desperately hoped Shaw would take him seriously as he placed his call to the FBI building in Washington.

"Come on, come on," he begged.

"Director's office, how may I help?" The voice was infinitely calm, absolutely assured of its own authority.

"I need to speak to the director immediately."

"Sorry sir. He is not here and is temporarily out of contact for the rest of the day. If you want to leave a message, I can pass it on as soon as he gets back."

"This is an emergency of national importance." Drywood bit down on the words.

"Yes sir, but he still can't be reached. He has made it clear he was not to be interrupted due to the importance of his meeting."

"He's with the president?" Of course he was. Where else would he turn off his phone?

He could pull rank and have security barge into the meeting. But to do so, he needed something solid. Pissing off Shaw by calling without proof would only get the phone slammed down on him. He hadn't been in Shaw's good books for some time now, and he knew the director did not want to hear of rogue nukes in his backyard. "Have him call me immediately the moment he is available, immediately."

Until O'Bandan got back to the branch office, he had no proof; even then, they had nothing solid that it was a bomb. He needed real proof—or he could act on his own authority.

As long as he got it right. His hand rested on the phone. If he was wrong, the consequences for his career could be harsh, well he could always take early retirement.

He picked up the phone and called the communication centre in the FBI headquarters building. The moment the operator answered, Drywood demanded to be passed on to operator's supervisor.

"Yes, Deputy Director."

"Jan?" He was stumped for a moment. His hopes rose a little. "Yes sir. How can we help?"

"Jan, we've got one hell of a situation in Arizona. A forensics team found a major radiation spike—weapons grade, they believe. Agent O'Bandan is on site and will send over everything they have collected. Now we don't have anything solid, but we need to get on top of this. On my authority…" *No, no…* She looked at the clock. *God.* She turned to get to the White

House direct line.

The White House

Senior Agent Mercer listened to Jan Mahoney's heated voice.

"You got the report on the 'messenger' waiting at the front gates of the White House?" she asked the Secret Service agent.

"We received the notification." Agent Mercer was blunt. He had little patience with what he considered nuisance calls, even if they came from the FBI.

"Has the messenger arrived?" Jan hoped they still had time.

"I have a confirmed on that. The perimeter guards just reported some woman wearing a red beret at the front gate."

"You haven't approached her yet?" Jan almost pleaded.

"The security guards at the gate—"

"Listen closely. The threat may be real. Take this seriously. Approach her carefully, and do not make any threatening moves that might be misinterpreted. She will have a transmitter strapped to her chest and a dead man's switch connected to the transmitter. Just don't assume that switch is a bomb. They have assured us that we can inspect it for explosives, so don't overreact."

"I read the report; you want me to take this seriously?" Mercer's eyebrow shot up.

"Yes."

"Well, I can't take her into the White House. And I am not about to let any possible terrorist anywhere near the president."

"If this is real, we are talking about a nuke sitting in an American city. We have to take this seriously." Jan ground her teeth together.

"I will hold her for interrogation and you get no to your Director to give me something more than hot air. Why didn't you guys give us more warning? I mean in view of the seriousness of the threat?" Agent Mercer wanted an apology, an acknowledgement of the FBI's failure. He wanted someone's ass to kick and to do it very, very hard.

"We are just getting a handle on this. Oh, just get onto it." She hung up. *Why hadn't we? What if we're too late?* They would find out later; right now, certain people needed to know what was going on.

Agent Mercer ran for the front door, speaking into his com-link for the guards to hold position until he had reached the gates.

If this is some fool stunt, if this is some… He shook his head, the fear and uncertainty in Mahoney's voice was all too real. And deep down he was expecting something bad to come along.

But this? You don't expect this. He still could hardly believe it, to have some terrorist come knocking on the front gate.

By the time he reached the gate, a half dozen agents were already there, fortunately staying well away. Their weapons at the ready but still concealed from the general public.

Mercer took two short breaths, wondering what the playbook would actually say if such a situation as this had ever been considered. If the threat was real, then the conventional protocols were out the window. It was still a hostage situation, *and* it was a nuclear threat and needed to be handled accordingly.

He walked up to the gate. "They told me to expect you." He tried to sound calm and assured.

"And yet you're still late." She spoke with a clear Midwestern accent, clipped but well educated. Her coat was expensive, and her shoes equally so. *So she's not some dropout from a hippy commune in need of a bath.*

"What are you waiting for?" She challenged him with her forthrightness. "We're behind schedule." She opened the front of her coat, exposing two boxlike apparatus made of metal and transparent plastic. Both devices were connected by wires. Another wire led from one apparatus into the coat, down the sleeve and emerged into her hand.

Damn this, we need more time. "I need to have that checked."

She grinned mockingly at him. "So where is your demolition guy?"

I think she's enjoying this. Mercer turned his head slightly. "Agent Coates, get over here."

"I'm not suited up..." He meant the heavy body armour demolition experts used when defusing bombs.

"Jesus, you're a pussy," the woman said. "You blind or what? Does this even look like a bomb? You won't even get an electric shock... unless you stick your finger in the wrong hole."

Agent Coates walked forward to inspect the devices. "Okay... no explosives I can see, and nothing holding a gas or liquid." His voice trailed off as he continued to examine the two items. "Looks straightforward... modified transmitter linked to an encryption module, with a few fancy bells and whistles attached. But I should take it apart to be certain."

"That isn't going to happen. You know the conditions: you take me to the president, and I give him our demands. If you interfere, I activate the dead man's switch, and they know you're not going to hold up your end of the deal."

"I didn't know we had a deal. Anyway, you're not going anywhere need the president. We are holding you—"

"*Listen.* You get me to Prescott, or you take the consequences. You talk to the asshole in charge, *now*, or you're the asshole who's responsible for what happens."

"What do we do?" Agent Coates asked Mercer. "Is this threat for real?"

"That's irrelevant; she doesn't get to the president."

"We are running out of time." She checked her watch. "Why don't you just ask the guy in the chair?"

"That's Mr. President to you." Agent Mercer turned to Agent Coates. "Find the FBI dick in charge and get some confirmation on the threat. Then get the chief of staff and the boss."

He turned back to the woman. "Move; we're not staying out here for everyone to post you on Instagram."

They walked up the driveway, one agent by her side and two behind her. They entered through a side door and entered a small room. Leaving the three agents to guard her, Mercer went to Abb's office, after being informed by another agent of the man's location.

He arrived just in time for the storm to erupt from within the confines of the office. Few might hope to find shelter from the rage of the chief of staff in full fury.

He gritted his teeth and entered.

"What do you mean, you don't know?" Abb shouted to one of his harried staffers. "What exactly do you know?" As the staffers saw Agent Mercer enter the room, their eyes suddenly begged for mercy.

Abb took note and looked behind him.

"We are waiting for an update from the FBI, sir." Agent Mercer answered to the staffer's relief. "We received an alert yesterday that a terrorist would present himself at the front gates. Fifteen minutes ago the FBI upgraded the threat alert, in connection to a possible nuclear threat to the country, sir."

"Jesus, talk about sleeping on the job. And you've just sat back and waited twenty-four hours for confirmation? Couldn't have gotten it when you received the warning?"

"At first the FBI considered it a crank call… I assume they had nothing to confirm the threat."

"Are we even certain this is genuine?" Abb's fury was only growing. "We need to know a lot more." Mercer looked him in the eye. "I think we'll find that the FBI is playing catch-up on this, sir. They will get back to us once they have something more. For now, they said to take the threat seriously."

"Does anyone actually know something I can take to the president?" The room was silent in reply. As the silence was becoming uncomfortable

Ethan Campbell entered the room to cut the awkwardness short.

"Sir," Campbell face Abb, "we need to see the president immediately." A few minutes later both staffers, followed by Agent Mercer, entered the Oval Office.

"Sir, we have a situation," Campbell said deferentially to Clayton. "We have just had confirmation from the NSA and the FBI of a serious threat. The NSA recently intercepted a message that hinted of a nuclear warhead being delivered to its target, but the target was undisclosed.

"Yesterday we received a message from what we believe to be the same source, informing us that a nuclear warhead has been sneaked into the US. The threat had not been confirmed. That was until an hour ago, when an FBI team found high radiation levels in a building, quite possibly from a nuclear device.

"A short time ago a terrorist operative approached the White house gates demanding to see you personally. She has a signal device with a dead man's switch strapped to her chest that she will activate if our instructions are not carried out. She is to hand over their demands to you face to face."

"That will not happen," Abb stated flatly.

"Why not?" Clayton inquired rather calmly.

"Sir, we can't let her anywhere near you." Campbell felt had let the president down. "The Secret Service doesn't believe the signal device is an explosive, but it could be hiding a small amount of a lethal virus. I take full responsibility, sir. I could have had a screen set up that would have safely allowed a face-to-face meeting."

"Get her in here."

"Sir—"

"Just do it, Ethan." Clayton spoke in a soft, almost tired voice. "They wouldn't have gone to all the trouble of sneaking a nuke into America just to attempt an assassination on me."

"We don't know that for sure," Abb objected. "Sir, if this threat is real, you need to know all your options. You'll need to be in constant contact with your national security team, and with her in the same room . . . it's out of the question."

"I'll excuse myself and say I need to use the little boy's room. We'll leave the intercom going so you can listen in."

"Sir, I think this is a bad idea. We need to consider all the possible outcomes." Agent Mercer agreed with Campbell.

"Agreed," said the national security adviser, "this could be a Russian ruse—"

"Russian… to what end?" Clayton turned to face him.

"If a nuclear weapon were to go off in an American city, it could undermine the public's support for our nuclear deterrent." Campbell paused. "To say nothing of creating further instability within the US."

"That's insane. What about all those Russians who died from the nuke—"

"Sir, one must remember the Russian mindset," Campbell pressed on. "They are pathological nationalists. Their new president was handpicked by Putin. He's an ultranationalist and will do anything to bring back the old glory days of the Soviet union, take back Poland, Hungary, Ukraine… If we are weak—or worse, consumed by internal division—it may be the opportunity he thinks he needs to win."

"Oh, for the love of God." Abb wanted to strangle someone, anyone. Campbell went on, "Sir, we know of Russian interference in both US and European internal matters . . . going back decades. We need to consider this possibility."

"Unfortunately, we don't have time for an investigation." Clayton paused as he thought. "Ethan, see what our people know to be facts… real facts."

"Yes, sir." Campbell pivoted on the spot and head for the door.

Clayton addressed Agent Mercer. "But for now we really don't have any other options. Let's see what she has to say." He walked behind his desk to sit in his chair.

With three agents behind her and Agent Mercer now at her right side, they brought the young woman in to see the president.

"For a man of the people, you're a hard man to get to see." She grinned impishly at Clayton.

"Even the White House has certain standards to uphold," Clayton replied with a certain coolness.

"Ache… Now that hurt." She couldn't help but grin; the main man wasn't a pushover.

"Now can we dispense with the usual un-pleasantries and get to the matter at hand? Do you have a nuclear weapon sitting in Los Angeles?"

"Never said we had anything in Los Angeles. Can we hold off on this? We have a schedule to keep." She looked around at a variety of glares and stares—and a bemused look from Clayton.

"By all means," he told the woman.

"Mr. President, you will order all members of the House and Senate to be brought here immediately. Then, with them present, you will comply with the people's demands on live TV."

"We will do no such thing," Campbell protested. "Imagine the panic if we told the public there is a nuke in an American city… the sheer panic. God only knows how many deaths that will cause."

"Then don't say anything. Keep them in the dark as usual. Just agree to our demands for justice, and it's all over."

"As if that is going to happen," Abb muttered.

"Even if we were willing to negotiate," Campbell said, "people would begin to wonder why we're considering your demands. Sooner or later someone is bound to leak the reason to the media. We can't go public with your demands and risk exposure. It's out of the question."

"This isn't open to debate," she fired back. "There is no negotiation to be had. Agree to our demands, and it's over."

"How do we know they have a nuke?" Abb said to Clayton. "This could be their way of inflicting massive damage on America without actually doing anything, sir. Ethan's right. We just can't let this threat be known to the public."

"So you're going to bury your heads in the sand? Well, I shouldn't be surprised. That's the government's usual response." She glared at the assembled faces.

"I'll meet you halfway," Clayton replied. "Agent Mercer; will you kindly have the House and Senate leadership escorted directly to the White House? Now what city is the bomb in?"

"So you can try to disarm it?" Her scorn was palpable.

"I'll make a deal with you," he said, ice in his voice. "I won't take you for an imbecile if you don't talk like one."

"Fine."

"If you give us the name of the city, we won't have a nationwide panic on our hands," Clayton explained to her.

"Merely citywide, right?" she sneered. "Just agree to our demands." "My word means nothing without congressional agreement. So whether you like it or not, we will be forced to negotiate. And that may take time, and the longer this drags on, the greater the danger of a panic. If I know the city, I can at least tighten martial law that'll reduce the loss of life. So will you provide us with the name?"

"And I'm going to do so as a sign of goodwill?" "What have you got to lose?"

"My major bargaining chip… What really matters to the corrupt State, you'll safely evacuate the rich."

Silence then fell upon the room.

Chapter 18

From a libertarian:

"Liberty includes the right to make bad choices."

"Then do not take me to task when, drunk and on drugs, I run your child over."

"So can I have all the heroin and Ice I want?"

"If I'm a terrorist, does that mean I have a 'get out of jail for free' card?"

The young woman sat on a chair in the corner of the room and waited, as Clayton calmly went over a few files left on his desk.

Abb paced the carpet like a caged bear, sending evil glances at the young woman, who lay comfortably slouched across a leather-covered chair.

"You want to spit it out before you choke?" the young woman asked with a smile on her face.

"You're beneath contempt," came Abb's reply.

"That's okay. I have nothing but contempt for corporate oppression."

"You're a damned traitor."

"Grow up, Pops. How can you be a traitor when your country has sold you out? Look around, old man. Once I had a lecturer who argued that he could not define evil. What was evil? he asked; he couldn't identify it. Well, I can. I see it every-day.

"I see it with the people who are made bankrupt and lose their homes because they can't pay their hospital bills. I see it in the lines of people waiting for their one hot meal of the day… people begging for food, while you have multibillionaires making tens of millions each year who won't give a cent to the neediest in this screwed-up country."

"And that justifies incinerating an American city?" Abb grumbled, glancing up as Brandon Keel entered the room.

"Isn't that the American way?" She grinned with honest malice. "You only listen when someone puts a gun to your head?"

"Sir, a moment." Agent Mercer placed his finger against his ear. "We have three Senators entering the White House."

"Kindly have someone brief them on their way to the Oval Office," Clayton stated flatly. "I don't have the patience to hear them whine about the situation, not today."

"Yes sir." Agent Mercer nodded before speaking into his sleeve. "You can justify your actions all you want," Abb sputtered, furious,

"but you're just another terrorist."

"One man's terrorist is another man's freedom fighter," she quoted flippantly.

"You obviously missed the president's observations on that subject," Abb responded.

"Oh, I heard it all right. That's why I know I'm a freedom fighter. In 1941 FDR made a speech about a world founded upon four essential freedoms."

"The freedom of speech, freedom of worship, and freedom…" Clayton began to clarify her meaning, only to be cut off.

"Yeah, the freedom from *want*. So you tell me. If you're working two jobs but can't make enough to feed your kids, wouldn't you take up arms against a corrupt state? Fighting for 'freedom from want'—doesn't that make you a freedom fighter?"

"That's utter nonsense." Abb hated intellectual debates.

"Right. After all, you only make thirty thousand a year, right, Chief? When was the last time you needed to beg for food?"

Keel almost managed to silence his gulp of amusement.

Abb glared at him. "You find this funny?"

"I'm not too sure who said it… I think it was Jefferson who said something about how we should have a revolution every two generations." Keel's smile hid his trembling hands. He did not have the fire that burned in Abb's belly and veins.

"That's one hell of a way to run a country." Abb couldn't believe the fool.

"You forgot 'freedom from fear,'" Clayton whispered softly.

"Sorry?" The young woman turned her head.

"FDR also spoke of 'Freedom from fear,'" he repeated. "How much fear will you create today amongst ordinary citizens? As a freedom fighter your struggle is with the *state*, the oppressor, the tyranny, not the citizens. You really haven't been taking notes."

"And what about freedom from fear of American aggression? Its naked aggression against the international community is apparent to everyone. Invading Vietnam, Iraq, Afghanistan—the criminal abuse inflicted on the Palestinians. And what about America's criminal interference in Iran, both past and present? I'm sure you forgot about that little episode, how the CIA overthrew the president of Iran in 1953, just so we could get their oil?" America had feared the socialist president would nationalize the oil industry. "For that matter, you have the criminal atrocities committed by the CIA all over the world." She turned her head to see who had opened one of the doors.

Jonathan entered the Oval Office and walked past the others to lay a file before the president. Clayton opened it and studied the contents, palming the small earpiece that Jonathan had secretly placed on the table. "Thank you," he said with a nod to Jonathan.

When Abb saw that Clayton was not interested in responding, he fired back. "And the atrocities we stopped? We stopped Nazi Germany. We stopped the spread of Communism. How many lives did we end up saving? While all you can do is complain.

"More often than not, we're the victims, Pearl Harbour, 9/11… we wouldn't have gone into Afghanistan if not for Bin Laden." Abb spat with growing fury. "I'll tell you what. I'll get you a one-way ticket. You can choose North Korea, Iran, Russia, or China in return for your cooperation. You get a pardon and a flight straight to the 'worker's paradise' of your choice."

She scoffed. "And that counts as your excuse?"

"You play the victim quite well," Clayton told the young woman.

"What?" She turned to face the president.

"You play the victim quite well, Miss Bernstein. May I call you Annette?"

She looked at him in shock. "What?"

"You really shouldn't repeat yourself," Clayton said; "it raises questions. Miss Annette Bernstein graduated from Harvard, no less, with degrees in—" Clayton saw the look on her face. "Face recognition, the marvels of science. You didn't think you could just walk into the White House and not be triple scanned?" His finger tapped the file in front of him.

"The police state at work," she said.

"Just trying to stop terrorists from placing bombs in public places," Abb snapped back.

"Don't you just love that plausible deniability crap?" she retorted. "You two should get a room," Keel muttered with bitter sarcasm. He spoke up. "If this were a police state, you'd be in some basement having your fingernails pulled one by one, followed by the Russian tradition of a bullet to the back of the head." Brandon spoke up.

"Although we could make an exception in your case." Abb happily offered.

"Let's not regress to the point of melodrama," Clayton said, raising a hand to stop the foreplay. "Now don't get me wrong. I accept that America's foreign policies have been hardly well thought out." He chuckled softly. "Incompetently planned, disastrously funded…" *I could give you a long list of bureaucrats and politicians I would've put in jail for criminal negligence.* "Having said all that, there have been provocations—"

"Non-existent provocations, like the Gulf of Tonkin incident that supposedly justified the invasion of south Vietnam, provocations invented to justify keeping minorities and nations under the control of the big powers," she replied with equal assurance. She knew the Cold War was all a conspiracy by the big powers to run the world.

"A real struggle," Keel said, underscoring the president's point, "even if most Americans were too high on their drug of choice to notice."

"You're arguing that the 'cold war' justified invading… Vietnam," she answered. "Well, then, I guess the government should hold its head high at the atrocities it's committed?"

Clayton was more annoyed with her by the moment. "Really, must everyone rewrite history? America did not invade South Vietnam, contrary to the views of certain professors and other 'useful idiots.'" There was no storming of the beaches of Normandy coming under Nazi machine-gun fire. South Vietnam never gave the North permission to invade the South. "As to who should lower their heads in shame, the fact that so many Americans had no qualm about letting millions of Vietnamese slip under the yoke of a communist dictatorship is the true shame of the Vietnam War. That was the true crime committed by America, which I have no doubt you fully support."

"And Iraq?" she sneered.

"What can I say?" Clayton shrugged. "In our defence, not everyone votes Republican, thank God."

"You really love your pompous lecturing, don't you? Telling everyone how inferior they are. That's your excuse for the atrocities committed by the CIA? That people are simply too stupid to understand how we're helping them?"

"Oh, if only we were all so lucky as to be living in a worker's paradise," Abb said.

"And that washes away all the blood of the innocent children?" she snapped back.

"Whilst you have taken it upon yourself to defend our children with a nuke?" Clayton retorted with equal stubbornness. "How magnanimous of you. But why? Is it empathy for the poor whilst living in your million dollar penthouse apartment? Are you another spoilt child of a decadent society trying to make up for all the myriad offences, real and imagined? No, I think not…

"Tell me, is this just to piss off daddy?" He grinned. "What did he do wrong? You received too many toys as a child? Not enough of them? What justifies the murder of a hundred thousand men, women, and children? I have to wonder why a young person with—I assume—a loving family, who is very well off, well-educated, would throw it all away. Maybe the Muslims are right, and we shouldn't let women out of the house until they turn thirty."

"You sexist—" She stopped. *The bastard's baiting me. Get it together.* Annette knew how women were treated in the Muslim world. Even now some were rarely allowed out of the house unless they were in the company of a male relative.

The door opened to end the debate prematurely as three Senators, each with a curious mix of confusion, outrage, and stunned disbelief stamped on their faces, filed into the Oval Office.

"Is it true?" Senator Holt demanded in outrage as if he had been personally assaulted while strolling down the corridor.

"Are we talking about the bomb or your bad record in government?" Clayton asked in a sweetly innocent voice that had Keel choking down a bubble of mirth, while Abb tried to grit his teeth even as his face went slightly pink.

The young woman sniggered at the sight of the Senator's red face.

"I will not be slandered in such a fashion," Holt snapped. "Answer the question."

"Indeed, Senator. The Secret Service often indulges in whimsical stories of woe to grizzled Senators," he replied whimsically. "It helps agents pass the time as they valiantly walk Senators to emergency meetings with the president. Now shut up and listen."

"God, it's true? We need to know our options." Senator Walker had come in behind Holt. "What do our intelligence agencies have to say about this total lapse in security?" he bellowed.

Another Senator spoke up from near the doorway. "Has the National Security Council been apprised of the situation?"

"Who is she?" asked Senator Holt, just noticing the young woman sitting on the couch.

Abb smiled benignly. "She'd be the terrorist."

"What kind of fool do you take me for?" Senator Holt barked out the words, just as the door opened and two more Senators entered.

"A bigger one than most?" Clayton asked in reply.

Holt's nostrils flared. "Sir, I have been a representative of the people for over thirty years, and I demand the respect that is due any elected official." "Thirty years in government," Clayton sniped at the 'elder statesman.' "Maybe that explains why the public has so little faith in its elected officials." There was a tiny chortle from someone in the room. "What?" Senator Holt turned in search of who was responsible and looked from one person to the next. This conversation was a little too unrefined for his cultured taste. As a veteran Senator, he expected respect, not this clown act.

To compound the Senator's difficulties, Senator Bell and General MacAdams were ushered into the room.

"So it's true?" Senator Bell demanded.

"It must be," Senator Walker answered.

"What do we know? Have the Intel agencies found anything?" Senator Bell continued her inquiry.

"To save time," Clayton said, silencing the room, "let me summarize. We have a nuclear device on American soil, and if any of you opens his mouth to ask another dumb question, I will borrow Agent Mercer's gun and shoot you in the one remaining organ that still works. I case you're wondering, I am referring to what's in your mouth." *How many times do you have to explain the facts before it penetrates?*

As he considered this question of the ages, another congresswoman was ushered in the room. He tried for a smile. "Now, I believe we have enough of our elected officials to at least see your demands."

"When you read them out to the public. How soon before the camera crew get here?" Annette was getting a little anxious.

"Why not now? What does it matter?" Clayton insisted.

"I was told not to—" She stopped. "You'll understand when you read out the demands."

"She's here to give us their demands?" Senator Holt stuttered in disbelief.

"She's not here for the laundry," came Clayton's flippant reply.

"We need to talk and in private." Holt turned to look at the young woman.

"Listen, I am not going anywhere." Annette stood up from her chair to answer him.

"It's not a request." There was fire and even brimstone in Holt's throat and nose.

"If you wouldn't mind, Miss Bernstein, just ask for a coffee or drink." Clayton stopped for a moment. "No, I suppose that wouldn't do; you'll be worried that we've spiked your drink. Feel free to read a magazine." Clayton gave her his most innocent smile.

She glared at the president, refusing to turn away. He simply returned her stare.

"We won't be long, and we still have plenty of time. Also the camera crews seem to be fashionably late. Plus, we still need the location of the bomb."

"I told you, I wasn't—" She huffed in exasperation. Then she turned and, escorted by Agent Mercer, left the room, feeling almost embarrassed— as if the adults had told the little girl to leave.

"You can't seriously be thinking of accepting their demands?" Holt stood straighter than he ever had. Surprisingly, he found it was not for show. This could not be allowed to happen.

"I am open to ideas." Clayton looked around the room half filled with Senators and a couple of Representatives.

General MacAdams spoke up. "What have our intelligence services got on these terrorists? Are we talking Islamic?"

"Ethan?" Clayton asked through the intercom.

"Right there, sir." Ethan was true to his word when he came through the other door, with an armload of files.

"We'll forgo the usual formalities and history lesson today, Ethan. Just tell us what you have."

"Yes sir." Ethan was not fazed by the president's demand. That was the trouble with working for a guy who actually had his shit together. Another president might need a score card; Prescott often knew more about the background than the man doing the briefing.

"At this stage we have some workable knowledge on the Chechen group and its Islamist affiliates who sent the message. We have several of our best analysts going over everything we know about them that may pinpoint any likely individuals involved in this case.

"For all that, we need to take into consideration—"

Walker glared at Campbell. "Wait, wait. All that could take days, weeks, who knows how long before you get something useful."

"We are aware of that, sir. But as I was about to say—"

Holt stepped in before Campbell could continue. "We know who they are; why isn't that enough? We can't wait around until they detonate this bomb. We spend billions on intelligence each year—"

"Senator, let him finish," Walker addressed Holt. God, even Holt should know how many years it took to find Bin-Laden in his Pakistani palace.

"Sir, with respect," Campbell plodded on, "we know the group and a number of key individual members. But this situation may be a lot more complex than we would normally expect." He sighed. "Let me explain. The intelligence community does know a great deal about our enemies—not everything, but a lot. We spy on them, we listen in on them, and that's what's got us really worried.

"For them to have successfully carried out a mission of this size with so little signal traffic, with every aspect so tightly compartmentalised— well, either we have new players hiding under an old skin, who have fundamentally reorganized this group into a totally difference organism, or we are facing something new and radically different... such as a nation-state taking an active part in the attack.

Campbell addressed the president. "Sir, I strongly advise you to consider Russian involvement. We have nothing concrete, but the lack of evidence doesn't remove how professionally this entire matter has been handled." He took a deep breath, about to advise the president to increase their defence level. It was time to put their nuclear arsenal on alert.

"Or they have learned to hide their tracks," Holt fumed." I've been on enough senatorial committees to tell when a bureaucrat is clutching at straws. Am I right? You've been caught with your pants down once more." *Damn those security leaks. The bloody Russians, the bloody Chinese, the bloody terrorists know more about how we operate than we do.* The old Republican had little patience for the "patriotic" whistle-blowers, especially the ones warning the terrorists to encrypt their messages and offering other useful tips.

"That's possible, sir," Campbell said and turned to the president." The truth is we have failed you, Mr. President, and the country."

"What about that message the NSA supposedly intercepted?" Abb's head was spinning.

"Good chance it was staged, to get us to accept that the threat was real. Ironically, if not for the FBI team finding that radiation spike, we would've dismissed the nuclear threat as a hoax."

"And if this radiation spike is the hoax?" Holt was not to be easily satisfied.

"The analysts have examined the readings on the radiation level, and it's just too high. So high they believe the terrorists must have done something to irradiate the building. It can't be anything less than weapons grade."

Senator Bell almost felt she was in a sick comedy. "So they had to actually hold your hand and lead you to the evidence—otherwise you wouldn't have even known about it? My God. What sheer incompetence." "Yeah, I guess we should be guarding Russian nukes more carefully," Holt shot back. "Maybe you should go over and volunteer." The cold warrior was rising to the defence of his nation.

"We have to do something," Walker bellowed. "The government can't be seen sitting on its hands."

He's very good at that, Clayton noted silently.

"How could you people have let this country down… yet again?" Senator Walker turned on Campbell with indignation. "National intelligence is supposed to prevent this. I will demand answers once this crisis is over."

That's it, start laying blame now, just in case it veers your way later on, thought Clayton. *Wouldn't want anyone to raise questions about limited funding or ignoring warnings by the intelligence community over limitations imposed on them by Congress, now would we?*

"Mr. President," Senator Walker said, "I recommend that we immediately raise our defence status to DEFCON one."

"Oh, how typical," Senator Bell snapped at the men. "We have no evidence, but somehow we have to blame the Russians. We have enough problems, but here we are looking for more…"

"Let's concentrate on the matter at hand, Elaine." Clayton's voice held an icy edge as if he had no wish to discuss the matter further.

"What can we do?" Walker asked the room.

"We need to get her to talk," Senator Holt spoke up. "She's one of them. We have to find out how much she knows."

"How do we get her to talk?" Bell snapped at Holt.

"A bribe—we offer her immunity from prosecution?" Senator Holt suggested. "The promise she won't spend the rest of her life in a sealed box with only a bucket for company."

"Wake up," was Bell's reply. "She's too committed to her damned course to be bribed."

"How do you know?" Walker was desperate for something to hold on to.

"She walked into the White House knowing her life was over, finished. For God's sake, she's a member of a group threatening to detonate a nuke in this country. Don't you think she's totally committed... utterly committed?"

"I would imagine," Clayton put in, "that one of their demands will be full immunity from prosecution; bribery would thus be doubtful."

"There are other methods," Walker stated darkly.

"Such as?" Bell turned to face Walker. "We do what is necessary." He persisted. "Then say it; are you talking about torture?"

Walker stared into her eyes. "We need to consider all our options." Bell faced him down. "I thought we don't resort to torture."

"We are talking about thousands, perhaps a million lives. And what if we're talking about New York? What would you do?"

"I don't know. But I do know we can't take that low road; if we do, we'll be as bad as they are." Bell was not about to allow Walker to ignore the dangers.

"Jesus, you're talking morality at a time like this?" Walker looked around the room for support.

"This is exactly the time, before we do something we'll regret." She almost stamped her foot in protest.

"She has information about a group planning to set off a nuke unless we agree to their demands," Walker barked back at her.

"But we don't even know what their demands are," she barked right back."

"It doesn't matter." Holt snorted like a rhino ready to charge. "She is threatening the US with a nuke."

"We are talking about torture. Not some gentlemanly interview by the FBI followed up by another dozen. You are talking about extreme, inhumane, *unlawful* measures, damn it." Bell was shouting. "It's wrong. We have gone down this route before, to our regret. We can't sell out our principles. We need to stand up for what we know is right, no matter the cost, or we're end up circumventing the law just for expedience.

"After our past mistakes we need to repair our moral compass, not turn a blind eye." She addressed Clayton: "If we behave like them, we lose, whether or not a bomb is detonated. Anyway, the FBI has acknowledged that torture doesn't work."

"They've never had a nuke ticking away," Walker snapped. "Extreme measures may be necessary."

"No, it's wrong. We can't do this… its more than violating her rights. This is about us, what we stand for. We may have to endure the worst for the good of the country—"

"What kind of crap are you talking about?" Walker shouted back into her face.

"I believe she is trying to convey the ramblings of a former colleague of yours, Senator. To stay true to our beliefs and our great nation, there are times when we may need to endure great pain or loss. It was a nice speech, got a standing ovation." He read the confusion on Walker's face. "OK, in short, if we have to choose between our principles and Los Angeles, we lose Los Angeles." Clayton smiled with calm certainty.

"That is ridiculous." Walker blinked in disbelief.

"Tell that to your sainted colleagues," Clayton answered.

"We do what we need to do! Can you imagine the outcry if we allow an American city to be incinerated just to protect our morals? Go play with your dolls, woman, and let the grownups deal with this." Walker began to wave his arms in outrage at the young woman.

"Look, we just need to keep all our options open, that's all. We'll try reason… first." Holt spoke up.

"And when that fails?" Walker turned to Holt.

"We consider our options."

"I say we put it to a vote." Walker offered.

"And who is going to 'extract' the information, you?" Senator Bell asked Walker.

"How are you going to get that trigger away from her without her setting it off?" Abb tried to claim down the heated voices.

"We jam the signal." Walker felt a ray of hope.

"There is something we are missing," Clayton muttered, almost to himself.

Campbell addressed the assembly. "Unfortunately we can't jam the signal."

"This is the White House, and we can't jam a phone call or whatever?" Bell was actually shocked.

"If we didn't have the equipment, we could bring it in. That's not the problem. We have been monitoring the woman's communications—"

"*What?* You're letting the terrorists listen in on our conversations?" Now Walker was in shock.

"No, sir. It's not like that at all. This is quite technical, but if you'll give me a moment, I'll explain."

"Just give us the simple view, Ethan," Clayton said, seeing the look of consternation from most of the others. "This is a room filled with politicians after all."

"Yes sir. She had a small, I suppose you can call it a microcomputer attached to a highly sophisticated encryption module that transmits a word or phrase at irregular intervals. It could be anything from… Tom, Dick to Harry every five, ten or fifteen minutes." Campbell looked around at the confused crowd. "So if we jam the signal, it wouldn't be long before the terrorists know."

"Then what the hell do we do? Give in to their demands?" another Senator asked.

"That is out of the question." Senator Holt would not be moved. "And watch a city being incinerated?" Bell countered. "We can at least hear them out."

"I don't know." Walker was now uncertain and as usual, when under stress, wanted his army of aides and advisers. "We need to debate this calmly and logically."

"Can't we string them along?" a fair-haired Senator spoke up from one corner to the room. "Isn't that what police negotiators do? At least until we can find the bomb?"

"Ethan?" Senator Holt turned to the man.

"It's in the playbook, and it is the best course of action, sir." Campbell felt defeated and now unable to even voice his opinion with full force, due to the intelligence services' failure and Clayton's icy tone. He felt as if he had no credibility left, a failure in every sense of the word.

"But how long can we keep stringing them along? I don't see this as the answer. We should get a full spectrum of advice." Senator Walker shook his head. "We need a consensus." Walker turned to the other Senators in the room.

God, to think these are the Titans that will stand guard over our democracy. The giants who will shoulder the burdens placed upon them by a grateful nation. Clayton studied their faces, filled with doubt and uncertainty. He shivered in defeat.

Where are the warrior philosophers of our time? Where are the leviathans of our age? Where, O God, are the poets of thought and deed who would defend the gates of our most holy of holies, so that our children may sleep the sleep of angels?

Snivelling worthless cowards, Clayton silently cursed them all.

"Ask her to come back in here," he told one of the Secret Service agents. The senators and congressmen cried out in disbelief up until the moment when the Secret Service brought back the young woman. Annette Bernstein, surrounded by her bodyguards, strode into a silent room, which made her wonder what she had missed.

"Now, I really need to see those demands," Clayton told her, "so that we can decide on a suitable response."

"You don't have a choice," she replied.

Clayton took in her stubborn look and said, "Then we can't go any further."

"You can forget playing your little games with me. I was told you'd try some silly little mind game."

"Look, what does it really matter?" Bell tried to smile and present an agreeable facade. "We are going to need time to come to terms with this. We're only going to get one shot when the cameras start rolling. How long before the camera crews are due?"

Bell turned to Agent Mercer, who spoke into his sleeve and then nodded as he received a reply. "We have three network crews waiting, ma'am," he replied.

Senator Bell stared at the young woman.

Reluctantly, Annette stood up and pulled out an envelope from her left-hand pocket, then took a step towards the president. She stopped when all three Secret Service agents pulled out their guns, instantly aimed at her head. Each had carefully positioned themselves for unimpeded lines of fire that threatened no one else in the room.

"I'll need to examine that," Agent Mercer stated with calm authority.
"Fine."

Agent Mercer slipped latex gloves onto his hands to carefully collect the envelope, before placing the envelope into a small boxlike device that sterilized the envelope and then the contents.

"I cannot believe this," Senator Holt stuttered in disbelief, "to see the day when a terrorist would enter the White House to hand over a set of demands."

When Agent Mercer was satisfied, he opened the envelope and extracted the paper. He inspected the paper and then placed it in a see-though evidence sleeve before offering it to the president.

"No… what fools we have been." Clayton's hand stopped in mid-air. "What utter fools we've been."

"Sir?" Agent Mercer blinked at the president.

"What were you told to do exactly, Miss Bernstein?" Clayton waved his hand is a gesture for silence.

"This won't work, whatever game you're playing," she insisted.

"Just tell me." Clayton looked at her with cold distain.

"Give you our demands. Then just make sure you go on live TV when you make the address to the country."

"Anything else?"

"Just make sure you do it in the Oval Office, for effect. Why?" "Yes, why is this so important?" Senator Holt demanded.

"At a guess, so they could take out what is left of the government." Clayton told him in a casual voice.

"The device is in Washington DC?" Agent Mercer stood dumfounded. *"No!"* Annette Bernstein nearly jumped into the air. "Why would he do any such a thing when you have agreed to our demands?"

"What are you talking about?" Holt shouted in his usual manner.

"You performed your task beautifully—an excellent distraction, Miss Bernstein. You kept us from thinking about the envelope." "Make sense, sir," Senator Holt hissed.

"You don't know that… I don't— Oh, this is a con, a scheme to get me to talk, right?" The woman shook her head.

"You really don't know the bomb is here?" Clayton marvelled at the absurdity.

"If the bomb is in Washington we must evacuate immediately." Senator Walker seemed to be almost jumping on the spot.

"We can't, Senator, we leave and the bomb goes off. Well played, my dear." Clayton nodded in congratulations.

"They told me to be careful in case you tried to trick me, but this won't work. So you can save the con job," she told Clayton.

"But you were told to release your little dead-man switch if we try to evacuate, correct?" he asked.

She made no response.

He pushed. "Well?"

"Back off... I know this is a trick." Annette glared back.

"Sir?" Agent Mercer addressed the president. He suddenly knew Prescott was right.

"Agent Mercer, remember that talk we had about the presidency? This qualifies, and anyway I'll never get to the door before she activates the dead man's switch."

Campbell cringed, his fears suddenly stronger. With one strike the Russians could indeed take out the US government and undermine American resolve. "Sir, you need to—"

"We can't stay," Senator Walker shouted as he fronted the general. "General, I demand you evacuate us immediately."

"You'll never make it," Agent Mercer declared in a harsh voice in an effort to control the situation. Didn't they hear the president?

"Annette, please . . ." Bell began an attempt to reach the young woman. "Give it a rest, this isn't going to work," Annette shouted, clearly furious at their deception. "And you're running out of time."

"Yes, you're quite correct; we need to get moving. General MacAdams, get your men to every TV and radio station in DC and have them continue to broadcast as if nothing is out of the ordinary. Second, all Internet services in the Washington area go down. You can, blame a... terrorist attack. You need to cut all communications into Washington, landlines, mobile phones, everything."

"Sir, I can't give any guarantees." General MacAdams spoke in his usual steely voice, even as he picked up the phone.

"Understood, we just need enough time to deal with this and keep Washington calm. Until then, ladies and gentlemen, make yourselves comfortable."

Senator Walker walked up to the seated president. "You can't be serious. We have to evac—"

"The young lady is not going to let that happen, so calm down." "What game are you playing?" Annette demanded.

"No game, just a tiny pause in procedure to give the general a chance to secure Washington, Miss Bernstein." Clayton paused. "We may go over the deadline by a few minutes, no more."

"Mr. President, we can't make an informed decision like this." The Senator from Alaska made his distress obvious.

They knew this was not how it worked. They had an army of advisers. The president had his cabinet, the NSC. The American government needed its political advisers.

"Abraham Lincoln did not need an army to make decisions, people," Clayton told the assembled men and women. "Take a seat, get a drink, and try to remember that we are adults and it is incumbent upon us to act as such."

They sat down and began to mutter and complain to themselves in hushed tones.

"Now, my dear, let's see these demands." Clayton stretched out his hand to Agent Mercer.

"You can't be seriously thinking of conceding?" Holt puffed up his chest. "To these filthy terrorists?"

"You don't have a choice," she told Holt bluntly. "Just accept the demands."

"And if I don't?" Clayton responded.

"You have to."

"No, I don't." Clayton smiled. "But I am curious." He put on his reading glasses.

"Let's see. First point, the US government agrees to confiscate all assets and property belonging to the top 1 percent. The properties are to be sold off and all the wealth redistributed to the bottom 50 percent of the American population." He looked up at the young woman and the crowd of Senators.

"Well, that's not going to happen." Clayton sadly shook his head. *What the hell is he thinking?* Walker almost felt as if he should hit

Clayton in the mouth. *Just offer the insane woman anything she wants; we'll straighten it out later.*

"You can't stop us. You will agree to our demands." She broke into Walker's thoughts.

"No. you fail to understand," Clayton said. "The government will not keep its word, my dear. You should know by now the government only keeps the agreements it wants to keep. Don't they teach history in Harvard anymore?"

"Of course they do." She blinked in surprise.

"Then you should know that the US government signed over four hundred treaties with the First Nations and broke every last one. Indeed, ask the South Vietnamese how good our word is." His smile widened. "Ask the Ukrainians. We agreed to honour Ukraine's borders, but when Russia invaded Crimea, what did America do? God, woman, haven't you realized its better being America's enemy than being her friend or ally?"

"That's simply outrageous," Senate Holt stammered in outrage. "Oh, sorry. So the USA hasn't gone back on its word, Senator? These ladies and gentlemen of Congress will agree with all your demands but will later renege and argue that they did so under threat." He swept an arm to indicate the gathered legislators.

"Then you do it." Annette replied in frustration.

Clayton chuckled. "I have no real say in the matter. At the end of the day it's Congress that decides."

She looked at him in disbelief as if she could not accept any of what he was saying.

"Now, let's see, what else?" He looked back to the list. "Justice for the Palestinians… stopping all support for Israel, agreeing to all sanctions against Israel in the UN. End of drone strikes… Stop all American oppression in all the Middle East…

"All American bases in the Mideast to be closed and all soldiers returned to the US…

"Admit its war crimes against Iraq, Syria, Afghanistan, Iran, and Vietnam…

"Publicly apologize for all its atrocities and acts of aggression against the innocent people of the world…

"And naturally full immunity from prosecution." He nodded. "Bring about world peace?"

Annette blinked at him, visibly confused.

"He didn't wri—" She stopped and suddenly looked foolish.

"Thank you." Clayton gave her a goofy grin; he had caught her out. "No, I put that bit in. But it did feel right."

Agent Mercer looked from the president to the terrorist. "Thank you" for what? For her confirmation that… she knew the guy who wrote that crap, he realized. She may know the asshole in charge. That's very useful.

"Will you take this seriously?" Senator Walker demanded.

"I need to speak to him." Clayton looked up from the piece of paper straight into Annette's eyes.

"There is nothing to be said, just comply." The words came as Annette's only reply.

"I still need to speak to him."

"Speak to whom?" Holt looked from Clayton to Annette.

"Why, my good Senator, the person who wrote this little note to us." Clayton held up the letter, even as his smile grew.

Abb looked closely at Clayton, he knew the man well enough to know that the more humorous he became the crueller and more devious he became. You didn't want him to be smiling at you; the more he grinned, the more lethal he was. His smile seemed innocent until he pounced.

You backed the man into a corner at your own expense. Enough media figures had learned that the hard way.

"Why?" Annette asked.

"Because your friends know we will never honour any agreement we make."

"Bull."

"Ask yourself why did you have to hand us the letter personally? Why not just send it in the mail? Email, text, Facebook… whatever. Why? To arrange it so that the majority of the government's leadership is all here in the Oval Office, all standing in front of the camera.

"Well played, my dear. But I still need to speak to the man in charge."

"Will you explain yourself?" Holt demanded with his eyes locked on Clayton.

"Wake up, Holt. The young lady may believe we will keep our word, but the terrorists know full well we won't. So they get us to make our little speech… humiliate America, have us begging on our knees. And then wipe out what's left of America's elected leadership with one nuke."

"Sir, we have to evacuate you immediately." Campbell began. "This could still be a ruse—"

"Ethan. Whether Russian or terrorist we still have time, they are working to a plan which means they want that speech," Clayton told him with conviction.

"You don't know that. They may be willing to negotiate," Walker insisted in a heated voice.

"They know we won't honour any agreement," Clayton stated in that calm assured voice. Then he turned to Annette. "The only way you are going to get anything solid out of this is if he talks to me."

"This is a trick—"

"No, this is reality, not some childish fantasy." Clayton's voice was ice cold. "You're playing with the grown-ups now. So step up to the plate. This won't work unless you accept that it's real."

A junior Senator looked towards the door. "We need to get out now—"
"No, you don't. You leave, and I swear I will release the button. This is a trick, I know it." Annette almost shouted at Clayton.

"Do you?" Clayton asked in a deadly calm voice.

"People, this is not the time to panic," Holt shouted.

"You're not fooling me," she insisted.

"Just give me a chance to talk to him. I believe I have something to offer."

"What?"

"Just arrange contact. You know I'm right: they know we'll never keep our word. Deep down you know we'll never honour any agreement with a gun to our heads."

Clayton pressed down on his intercom. "Jonathan, could you come in?" He was still speaking when Jonathan entered once more. "Sir?"

Jonathan tried to sound calm.

"The media?"

"At your convenience, sir."

"Show them in." Clayton turned to the young woman. "Miss Bernstein, we don't have much time."

"How do I know you won't try to track him down?"

"I have been told you are carrying a rather sophisticated communications device that is encrypted." Clayton pointed to her belt. "And if it doesn't suit I can assure you we have the communications capability to reach your leader. You need to contact him now, while you have the chance to get something out of all this." Clayton paused, trying to think of something to add. "And I am sure that your people have taken steps to protect themselves. As I said, you're playing with the grown-ups."

"Suppose you're right; why would he agree to call?" Annette demanded. "You will just have to convince… him. Ask him what he wants most of all. What is the one thing he wants more than anything?" "I'll need some room."

"Agent Mercer will escort you outside. You can still see us through the window if we try to make a run for it. Just tell him to contact us. Agent Mercer will give you the number for a direct line he can use. I am certain your friend will secure his own line of communication."

As she walked out, she heard Clayton call General MacAdams over to speak to him in a soft voice, directing his attention to a writing pad on his desk. He ignored the media crews as they carried in their cameras with bewildered looks. This was all rather unusual.

The camera crews had not even taken a dozen steps when the director of the Secret Service stormed into the room. "Sir, if you are right, we can't let you stay in such an exposed position." He had just arrived at the White House and was furious that his agents had not removed the president the instant the threat had materialized.

"I fear the young lady will object."

"Sir, we can deal with her. We can jam the signal—" "As I understand it, there is some risk in doing so."

"It's a small risk, sir. We have monitored the timing in the transmissions, once we jam the signal we should be able to get you into the bunker before the terrorists realize she has been taken out of play."

"The risk to Washington is too great, director. We may get to safety in time, but the city will not. Stay focused; we need to find some form of leverage." Clayton was not about to let the Secret Service pull him out of his chair and into the bunker or onto Air Force One at the price of Washington DC. "And may I point out that the nuke may not be in Washington."

Holt's eyebrows went up in alarm. *You were damned sure a moment ago.* Clayton turned to face Senator Holt. "Senator, your politics are crap, but you know people. What do you make of our young terrorist?" Senator Holt looked at the president, stunned at the backhanded compliment for a moment, and then nodded. Politicians might well be bent, but they didn't have to be cowards. "I would say she is committed to her cause—she believes. But you have raised doubts. Yeah, I'd say this is not the way she expected things to develop. And she isn't as closed-minded as she seems. Is that what you wanted to know?"

"Confirmation can only help, Senator."

"Many politicians say they will make America great again.

How, exactly?

Maybe if they stopped selling out America for thirty pieces of silver?"

Harold Blunt

Chapter 19

Annette Bernstein returned to the Oval office, escorted by her now constant chaperone, Agent Mercer.

"I sent the message," Annette told Clayton with a sombre face. She was beginning to take this seriously. "I received a reply to continue with the timetable."

"We can't if you're right, we need to move," Walker told Clayton. Even Senator Bell nodded her head in agreement.

"We are America's representatives, we do not run." Holt shouted to the crowd in frustration and disbelief. Everyone seemed all too willing to concede to the terrorists.

"Agreed, let's get this started," Clayton told the gathering and turned to the camera crews. "Gentlemen, when you are ready we will begin."

Each camera crew gave the signal to begin.

President Prescott, surrounded by Senators and congressional representatives, looked into the camera lenses of the media. Then he calmly stated that a nuclear bomb was hidden within the capital city, before assuring the American people that the only bomb was in Washington DC; the rest of the country was safe, and he expected the terrorists to make contact shortly.

He left out any demands made in the letter.

Clayton then asked the media to wait in the outer office. "Now, we wait," he told the assembly.

Time once more dragged as they impatiently waited for a reaction from the terrorists.

The light on the private line blinked, and the entire room went silent. With considerable self-control Clayton turned on the speaker. "President Prescott, you did not read out our demands." A clear voice with an almost metallic tone came out of the speaker.

"A little incentive for you to call," Clayton replied

"Very well, but before we begin, you will bring back the media and read the statement provided. It will be useful if we have a live record for posterity."

"I would like to discuss a few matters first." Clayton would not be diverted.

"No, call them in. You can say what you want after the media has broadcast the statement."

"This will go better if we discuss this personally," Clayton told the voice.

"I am sure it would be for you, but first you will read out our demands or I hang up."

"As you wish." He looked around the room. "Gentlemen, would one of you be kind enough to ask the media to come back?"

The media filed in, now short one of the camera crew who had found a more important story to cover.

Clayton spoke into the small speaker as the media switched on their equipment. "How would you like to be addressed?"

"You may call me Ahmed," The uninterested-sounding voice responded.

"Splendid, first name basis, that's a good start." Just then the media crews gave the signal to begin.

Once more Clayton addressed the nation, putting on his reading glasses, and began reading the list of demands.

But he then paused halfway down the list. "Now, before I finish reading out all the demands, I would like to ask Ahmed to select two hundred Muslim cities, each with a population of over one million." Clayton spoke loudly towards the intercom.

"What?" The metallic voice responded to his demands.

"I need the names of two hundred Muslim cities," Clayton repeated himself.

"Why?" The voice sounded suspicious of his intent.

"Come now, your threaten to incinerate Washington in a nuclear fireball; what do you think?"

"You can't be serious. You promised to—" Ahmed began in sudden horror.

From the corner of his eye Clayton saw Annette Bernstein all but jump out of her seat, only to be blocked in her advance by the imposing figure of Agent Mercer.

"I really would like you to give me the names of two hundred Muslim cities." Clayton seemed to just whisper the words, yet they drove an ice pick into the groans of many of the men present.

"This game will not gain you anything." Ahmed's metallic voice sound wobbly.

"I see. You think we haven't the balls to retaliate? That's fair enough, so select two cities and you'll have your proof." Clayton calmly replied.

"I will not."

"Come now, just two cities. You can name two off the top of your head."

"You are insane," Ahmed's voice hissed over the intercom. "Debatable, but I think we should continue this in private. Gentlemen, if you would kindly leave the room. Once we have finalized this, you can come back, and I'll read out the rest of the terrorist's demands. Thank you for your time."

Once the media crews had left, Clayton scratched his nose.

"Very well. General MacAdams… what are my options to mount a nuclear strike on the cities of Tehran and Jerusalem?"

"Uh…" The general seemed to draw a laboured breath. "It depends on whether you want to employ a cruise missile or an ICBM, sir. An ICBM may worry the Russians and Chinese. We'll need to make sure they know who we are targeting. A cruise missile from a sub wouldn't worry the Chinese or Russians too much, but we would have to get the subs into range.

"A further option is to use bombers launching cruise missiles— although since they'll be carrying nukes, we'll have to be careful not to overfly certain countries."

"But… you will lose Washington." The voice on the intercom betrayed some concern. "Are you willing to sacrifice an American city for Israel?" "Israel is not the issue. You dare to threaten the US, you have the gall to put a gun to our head, and you think you can get away with it?" Clayton snapped.

"You will not do this," the disembodied voice declared.

"General, a cruise missile strike by sub, how long will it take?" Clayton's voice was steel.

"Three to four hours should be enough. We have a navy sub that would be able to take out Tehran in under four hours. A sub in the Med won't even need two hours to be in range of Jerusalem."

"Ahmed, kindly give us four hours, then watch your local new outlet. Or just keep up with the Internet. You get to watch Tehran burn a couple of hours after Jerusalem."

"Mr. President, we should stretch that a little. Most communications will be out. It'll take time for TV… commercial TV, the conventional media to show the results of a nuclear strike," the General stated matter-of-factly, as if the idea of incinerating two cities were all in a day's work.

"Are our demands so unacceptable that you are willing to lose Washington?" Clayton heard a hint of a plea.

"What demands? We both know you intend to destroy Washington anyway.

"Oh, by the way, I have already transmitted the launch codes. Even if you detonated the bomb this instant, NORAD will automatically launch two hundred missiles at randomly selected Muslim cities." Clayton blinked, was NORAD still the command and control centre for North America's nuclear defence? He'll have to ask MacAdams when he had the time. "But I would very much prefer that you selected the targets."

Ethan froze in sudden realization. This was why Prescott had cut him out. Prescott already had a military response. But instead of their nukes aimed at Russia, they would strike the Middle East.

"You almost had me fooled," said the voice from the box." You want the time to leave Washington."

"Your young lady is still here and can easily warn you if I try to leave the Oval Office."

"You will try to jam the signal."

"We are aware of your safeguards against jamming, and do feel free to keep in contact with the young lady. She will be right here with me in the Oval Office." Clayton then smiled at Annette.

"You can't be serious. This is madness." The note of concern was growing.

"Call me when you have confirmation of the detonations." Clayton pressed the intercom button, ending the conversation.

Even before he had lifted his finger, Clayton received a howl of condemnation from both senators and congressmen. "You can't do this. You have no authority to—"

"I have all the executive authority I need, gentlemen. Feel free to make use of the cafeteria; just be back in twenty. Unfortunately, we may need to make some unpalatable decisions," Clayton offered as he lowered his head to examine some notes lying on his desk.

With gaping mouths they stared at each other. The most powerful men and women in Washington, and they were being totally ignored.

Realizing that they looked ridiculous, they closed their mouths, bracing to once more express their considered opinion. Thus Agent Mercer slipped out of the Oval Office without drawing any attention and then rushed into the Secret Service command centre.

"Coates, what the hell have we got?" Mercer was not out of breath, but sounded rushed.

"Not much." Agent Coates looked at Mercer. "Truth is, we have nothing."

"Well, we got the details of the nuke yet?" "Unchanged," Agent Coates stated flatly.

"How bloody long does it take to find out the nuclear yield of one of those things?"

"The Russians haven't been overly cooperative. They're still holding to their story that the nuke was home-made."

"This is no time—" Mercer snapped but then paused for a moment. "OK, OK, do they really want to play games?"

"Yeah, I know. Well, the director's been on the phone burning the Russian ambassador's ear. Told him he'd better get the bomb's details over to us now, or he'll make damned sure there won't be enough of the Ambassador to send home in a shoebox, even if the Russian embassy is outside the blast radius." Coates actually believed the director would do it. If he was still around, Coates decided he'd help.

"Well, what about our fantastic spy satellites. Shouldn't they tell us the blast radius? You know, from the bombs they set off in Russia?"

"Not necessarily. Some of the modern versions can have their yield lowered so they can create a smaller nuclear explosion. There's no guarantee the ones in Russia used the maximum setting. I doubt the terrorists had someone reading the instruction manual as the time." Agent Coates shrugged helplessly.

"Look, if the bomb went off, could the president be safe below ground? We're talking about a small tactical nuke, right? Not some megaton whatever?"

"You don't want to use Marine One?" Agent Coates asked. The presidential helicopter could get the president well out of the blast area within several minutes.

"It's too risky. One, we got that crazy bitch in with the president. Second, who knows, they may have eyes on us, and seeing the bird take off may be enough to tip them over the edge. So?" Mercer stared at Agent Coates.

"I'm not an expert on Russian suitcase nukes, and the White House wasn't designed to take an ICBM warhead. But if he's in the bunker, no problem." Both men knew the Presidential Emergency Operations Centre was buried a good 120 feet below ground. "So do we take him down now?" "Not right now. I honestly think the man has a plan." Just wish he'd tell the Secret Service. "Just be ready to go at a moment's notice." Agent Mercer walked back to the Oval Office.

Inside the office, Clayton watched the clock slowly click over the minutes until Congressman Sebastian Bradbury entered the room. "As always so fashionably late, Sebastian, must you always make such a dramatic entrance?" Clayton gave the Congressman a small grin.

"It's the showman in me."

"What's it like out on the streets?" Clayton asked.

"A little congestion with the possible build-up of another protest march. Now what's the emergency? And don't tell me we're under nuclear threat. I know you put them up to it. That Secret Service guy should be in the movies. Hell, I'd never have thought you'd get this place to liven up even a little."

"Oh, I haven't needed to do much to liven this place up." Clayton then filled in the congressman, whose skin seemed to actually turn a shade paler.

"No way." Sebastian Bradbury looked around the room.

"So where are the other members of Congress?" Clayton noticed the lack of political appointees.

"I haven't seen anyone."

"Agent Mercer, we really need to get moving," Clayton told the agent. "Yes sir." Mercer spoke into his wrist cuff. Then he waited a few minutes, nodded twice, spoke again for verification.

"Sir, they…" Mercer glanced at Annette.

"Go on," Clayton prodded.

"I have confirmation of at least three congressmen making a beeline for the side entrance. Another two are heading for— Do you want security to try getting them back?" Agent Mercer glanced at the young woman still seated in her corner chair.

"No, I am sure they have pressing matters in their constituency." He then smiled brightly to the infuriated young woman to offer reassurance. "Relax, I'm not going anywhere," he calmly informed her

Then he chuckled as he saw Nat Coldlock enter the Oval Office followed a few moments later by Bell and a few stern faced congressmen.

"Well, I never would have believed it." Clayton laughed as an angry faced Holt brought up the rear.

"What's so funny?" Holt asked with a hint of suspicion.

"You grew a pair." Clayton grinned in genuine surprise.

Holt snorted. "I may not agree with everything you stand for, but this is my country, and I'll be damned if I run and leave you to deal with this alone."

Clayton nodded. "Please, take a seat."

The politicians each took a seat, as there was now plenty of room, although Bell kept glancing at Annette with a confused look, as if to say, *What is she still doing here?*

"Look, let's drop the ideology and do something constructive," Clayton told Senator Holt. "One dollar in tax cuts for every two dollars we cut in wasteful expenditure."

"God, in the middle of all this, you want to talk tax reform?" Holt looked as if he was a fish with his mouth open.

Clayton grinned wickedly. "What better time? It kind of puts it all into perspective."

Holt actually blinked. *The guy may be crazy, but he's right.* Their differences did seem rather trivial right now. "You're talking peanuts... a few billion, perhaps."

"It's a starting point, besides you are the one talking about small government."

"Ten percent tax cuts in exchange for—"

"Enough shit, enough," Bell snapped at him. "You're reaching retirement, so you can make some effort to balance the bloody budget for once." She locked eyes with him and refused to turn away.

"One dollar-fifty tax cut for every dollar cut in waste reduction." Holt replied to Bell's outburst.

"Three dollars in waste reduction for one in tax cuts and as a sweetener I'll add... let us say, a little 'barracuda' to help my cut as much waste—and government wages—as you please. You don't cut the programs or their effectiveness, but any waste you identify is all yours to chew on."

"Okay, one dollar in tax cuts for two dollars in cutting waste ?" "Okay. But I still think you're senile." Clayton told Holt with a straight face.

"You really know how to ingratiate yourself with your colleagues." Holt wondered what was rattling inside Clayton's mind.

"I try my hardest."

Holt lost his chance for a witty reply as the intercom came alive.

"Sir, it's that madman," Kath, Clayton's secretary, informed him with considerable disapproval; obviously she believed the president shouldn't be talking to such people.

"Thank you, Kath."

The voice on the intercom spoke up. "President Prescott." "Yes, Ahmed, you're a bit early. Do you have the names?"

"No, I propose the following. All American troops are to leave the Middle East. After all, you have already pulled most of your soldiers back to your own land.

"Cut all ties to the criminal Israeli murderers. In return I will not detonate the device. I will tell you how to locate it, and your people can disarm it." There was no edge of desperation in his voice, but his words seemed in a rush to get out.

"Wait, what about the social change… economic justice?" Annette demanded from her corner.

Ahmed apparently did not hear her. "What do you say, Mr. President?" "No, that won't do at all. Do your worst." Clayton's even voice shattered the calm in the room. Jaws dropped, and cries of disbelief arose across the room.

"What? You can't mean that," Ahmed replied.

"Of course I mean it."

"Why? I will tell you where the bomb is. Why are you doing this?" "What happens the next time? The next sneak attack with another nuke, only the next time they detonate it without warning. No, better this way."

Ahmed cried, "You are insane!"

Clayton smiled. "Aren't we all?"

"What do you want?" The metallic-toned voice demanded over the intercom.

"What do I want? Oh, I don't know. A quiet Sunday, now and then… that would be nice. More walks in the park. Whipped cream on my ice cream would be nice. I haven't had that in a long time."

"My God," Senator Coldlock bellowed, "he's mad… the president… Prescott is insane!"

Suddenly it all became so clear to him. Prescott's irrational treatment of the health care providers, giving them tinfoil hats, and all the other insane policies… like the death penalty for drug dealers. "You have to stop him," Coldlock demanded of Agent Mercer, even as he was lunging for the nearest agent's gun. After this foolish mistake, he found himself in the air and then flat on his back with the barrel of the same gun staring him in the face.

"Can't you see he's lost it? The stress is too much!" Nat shouted as his finger pointed accusingly at Clayton.

"Calm down." Agent mercer told the terrified young man.

But the contagion was spread by now, and all were looking at Prescott with uncertainty and even fear. The Secret Service agents sent nervous glances at each other.

Holt took a step forward to the desk. For the first time in a long time he was lost for words. He finally stammered, "Sir, we need… we need you to justify—"

"No, you justify selling out this country," Clayton hissed.

"What?"

"You heard me. Look at you—all aquiver and eager to run, as usual. 'We do not make deals with terrorists,' remember? And here you all are… a little pack of jellyfish ready to make any deal to save your skins." Clayton looked from one to the other, staring them down.

"He's mad. You have to stop him!" Coldlock shouted.

"Shut him up," Senator Holt snapped at the agents. Then he turned to Prescott. "You can't just let Washington burn; that is criminal. It's a dereliction of your duty to protect this country."

"This is the only way," Clayton replied. Politics aside, Holt was the most senior, the elder statesman, the natural leader.

"There must be alternatives." Holt would not waver. "Think of the people."

"There is no alternative but to face up to terrorism, no matter the cost."

"But… no matter how extreme our response has been, the terrorists have never listened to us before," Bell pointed out.

"That's because we've never offered a valid response before." Clayton addressed the confused assemblage. "No one has ever believed we would do what needs to be done. Well, not any more. They need to know that they will no longer escape retaliation. After this, none will ever doubt our resolve to do what is necessary."

"This is necessary?" Holt tried to think, to find a refutation for the man's insane words.

"The only way to deal with terrorism is through true terror. Not an eye for an eye, but a city for an eye. An entire country for a hand. A continent for the life of one American, that is the only answer.

"Only when the supporters of terrorism—the nation-states that fund terrorism—understand the true cost, only then will this end.

"We crushed al-Qaeda, and then came the Islamic State and after them…" Clayton sighed. "There will always be another threat. It'll never end until the nations supporting terrorism are made to pay—and made to pay too great a price. Only then will we have peace.

"If that means two hundred Muslim cities, two hundred *million* Muslims, then so be it.

"Think, they want World War Three. Then let them taste the ashes of that catastrophic cataclysm.

"Today the Muslim world will learn to fear the US." Clayton stared into Holt's eyes, challenging him to question the power of his argument.

"But… to lose Washington," Holt said. *Give me a reason not to believe you're insane.*

Bradbury said, "There must be a more rational approach. He's willing to negotiate." He sounded willing to make a deal.

"No one's making any deals today, Sebastian."

"But think of the loss of life," Bell pleaded. "Is he asking for so much?" "Half an hour ago you opposed using torture for the sake of our principles, even if that meant letting a city be nuked."

"That was different." She wanted to shout, *When has Israel done anything for America but given it grief?*

"No, it's exactly the same. Unlike the good Senator Walker, you understand that to protect our principles, indeed our way of life, sometimes we must endure great loss." Clayton stared at Senator Bell, who suddenly felt sick with guilt over her highbrow words.

"That's not good enough," Holt hissed, rage filling his words. "Your first duty is to protect the nation and its people."

"That is exactly what I am doing."

"By destroying Washington? What the hell are you trying to prove? That you're some kind of wannabe hero, facing the end of the world, standing on his feet." Holt was nearly trembling with uncertainty and confusion. "This is insane. How can sending any kind of message justify the loss of a city?"

"To say nothing of the horrors you will inflict upon the world," Bell said. "It's a crime against humanity. You will be responsible for the slaughter of two hundred million human beings. You can't do it." "Spare me your excuses," Clayton snapped at them

"No, what is this about? What is this really about?" Holt slammed the palm of his hand down on the table. "It's not about standing up to terrorism." The words surged from Holt's primordial soul, for all his years it was still a caged animal that lurked under his veneer of civilization, relying on instinct more fervently than any highbrow conscious thought. Sniffing, tasting the air for the other's weakness, the sweat of fear, the heady scent of arrogance, it would not be fooled by the foolishness of thought.

"It's about not running away," Clayton yelled back. "I'm sick of this country putting its tail between its legs and running. That's all we've been good at for the last seventy years. Vietnam, Beirut, Mogadishu, Afghanistan, Iraq, Syria, Ukraine… On and on, all we do is run away from the principles we are supposed to believe in. Well, today this country stops running."

"You are wrong, sir," Bradbury answered, resorting to a rote maxim." We will always stand and fight when the cause is just."

"And when China tells us to run along and leave Taiwan to China's tender mercies, will you stand and fight or run? Only when they believe we have the stomach for war will they fear and respect us.

"Soldiers are expected to fight and die for this country, yet we automatically exclude the public from sharing in that burden. They are never asked to stand up and be counted… What was it you said, Senator Bell? 'We can't sell out our principles. We need to stand up for what we know is right.' Well here we go; time for the people to stand up and be counted. It's time for the people to learn to shoulder the burden."

"A lot of Americans would disagree with you." Bell held herself erect by leaning on the table.

Clayton stood to stare straight into her eyes. "And they are the ones most likely to spit on the American flag and piss on your principles."

"There has to be another way," Congressman Bradbury whispered. "There is no other way, no alternative except to surrender, to be the snivelling cowards they think we are. Well, as the president of the United States, I refuse to go on my knees. Do you agree with my course of action, Senator Bell? Congresswoman Bradbury? Or are you just going to run like all the other 'defenders of America'?" Clayton sneered into their faces, mocking and challenging them to stand up for their beliefs, such as they were.

Holt knew what Clayton was doing, drawing them in. In a way he was trying to seduce them with his logic. But it was pure logic without emotion. How can anyone emotionally justify such an atrocity? "The children," he said, with a gasp that sounded like a sob, "think of the children."

"Yes, think of the children," Clayton echoed. "Think of the millions of American children, the ones we're sworn to protect, threatened every day of their lives because we don't have the courage to act today. This is the only course of action. If they think they can blackmail us, all our children are at risk. One small tactical nuke, which may or may not work, balanced by whatever horror terrorists or nations may decide to inflict on us tomorrow because they think we haven't the stomach to act. So give me your alternative; go on and tell me you have the answer, or else stand aside."

The old and young both looked at each other.

"You're the president of the United States," Holt half whispered.

Senator Bell nodded to herself, half acknowledging defeat.

Congressman Sebastian Bradbury silently took a seat.

"Good, we're all in agreement." Clayton smiled, and they would swear he looked like a piranha.

Annette broke the brief silence. "For God's sake, Ahmed. Tell him the truth before it's too late. It's a hoax!" She turned to the president. "It's a hoax—don't you understand? How could we get hold of a nuke, for God's sake? I joined a group of online anarchists. I joined Anomalous America to save this country, not to blow it up, you bloodthirsty bastard." She collapsed into the leather chair, on the verge of tears.

"You believe her?" Holt was not sure about anything anymore.

"Of course," Clayton told Holt. "The lies you tell yourself are the ones you most want to believe." *Just as the ugliest lies are the ones you tell yourself, to convince yourself your actions are just and proper, no matter how evil they are.*

Ahmed spoke: "You truly are mad. I will tell you where to find the device. What else do you want?"

"What?" The word came out as tortured screech of disbelief from Annette.

"The threat is quite real, my dear," Clayton told Annette.

"No, you're wrong. It's a hoax; tell him." Annette was addressing Ahmed.

"It's no hoax; this is for real." Clayton informed the young woman. "Then... this is real? No— Please... God, you can't launch those missiles," she pleaded, desperate to stop the insanity.

"Don't panic, Miss Bernstein," Clayton responded. "I will not order a launch."

"What?" Ahmed's voice crackled in disbelief.

"I will not retaliate. There will be no nuclear response. Feel free to do your worst."

The faces in the room plummeted from angelic bliss to the depths of hellish anguish.

Bell jumped out of her seat. "What? After all that, you're going to do nothing?"

Holt clutched his chest.

"Then why go through this charade?" Ahmed demanded. Silence was the only response. "Why?"

"That is not the question. The question is what will you achieve? What will you reap from the seeds you will sow this day? Think; the hatred here for the Islamic world will be such that America would rather sacrifice a hundred million Muslims than give one inch of Israel to the Palestinians.

"You will ensure that America will incinerate the Arab world before allowing you to lift the black flag of Islam over any city or town.

"America will never forgive or forget what you have done. It will oppose everything you hope to achieve. You will have made an implacable enemy for generations."

"You're mad." Ahmed whispered the words.

"And there will be no lily-livered coward to accuse America of any act of aggression. There will be no traitorous apologist to denounce our actions. You will feel the fury of an outraged America as it lays waste to your world.

"The next president may or may not retaliate with nukes; he may target only five cities. Then again, you imagined, it didn't you? That's what's terrifying you this instant: two hundred Muslim cities incinerated, two hundred million Muslims dead in one day... can the Arab world survive, or will it sink into a new dark age?

"Imagine a hundred years spent just to rebuild what was lost. The radioactive fallout, how many deaths, how many deformities? How much of the Arab world will be in ruins for generations? That's what I wanted you to see.

"For decades fundamentalist Islam has wanted a war. Well, you'll have one—a real war, the likes of which you can't even begin to imagine. You may think of Americans as weak and cowardly, but I tell you we are geniuses at finding new weapons of destruction, new ways to kill, new horrors and torments.

"In the past you have only felt the feather touch of our weapons. But next time, I daresay, we will do unto you as Rome did unto Carthage. We will seal your wells and salt your lands so that nothing grows. Your Islamic states will be as desert from end to end. Come, embrace your future, taste the ashes that'll be your world. And know your name will be cursed by your own for a thousand years to come.

"A small tactical warhead, I imagine will incinerate possibly a third of Washington, but America will survive." Clayton snorted with a foul grin. "Hell, getting rid of all the lobbyists may actually be a godsend."

Annette stared at Clayton in horror.

"You have nothing prophetic to say, Miss Bernstein?" "What is there to say?" She could only whisper.

"Finally." The president turned the chair so he could look out the window.

One of the Secret Service agents tapped Annette on the elbow, with a tilt of his head to indicate she was to follow him out.

Mercer addressed the president. "Sir, I must escort you to the bunker—" Clayton put up his hand to stop him. "Not this time. This is about the office of the president, Agent Mercer. The office of the presidency." His eyes locked on to the young Annette. "I am staying right here with the young lady."

"You're insane," Annette said, surging to her feet. "You want some insane war?"

"No, but there can be no negotiation with terrorists. Funny, people keep saying that they will not be intimidated even as they wimp out in fear. We must stop being afraid and make the terrorists afraid. That is what America, the West, has never understood. That is how you fight terrorism." Clayton looked around the bewildered room with a grin that was pure evil.

Clayton then looked at the intercom. "Ahmed, because of 9/11 the West has around twenty thousand dead, compared to nearly five to seven million Muslims so far, the tens of thousands in Afghanistan, the hundreds of thousands in Iraq, the million or so in Syria—the list of dead goes on and on. So how many more will today bring? Are you prepared to accept a hundred million dead Muslims to gain your grand prize?

"The Muslim world has long argued that the West is out to destroy Islam. Well, today is the day it begins. Do it."

"You're wasting your breath. You cannot break us. Even if the war lasts a hundred years, we will not give in." Yet Ahmed's voice was shaken.

"You already have—in Iraq. You are so eager to believe your own propaganda, you'll believe anything. Along with the US 'surge,' there was the Sunni 'awakening,' remember? Many Sunni Iraqis were so sickened they came to us, grovelling to the Great Satan. We gave them guns and paid them, and we crushed the 'lions of Islam,' we crushed al-Qaeda in Iraq.

"Then the dictator Assad of Syria broke you again. Millions went crawling to Europe, millions running away in fear.

"You were broke then, and we will break you again and again… and this time the cost in blood will be tenfold. Do you understand? When the slaughter becomes so great, when hope is gone, when the cries of your children die as your children die of hunger, when your rivers run red with blood—then you will be broken, when the pain is so great that your own will turn against you just to stop the butchery.

"It's all a question of pain, enough suffering that it will make your young men cry as their world burns, as they see nothing but a world of ash.

"Come on, do it. You will make us stronger than you can imagine. There will be no more cries for compassion, understanding, or mercy—just screams of revenge… hate… anger. You will fan the very fires of vengeance that only the blood of your people can quench." His voice shook with passion.

But Holt heard delight in it. *Madness… sheer madness.*

"What you have never understood is that we have always had the power to turn your world to ash but have never had the fire in our bellies to do so. After this Americans will scream for blood."

The legislators in the room sucked in their breath. Their hearts lodged in their throats as their fear sucked away reason. Only Holt looked Clayton straight in the eye as if he was in agreement with the president's refusal to back down, even as he saw the madness shining from Prescott's eyes. *My God, he'll do it; he won't back down.*

"I—" They could all hear Ahmed's heavy breathing. "I will not give the order to detonate the device. I will still give you its location. The rest is up to you."

"Yes!" Annette cried out.

"Mr. President, I think you have made your point." Holt stated with his back as rigidly straight as a Queen's Guard on parade.

"Sir. The mere suggestion of our response… surely that will be sufficient? We can't surrender all those lives now. Sir… Mr. President?" Bell half whispered as if afraid she might spook Clayton into provoking the terrorist.

"Sir?" Mercer wanted to get the president below ground, but his feet would not work. The very earth seemed to be holding his feet.

"Go ahead," Clayton addressed the intercom, almost waving away Mercer's request.

"The device is in a van. I can give you the tag number and its route around the beltway."

Agent Mercer wrote down the details and was out the door, even as he called for the other agents to escort the president to safety. He was reading out the licence plate into his sleeve as he ran the short distance down the corridor to confront the Secret Service director.

"We can't take any chances," Agent Mercer declared to the older man, even as agents were communicating with various agencies trying to locate the van circling the White House. Both knew it would not be long before either a police officer or a traffic camera would spot its licence plate.

"The FBI will take the lead on this one," the director informed Mercer. "Screw that. The Secret Service exists to protect the president." "He is being secured as we speak."

"Yeah, well, he did his job. Now we do ours. I know the FBI handbook on this, and they aren't ready to deal with this. We can do better." Mercer wanted them to take the lead with a passion.

"And we are?"

"Director, this is our backyard, and we have the best snipers in the world. We know the terrain. I've learned one thing from the president, and that is to think outside the box. The FBI isn't about to throw away the handbook on this one. Their first instinct will be to isolate and contain the situation.

"Sir, with something like this, you need time to process it, accept that it's real. They won't go in hard and fast enough. I've spent the last hour with the president. I know this is real. I know there is a nuke in that van. And I know we have to do something really crazy to pull this off."

"How would you do it?"

"Well, that's the thing. What have we got on the streets right now?" "The usual… protestors."

"Oh, that is so beautiful." Mercer grinned. He could almost kiss the nearest protestor. "We'll need the entire White House staff to pull it off— and eggs, tomatoes… yeah, lots of eggs." Luckily the White House had a very large staff and a large kitchen. And the FBI could play a part in this as traffic cops, he realized, with a wicked grin spreading across his face.

"Mercer," the director almost yelled.

"Sir?" Agent Mercer looked at him in surprise.

"Don't smile like that. You reminded me of the president when he's about to give me heartburn."

Misha watched the News channel on the small screen on his iPhone. And once more wondered why he had not received the transmission from Ahmed that he had been promised.

"Still nothing?" Aloth cried out as he sat in the driver's seat of the van. "Nothing as yet." Misha began to sweat even more in the tight confines of the van. But it was not the heat but his still-growing concern. *Why hasn't the American leader read out the list of false promises?* The news channels still showed their boring daytime dramas of local news as if nothing was happening. *How much longer can we wait?*

The van slowed even more in the heavy traffic, before stopping with a savage jerk that nearly sent him flying.

"What happened?" Misha asked as he straightened in his seat. "Protestors, they are blocking the road," Aloth snapped back, the tension was evident in each word.

Misha gently touched the device's detonation pad. He was tempted to activate it, but they had orders to wait. First let the American leaders embarrass themselves by pleading for mercy, and then wait for the call from Ahmed.

Well, they could wait a little longer. He raised his head to look through the windscreen. Ahead were a number of protestors, with, police blocking the road. A few more drivers began honking their horns.

"What do you see?" Misha demanded.

"Even more protestors. They are pests." Aloth looked into his rear-view mirror to see another smaller crowd of protestors marching through the traffic to join the main protest group. Some of the protestors were throwing eggs, a few tomatoes, banging on the hoods of cars. One or two held up placards. More eggs were thrown, resulting in one driver jumping out of his car to shout abuse.

The first few protestors passed the van, yelling, "Death to the pigs, power to the people, down with the rich!" One banged on the side of the van. A tall protestor walked in front of them, waving his arms in the air. He then lowered his arms as his left hand went into his pocket to pull out an egg. Agent Mercer smiled pleasantly as he glared directly at Aloth.

"Don't you dare, you fu…" Aloth screamed as he saw the man pull his arm back to throw the egg at the windscreen. Only a tiny fraction of his brain noticed an oddity: the protestor wore quality black slacks, and his white shirt looked to be well ironed. An oddity, when the protestors as a rule looked dirty and shabby.

Even as he hurled the egg, the windscreen shattered. At the same moment Aloth's head was flung back by the large-calibre round fired by the Secret Service sniper from a second-storey window of a nearby building.

Not even a second later the hinges and lock of the rear doors were blown apart by small explosive charges. Misha never felt the small explosions, nor did he see the two large men tear away what remained of the doors. He only caught a glimpse of the two women and one man as they stood up and opened fire, hitting him several times before he could even register the thought that he was dead.

Secret Service agent Mercer ran around to the rear of the van. He looked inside the vehicle. There had been no attempt to take the men alive. They had used the element of surprise in nothing short of a cold-blooded execution, giving the terrorists no time to react.

Chapter 20

Change without vision is chaos

—Martin King

The presidential convoy came to a stop in a small street in a quiet suburb. The president of the United States climbed out of the limo. Followed by Abb and Jonathan, he walked out to where teams of workers were beginning to unload solar panels from a large eighteen-wheeler.

The supervisor, Cox Jeweller, stepped up to meet them. "Mr. President, it is an honour to have you here today."

"It's my pleasure, I would not have missed this for anything," Clayton told him.

The small group, circled by Secret Service agents, quietly watched as the large truck was unloaded. Already individual workers were being organized into teams.

"If you'll excuse me for a moment, sir. Mr. President." The supervisor almost pleaded for understanding.

"Don't let me hold you up." Clayton sent him on his way.

The supervisor walked over to where four groups of men and women waited, while Cox studied his outdated clipboard; he really should have carried an electronic tablet.

"Okay, Joe, your guys have house one; Andy, number three; Lara, you got four. Lucky last, Freddie, you get five." The supervisor sent them on their way before turning and walking back to the president.

"The second house doesn't qualify, sir. It's rented, and the owners don't want to pay for the installation." Cox checked his clipboard.

"That's even with the free panels?" Clayton inquired.

"Guess he feels the money for installation can be better spent." More like kept in his pocket. "But things are moving right along; we expect to have the entire street done in under three days. You know, sir, doing the whole street all at once ain't bad. We're cutting the cost of installation by thousands." Cox smiled with approval. There was no time and money being wasted by making repeated visits to the same street.

"Yeah, this is the way to go, sir. Mr. President." Cox spoke while watching a tall woman in her early forties in a dark expensive suit approach the president.

"Mr. President," she said.

"Miss Castello, isn't this a sight?" Clayton smiled like a little boy. "We're going full steam ahead, as they use to say in the wonderful days of steam."

"Sir, this is only a trial run. The actual implementation is still months away."

"I am aware of that; relax. I'm not going to push up the schedule you outlined, Miss Castello."

"Thank you, sir." She glanced at him sideways as they watched the panels being unloaded. "You do know this won't fix everything. There are tens of millions without housing—"

"I have some of my people talking with the banks to see how willing they are to give use a large number of their worthless houses for a minimal amount."

"Nice one." *He really is serious about government going into business.* "And I think we can help. At the moment we have more than enough to get the solar panels scheme off the ground. We could put some money into your… house acquisition."

Jonathan said, "The new Congress may see it as an attempt to acquire funds inappropriately, sir."

"Unfortunately, Jonathan has a point," Clayton said, giving him a nod. "Best we commit all funds to the solar panel scheme. Half our profits, on the other hand, will go to a futures fund." *The interest it provides can go to either paying off our debt or buying more cheap housing.*

"Yes sir. It's just that the money could come in handy if the tenants can't pay the rent." *If they've got jobs in the first place,* she was thinking.

"They can't then we make sure they keep the property in good condition until they can pay rent." Clayton seemed unperturbed.

"And if they can't?" She was not about to be put off so easily.

"Then, when the houses are worth something, we sell them at a profit. This is a new day for all of us. Your government is in the business of making money, Miss Castello. The people we put in charge of these projects will make money, or they can kiss their ass goodbye."

"Fair enough, sir." She scanned the worksite. "I've been informed that the city council is looking into whether they can use the installation program to create a microgrid or three in the city."

Clayton stared into her eyes. "Go on."

"It's an idea, more a rumour. If they established a microgrid using the solar panels, then maybe they could power City Hall, town libraries and such… using electricity from our panels." Castello shrugged. "No surprise, sir. I expected people would be trying to stick their fingers in the pie. Don't worry; I'll cut them off," she said with a wink.

Clayton nodded and turned to the rather concerned supervisor. "You and your people are to be commended. Thank you for your work, Mr. Jeweller." Clayton shook hands with the man before walking to the passenger side door of the limo.

"This is a good day, people. We keep going at this rate, in a year the government will have so many solar panels on houses that no one will be able to undo our work." Clayton beamed in delight as he said his goodbyes to Castello and stepped into the vehicle to sit on the padded rear seat.

Once Jonathan was seated, he addressed Clayton. "Sir, the latest polls have come out. It looks like the public is right behind you on the health insurance scheme, and you're even getting some traction on your gun policy along with the death penalty for drug dealers."

"The polls… Well, that comes as a shock." Clayton stared at Jonathan who sat in the rear-facing seat. "That is quite surprising, given the opposition from so many quarters."

"Well, sir, it appears that the public is now more supportive of your more… far-reaching policies," Jonathan repeated.

"And that still comes as quite a shock." Clayton looked out the window to where the work crews were busy with ladders and their tools. "Can you see it? That is the future coming to life… if we are fortunate, if we can build up a full head of steam."

"Yes sir." Jonathan paused. "I must say I thought you would react more favourably to the news."

"Huh? Oh, sorry, Jonathan. I was just basking in the moment."

"Yes sir. Just… we don't have much time. You know how important it is to get a strong start." *On issues that could still blow up in your face if you're not ready.*

"Yes, we should begin considering our options." But Clayton's tone was still a bit dismissive, his attention on the work outside the window.

"But we need to stay focused on the solar program and reducing the street violence first."

It was then that Abb spoke up. "The number of violent incidents has gone down a little since the nuclear scare. Guess they are re-evaluating what matters most."

"The violence hasn't dropped that much," Clayton noted sourly, "and it could just as easily pick up."

"That may be the case, sir," Jonathan answered. "But by advocating your polices they may also distract the public from their immediate concerns. It could make the anarchists' job of motivating the disenfranchised all the harder."

"Let's leave it for now. This is what's important. We'll go over our options later."

Jonathan persisted, fighting a growing sense of defeat. "Yes, sir. It's only that we need to move—"

"Leave it for now, Jonathan," Clayton cut him off.

"Yes sir." Jonathan's voice held a note of sadness.

Much to Abb's surprise, thus he spoke up, "Mr. President, Jonathan has a point. We need to move if you want to implement any reforms. The longer we take to begin, the harder it will be." *You've the one saying we don't have time to waste. And now here we are watching the grass grow.*

"This has been a great start," Jonathan began.

"Exactly," Clayton said. "We have begun something, something we can be proud of. But this isn't the end of the fight. It's barely the beginning. Once the power companies realize I am serious, they will fight me tooth and nail."

"I don't understand, sir." Abb shook his head. "Why are a few solar panels so important to you? Health should be our major priority." Although he was not enthused over Clayton's gun policy, he could more than agree with his health policy. Even the drug policy, if he was honest with himself.

Clayton looked from one man to the other. "Have either of you considered the future?" Clayton sighed softly. "In the 1900s an economist once came up with the 20/80 per cent economy. You know of it?"

"No." Abb admitted.

Jonathan smiled knowingly and thus responded. "That's where the top 20 per cent own 80 per cent of the wealth. Apparently the economy can run on that kind of massive inequality… provided you have decent health and education for all."

"Wasn't that when they were using leeches to cure cancer?" Abb scoffed at the idea. "Too bad they didn't have social media back then, or else a few hundred million Americans could've told the dick where to stick his formula."

"Anyway," Clayton remarked, "that is the theorized limit of inequality. And therein lies my concern. Can you imagine social inequality getting close or even worse than the 20/80 scenario?"

Jonathan blinked in disbelief. "Sir, the likelihood of such a development is unrealistic. For any economy to function, people need to spend. We couldn't—"

"Aren't we already on the verge? Aren't we seeing massive inequality unseen in the industrial age? Along with seeing our education, health care… all our infrastructure crumbling." Clayton looked out the window once more.

"But sir, it doesn't have to be like that. The economy will pick up eventually." Abb's voice trailed off.

"And collapse yet again, Abb?" Clayton asked the man.

"Countering that view," Jonathan answered, "there are many who believe the ongoing automation process, all the new technology, will eventually create a lot of new jobs. It could be a new golden age of prosperity."

"Jonathan, we have all read the reports. Look, I know full well the economy is a complex beast. And the economy will pick up, and eventually automation may create new jobs. But so far the few new jobs have been consistently casual and low paid."

Clayton sighed as he kept gazing out the window. "Since the 1970's American productivity has increased nearly a hundred per cent while wages have barely risen 10 percent.

"People, automation may continue to increase productivity, yet where is the wages growth? Just when will we see *real* and *ongoing* wages growth for low- and middle-income people?"

Clayton shook his head. "Have either of you ever considered that we may rarely… if ever get enough GDP growth to force real ongoing wages growth? We are a developed—hell, an overdeveloped economy. No one seems to understand what that actually means. It's as if they actually believed we could achieve a 3 to 10 per cent growth on a multiyear basis. What if we have hit 'peak trade'? And even with full employment, the American pie of prosperity will not provide enough."

"Sir," Jonathan addressed Clayton, "such an unbalanced economy as that is very questionable to sustain. I mean, if only a small part of the population had most of the wealth… then money would eventually become worthless. People would simply find other forms of exchange, like barter. I can't see it."

"That is why it may well happen. Like you, Jonathan, far too many may not accept the possibility, no matter the evidence." Clayton exhaled through his nose. "And that may well bring about America's complete financial collapse—"

"Financial collapse?" Jonathan sounded shocked. "Are you certain you realize—"

"In the past, we have had a large middle class for the government to tax. We had a big enough cash cow to bleed to get the economy running again. So how will the government deal with the next economic downturn without a large middle class? Ask the rich to pay extra taxes?

"Look how close we are to a total collapse with our 'little' GFC Mark Two. Face facts: the chances are good that the bankers, Wall Street, or some other high flyer will succeed in destroying or crippling our wondrous economic system the next time around.

"Okay, the rich can fly off to their estates in Brazil or wherever. But what about the rest of us who will have to pick up the pieces? And that's where 'a few solar panels' come in. This isn't about cheap electricity. This isn't so much about freedom or even choice. This is about survival, being independent enough from the system to get back onto our feet after the event. Providing power is a good starting point to rebuilding the nation."

"You actually subscribed to such a possibility?" Jonathan almost stammered.

"We've survived downturns, recessions, and depressions in the past." Abb agreed with Jonathan.

"I can't see the future, Abb, but I have studied the past. Greed all too often wins out over common sense."

"That's one hell of a negative way to look at things," Abb countered with a sinking feeling.

"This is America. I can be as pig-headed, ignorant, and as legally stupid as I want." Clayton chuckled, but then sighed. "Perhaps I am being pessimistic. But even if greed is checked, will that end poverty? We'll still need ways to compensate our workers for being paid poverty wages without the government supplying more and more handouts—and one way is to provide cheap power, some form of transport, and a roof over their heads."

He looked from one man to the other. "And won't that not only benefit them but also put less stress on America's support systems?" And if the shit hit the wall at least they would have a good start to rebuilding their lives. Clayton scratched his chin. "The two of you may think I'm overreacting. But have either of you noticed how 'agitated' the public has been lately?"

Both men looked away. Neither could bring himself to mount a defence.

Jonathan finally said, "Then take your concerns to the people, to the new Congress."

Clayton gave a dry chuckle of contempt. "Oh, Jonathan, if only I had your faith. We achieved this small victory with the solar panels not because of Congress but because there was no Congress to block us. We've succeeded so far because the power companies could not promote their own interests; they haven't been able to sic their dogs onto us."

"That's a little unfair, sir," Abb countered. "I am sure many would rally around your proposals."

"A few, perhaps, but in the end the majority will block any agenda that doesn't serve their interests." Clayton locked eyes with Abb. "Come on, I wasn't joking. America is one of the most legally corrupt country in the world, and you know it. Just because it's legal to take a bribe, that doesn't make it right or good for this country. And a bribe's a bribe, no matter what you call it."

Both Jonathan and Abb looked straight ahead.

Abb grunted then spoke up, "We may take issue with how some things are done, but people do have the right to donate money to the person of their choice—to a politician they think is doing a good job."

"Like those who give the maximum allowed to every member of Congress, both Republican and Democrat? Are you telling me they believe in the death penalty and are against the death penalty?

"They are in favour of abortion, while being against abortion? They favour gun control, while being against gun control? They're in favour of everything and against everything, really?" Clayton asked in mock disbelief.

"Some Congress members believe in their policies."

"And just what policies are those… to bring about the collapse of the United States of America? You think ever-growing inequality is good policy? Well, imagine that. Even when we've had Nobel-Prize economists warning us about the dangers of inequality, Congress was right to ignore them. I can only suppose that allowing the rich to avoid paying real taxes is an act of patriotism? Following in our forefathers' steps: 'No taxation without representation.'" Clayton mockingly raised his left hand in a grandiose manner, even as he sneered at his own words.

"Congress has known for decades that we needed to improve health and education and to make tax policies that discourage inequality. God, just look at all the loopholes, all the legal tax avoidance—and what has Congress done in all the decades? Nothing, because they have been too busy collecting their thirteen pieces of silver."

"Sir, the evidence of that—"

"Abb, the less taxes the rich pay, the greater the proof that there is legalized corruption within Congress."

"Isn't that even more of an incentive to govern by referendum?" Jonathan tried to soften his pleading tone. "We could replace Congress with a 'people's council'?"

"Out of the question," Clayton declared.

"But you were in favour of such an option. Just think what you could achieve by taking your ideas directly to the public, sir. Show them what a few referendum votes can achieve before Congress is reinstated and undermines your policies."

"Lovely thought." Clayton snorted at the idea, and then grinned at Jonathan. "But you really don't want to go there."

Jonathan looked puzzled. "Sir, the public is behind you, there is no danger, you have massive public support."

"And that is why I cannot and will not use it." Clayton spoke with conviction.

"But you can implement vitally needed policies… real change." "Exactly, that's exactly why I can't."

"I don't understand, sir." Jonathan pleaded for an answer.

"Just leave it, Jonathan."

Abb felt offended that Clayton had not confided in him. "Sir, you went through all this. *We* went through all this for you, and I think we have a right to know why you won't act."

Clayton softly sighed in sympathy with their request. "By doing it I could actually do further damage to our social fabric."

"Why would putting your policies before the public a danger to the nation's social fabric?" Jonathan was confused, even bewildered.

Clayton nodded to himself as he turned to once more look out the window. "Because, Jonathan, people rarely consider the consequences of their actions."

They sat in silence as the presidential limo travelled towards its destination. Finally Clayton turned away from the window to face both men. "It's complicated, Jonathan. How do I explain this without five years of lectures on history?" He was speaking softly. "People think change is good… and yes, change is often unavoidable. But too few see the negative side."

"But change is inevitable, sir," Jonathan said." If there is no change then we stagnate, in the long run it's for the best."

Clayton smiled his toothy grin. "Tell that to the Chinese communist government. I don't think they are in favour of changing governance."

Jonathan gave Clayton a less than appreciative look.

"I was being only half flippant. Tell me, do you believe in equality, Jonathan?"

"Yes, of course."

"Then you believe we should not discriminate against someone because of their gender?"

"Absolutely."

"You believe we should not discriminate against someone based on their age?"

"Yes."

"You believe we should not discriminate against someone over their sexual orientation?"

"Yes."

"Then you support the rights of paedophiles to have sex with children?" "Ye… What? No, of course not. No one can support such filth." "But you just stated that you believe we should not discriminate against someone because of their age and sexual orientation."

"But that's totally different. We're talking about molesting children.

How could anyone support that?" Jonathan looked to Abb for support.

"No, I am talking about change and the results and consequences of change, whether we like it or not." Clayton went on: "Fifty years ago homosexuality was illegal; then it was legalized, and now it's embraced. Fifty years ago drugs were evil. Now people want to legalize all drugs. Twenty years from now why won't paedophilia be legalized?"

"No, sir, that is just so wrong." Abb jumped to support Jonathan. "So was homosexuality. Can't you see the logic? Change comes, even if we don't like the results."

"But paedophilia?" Now Jonathan spoke up. "It can't be legalized." "Oh, I wish that were true. Unfortunately it has to be, one day. Now that homosexuality and lesbianism are fully accepted, then all other forms of sexual behaviour have to be accepted. How can we deny one small group the same fundamental rights we give to everyone else?

"My friends, while sex was limited to a man and a woman, we could oppose other forms of sexual behaviour, but not now. The only form of sexual behaviour we can still outlaw is bestiality... on the basis that it is cruelty to animals and cannot be consensual."

"But not with children—they are children."

"Jonathan, fifty years ago children were more innocent. Now children are having sex with children every day of the week. There was that sorry incident of an eleven-year-old girl giving birth with her twelve -year-old boyfriend in France a few decades ago. Did the boy go to jail for underage sex? Did the girl?

"What I am trying to show you is that change leads in directions we do not think it will lead. And holding referendum elections—"

"Sir, they are children. How can they know, understand?" Jonathan refused to listen.

"Yet America supports the rights of transgender children, correct? We accept seven-year-old boys going into the girls' toilet, likewise a nine-year-old girl wanting to be a boy. You're telling me they don't understand their sexual nature?"

"But—but—" Both Abb and Jonathan were stammering in disbelief. Clayton waved away their concerns. "We can't hide behind age or use it as an excuse. As long as sex is consensual, what right do you have to discriminate against someone based on their age and sexual orientation?" "*No*, you are wrong."

"Oh, Jonathan." The tone of Prescott's voice was gently mocking. "What was it they used to say? 'Don't be a homophobe'? Well, don't be a paedophobe. Imagine America twenty years from now. Will some lawyer go before the Supreme Court and demand an end to 'this age discrimination' against his paedophile client? And why not? I can hear millions of libertarians crying out; 'Why can't we do as we please?' We are a liberal society. Why shouldn't a twelve- or thirteen-year-old come home with his forty-year-old lover for a bit of anal?

"Why shouldn't polygamy be legal? If you're rich enough, why can't you have a harem? You're rich enough, why not have five wives? And if one of them is only interested in being your wife for one day a week, well, why not? And if another wife has five husbands, one for each day of the week with the weekends free—well, what's your problem?

"That half-naked pop singer, the one photographed kissing so many men and women—she could have two husbands, two wives, two boy lovers, and two girl lovers all waiting for her in her purpose-made gilded harem, and why not?" Clayton's voice was lightly tinged with the frustration of defeat.

"That's disgusting." Abb felt almost sick.

"Equally, why shouldn't twenty-five to thirty-five per cent of Americans spend their lives in a narcotic-induced catatonic bliss? Just like the top one per cent should have the right to pocket billions from the less fortunate.

Don't they have the right to engage in 'the pursuit of happiness'? If making themselves rich makes them happy, why not?

"And let's not forget euthanasia. Once we were against it; now it's 'to end the pain and to die with dignity.' And tomorrow if we have individuals who are not terminally ill or in pain but demand the right to die, then why not?" Clayton remembered a story about an Australian doctor who apparently assisted a health man to end his 'intolerable depression' or something like that. "How long before we have perfectly health thirty-year-olds being legally put down simply because they are bored with living?"

"The public will never allow it . . . paedophilia." Abb could stand no more. "The law can't be twisted like that. It is meant to protect people."

"And it will, even if we don't want it to," Clayton snapped back, but not unkindly.

Abb would not be silenced. "That is insane, the Constitution—" "Will demand it," Clayton told him.

"No, that is wrong." Now Abb was almost pleading. "If we have to, we can change the Constitution."

Clayton laughed. "Oh, yes. We so love and worship the Constitution… as long as it suits us. And when it doesn't, we're just as eager to wipe our asses on it." Oh, Brian, you are so right. Clayton thought back to his talk with his old friend from university days. "And that is what scares me. We are indeed a nation of laws—laws that we have changed at our convenience. They have been rewritten for the convenience of the rich, the powerful, and the uber-greedy, uber-selfish.

"And now you want the masses to have a turn?

"Imagine for a moment a future where we did have national referendums. Can you imagine the harm the sheep of America would do to this country? You see a bright… a great and wonderful future created by a well-informed, enlightened, and educated public. I see a people too selfish and too self-centred to overcome their weaknesses, bigotry, and prejudices.

"People, it's easy to vote for something you get for free. It's a lot harder to vote for something that will give you pain in the here and now and only in the future will it yield benefits to you… or your children. That is, if the rich don't just lead them straight to the slaughterhouse after fleecing them first."

"But if you don't want change?" Abb stated flatly.

"I accept that change is inevitable. But I hope for change without change, Abb. Change that will not create even more social upheaval… will not fracture this country even more.

Understand me, change without vision, without direction, often leads to chaos. We need a plan, an idea, a vision. We've had more than enough chaos. Rule by referendum requires adults, grown-ups. And where are you going to find them, Abb?

"Honestly, look at the clowns they've elected to office. And you want to give them the power to change the law? The clowns in Congress are bad enough, but to give the idiots on the street real power… God save America… they'll be selling machine guns, rocket launchers, landmines, and every type of drugs and have rampant child prostitution on every street corner." *It'll be giving the kids the keys to the liquor cabinet . . . then shooting them up with heroin.*

Jonathan looked at Clayton in near shock. Suddenly he saw it all. Prescott had never intended to try for the Federal Health Insurance scheme, the death penalty for drug dealers, gun control, or the rest. "It's all been a bluff… to get business to donate to the solar scheme? This has all been a con?" All the threats, all the mad behaviour, all the speeches, it had all been… The enormity of the deception struck home.

"I believe in universal health care and a lot more, Jonathan. But let us be realistic. This was the best we could hope for. Maybe one day Congress will indeed act in the national interest." But Clayton's voice held no conviction, merely the acceptance of the ugly reality that was the members of Congress.

Two Days later in the White House

"Out with it; you have been as silent as a mouse all day," Clayton told Jonathan as the younger man picked up a file left on one of the couches in the president's study.

"Sir?" Jonathan straightened in surprise. "Oh, it's nothing."

"Then why the look of misery on your face?" Abb offered from the opposite leather couch. "Out with it man."

"I understand your concern, sir. But I don't see it. They will never allow such excesses as those you fear. The vast majority of the American people are decent, caring—they will do the right thing."

"Jonathan." Clayton grinned sadly, showing some sympathy for the young man. "Take a good, hard look at most of American society, and what do you see? Look at our children—the ones we should do everything we can to protect, not just because they are our future, but because they are our children. Yet how many of our children are homeless? One estimate puts the number at ten thousand children in every major city... perfect prey for the 'chicken hawks.'" The paedophiles had the nerve to call themselves that, as if preying on children were the natural order of things. "If the parents of America gave a damn would they let that happen?"

"And all the parents who do love their kids?" Jonathan answered seriously. "Who are worried about guns, drugs, and all the problems kids face today?"

"And yet there so many guns on the street, so much drug abuse. Jonathan, they want the drugs, the gun madness, the pornography, prostitution, and paedophilia. My God, man, it's the Hollywood dream come true, unrestrained libertarianism.

"They want it, Jonathan. They want this selfish society as it is, with all the perversions running rampant through-out the nation. They want the hypocrisy that is the government of today.

"Do you truly believe inequality or racism is some deliberate government policy? No, it's what they want. Why else do they allow a near perpetual gridlock in Congress? They choose the traitors who make Congress all but unworkable."

Clayton took in a deep breath. "I can put in a thousand anti-discrimination laws, but that won't change what is in people's hearts. I can give America the best health care… the cheapest and best health care in the world, and the only thing stopping me is the American people."

"And not the insurance companies, the Doctors?" Abb asked from his corner.

"Last time I looked, they're Americans too," Clayton responded. "They want things as they are… millions want a divided country.

"When we talk about health reforms the AMA starts screaming about… 'Reds under the bed.'

"When we talk about gun control, these the NRA screaming… 'They'll take you guns way.'

"Climate change… 'All lies, all a Chinese conspiracy.' I am talking about the politics of division, people. They see the benefits of dividing… and thus sabotaging… this country for their profit.

Jonathan lowered his head. "But what about all those people on the streets crying out for justice?"

"Fair point, but how many are out there because they've lost their jobs, lost the money to buy their guns, drugs, and whores…" Clayton paused for a moment.

"Yes, Jonathan, the rich are organized, focused on getting what they want, so yes, they are not without blame. But how many of the middle class were happy with how things stood?

"They got what they wanted, and better still, they could blame the government—even if they are the ones who elect Congress." He sneered with quiet contempt. "After all, the people need someone to blame when they screw up—to blame for their failures, their flaws, their refusal to act. The American anthem of today: 'Why should I take the blame for my own actions or inactions?'"

Clayton saw the looks on the two men's faces. "Oh, come on, people. You're a loser, so who better to blame for your inadequacies than the government? Why do you think we have an entire industry based on conspiracy theories?"

"Maybe if the public were better educated? You have been critical over the failings of the media." Jonathan almost felt as if he was pleading for understanding.

"Ignorance can only go so far as an excuse." Clayton shook his head. "People… know that thirty thousand Americans are killed by guns each year… they know nearly a thousand children are killed with guns each year, *they know*."

"And most Americans want it to stop." Jonathan pleaded in their defence. "It's just . . . They don't know how."

"Wrong, they know exactly how to stop it. They just need the *will* to get organized. To organize an anti-NRA, that will target politicians with threats like the NRA does. Organize the 'loving' mothers and fathers into chapters of 'save our children from guns' in every State.

"Organize a campaign to have Google, Facebook, Microsoft, Amazon… all of the so-called liberal companies… donate to a fighting fund that would promote a long-term strategic for gun safety.

"They know they need a well thought out campaign to win people over, to offer alternatives, to fight the gun merchant's propaganda.

"They won't even try to stop the online conspiracy trolls with their lies… take the Sandy Hook massacre with their endless accusations that it was some goddamned government conspiracy. How many idiotic assholes *want* to believe the government murdered twenty first-graders to stop them from keeping their bloody guns?

"Next year, if I put my health care propose before the House, would there be hundreds of thousands calling their representatives screaming that either they pass the reform or the bastards will be castrated come election time?

"No, the mothers of America are more worried about what the latest contestant in some reality show is wearing or how her nails are painted than the lives of their own fucking children. —Sorry… I get so frustrated." They could see that Clayton was actually trembling with fury and frustration.

"Sir, don't you think that's a little unfair? Jonathan asked. "Most people don't think they can achieve much."

"Yet when women wanted the vote, they got out and organized… marched, didn't they? The gays marched until they got equality. So will they organize, fund, and march against gun violence? No. The self-absorbed bitches of America love their guns more than they love their children."

Now Abb felt he had to offer something. "Sir, you know that's not true. Most want gun control, but the obstacles are considerable."

"I see, we're back to the special interest groups and the lobbyists, with all their influence and money, that are truly responsible, right?'" Clayton steadied himself. "After all, how does a small community match up against the multinationals, Walmart, the oligarchies and cartels? The paid-for politicians and… a Supreme Court that panders to their desires?"

"Yes sir," Jonathan answered with a nod.

"No sir," Abb responded, with anger and sadness. "If the people wanted, they could have put an end to such arrangements decades ago. It's as you said, just a matter of getting organized, and wanting it."

Abb then looked at Jonathan. "Excuses can't cut it forever." Hell, they could've put an end to buying politicians ages ago if they were serious. All they needed was the commitment.

"So we can discount your 'coup' by the wealthy elite that took place in the eighties, sir?" Jonathan said, reminding Clayton of his own words.

"My point exactly, Jonathan. In all the time since, what have they done to 'retake' America?"

"Donald Trump… for president?" Jonathan gave his response before he had considered his words.

Clayton choked on his laughter. "And look how that went. We may end up paying off the national debt by the next century." He sneered with a passionate loathing. "God, 360 million Americans and all they could find was a liar, hypocrite and con man, versus a woman most Americans distrusted with a passion." Clayton softy sighed. "How can you 'make America great again' when Americans are so small?" *Interested only in themselves.*

"Uh—" Jonathan spoke the word in defeat. "I'll take care of these files, sir." He collected several more files and turned to leave the room.

"I don't buy it." Abb turned to Clayton, stopping Jonathan in his tracks. "I've seen you stare down a nuke, and now you're worried about something that may happen in the future… all because we're not hugging each other. Do you have any reason to believe any of your fears will materialize? There has to be more to this."

"You really think so?" Clayton looked Abb squarely in the eye. "Isn't there? I have heard what you said. And yeah, there are some who have too great a sense of self-entitlement that's made them spoilt, selfish . . . self-indulgent and self-serving—that old 'me, myself, and I… and screw America.'" He wasn't blind, Abb told himself. He had seen it, seen the erosion that Clayton had spoken of.

Even the TV seemed to show more of it every time he turned it on. When he had been a child, the TV was full of positive influences— cartoonish as they may have been. The police were honest, and each week they won the good fight.

Now half the cop shows were about corrupt cops selling drugs. Even the costumed superheroes, "the epitome of American values," now committed murder. Thugs masquerading as our heroes. But that was more to do with the bleeding-heart liberals of Hollywood than the hard-working Americans of the heartland.

Abb said, "But at America's core there are millions who are good, decent people. Who can be relied upon to do the right thing. So I ask you, where is your evidence the public will sell out the country? May I remind you that this nation was built on individualism? It took World War Two to get both political parties to read off the same page. We have gone through bad times before."

Clayton gave them one of his costmary pauses as he considered his reply. "Abb, you are truly amazing. You have a knack for hitting the nail on the head." Clayton began walking the room, as if he was back in his lecture hall addressing his favourite students. Both looked at him blandly.

"We came together for World War Two, yet we tore the country apart over Vietnam. I suppose it was the 'sixties, the counterculture. Everyone that was around back then thought of it as a great period, all that 'sex, drugs and rock 'n' roll,' and let's not forget it ushered in equality for women and, supposedly, for minorities.

"But everybody forgets what truly took place. Americans went to war with America… with the deliberate intention of undermining our nation. It was the first time sections of the public had not merely refused to support their government but actually undermined its war effort.

"Right or wrong, sections of this country undermined this nation in a time of war. Let's forget the semantics of whether Congress should or shouldn't have declared war. American soldiers were fighting for this country in Vietnam, and they were sold out—betrayed. As were our most cherished beliefs for a treasonous agenda."

Abb stood his ground as defiantly as he could. "There were a lot of reasons why Americans were against the war. But there are still millions of good, honest Americans, loyal to this country, willing to fight and die for this country now and in the future." He stopped, not wanting to go overboard with the praise. "Sir, I think you need to have faith, trust in the people that they will do the right thing by their government."

"Loyal? Willing to fight and die for this country? Abb, you really haven't been listening. Do you realize how ludicrous that sounds? Americans are now more willing to burn the flag than serve under it."

"Sir?" Abb cried out, unable to endure the cruel jabs against the people of his country.

"Sit, sit." Clayton raised his hand in a stop sign, before he pointed to a chair.

"With all due respect, sir, how can you say that Americans are disloyal?" Abb coldly stared into Clayton's eyes for a few seconds, even as he sat in his chair. "They are still loyal to the core principles of this nation."

"Yet every time they are tasked with defending those core values, they fail."

"I beg to differ. There is no proof." Abb sat straighter in his seat. "And I beg to argue there is an abundance of proof from Vietnam,

Afghanistan, Iraq, and so on." Clayton saw the looks of disbelief written large on their faces. "OK, this does not go beyond these walls. Understood?" Clayton told both men.

"Understood," Abb responded.

Jonathan merely nodded once.

"Indulge me if you would for a moment. Let us begin with the Iraq war. Prior to the invasion General Shinseki testified before Congress that America needed seven hundred thousand troops to invade and secure Iraq . . . *secure* Iraq, gentlemen. Not merely invade but *secure* the country.

"From day one we never had enough men to secure Iraq. I remind you we had enough men to secure the ministry of oil, but not enough to secure the Baghdad Museum. We had enough men to secure the ministry of oil but not enough to secure those Iraqi Army ammunition dumps— ammunition used to kill American soldiers.

"Further, towards the end the US Army was so desperately short of manpower that it was taking in men with criminal records. Just where were these 'loyal, patriotic' Americans of yours? The army was so short-handed that it had to send the same men on repeated tours of duty in Iraq.

"Now I will never defend that idiot Bush or that traitor Rumsfeld. But the question remains, why didn't Rumsfeld commit the manpower? Did he criminally commit America to a war without sufficient manpower out of blind arrogance? Or did he know he wasn't going to get the men needed? In other words, did he know he would not get the volunteers and he wouldn't get the support needed for a draft?" Clayton looked from Jonathan to Abb. "Now, does anyone wish to argue that we have all the manpower we needed in Afghanistan?

"Then there is Vietnam. Just six months after the first Marines arrived, university students were protesting against American involvement. Right or wrong, they undermined the war effort. They were the ones who tried to make the war 'unwinnable.'

"How can any government conduct a war when its citizens' first act is to betray the war from day one? Whatever their political views, they sold out the elected government of the day.

"Worse, much worse—unforgivably—we had mothers of American soldiers who were marching against the war, demanding that their sons come home. What do you think they were telling the North Vietnamese? Weren't they saying; 'Just hold out long enough, kill enough American boys, and you'll win'?

"When they were crying out 'Ho, Ho, Ho Chi Minh is going to win,' what the hell do you think they were telling Hanoi? Didn't their actions give aid and comfort to the enemy? Just how much support did the North get from the mothers of America?

"Think it out, how many American soldiers died because of the people's support for Hanoi? By encouraging them to fight on... delay going to the negotiation table? Simply because they saw Americans for what we are." Clayton's voice dropped to a whisper, making both men cringe just a little. "The reality is that the public's opposition to the war ensured we never committed the manpower needed to win."

Jonathan was shocked. "Sir, at the height of the war we had around six hundred thousand men serving in 'Nam."

"Oh, how innocent you are, Jonathan. Of the six hundred thousand, how many were doctors, nurses, chaplains, lawyers, clerks, mechanics, drivers, generals, and their bloated staff?

"One estimate put actual America combat troops at around ninety thousand. Remember, they had some combat units operating at 70 per cent strength due to casualties. That, my dear Jonathan, is how much support Americans gave their soldiers."

"That's an interesting view," Jonathan said with a shrug. "But some could argue that it's a one-sided view of history. Maybe we just aren't the warmongers so many want us to be and that we insist on a genuine need to intervene. Remember, some never accepted that the Gulf of Tonkin resolution gave America the right to enter the Vietnam War . . . They believed our warships were not attacked."

"They were there, were they?" Abb snorted. "They saw what happened?"

"Their position merely showed their hypocrisy and ignorance." Clayton added his own view. "Prior to Vietnam, America had the policy of 'containing communism.' That was the state policy of the duly elected government of the day. It was clearly and loudly proclaimed. We more or less fought the Korean War because of that policy.

"Before Vietnam there were thousands all across America screaming 'better dead than Red.' Yet within a year of our Marines landing in 'Nam it was 'Comrades, let us unite with our socialist brothers and bring down the capitalist establishment.'"

"Well," Jonathan responded, "others were protesting against of the abuses, the atrocities… the Ma Li massacre. They didn't want America involved in such bloodshed."

Abb protested, "Jesus, Jonathan, you mean war isn't a slaughterhouse? How many civilians were slaughtered in World War Two from Allied bombing raids alone?" He still remembered reading about just one British air raid that used fire bombs. An entire city had gone up in flames with tens of thousands burned or suffocated to death in one night. "Let's get real. The majority were upset because they saw it live on TV while having dinner. If it had been out of sight, it would have been out of mind. Hell, we assassinate hundreds of terrorists with drones each year, and I haven't heard a word out of the bleeding hearts." *Pussy shit, the lot of them,* Abb grumbled.

"That is no excuse, sir. Americans expect their soldiers to obey the Geneva Conventions," Jonathan stated with conviction. "Doesn't that tell you something about the American people? You think the Russians, Syrians, Chinese, Iranians, or Nigerians would give a damn about how many innocent children their soldiers kill in their own country or in some overseas conflict?" He hoped to give Clayton food for thought.

"Hypocrisy has its limits, Jonathan," Clayton stated coldly. "Hypocrisy? Where is the hypocrisy in doing the right thing?"

Jonathan felt a jolt of shock.

"Because they were not doing it for the right reason." Clayton smiled at Jonathan. Yet Jonathan's comment saddened him. Didn't he see the truth? See what was really going on? Much of the anti-war movement never gave a damn about Vietnamese casualties. It had always been a cover to hide the real reason.

He had little patience left for all the lies.

"Have you ever considered how many of those war crimes committed in 'Nam were the fault of the American people?"

Jonathan's brow crinkled in disbelief. *What the hell is he talking about?* "Jonathan, you brought up the My Lai Massacre, and that's a perfect example. At the court-martial of the commanding officer, a Lieutenant Calley, his own defence counsel pointed out that if the Army had not been so desperately short of officers, he would never have graduated. Nor would the Army have given such a junior officer such a senior command position. "I could give you a two-hour lecture on the Army's failings due to political interference, poor morale, and hopelessly poor officer material. Most of which was due to your 'loyal Americans' undermining the war. Denying the men the army needed… undermining its morale… all of which did affect the conduct of the men who did serve their country, as opposed to your 'compassionate public' pissing on the flag."

Jonathan tried to remember the little he knew of the Vietnam War to rebut the argument. But he knew he was at a disadvantage. Clayton was not just an excellent debater; far worse, the man had studied and almost breathed history. That was Jonathan's weakness: he had not spent years studying history with anything like the analytical detail and passion of the man in front of him.

Clayton smiled his little smile. "I am not defending the stupidity and incompetence of the administration. But when did government incompetence justify betrayal?"

"And those who argued that the war was unwinnable?" Jonathan wondered.

"And yet they won the guerrilla war against the Viet Cong. A handful of soldiers and marines… denied the numbers they needed for a quick victory, denied a valid strategy due to an incompetent general. Undermined by traitors and cowards, and they still won the ground war—until the final betrayal.

"Understand, gentlemen: we had won militarily in Vietnam; the Viet Cong had been all but wiped out. We had won militarily in Iraq; al-Qaeda in Iraq had been reduced to a handful. Yet somehow we lost; you want to explain why? Was it not because of the American people's betrayal of the government when it needed their support the most?

"We didn't lose in Vietnam or Iraq; we lost in the USA. Face the truth; the American people cut and ran. They have no loyalty and no commitment. Both Vietnam and Iraq were just starting to stand on their own feet when we ran out on them.

"That is what's so galling . . ." Clayton stopped and leaned back in his chair. "At that critical moment, when we finally have victory in our grasp, we just let it slip away. In that critical moment when North Vietnam crossed the DMZ and invaded the South with twenty-two North Vietnam Army Divisions—an Army larger than our own—we wouldn't even provide the South with fuel for their trucks." Denying the South fuel for transport crippled the South Vietnamese army, which went into battle piecemeal and were defeated.

"We wouldn't even provide air support. And you want to trust these fickle Americans?" It had always angered him how easily liberal America had rewritten the Vietnam War. How easily it had given the impression that it had been the fault of the South rather than America's betrayal. It was as if they never saw the pictures of the North Vietnamese army tank knocking down the gates of the presidential palace. As if it was a Viet Cong tank made of bamboo.

"Yet so many believed the war was wrong." Jonathan persisted.

"Yes, I suppose it was inevitable that we would surrender in the end. So many put so much effort into betraying this country, there was no alternative. They had to sell out Vietnam, just as they sold out Iraq. Remember that lovely quote to justify running out on Iraq? 'The price in blood and treasure is too high.' *Treasure*, Jonathan. Did we complain how much World War One and Two cost?

"Say, China invades Alaska. Do we say, 'Sorry, but it'll just cost us too much to liberate Alaska, so it may as well stay under Chinese control'?"

"Sir, with respect," Abb declared solemnly, "it wasn't entirely the public's fault. Many Americans wanted out of Iraq, that's true. But it was Obama and the Iraq government that sent our forces out of Iraq."

"Yes," Clayton went on, "and five years later when the Islamic State was at its height, how many in the West were opposed to sending in ground forces because of America's 'failure' in Iraq? And how many Americans went on and on about the 'failures' of Western armies in the Middle East?

"What failures? We won the Gulf War. We liberated Kuwait, remember?" He looked at their blank stares. Oh, yes that's right. If we don't have enough dead American, it doesn't count as a real war. Just go tell that to the widowed spouses of the Iraq soldiers who did die. "With only a handful of soldiers, we won militarily in Iraq, contrary to all the statements made by the liberal media. A victory thrown away by their liberal darling... a man elected by the people to get America out of Iraq, no matter what cost endured by our soldiers."

"With respect, sir," Jonathan argued with conviction, "if Obama had left troops in Iraq, do we know it would have changed anything?

"We can debate possible outcomes all we want. But the facts are that President al-Maliki and his Shia militias alienated the Sunni tribes. It was their brutality that allowed Islamic State to march in and take much of Sunni Iraq… resulting in our 'defeat' in Iraq.

"Sir, al-Maliki was no President Lincoln. I doubt he was worthy of shining Lincoln's boots." He saw Abb give him a strange look. "That wasn't racism, sir, just the truth. Look how President Lincoln treated the South after the Civil War. We should all give thanks we had men like Lincoln, General Grant, and others of conviction. President Lincoln and his successors did more than win the war; they won the peace."

Jonathan allowed himself a grin. "He did so by word and deed. President Lincoln bound up our wounds and healed our hearts by giving the South the best terms he could." Clayton wasn't the only one who could play with words.

He went on, "His greatness was the hand of friendship he offered to the South. Can anyone say the same about that thug, al-Maliki, a poisonous little toad with his Shia death squads and Shia militias, killing god knows how many Sunnis?

"Sir. America didn't sell out Iraq; the Iraqis did that on their own, no matter what lies they tell themselves. Even now, look at how they're murdering their own… in the name of their God of love and compassion." *Maybe the critics are right about the Middle East, and Islam just can't cut it when it comes to democracy. It sure as hell has no respect for human life,* Jonathan concluded.

"Isn't that reason enough to have stayed if we could have influenced al-Maliki?" Clayton countered Jonathan's argument. "According to some he was afraid of a military coup. If we had left a suitable praetorian guard, if you will, to assure Maliki that the US would support his government against any Sunni coup, it might have moderated his actions." Clayton shrugged. "True, we will never know, but my point remains, did America give Vietnam and Iraq the support they needed to stand on their own feet?" "It wasn't that simple," Abb wanted to believe. "Many were tired of the Iraq war."

"They were 'war weary'? Oh, the poor, poor public. We committed only one per cent, one… entire… per cent of Americans to war, the same young men sent on repeated tours… whilst the fat, selfish 99 per cent sat at home watching TV. The poor dears," Clayton sneered, "they must have been so sick of watching TV. Oh, the misery they must have endured, the blisters on their asses… oh, the pain of it all. How could they have gone on?"

"We still lost over five thousand soldiers in both the Iraq and Afghan wars."

"And we lost over *three hundred thousand* from guns inside the US during the same period, and I don't recall the fags of America marching in protest over that even once."

Abb tried to breathe deeply. He could not come to terms with what Clayton was implying. No, that couldn't be right. Clayton was declaring that Americans were utter wimps. No, he could not accept the argument. He fired his last shot. "That may well be true, sir. But we still have no real justification for our involvement in Iraq or Vietnam."

"Really? I would argue that 'Nam was one of the most justifiable wars that we have ever fought."

"You're kidding!" Abb's eyebrows shot up in absolute disbelief. "How can you possibly say that? You can't stretch reality to argue it was in our national interest."

"Which is why the Korean War and 'Nam should have been two of our greatest moments and not the disasters they became."

"You have lost me. If they were not for our national interest, then why?" "For a principle, Abb, for a goddamned principle." "What?" A laugh choked Abb's voice.

"Yes, we should laugh." Clayton smiled sadly. "The very idea of Americans fighting for democracy is truly absurd."

"Sir, I protest!" Abb all but snarled in outrage.

"Oh, come on, Abb. When has America ever fought for democracy? For self-interest, oh yes. But for Democracy, well that's entirely a different matter."

"We have fought for…" Abb was feeling dizzy, tried to stand straighter in outrage.

"Abb, name the nations we have liberated in the name of democracy. And don't you dare suggest we entered World War Two in the name of democracy. We fought because we were attacked. Millions of Americans believed in isolationism, tyranny could rule as long as we were left alone."

"But Vietnam wasn't a democracy," Jonathan pointed out.

"Indeed it wasn't a democracy. —But wait." Clayton stopped speaking and gave them the look of someone who had just had a light-bulb go off in his head.

"Before the Korean War the North was a dictatorship, and South Korea was another dictatorship. After the war the North became a state of horrors, and the South was still a military dictatorship. Yet, today the North is a hellhole, while South Korea is a democracy. Why? Was it because for once we didn't run?" Clayton looked from Abb to Jonathan with a hint of sadness in his eyes.

"Look, to you and me, ten years is a long time, but to a nation what is ten years—or twenty or thirty years? And the fighting was all but over… that's what's so galling." The words came out silky smooth.

"But back then Vietnam wasn't a democracy. The people couldn't tell what was in the future." Jonathan's words sounded hollow in his own ears.

"Did they even try? Did 'Hanoi Jane'"—Clayton referred to an actress of the time who had supported the North Vietnam war effort, even being photographed in the seat of an anti-aircraft gun that may well have shot down American planes—"and her university 'comrades' go to the government and say, 'We will support America's efforts if we all strive to establish democracy in 'Nam'?" Clayton hissed out his anger as he screwed up his face. "Did they offer any solution other than blaming the government?" Clayton's little smile was the one that warned of storm clouds to come, the smile that worried Jonathan more than a little.

"Imagine if the 'loyal' people of America had supported the government and allowed it to support South Vietnam when it was invaded in 'seventy-five, where would it be today? Still living under the jackboot of a discredited dictatorship, being denied their basic human rights, or under a valid democracy? Did we give them even one plane to provide air support?"

"And to the millions who simply said, 'Vietnam was wrong, immoral, and unjust,' whatever the stated policy?" Abb persisted even against Clayton's rapid fire replies.

"I respond with the words of Ivan Beckett:

> "'War is not right, war is not wrong.
> War is not just, war is not unjust.
> War is not moral, war is not immoral.

"'To argue that war is right, moral or just is to argue that the killing of hundreds, thousands, millions is right, moral and just.

"'To argue that war is wrong, unjust, or immoral is to deny yourself the right to defend yourself, your family, friends, allies, and country, and the principles you believe in.'

"Although I would rephrase that by saying, 'The principles Americans *supposedly* believe in.' After all, we know Americans don't believe in the principle of democracy."

"That's…"

"The truth, Abb, is that Americans believe in democracy only for themselves—and certainly not for the inferior.

"Come on, we know the truth: we know democracy is only for the real people—white men." He whispered in a subtle, seductive mockery of a Southern voice: "'The niggers, gooks, and ragheads—they're not real people. Ugly subhumans, monkeys without tails—they ain't deserving of it, not like the pure Aryan race. Democracy belongs to the white folk.

"'We all know that only white folk are capable and deserving of democracy. The niggers, the gooks, and the subhumans really don't deserve democracy or human rights. Come on! You know niggers have never achieved anything unless us whites—the pure Aryan race—have done it for 'em. No filthy nigger, smelly gook, hairless monkey without a tail, raghead, or greaser is good enough—'"

"Sir, I must protest." Abb's eyes flared in outrage. *He can't be serious, he just can't.*

"Of course you must. But that doesn't change the facts; personal views don't change historical facts."

"You are going too far. We have a long tradition of supporting democracy. Look at Latin America . . ." Abb's words turned to ash in his mouth even as he spoke them. Many in Latin America would laugh at the suggestion of America supporting democracy. America had simply supported too many right-wing military juntas in the 1970s for anyone to believe that story. Then there were the military interventions in the 1900s to protect American economic interests.

Jonathan looked at Abb in disbelief. *Tell that to the Ukrainians, the Balkans… the Arab world.*

God, where does America support democracy? Hell, we have enough Americans saying Russia has every right to take as much of Eastern Europe as it wants… as if they have no right to choose their own government.

Yeah, we're all big believers in democracy… for ourselves.

"Then why didn't JFK or President Johnson just say that about Vietnam? 'My fellow Americans, we're not just fighting the 'commies' but will work towards establishing a democracy in the South.' Why didn't they, Abb? Was it because they knew what the answer would be? That Americans never gave a damn about the monkeys without tails." Clayton's voice hinted at the man's sadness. "That's why the youth of the sixties could so easily sell them out—use them to justify their little counterculture revolution.

"Face it, Abb. Most activists weren't fighting to defend the people of Vietnam; they just wanted to bring down the 'establishment.' As one activist stated, 'If there hadn't been a Vietnam, we would have had to create one.' That was the true reason why 'Nam was wrong… It needed to be wrong, to justify burning the flag and overturning the government.

"'Nam needed to be wrong to oppose the government—so what if it meant betraying the soldiers and the Vietnamese who fought by our side? After all, the US soldier was a 'motherf…ing baby killer'; the Vietnamese were just monkeys without tails. Weren't they expendables for the cause?

"There are those that believe America's soul was poisoned… or at least blackened… by the Vietnam War. I do not. I hold that it was the upheaval created by the counterculture. They wanted change, and they used 'Nam to achieve that change. They started the rot that is poisoning us today.

"Be honest, Abb. Ethically, morally, socially haven't we been sliding downhill since the 'liberation' of the sixties?"

Abb walked around the room, trying to come to terms with Clayton's words. "All right, Americans haven't been overenthusiastic in following their government into war." Abb sighed almost in defeat. "But why should Americans blindly support their coun—their government?"

"You're not listening, Abb. I'm not just talking about lack of support for the government but an actual desire to believe the worst about their government, their country. A desire to believe it is evil."

Abb's jaw dropped; Jonathan blinked and blinked again. Both wondered if Clayton was losing it.

"You see where I'm going with this? Everybody asks, 'Can we trust the government?' Well, can the government trust the people?" Clayton shook his head. "Look around, it's always about the individual, his rights. Screw the government. Screw America. It's all about the individual… America's

Achilles heel. It's all about 'my rights, my freedoms…' 'I have the right to bear arms,' but I don't have the responsibility to secure them."

Jonathan slogged in despite his sense of defeat. "And when the government hasn't been all that honest with the public? Remember the scandals, Watergate, the Pentagon papers, NSA, drone combat…"

"Isn't that proof that the government isn't this conspiratorial, all-encompassing secret empire they wet their panties over?" Clayton shot back. "If those scandals had happened in Russia or China, would they have come out or been buried, along with any witnesses?

"Look, I have no doubt we've messed up and messed up baddy. And we'll mess up in the future.

"God, after 'tricky Dick' Nixon, the idiot Bush, the sissy Obama, and the liar Trump, what do you expect? But how many of our rash actions have to do with unwanted pressure? First we had the Cold War, then the war on terrorism."

Clayton turned to face Abb. "Liberals have long castigated American over interference in the affairs of other nations, but what would it have been like if we had no Pearl Harbour, no 9/11, no Cuban missile crisis?

"How different would the world be today if the American public elected giants, titans instead of pygmies, whimpering sissies, trumpeting clowns?" *In truth it should've been expected*, Clayton thought, *given the ridiculous system of government we employ. We pick some poor bastard out of a line-up and declare him president with no real training. Okay, he might have been a governor of a State once, so I guess that's all right. He's got all the executive experience he needs. Bullshit.*

The poor bastard should be elected in the midterm elections, Clayton had once joked. That way the president elect could have two years to sit and watch the current president and learn. Well, at least he'd get a better idea what to expect. Travel the world. Go to school and learn instead of starting cold turkey. Have the time to select his people.

"Be honest, the NSA intercepts and Guantanamo just showed how unprepared and impotent the government truly is. That is the US's greatest secret." Clayton knew the lawmakers of this land spent little time looking to the future. Always reactive, never proactive, we're defeated even before we begin.

He had often wondered whether the NSA spying and Guantanamo would have occurred if the lawmakers had dealt with the issues of terrorism prior to 9/11. Then again they probably would have messed it up yet again. "When the government overreacts, stupidly, even with the best of intentions, it is vilified. Yet we have traitors who act with deliberation, forethought, and malice, only to be praised."

The room was silent for a few moments, as they considered the president's words.

"Treason is not just about selling secrets to the Russians. Treason is about betraying your country for your political views, for your greed; that's what Americans don't want to understand.

"Abb, what's the difference between giving our secrets to Russia in the so-called name of patriotism and just selling American secrets to Russia?

"What is the *true* difference between destroying America's economy out of greed and supporting a naked act of aggression from China that would cripple us economically?

"What is the *real* difference between pushing 'fake news,' deliberately lying and thus dividing us, undermining our solidarity… for their profit, and supporting a Russian cyberattack on America?

"How is sending *trash* to fill the seats in our Congress an act of patriotism?

"God almighty, if that isn't enough…" Clayton sat back in his chair as he looked away. "We have the Republicans going on for decades about voter fraud, in their efforts to make voting harder for the niggers"—he spat out the word in disgust. "Even while they're stacking the deck with their gerrymander. Aren't they undermining faith in democracy? Aren't they engaging in treason against democracy in the hope of getting more Republicans into office?

"It just goes on and on… all those conspiracy factories spouting any bogus story, no matter how harmful.

"Abb, Jonathan… look around, truly look around. You see millions of loyal Americans, and so many are. But I also see a growing number of Americans being so greedy, so selfish, *so* self-important that they want, actually *want* to believe in every lie, every conspiracy, in anything ugly to avoid the truth.

"Each year I see more suspicion, more paranoia that is undermining this country, if not outright betraying it." Clayton stood up in frustration. "Only in America is selling out one's country legitimized, glorified, and justified in the name of libertarian freedom. In the name of individualism, betrayal has become patriotism. The poet Bungert was right:

> 'The 'Sixties began the age of social change.
> That brought about our descent into totalitarian individualism.
> Our Founding Fathers believed in enlightened self-interest.
> Now we believe only in selfish self-interest.'"

Clayton sighed. "And with each year it keeps getting worse, and that, gentlemen, is our ruin. It has become our fundamental flaw. And that is why I cannot call upon the people to act. I simply do not trust enough Americans to act in our common interest."

"'Right or wrong, my country is still my country.' How many Americans would have those words on their dying lips today? One in ten? One in ten million?"

Harold Blunt

Chapter 21

War is not right; war is not wrong.
War is not just; war is not unjust.
War is not moral; war is not immoral.

To argue that war is right, moral or just is to argue that the killing of hundreds, thousands, millions is right, moral and just.

To argue that war is wrong, unjust or immoral is to deny yourself the right to defend yourself, your family, friends, allies, and country, and the principles you believe in.

War is necessary or it is not necessary.

Was the Vietnam War necessary for the United States? No. Was the Vietnam War necessary for South East Asia?

Perhaps, some have argued that the Vietnam War gave the countries of South East Asia time to fight and destroy the communist insurgences within their own lands.

Was the Vietnam War necessary for South Vietnam? Absolutely, no people should have to live under tyranny, either ideological or religious.

And if you think they do then pack your bags and go live in the worker's paradise of North Korea.

—Ivan Beckett

How does science provide morality? Provide belief in what is right and wrong?

It doesn't.

Indeed, does science strengthen or does it undermine our moral compass?

—Stanley Crook

The White House

He watched the TV. It was now the third day that the new wave of protestors had been out in force.

Abb turned away from the TV to address Clayton. "You really have to see this." Abb wanted Clayton to take in the sight of the long lines of people marching along the sidewalks.

The voice of the reporter was easily heard. "It is estimated that there must be close to ten thousand in this march alone, clogging Wall Street. As far back as I can see we have more people slowly marching up and down the street."

The traffic was crawling along the road.

Clayton studied the long lines. "It's impressive. I didn't think that many people would come out."

"They do seem to feel your reforms are worth the effort—even talk of dissolving the House and Senate for a few years."

"And yesterday there was a bigger march calling for my impeachment." Clayton looked down at the papers on his desk. "And the anarchists… how many 'one per-centers' have they 'offed' this week?"

Abb coughed on that. The rich still had a giant target painted on their backs.

"All we need is a spark," Clayton said, "and we can have a firestorm that will turn the country to ash. Now, where are the latest reports on the financial data from the banks?" He wanted to see how the banks' fortunes were faring. Could he get the Fed to threaten to do something nasty to the banks if they didn't donate more unoccupied houses?

That was vital; it was crucially important to provide housing to the homeless. It was the first step to obtaining jobs and thus a future that would benefit America.

Abb stood up. "I'll get right on to it with all haste and with the straightness of an arrow loosed from a bow."

"Oh God, don't you just hate a chief of staff in a good mood?" Clayton grinned as he looked down at the collection of papers in mock disgust.

Sometime later Abb entered the Oval Office with several reports tucked under his arm.

"Abb, you could have just asked someone to deliver the reports. I didn't expect you to be an arrow that returns to the bow." Clayton joked, then frowned a little at the unsmiling face.

"Abb?"

"I've just been informed that Jonathan has handed in his notice of resignation."

"On what grounds?" Clayton seemed in a state of disbelief. "I have no idea."

"Ask him to come and see me, please."

Abb nodded then left the room, a few minutes later he located Jonathan and delivered his message.

Jonathan entered the Oval Office with a hint of trepidation.

"I have been informed of your decision to leave. I hope it was not over anything I said. I may have been harsh, but it was in no way directed at you."

"No, sir. It's not you. Well, not you… directly." Jonathan stood before the seated president. He held a few files in his hands almost as protection, like a schoolboy facing his headmaster. "You were right. I—sir… I thought about what you said and then wondered what was I doing here. Was I here to help my country or for my own benefit? And honestly, I have to admit that I could do more outside the White House. Commit myself to doing something worthwhile. In a way I have taken on board what you said."

"So what will you do?"

"Honestly, I don't know. But I need to stand up and fight for something I think is worth it. You know… fight the good fight." Jonathan grinned impishly. "I actually do believe we can do better. I know you have a lack of trust in the public, sir, but I still have hope for the future. After all, isn't that the American dream?" He spoke with an air of conviction. "Sir, if I may, change is already upon us. You've been telling enough people to look out the window. I ask you to do the same.

We are on the edge of massive change, whether we like it or not. The question is whether it can be managed or if it becomes a revolution. Sir, America needs a leader."

"Jonathan, Jonathan." Clayton sighed once. "This country is so fragile, the people so weak." He sounded as if the weight of the world was on his shoulders.

"Sir, I accept that Congress has failed this country, sold us out, I accept all that. I heard what you said, I truly did. But have you considered that it is not the people that are betraying America, rather it's their defeatism? Perhaps that's a little too harsh; maybe *disillusionment* suits better. Too many are lost… without direction . . . I don't know, maybe, maybe, it's like they say: 'No more mountains to climb, no more rivers to cross.' We need direction or purpose."

"A common enough complaint," Clayton nodded to himself, "but is that really sufficient to excuse our more selfish behaviour? Especially when we do have so many mountains to climb… racism, inequality, intolerance— making America great by being a great people.

"Greatness comes from doing great thing… not making empty promises.

"Jonathan, I do recognise America's potential…" Clayton trailed off, there was a sadness to his words, a resignation.

"That's why you have to guide them, the public. You're the only one with a strategy, a real plan to get things moving. I don't care how insane some of those ideas sound." *I don't even care if you do or don't believe in any of them.* "But you're all we have got. The truth is you have to act. Congress won't, the rich won't. You're all we have left to save this country."

Jonathan glanced down. "Sir, you have to be our Abraham Lincoln, our George Washington… Leadership is the role of the president, and if the people will not follow, then—well, screw them. Screw the whole damned lot of them. But you have to give them your best." Jonathan almost gasped for air; he hadn't realized he was barely breathing as he spoke.

"Jonathan, do you know what you are really asking for? It's not just a few solar panels or needed changes in the tax code. If things go wrong, we could damage the whole system. My fear… my fear is that we could shake the crumbling bedrock of America and quite possibly for the worse."

Clayton shook his head. "You see the very best in people, Jonathan. That is what I've always admired in you. But how do you ignite a belief in a spent people? And after that, how do you instil the faith and loyalty in the government that we'll need to achieve success?

"As a people we have a hole in our soul, Jonathan. Individualism is so ill-suited for patriotism. Look at us, Jonathan, truly look at us, and tell me we will succeed."

"I can't say that, sir, but some of your ideas make sense. And someone has to try. Can you live with yourself if you don't try?"

"And the risk?"

"Life is a risk. With respect, sir… is it their lack of faith or yours that is holding you back?"

Their eyes communicated far more than words; a pair of young eyes eager for hope stared into a pair of sad tired eyes—eyes that were far too old to shine with any true faith.

"'All evil needs to flourish is for good men to do nothing,'" Clayton quoted with a sad smile. "Right, Jonathan?"

"I know I'm coming up with all the clichés, sir. But when that is all you have, then that's what you use. And I do believe that there are good people who will listen to you, this country still has potential."

"It's not me that needs reminding," Clayton whispered.

"Anyway, I've had my say. And it has been an honour to serve under you, sir. And I truly wish to thank you and will try to honour what you have taught me." Jonathan thought he saw a shadow of sadness cross the president's face. For a moment he could feel the sting of a tear in his eyes.

"Well, thank you for all your efforts. And may I say I am grateful for your service." Clayton offered his hand to Jonathan.

With great relief Jonathan shook the old man's hand. "Thank you, sir. This is very kind of you."

An hour later Abb returned to the Oval Office and quietly listened as Clayton explained the reasoning behind Jonathan's leaving.

"I know you're disappointed by him going." Abb knew Jonathan had upset Clayton. "But you have to do what you believe is right."

"Do I?"

"I was taking about Jonathan… but I guess that should apply to us as well."

Clayton softly snorted. "We so easily ask ourselves to do the impossible." "Sir?"

"How can I or anyone be certain? After all I don't hear voices." "Voices? What voices?" Abb actually sounded worried.

"It's something I used to say to my students. It always struck me as odd that so many people—especially atheists—believe they hear the voice of

God." Clayton shook his head with a sting of sad pity. "After all, Abb, only the Divine can be truly right beyond question." He grinned. "So unless you've got a direct line to God, just how can you be absolutely sure you're right? We are so presumptuous and arrogant, yet we refuse to acknowledge it. How do I know I am right?"

"Because you can still ask yourself that… I think that's one question that's pretty easy to answer." Abb replied quickly, hoping it was enough.

"No, Abb, it's the hardest question to answer. Consider the failures that were Obama, Trump, and Congress. They all thought they were so smart, so right."

"You're nothing like them."

"You're sure?" Clayton paused for a moment, deep in thought. "You remember your university days?"

"Oh, yeah. Had a real good time, that's what I tell everyone."

"Yes, with all these smug intellectuals—and we think Congress was stuck up. Just about everyone thought they were so goddamned smart, especially our illustrious scientific community.

"There was this particular theoretical physicist who truly got up my nose with his arrogant certainty. He was one of those in favour of replacing God with the religion of science. Now that wasn't what was annoying me, mind you. It was the stupidly of his intellectual debates. He'd jump at the first opportunity to utter his favourite lines in any debate—the *same* bloody lines, every time, whenever his opponents would bring up God to legitimize morality. He'd tell everybody how wrong they were, with his clichéd line about morality and religion.

"He'd ask the audience, 'If you didn't believe in God, would you then go out and kill your neighbour?' And the answer naturally would be no. Then he'd go on about how it wasn't morality and religion; it was actually rationality and empathy that stopped you from killing.

"I got so fed up with the guy.

"It was such a loaded question; it was such bullshit. Of course you're not going to kill your neighbour, whether you're religious or not, you need a motive. The question should have been, What would stop you from killing your neighbour if you had a motive to do so?

"And the answer is not rationality or empathy; it's fear. Fear of God's wrath… thus was born our morality. Fear of the police arresting you… the law. Hell, how many would shoot their neighbour if his dog kept on barking all night if not for fear of God or the law?

"What an idiot, Abb. We have over two thousand years of written history, most of it written *in* thy neighbour's blood. Our history, from Babylon and the enslavement of the Jews to the bloodbath that is the Middle East, is all about killings, atrocities, rape, and murder. So where the friggin' hell is rationality and empathy in all that?

"After Russia invaded Poland, Stalin had thousands of Polish officers murdered. He considered them a threat, so he coldly, logical, and rationally had them shot.

"The Islamic State terrorists coldly, rationally tortured and murdered thousands to instil fear.

"Millions of Jews were methodically rounded up, systematically trucked away, and with ruthless rationality gassed.

"Here was this renowned theoretical physicist, and it was as if he had never read a book in his entire life.

"We have done nothing else but butcher or enslave neighbouring tribes since the dawn of written history. And that ignorant . . . If not for fear of the police, I probably would have shot him just to shut the asshole up. He was so wrapped up in his belief in science, living in his ivory tower. Never seeing—" He stopped and returned to the present.

"Never seeing the real world?" Abb inquired.

"Yes, so I gave it to him with both barrels, that science was actually the problem." Clayton smiled as he remembered. "I had a great night. The science nerds were huffing and puffing with indignation at the idea that science was the threat...

"And yes, yes, I know. Science isn't evil, it's neither good nor bad; what matters is how we use it. But I just wanted to shove it up his ass. I laughed in his face and asked whether science could teach morality." *Or mercy, compassion, or honesty for that matter,* Clayton silently added. "Whether it had any principles you could live by. Castigated him for the absurdity of his ideas, argued that science was a threat to society itself by dictating that there was no God. Argued that people would rape and murder to get what they wanted since they wouldn't face punishment in the here and now or in the afterlife.

"If humanity is wiped from the face of the planet, it won't be from a comet; it'll be human stupidity in employing science."

"I see." Abb thought he understood.

"No you don't. I ridiculed and belittled him because of my own views. I attacked him because of my prejudice."

Abb looked at Clayton with a peculiar look. "I didn't take you for a religious man."

"It had nothing to do with my religious beliefs. I was wrong because I believed I was right and he was wrong. And yes I believed I was right because I had to be right... for the good of the country."

"Sorry?"

"How many times have we stated the obvious? We need to believe in something greater than ourselves. Science is an admission that we are not at the right hand of God but just some noisy animal. Whether God exists or doesn't is irrelevant; we need him. I thought, for America, as a society, it needs him to exist. We need a set of principles, standards, some sense of morality attributed to a higher power. I thought we needed to believe in some kind of justice. We needed there to be something more than just evolution."

Abb asked, "God allows us to separate ourselves from the animals by allowing us the... illusion or the reality... of morality and conscience?" It was something he thought Jonathan would have said.

"Close enough. I always thought that we need to believe in something higher than simplistic libertarian individualism." He chuckled softly. "Give us something else in life, and maybe that'll keep our base nature in check. It's not as if science and business were doing a great job."

"And believing in our country doesn't cut it?" Abb asked. "If only Americans believed in their country, Abb, if only."

"Well, a lot of atheists believe the country does just fine without God." "You just provided the rebuttal. Some believe the country is doing OK, but go ask anyone on the street how great the last fifty years have been in

'Godless' America?"

"So we need God whether he exists or not. But isn't that a bit hypocritical? It's like having belief under a false flag... or whatever."

"Who knows? If we practice faith, we may acquire it." Clayton grinned at Abb. "But you are correct.

"And thus it showed how wrong I was. I justified my attack using my belief that we needed God. In my pompous arrogance I believed I was right, not necessarily because I was right, but because I wanted to be right. So how do I know I'm right to risk the well-being of this country?"

"OK, maybe you can't know." Abb knew that without doubt, his years in politics amounted to one thing: never doubt yourself. That was the problem... too many small impotent men with giant egos. *So unlike you,* Abb silently told Clayton, a big man without an inflated ego.

Is that what made Abraham Lincoln great?

"But it's not up to you, Clayton. It'll be up to some nerd doing your autobiography fifty years from now… And guess what? He'll get it wrong. And you know why he'll get it wrong?"

"Because he'll be looking at my history through the moral lenses of his own time." Clayton shook his head in disbelief and gave a small chuckle.

"Look, you're not Obama, worried sick about your next orgasmic media moment." *God, how that man had loved hearing himself talk.*

"And you're not Trump, so pathetic he needed to find enemies everywhere to hide how inadequate he was." *Egotistic prick.*

"If I may say, you're as big a man as President Caine." His heart swelled with pride at the mention of his friend's name. "So you're big enough to carry out your duty to this country. And that means, I think, you have no choice but to act… You just have to be honest enough to give it to them straight." The words came out like a thunderbolt, before Abb even realized he had spoken them.

"Sooner or later, it's up to them. America is still a democracy. After all; the people get the government they deserve." With a ridiculous grin spreading all across his face, he joked, "And they deserve whatever they get… until the Republicans deny them the right to vote." *And if they reject you and vote in a clown, that's their fault, not yours.*

"And may I add, I have never been a strong supporter of gun control, but you have brought me around to the idea that a few safety precautions aren't a bad idea. If you can present a real argument that brings someone like me around, then, sir, I think you can sleep easy at night." Then Abb gave Clayton the brightest smile he had given in a long time.

They talked for a little while longer, before Abb retired for the day.

As Clayton was about to call it a night, the private line rang.

"Sir, a call on your private line."

"Thank you." Prescott took up the receiver and said hello.

"Sir, I am sorry to bother you."

"Quite understandable, Alex." The president leaned back in his chair. "Sir, we have a problem."

Maine

The limo's driver guided the vehicle down the smooth private road leading to the mansion, surrounded by the immaculately tailored lawns and sculptured trees. The level of security was evident in its apparent absence.

An expert in security, the driver nodded in approval. The security was so high-tech, it could easily surpass the level in the White House.

The passenger climbed out and entered through the double doors and stepped into the meeting room. It was dominated by a large table surrounded by chairs, several of which were already occupied.

As he sat, only a few nodded to the new arrival.

They were not there for pleasantries. Silently he took his seat. When all the seats were filled, they began.

"He's gone too far. We have to get rid of Prescott." "Agreed, but it won't be easy."

"Not as difficult as you may think. We can target him on not protecting the citizens of Washington from the nuke."

"The media will—"

"Need to be careful, he is overly popular at the moment. The public will not take kindly to what they will see as an attack on 'their president.'" "Agreed, but our people have found a very interesting connection between Prescott and Dr. Quaice. A connection that I believe we may be able to exploit, if we are not too obvious."

"It will have to be earth-shattering. He's the public's favourite right now. Hell, there have been calls from liberal groups for him to present his reforms to the public."

"It's all in the packaging."

A Dirty Street in Los Angles, California

Andrew Drywood pulled his heavy bulk out of the old truck and walked into the sad house with drooping sides. Dressed in worn jeans and a rumpled grey shirt, he followed the driver into the main bedroom. Inside was a bank of screens showing several sides of the house facing the one they currently occupied. Lying on the double bed were several pieces of surveillance equipment.

"Agent McPherson, sir." A tall man with long blond hair shook hands with the deputy director.

"Agent." Drywood nodded. "So how are we going?"

"We have a wiretap on the landline. The computer is another story. It's highly encrypted and will probably self-destruct if someone tries to access it without the right code."

"So how do we access it?" Drywood began to worry.

"If he keeps to his routine, the target will go out for the evening. Then we'll go in and insert a virus in all his memory sticks. Once he inserts one into his computer itself… we'll have complete access."

"Good, good. So what do we know about Mr. Cobbett?" "Unfortunately, little more than what we already knew. We have his van on camera a block away from the murder scene." That had been nowhere near enough to actually suggest his involvement, McPherson knew. But that had all changed when Drywood had focused their attention on whether Cobbett had any history of political cyberhacking. When they had found such activity, everything changed.

They had dug deeper and found that he had had some minor relationship with the victim before she had become a star.

Cobbett fitted Drywood's theory of a murderer with personal links to the victim and the anarchists; thus they were going the extra mile. And with results: under surveillance they had already identified three members of two serious hacking groups.

One member had even attended the same university where Clayton Prescott had lectured.

With luck they might have the first real lead in cracking the case. They might even make Drywood's day if this guy is hardwired into the anarchist network, Agent McPherson thought as he watched Drywood walk over and study the screens as if he could actually see into the house.